MARCHING INTO THE DARK

"Buildings are stone or cement with steel reinforcement. Remind everybody about ricochet casualties. As far as tactics, we don't want bodies. When that changes, we'll be sure to mention it."

"So who are we shooting?" Henke asked.

If he'd had epicanthic folds and the ability to hold his opinions to himself, Major Harjalo would have been at least a colonel. "Dear me, the admiral must have forgot to mention that. The task group intelligence officer doesn't know. Admiral Lee declined intelligence gathering prior to landing to preserve strategic and tactical surprise, which is supposed to be our most priceless asset. A few people down there don't like United Steel-Standard or each other. They may not like us. The admiral doesn't expect to see anyone shoot at us, but his data is falsified or stale. The paper says we establish an Imperial presence. Beyond that, your guess as to what we're supposed to do is better than mine, Paul, yes?"

By Robert Frezza
Published by Ballantine Books:

A SMALL COLONIAL WAR
McLENDON'S SYNDROME
FIRE IN A FARAWAY PLACE

A SMALL COLONIAL WAR

Robert Frezza

A Del Rey Book

BALLANTINE BOOKS • NEW YORK

A Del Rey Book
Published by Ballantine Books

Copyright © 1989 by Robert A. Frezza

All rights reserved under International and Pan-American Copyright Conventions. Published in the United States of America by Ballantine Books, a division of Random House, Inc., New York, and simultaneously in Canada by Random House of Canada Limited, Toronto.

Library of Congress Catalog Card Number: 89-91892

ISBN 0-345-36200-4

Manufactured in the United States of America

First Edition: February 1990

Cover Art by Stephen Hickman

14 13 12 11 10 9 8 7 6 5 4

PRINCIPAL CHARACTERS _____

1st Battalion, 35th Imperial Infantry (Rifle)
Lieutenant-Colonel Anton Vereshchagin ("the Variag"), commanding
Major Matti Harjalo, battalion executive officer
Battalion Sergeant Yuri Malinov
Surgeon Claude Devoucoux, battalion medical officer
Major Saki Bukanov, battalion intendance officer
Quartermaster Sergeant Vulko Redzup
Senior Communications Sergeant Timo Haerkoennen
Lieutenant Lev Yevtushenko, reconnaissance platoon leader
Corporal Victor Thomas, 1st section reconnaissance platoon
Lance-Corporal Vsevolod Zerebtsov, 1st section reconnaissance platoon

A Company, 1/35th Infantry
Major Piotr Kolomeitsev ("the Iceman"), commanding
Lieutenant Detlef Jankowskie, No. 1 platoon leader
Platoon Sergeant Arkadi Peresypkin ("Pertsovka"), No. 1 platoon
Section Sergeant Daniel Suslov, 1st section No. 1 platoon
Superior Private Nicolas Sery, 1st section No. 1 platoon
Corporal Kirill Orlov, 2nd section No. 1 platoon

B Company, 1/35th Infantry
Captain Chiharu Yoshida ("Tingrin"), commanding
Lieutenant Hiroshi Mizoguchi, No. 5 platoon leader

C Company, 1/35th Infantry
Captain Raul Sanmartin, commanding
Lieutenant Hans Coldewe, company executive officer
Company Sergeant Rudolph "Steel Rudi" Scheel
Senior Cook Katrina "Kasha" Vladimirovna
Section Sergeant Aleksei Beregov, 2nd section No. 9 platoon
Superior Private Charles Fripp, 2nd section No. 9 platoon
Corporal Roy "Filthy DeKe" de Kantzow, 2nd section No. 9 platoon
Corporal Isaac Wanjau, 2nd section No. 10 platoon
Sublieutenant Edmund Muslar, No. 11 platoon leader
Recruit Private Jan Snyman, medic's aide, No. 11 platoon

D Company, 1/35th Infantry
Major Paul Henke ("the Hangman"), commanding
Sublieutenant Sergei Okladnikov, No. 14 platoon leader
Sergeant Platoon Commander Konstantin Savichev, No. 16 platoon leader

Other Imperials
Vice-Admiral Robert Lee, commander Imperial Task Force Suid-Afrika
Rear-Admiral Isoroku Irie, deputy commander Imperial TF Suid-Afrika
Colonel Alfred Lynch, TF ground force brigade commander
Captain Francis Dong, aide to Colonel Lynch
Captain Carlos Gamliel, TF chief political officer
Captain Gabriel "Rhett" Rettaglia, TF chief intelligence officer
Senior Censor Liyu Ssu, TF chief censor
Lieutenant-Colonel Eva Moore, commanding 15th Support Battalion
Surgeon Natasha Solchava, Hospital Company, 15th Support Battalion
Lieutenant-Colonel Uwe Ebyl, commanding 1st Battalion, 3rd Light Attack
LTC Kosei Higuchi, commanding Provisional Battalion, 13th Infantry (Gurkhas)
LTC Jisaburo Kimura, commanding 2nd Battalion, 64th Infantry (Baluchis)

Boers
Albert Beyers, lord mayor of Johannesburg
Hanna Bruwer, schoolteacher
Christos Claassen, banker and Bond member
Christiaan de Roux, pharmacist and Bond member
Daniela Kotze, farmer
Pieter Olivier, accountant, Bond and Order member
Hendrik Pienaar, farmer and militia officer
Koos Gideon Scheepers, manager, Bond and Order member
Louis Snyman, religious minister, Bond and Order member
Willem Strijdom, religious minister, Bond and Order member
Hannes Van der Merwe, student and militiaman

Cowboys
Bethlen Andrassy, rancher, Landrost and Council member
Ian Chalker, rancher and Council member
John Henderson, rancher

Kirk Hunsley, secretary Reading District Council
Janine Joh, rancher and Council member
James "Big Jim" McClausland, rancher and Council member
Jeffrey "Jeff" Newcombe, president Reading District Council
Thomas Tsai, rancher and Council member

Mercenaries
Louis "Louie" Hain, nominal private
Daniel "Danny" Meagher, nominal major

United-Steel Standard
Yugo Tuge, planetary director

Others
James Branch Cabell, American author, deceased
Samuel Langhorne Clemens ("Mark Twain"); American author, deceased
Jopie Fourie, South African Army captain and rebel, executed
Kemoc, Irish saint, deceased and gone to heaven
Karl May, German author of American western tales, deceased
Damon Runyon, American author, deceased
Quintus Sertorius, Roman general and successful rebel, deceased
Spartacus, Ashcroft laborer and rebel, deceased
Karl von Clausewitz, German philosopher, deceased

Order of Battle (L-Day + 14)
1st Battalion, 35th Infantry (Rifle)

MAJ Harjalo Executive Officer	LTC Vereshchagin commanding	B/SGT Malinov Battalion Sergeant

A Company

LT Malyshev Executive Officer	MAJ Kolomeitsev commanding	C/SGT Leonov Company Sergeant

No. 1 Rifle	*No. 2 Rifle*	*No. 3 Rifle*	*No. 4 Mortar*

LT Jankowskie
P/SGT
  Peresypkin
	S/LT Degtyarov
	P/SGT Gledich
		LT Hara
		P/SGT Tributs
			SGT/PC
			  Sjurssen
			P/SGT Sausnitis

B Company

LT Sversky Executive Officer	CPT Yoshida commanding	C/SGT Rodale Company Sergeant

No. 5 Rifle	*No. 6 Rifle*	*No. 7 Rifle*	*No. 8 Mortar*
LT Mizoguchi P/SGT Gurevich	(Sversky) P/SGT Aittola	LT Kiritinitis (A)P/SGT Ngo	SGT/PC Miller P/SGT Soe

C Company

LT Coldewe Executive Officer	CPT Sanmartin commanding	C/SGT Scheel Company Sergeant

No. 9 Rifle	*No. 10 Rifle*	*No. 11 Rifle*	*No. 12 Mortar*

LT Karaev
(A)P/SGT
  Beregov
	SGT/PC
	  Gavrilov
	P/SGT Sucre
		S/LT Muslar
		P/SGT Lebanik
			SGT/PC Traone
			(A)P/SGT
			  Mekhlis

D Company

CPT Schwinge
Executive Officer

MAJ Henke
commanding

(A)C/SGT Poikolainen
Company Sergeant

Mech Mortar	*No. 14 L Attack*	*No. 15 L Attack*	*No. 16 L Attack*
SGT/PC Fischer	S/LT	S/LT Muravyov	SGT/PC
P/SGT	Okladnikov	(A)P/SGT Liu	Savichev
Bushchin	P/SGT Zakusov		P/SGT
			Kuusinen

Reconnaissance	*Engineers*	*Quartermaster*	*Aviation*
LT Yevtushenko	LT Reinikka	CPT Bukanov	LT Wojcek
P/SGT Drake	P/SGT	CPT Heinlein	F/SGT Laumer
	Pournelle	QM/SGT	
		Redzup	

(A) = acting rank

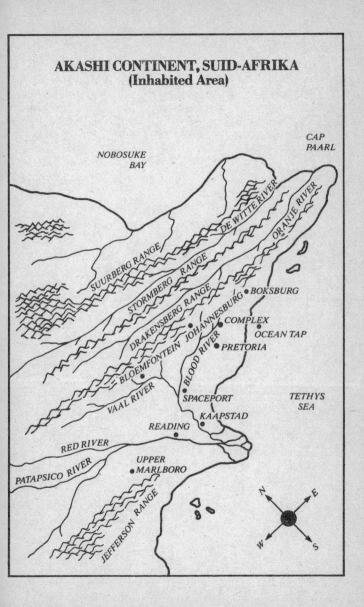

AKASHI CONTINENT, SUID-AFRIKA
(Inhabited Area)

CAP
PAARL

NOBOSUKE
BAY

DE WITTE RIVER

ORANJE RIVER

SUURBERG RANGE

STORMBERG RANGE

DRAKENSBERG RANGE

BOKSBURG

JOHANNESBURG

COMPLEX

OCEAN TAP

BLOEMFONTEIN

BLOOD RIVER

PRETORIA

VAAL RIVER

SPACEPORT

TETHYS
SEA

KAAPSTAD

READING

RED RIVER

UPPER
MARLBORO

PATAPSICO RIVER

JEFFERSON RANGE

N
E
W
S

PROLOGUE

Suid-Afrika

HUDDLED, DRESSED AS SOLDIERS, THEY MOVED UP TOWARD A plateau rich with plants from Earth. Square flashes of brown leather bearing a Lake District brand were sewn to their shoulders with wide stitches. Gaudy camouflage designs glistened like flowers against the drab filaments of the fern forest.

Ahead of them, point man and proud of it, Louie Hain spat sideways. Moving his hand to wipe away the sweat plastering his hair to his forehead, he listened to the buzz of voices and the click of metal. His fellow slum rats were tolerably good for instant mercenaries, even the two gerbils who spent their time holding hands. This was their second slash and burn; they hadn't screwed up the first one too badly.

Three or four more, Hain thought, and the Dutch hayseeds might get the idea. Stubborn they were, like Amish at home. Right now, most of them didn't seem to know there was a war on, one the Steyndorpers had started by running Chalker and Henderson from between the rivers.

They would learn quick enough. Ian Chalker had shown Big Jim McClausland off. He wouldn't take kick-all from farmers. As big a planet as Suid-Afrika was, if Boers could run a man like Chalker, there wouldn't be much place on it for Louie Hain.

The air was humid hot, hot as hell in August. Dripping with moisture, Hain cradled his rifle. Strange that after a century's worth of space flight they didn't invest in better ways to kill people. He stopped to light an Earth cigarette and give the city boys a minute. The merc officer wearing the three circles of a captain waved him on irritably. Shrugging, Hain ducked under the thorns clinging to the underside of a frond. He crushed dry ferns underfoot.

Hain had jacklit his first deer at thirteen in an unburned slice of western Pennsylvania, half a lifetime away. The job would do

1

fine for the time being. The cowboys paid regular, and the food wasn't bad. As for being point, point man got first pick. There might be a woman this time.

The captain hollered again. Someone was going to catch dirt. Hain licked his lips and went to fish out his canteen.

His hand stopped. A familiar patter of four hooves on the other side of the crest stood out from the quiet cursing and the rattle of metal on metal. "Well, goddamn," he muttered.

He ran to the top. A gray-bearded man in a black coat sat astride a little brown pony. "Old Amishman's going to get himself killed like that," Hain thought aloud. An instant later the assault rifle in the crook of the Afrikaner's arm leveled and half a clip tore Hain's chest away. The stub of the cigarette slid from his mouth.

Automatic rifle fire from the crestline raked the mercs struggling up the slope, and a burly Afrikaner heaved a satchel charge at the sound of their voices. Fumbling with safeties, two of the mercs tried to charge the ambush and died. The rest froze or fled. Eight horsemen led by the gray-bearded man cantered past Steyndorp riflemen to cut down the survivors.

The youngest rider outstripped the rest, flaxen curls peeping out from under a floppy hat. Spurring his horse up behind the nearest of the fleeing mercenaries, the boy stitched a pattern from the man's left hip up to the right shoulder. Recoil carried his shots into the sunlight. He reined in and fumbled for another magazine.

One of the mercs looked back to see his comrade slide over at the waist. With an incoherent scream, the mercenary turned and ran back firing wildly. The boy's horse thrashed, the young Afrikaner slipping from his saddle. A three-round burst from the gray-bearded man blew away the side of the mercenary's head. He toppled, his face masked in crimson.

When the gray-bearded man returned, he leaned over at an impossible angle and fired a single shot between Hain's sightless eyes. He watched the body jerk. Medals taped down, from a forgotten government, a forgotten war, bounced softly on his chest.

He heard a voice in Afrikaans. "Hendrik! Where is Piet?"

Hendrik Pienaar didn't answer. "Amateurs," he whispered instead to Hain, savoring the taste of the English word. His Steyndorpers were amateurs too, God rest them, but Pienaar was a professional still.

The Steyndorp kommando stripped the cowboys' mercenaries

of weapons and field gear. They left the bodies for the crawling amphtiles to eat. Piet and his blond grandson came back lashed head to foot on the same horse.

NADIR

'We're having a war, and we want you to come!'
So the pig began to whistle and to pound on a drum
'We'll give you a gun, and we'll give you a hat!'
And the pig began to whistle when they told the piggies that

excerpt from *The Whistling Pig*, anonymous

In Ashcroft Orbit, Outbound

VERESHCHAGIN PACED THE LENGTH OF HIS COMPARTMENT, three meters square. It took very little time.

Anton Vereshchagin was a man of medium height. Crisp features and a jutting nose made him look taller. As senior officer aboard the assault transport *Kaga*, he had a cabin to himself. Only the vessel's captain shared that distinction. With well over seven hundred men squeezed on board, Vereshchagin's battalion was packed like tinned fish. The timetable the vessel had been given precluded more comfortable arrangements until they began moving men into the cold sleep of the ice box. It was hell in a little tin basket.

The wall announced its presence. "Lieutenant-Colonel Vereshchagin, the last shuttle is arriving in the landing bay. Battalion Sergeant Malinov has requested your presence."

"Thank you," Vereshchagin remarked to the wall. He opened the door and stepped smartly down the passageway, squeezing past a file from A Company and a lieutenant headed in the opposite direction.

The battalion sergeant was waiting at the landing bay with a corporal's guard. Vereshchagin cocked an eye and said nothing. Yuri Malinov was a tall, erect man with iron-gray hair cropped closely. Otherwise superb, he was unnaturally reticent.

Grinding sounds indicated that a shuttle was coupling to the loading lock. When the hatch opened, Raul Sanmartin stepped out, straightened, and saluted briskly.

Vereshchagin returned the salute without comment.

Slender, painfully so after the desert, Captain Sanmartin had recently come in possession of Vereshchagin's C for Chiba company, his predecessor having made the error in judgment that cost him his life.

"We have six altogether," Sanmartin was saying, "one under restraint. Superior Private Prigal."

Vereshchagin could hear Superior Private Prigal faintly. Prigal was a driver in Muravyov's No. 15 light attack platoon, and Lieutenant Muravyov was doubtless an unhappy man.

Vereshchagin eyed Sanmartin as he might have eyed a piece of wood, seeking the fineness of its grain before setting knife to it. "How many unaccounted for?"

"None."

That was far better than Vereshchagin had expected. Many, many years ago, before the battalion had become Vereshchagin's, when leaving Earth there had been twenty-nine deserters and something of a small mutiny. He deliberated. "Very well. Battalion Sergeant, I think that under the circumstances, Prigal need not wait."

"Sir." Malinov replied.

Sanmartin nodded and made a stiff-fingered motion with his left hand. Two soldiers jerked Prigal through the opening. Prigal managed to curl his arms around the shuttle door frame. For a few seconds he clung, squawking fit to raise corpses. Then he turned his head far enough to notice Vereshchagin tapping on the back of his hand the pipe that he never lit. Vereshchagin raised his left eyebrow.

"Oh, hello," Prigal said weakly.

The battalion sergeant clapped his hands, and his guard whisked the unfortunate Prigal off the door. They planted him on the deck in a position resembling attention.

"I bring this field court-martial to order. Superior Private Prigal, stand at rest. Would you care to have me formally read charges?" Vereshchagin said.

The accused shook his head rapidly from side to side.

"Captain Sanmartin, will you take oath?" Vereshchagin requested formally.

"I do."

"Where did you find him?" Vereshchagin asked.

"In an establishment on the RuePissarro, barricaded in one of the rooms."

"What did our superior private have to say for himself?" Vereshchagin inquired.

Sanmartin paused, then said, "He claimed to be sniffing out a plot against His Imperial Majesty that took priority over his duty to move with the battalion. He also stated that he was someone other than Superior Private Prigal, I am not entirely sure who. He may have come up with other explanations while we were breaking down the door. I would have to ask."

Vereshchagin allowed his eyes to close. "How did you find him?"

Sanmartin coughed politely. "The superior private left himself an audit trail."

Vereshchagin inclined his head a few millimeters. "Prigal, are you listening?" he asked kindly.

Prigal suddenly realized he had an audience. "Ah, sir, I was just on my way to report to the landing pad when I was attacked and forced to drink vile liquor. Then there was the plot, sir—"

"Prigal. Please, do not add mendacity to your other accomplishments. Have you anything to say in your defense or in mitigation?"

Sobering quickly, the accused stood mute.

Vereshchagin recalled the city below, the RuePoussin and the cobbled plaza of the Place Watteau, where against the flow of thin crowds, the horizontales moved in chakras and veils as bright birds of passage, luring men like Prigal.

Outside the barriers to the desert, willie-willies joined and spun away, gouging furrows into ruddy sands. Inside the city, Ashcroft's oligarchs didn't speak to soldiers, didn't look at soldiers. Most of the "parasites" veiled their hostility in indifference. The rest were being cleared out on the *Lisbon Maru*. Vereshchagin's battalion had put down their insurgent slave labor, but the parasites had lost more than the cacos—the cakes—that Vereshchagin's men had shot down, because they had more to lose. Inside the city, brick-red dust lay pasted as a glaze. The desert had crept into the city and stayed.

Yet even on Ashcroft, some men found some things worth clinging to. When the battalion had mustered on the landing pad, one lad had broken ranks. Vereshchagin remembered him quietly sobbing, pinned to the tarmac by three of his comrades, his soft blond hair fanned by the demon breeze. One always coaxed soldiers on board the transports with patience, because the time differential and the icebox meant no return; the world left behind would prematurely age.

In Ashtoreth bei Hebron there had been a girl who had made a very young lieutenant wish that he might stay. That lieutenant had not stayed, and his name had been Vereshchagin. Her children would have children older than that lieutenant had been. Departure was a final step, a step not taken lightly even on Ashcroft, which did not excuse or diminish Prigal's conduct.

"Superior Private Prigal, this field court-martial finds you guilty as you have been charged. Captain Sanmartin?"

Sanmartin hesitated for a second. "The offense is capital."

Vereshchagin tapped his pipe softly against his thigh. "What should I do with you, Prigal? You do realize that Captain Sanmartin should have shot you when you made a complete nuisance of yourself."

"Yes, sir. I mean, I don't know what you should do with me, but I understand, sir. I'm sorry, sir," Prigal said, slurring his words.

"Battalion Sergeant?" Vereshchagin asked.

Malinov rubbed his chin. "We could start the former superior private in the starboard washroom. For five, six months."

"I concur, Battalion Sergeant. Shooting is much too good for you, Prigal. You must first earn the right to be shot. Do you understand me in this, Prigal?"

"Yes, sir. Thank you, sir."

"Excellent. Bring yourself to attention, Superior Private Prigal. We shall talk again in a week, Recruit Private Prigal."

Prigal left in the arms of his escort to polish the starboard washroom, centimeter by centimeter. The two other members of his armored vehicle crew who would join him in the washroom would not thank him kindly for it. Five other defaulters followed Prigal in various stages of disarray. Then a ship's crewmember secured the aperture.

"Was there difficulty with the others?" Vereshchagin inquired of Sanmartin quietly.

"No, none. My four were waiting on the landing pad. Detlef's pedaled up on a cycle as we were buttoning up."

Vereshchagin nodded and waited. One of Sanmartin's teams had overstayed in a body, and therein lay a tale.

"Purnamo's little establishment was thoroughly torched," Sanmartin volunteered.

Vereshchagin smiled.

At some point, Vereshchagin's reputation for probity had ev-

idently touched the city garrison commander's business interests
too closely. While it would be a long while before the battalion
forgot Major Purnamo, it would now be an equally long time
before Major Purnamo forgot the battalion.

"Admiral Nakamura will undoubtedly be irate, not that this
will matter. What else of interest?"

"The brothel owner wanted to affix a lien to Prigal for his
bill."

"You persuaded her otherwise?" Vereshchagin's cheek dimpled slightly.

"I told her the expenditure required your personal authorization, and I offered to knock down a few walls to see whether
she was harboring any other deserters while we were waiting."

"Simple, imaginative, unorthodox, forthright. I value this in
you," Vereshchagin stated, and paused. Despite his record as a
company officer, Raul Sanmartin was not a known quality.

"Raul, the essence of punishment is twofold. It must persuade a man that he is shamed by his actions, and persuade him
that he may regain self-esteem in undergoing punishment. You
overplayed your line. We only shoot the ones we cannot alter,"
he said, indicating dismissal.

Sanmartin stood still for a second, then moved out to find his
company.

FORTY-SIX HOURS LATER, HE LAY EXHAUSTED, ORIENTING HIM-
self to a space half a meter high and half a meter wide, his
bergan and the ruck with his personal possessions hung at the
far end.

His company sergeant, Rudi Scheel, had selected a location
immediately below an air louver, which did much to mitigate
the odor a transport rapidly acquired. Company Sergeant Scheel
tended to treat his company commander as a beloved, brilliant,
but not very well pinned together younger brother.

Soft breathing from Sanmartin's executive officer in the hammock below penetrated the whine that a fusion ship never
seemed to lose. With his eyes shut, the cherubic look on Hans
Coldewe's face would fool saints and martyrs.

On Ashcroft, some men had lost sanity, a few had lost the
will to live. Lieutenant Coldewe had developed a sense of humor, which was worse.

But it had been Hans who had snipped a lock of hair from
Vilho Isotalo to cremate.

Corporal Isotalo had been C Company's last casualty, gunned

down in the street of the city he had helped liberate and saw again so briefly. When the reaction squad arrived, he had been staring to the sky where the ship waited, the citizens walking past with an air of elaborate unconcern.

Unfortunately for passersby, Admiral Nakamura had hand-picked his reaction squad from newly arrived Imperial security police. If the infantry played the game rough, the blacklegs played it rougher. Debarking in the street, the reaction squad rounded up the first twenty well-dressed male citizens they saw and shot them, beginning with the man who had been careless enough to be found kicking Isotalo's corpse.

An hour later, the names of one hundred and eighty more citizens were posted on a mass detention list. Three hours later, a man wrapped in a fur-bordered cloak was dumped on the access ramp in front of Admiral Nakamura's headquarters. He had been shot with a wave pistol on wide aperture at close range. He lived long enough to confess. Examination of the weapon which had been carefully tied around his neck corroborated his testimony.

The hundred eighty citizens were released with Admiral Nakamura's personal thanks for their assistance. The admiral apologized for the inconvenience.

The following day, C Company began the labor necessary to ship the battalion off-planet. They left behind the refuse of the insurgency for the regular police and the blacklegs to clean, bound for a world that called itself Suid-Afrika.

"Hans, a new planet, a new war," Sanmartin whispered softly, only to himself.

ACROSS THE SMALL TABLE, FRAMING A REPLY, CLAUDE DEVOU-coux shook his head. Vereshchagin considered his physician gravely.

"The voyage is awkward, Colonel. Eight months in space is a very long time. Hibernation units are simply not intended for such. Moreover, climactic conditions on Ashcroft were very bad, very bad. Most of the men have little fat."

"What other bad tidings do you bear, Claude?" Vereshchagin asked.

"Physical conditioning will be a great problem. The battalion sergeant tells me that for the first part of the voyage half of the gymnasium will be needed as storage space. The vessel's captain tells me we only have rotation for seventy-seven percent of

Earth sea-level gravity. We may expect some calcium loss. May I ask what you have decided?''

Vereshchagin turned to his battalion sergeant. "Yuri?"

"Sir. A and B companies have the 1200 to 2400 cycle, with the engineer platoon, the reconnaissance platoon, and aviation administratively attached. C and D are with the quartermasters on the 2400 to 1200," the battalion sergeant said, naming separate day-night schedules the two halves of the battalion would follow. Hot-bunking—two soldiers sharing every space—was not especially well thought of. Soldiers have little enough to call their own.

"To make space, A and C companies will go into the icebox, every last man," the battalion sergeant continued. "Number fourteen and number fifteen platoons from D will go in as well. We will fill out with aviation, reconnaissance, and odd bodies from quartermasters. We will stagger out the rest."

"Sufficient, doctor?" Vereshchagin asked.

"I foresee no difficulty."

"Battalion Sergeant, what other health concerns have we?"

"Sir. Water recycling. The equipment was not broken out of storage until we boarded. It does not appear to be functioning properly."

"Soldiers always complain about the taste of water recycled from urine," Devoucoux commented wryly.

"Please look into the matter thoroughly, Claude." Vereshchagin turned to the fourth man present, the battalion's executive officer. "Matti, do you have anything?"

Matti Harjalo stretched out his arms. "As mentioned, the gymnasium is a problem. We need a football field. I would mention Reinikka wants me to play midfield. He claims engineers are all intellectuals."

Major Harjalo had soft eyes of gray-blue in an oval face. The battalion being short more than a few officers, he doubled as operations officer. He was built more solidly than his appearance suggested, which sufficed to make his progression down a football field suggestive of a wrecking ball.

"Agreed," Vereshchagin said, tapping his pipe against the heel of his hand. "Yuri, how long before we eat up what is crated in the gym?"

"Seven weeks, three days."

"Unacceptable. Move the boxes somewhere."

"Sir."

"What else?"

"The ship's engineer intimated he would be happy to present some lectures. He seemed to feel we have not enough to keep ourselves occupied," Harjalo volunteered.

"What did he suggest?"

"Binomial theory, the ship's propulsion system . . ."

"Enough. I hope that you did not disabuse him too roughly."

"I asked if he was willing to administer the coercion necessary and invited him to attend one of Raul Sanmartin's presentations on nudibranchs instead. He had a most perplexed look."

"I would not doubt. Have we other business?"

"The battalion sergeant has brought to my attention one other problem."

"This is?"

"When are *you* going into the box, Anton?"

The only two persons who would be gainfully employed for the entire voyage were Battalion Sergeant Malinov and Devoucoux. As executive officer, Major Harjalo kept his eyes on such things.

Vereshchagin sighed. He thought for a moment. "I will go down now with A and C. Get things organized, then put yourself under and let Paul take over for a while."

The Hangman, Major Paul Henke, could easily handle anything that would come up.

"Is there anything else? We have taken up enough of our time, then," Vereshchagin said.

IN THE ICEBOX, SPACES WERE LAID RACK UPON RACK, TIER UPON tier, like caskets in a morgue. When Vereshchagin felt the pinprick on his arm, he waited for his body to cool, considering Suid-Afrika.

Kaga would rendezvous with a freighter carrying a veteran light attack battalion from Canisius, and with six ships from Earth carrying two more rifle battalions, a brigade headquarters, a support battalion, a gun-howitzer company, an engineer construction company, a cadre for locally raised battalions, heavy air transport companies, ground-attack aircraft, police, odds and ends. The main task group would be accompanied by a frigate and three corvettes to provide space-borne fire support.

No task group was ever large enough, particularly for an entire world. What Vereshchagin found disturbing was the policy statement that the task group would occupy points of settlement "to protect Imperial interests."

Apart from landing-port facilities and one offshore energy

tap, Suid Afrika's only strategic points were mining, refining, and metallurgical facilities, which could be taken and held by a reinforced battalion or two. But Admiral R. E. Lee, the task group commander, envisioned something quite different. The occupation of nonessential points was a bloody business in Vereshchagin's opinion. It tempted people to resist. The thought lay like a dead weight in his mind until he felt himself sink into chemical sleep and five months passed from his life.

Suid-Afrika Orbit, Inbound

KAGA CAME IN ON A FAST ELLIPTICAL ORBIT, WASTING VIRTU-ally all of its remaining velocity on a swing around the system's star. Freed of that enormous burden, it coasted to a stationary orbit on the side of Suid-Afrika opposite Akashi Continent behind the freighter *Reykjavík Maru* from Canisius. The "Ode to Joy" from Beethoven's *Ninth* drifted over the ship's sound system, followed by Haydn and Mendelssohn.

Vereshchagin's men turned in coveralls that were bone-dry from cleaning in hard vacuum. They resumed combat gear to wait. The Earth ships arrived eighty hours later, bellwethered by the frigate *Graf Spee* with her corvettes attached.

As they boarded the transport *Shokaky*, Vereshchagin and Harjalo were met by a lean major with white streaks in his hair. The major saluted and then stuck out a hand to shake. "I'm Rettaglia, task group intelligence officer. I've appointed myself your tour guide." He nodded at a few of the staff officers scurrying through the corridors. "Things are a bit confused at present. The brigade commander, Colonel Lynch, will have conduct of ground operations. He's waiting to hand you your operations plan."

Matti Harjalo stole a glance at Vereshchagin. "How much of a plan has he worked up?"

"All of one, I'm afraid." Rettaglia motioned them down the passageway and was almost run over by a harried-looking lieutenant with a clipboard. He added over his shoulder, "Gamliel, the political officer, will be present. Watch him. To answer the question you haven't asked, when Colonel Lynch called his fourth planning meeting two weeks ago, Admiral Lee remarked that we were having planning meetings to plan meetings. Colonel Lynch hasn't called a meeting since."

"I see," Vereshchagin said.

They were met at the door to the ship's conference room by Colonel Lynch's aide, a captain named Dong. Lynch and Gamliel were seated inside. Rettaglia made introductions. Lynch was stout with a very pale complexion. Gamliel had sharp features and a round, pock-marked face.

Lynch stood up and exclaimed, "Welcome aboard, Vereshchagin. I trust you're eager." Dong passed over copies of a thick operations order.

"I am sure this will be most interesting for us," Vereshchagin replied, glancing at the document.

Lynch placed himself in his chair heavily. "The other units have been briefed. I expect you will be able to carry out your tasks with equal diligence. I see that you were on Ashikagi with Admiral Nakamura. That must have been an interesting situation."

Vereshchagin seated himself, murmuring politely, "The cacos—the cakes—were in rebellion against the oligarchs and in full control of the planet. They continued in rebellion after our arrival. The oligarchs were only slightly less hostile. Admiral Nakamura felt that he should have been given two more battalions. Fortunately, we were able to resolve the matter."

"Major Purnamo was a classmate of mine. Did you know him?" Gamliel asked.

"Quite well. Too well," Harjalo replied.

After an awkward pause, Lynch said, "I would like to see your most recent status reports, I assume you brought them."

"They weren't requested, so I'm afraid we didn't," Harjalo said blandly. He flipped through the operations order. "The intelligence analysis here is a pile of stuff."

Lynch's face colored perceptibly.

Rettaglia smiled. "My regrets. In order to preserve strategic and tactical surprise, Admiral Lee did not allow me to initiate local intelligence-gathering prior to landing."

Vereshchagin tapped the operations order in his hand lightly. "Colonel Lynch, may I make one small suggestion? The climate down there is extremely hot and humid, which will severely affect operations. After eight months aboard a transport rotating in and out of hibernation units, my men are not in the best physical condition. Let us push the schedule of landings back seven days so we can acclimatize ourselves in some uninhabited area."

Gamliel made a slight gesture with his fingers.

"No, Admiral Lee would never contenance it," Dong said. Out of the corner of his eye, Vereshchagin watched Matti

Harjalo's face tighten. "A second point, the USS manufacturing complex is listed as one of our primary first day objectives. With your permission, I will airdrop a company there."

Lynch put his hand down on the table sharply. "Impossible. A night drop on Complex is completely out of the question. We could never support them."

"Frosty hell," Harjalo said bluntly, "we can at least put people down on the Complex. You have a platoon airdrop on the ocean tap listed here. There isn't room on the ocean tap to swing a rope."

Gamliel started to say, "The ocean tap won't be defended . . ." He stopped when he saw Rettaglia grin broadly.

"What kind of weather patterns do we have out at the tap? Are there morning updrafts?" Harjalo asked. "Do we even have a recent photo?"

There was a slight silence. Dong said, "It's too late to alter the shuttle schedules."

Looking over at Gamliel, Rettaglia asked smoothly, "With Colonel Lynch's permission, Louis, why don't you fill them in on the political situation?"

Gamliel cleared his throat. "United Steel-Standard was originally chartered to exploit Suid-Afrika's fusion metal deposits. The corporation was facing adverse tax consequences at a time when the Guardianship Council wanted to move the metals markets."

Rettaglia interjected, "The Imperial Government agreed to give them a credit on their excess shipping and development costs. The Lower Diet characterized it as a license to steal."

Gamliel paused noticeably before continuing. "USS planned to supplement a small permanent staff with unsubsidized emigrants and filled dead space on the carrier ships with members of five disparate religious sects. USS hoped that the sects would provide food for the permanent staff and become a consumer market."

"Cheap labor," Harjalo commented.

"The sects were very undercapitalized. The experiment was unsuccessful," Gamliel told them.

"They died, mostly," Rettaglia commented.

Gamliel dabbed at his chin with a small handkerchief. "A better organized colonization attempt was made in cooperation with the government-in-exile of the former Republic of South Africa, using Afrikaner refugees who survived the crack-up and the Bantu Wars. The exiles had skills which allowed USS to significantly reduce the staff being paid isolation wages."

Rettalgia interjected again. "Although USS set up a counterbalance by introducing the so-called cowboys, it didn't occur to them that they were handing the Boer miners a stranglehold over their production. The Boers remember their history, and they've never forgotten or forgiven *Jan Companie*, the United East India Company, to which USS bears more than a passing resemblance. When USS terminated the 'Zutpansberg Seven' for labor agitation, the Boer elite decided to alter the distribution of power. They began with a general strike. After enough ships grounded without loading, the USS planetary director negotiated an arrangement and honorably committed suicide. I understand that negotiations were materially speeded when a Boer militia kommando started using USS industrial robots for target practice."

Colonel Lynch said, "Major Rettaglia, would you please stick to the point and avoid interruption."

Gamliel continued, "The agreement provided for import schedules, prioritized employment of Afrikaners, a wage-price understanding, and diversion of some production toward local needs. USS attempted to evade fulfillment of these terms, which led to several years of production slow-downs. With a deteriorating bargaining position, a second USS planetary director capitulated abjectly. The USS Directorate did not approve."

"Tell them about the cowboys," Dong suggested.

"The cowboys initiated a final crisis. Although they were intended as a counterweight to the Boers, USS exploited them in a short-sighted manner. Sagging margins led USS to cut passage fees below cost and export agricultural produce to the newly opened Zaibatsu planets. The amount of land cultivated by the cowboys doubled at the same time the expanding Afrikaner population began turning to agriculture. The cowboys found themselves pushed out of markets on-planet at the same time the Zaibatsu markets went soft. Deficiencies in survey and the inadequacy of the USS governmental structure turned disputes over land tenure and contract interference into armed clashes." Gamliel tucked his handkerchief away.

"On Earth, the USS Directorate determined to break the Afrikaners and supplied the cowboys with mercenaries under the guise of labor guards. Internecine feuding on-planet became general, and USS governmental authority collapsed. USS belatedly enlisted Imperial Government support. However, the

Guardianship Council voided the charter for the planet before dispatching this task force," he concluded.

"Colonel, what precisely is our objective, and what is USS's status?" Vereshchagin asked.

"We are to restore order and cooperate with corporate officials," Colonel Lynch informed him.

"I see," said Vereshchagin. He closed his eyes and said, "The loading schedule here is very sketchy. If you would allow me to make some slight modifications to the plan overall, I believe that I can guarantee successful completion of my assigned mission. Otherwise . . ." Vereshchagin let his voice trail away.

Rettaglia said innocently, "Lieutenant-Colonel Vereshchagin and Major Harjalo haven't met Admiral Lee yet. I am trying to get them on the Admiral's schedule."

After a moment, Gamliel nodded almost imperceptibly. Dong asked, "But what about the shuttles?"

Lynch pursed his lips and thought for a minute or two. Then he said, "All right, Vereshchagin. Go ahead and work up whatever small changes you think are necessary. But no changing the shuttle schedules and no air drop on Complex!"

"Thank you, sir," Vereshchagin replied, patting Matti Harjalo's arm lightly.

Rettaglia took them back out into the passageway. "Brigade staff will be handling the landing. They're rather new at it. I'll take you around to meet key personnel." He added with disarming candor, "Although the Council voided the USS's charter, the corporation was allowed to retain concessions which blur the distinction that direct Imperial rule was meant to draw. The fact is, USS hasn't articulated its policy objectives, and the Guardianship Council was reluctant to impose any. I do think you'll like Admiral Lee. He's a very sharp officer. Of course, he's never had any duty with line troops and has not involved himself in the operational planning. He sees Suid-Afrika primarily as a political problem."

"I see," said Vereshchagin.

VERESHCHAGIN PAUSED TO CONSIDER THE SEVEN MEN HE HAD brought together in *Kaga*'s tiny stateroom.

Lev Yevtushenko, the lieutenant from the reconnaissance platoon, was squeezed into a corner. Beside him were Malinov, Harjalo, and Vereshchagin's four company commanders: Major Piotr Kolomeitsev, the Iceman, brooding under a polished veneer; Captain Chiharu Yoshida, a dilettante in a trade that rewarded cold, hard professionals; Sanmartin, pallid and ill at ease; the Hangman, skeletal Paul Henke.

Harjalo reached down and turned on his magic map.

"Corvette *Achilles* has given us three mapping passes over Akashi Continent. Akashi has been divided into 10,000-meter squares for plotting fire control. The battalion sergeant has the control key." He colored a square in and narrowed the focus.

"Background. Once upon a time United Steel-Standard was chartered for this place. The only thing that would bring somebody like USS to a pigpen this far out is fusion metals, and that's what's here. USS tried to work the mines with temporaries and settle the soil with deadheads."

He paused to refresh himself from a mug of tea gone cold.

"That didn't work," he said presently, wiping his mouth, "so they got cute and brought in the Afrikaners, the Boers. After falling out with the Boers, USS filled the southern part of Akashi with graziers, they call them ranchers or cowboys. Then they helped the ranchers import mercenaries so the ranchers could feud with the Boers and each other. USS lost control. That was six years ago local, and before that USS was giving guns to at least three or four sides. USS went crawling to the Diet, the Diet tapped us.

"Objectives. The spaceport where we come down is here, up near where the Blood River joins the Vaal. Twenty kilometers north is the first of three sets of hills, from south to north the Drakensberg, Stormberg, and Suurberg ranges. The easternmost extension of the Drakensbergs juts into the sea as the Cap Paarl peninsula."

He lit up the middle of the peninsula. "The main USS manufacturing complex is located here on a spur off the main Johannesburg-Pretoria road. Seven kilometers offshore is an ocean tap that uses the deep-water temperature differential to produce electricity for everything and everybody. These are our two first-day objectives. We want them intact, especially the fuel-alcohol farm separately housed on the south side of Complex. Otherwise we walk a lot."

He waved his hand, and three large green blotches appeared on the map. "Our three second-day objectives are main Afrikaner population centers. Pretoria is where Complex workers reside, eleven kilometers southwest of Complex on the alluvial plain. Johannesburg is where the mining operations are run, northwest in the middle Drakensbergs. Bloemfontein is west in the altiplano. Farming communities radiate from there like spokes all through the Highveld. The riverport, Kaapstad am Vaal, is somebody else's problem.'' Harjalo highlighted the areas in a deep emerald to illustrate his points.

Yoshida shifted his feet. Despite the constant hum of the engines, the slight noise was unsettling. Harjalo looked at him sharply. Yoshida's expression didn't change, but the back of his neck turned very red.

"We do not intend to sit around and wait for day two to roll around," Harjalo said flatly, turning his back to Yoshida.

"Day three?" Yevtushenko asked.

Harjalo snorted. "Who knows? We wait until Brigade figures out what they want. We'll document some civilians and do weapons control. There are communities and individual farms all over the potato patch, along the Oranje River and its tributaries, up into the Karoo, but nobody's been silly enough to identify these as mission objectives." He lit the map up in a rash of green. "When things get dull, Lieutenant Reinikka's engineers and I will graciously give Piotr's number three platoon a rematch."

"Utilizing a few extra referees, I trust. And what of the other battalions? What missions have they?" Major Kolomeitsev inquired with calm grace.

"Lieutenant-Colonel Kimura's battalion is going to take the spaceport for us and head south to pacify the riverport and the rancher country," Harjalo said, tapping his fingers. "Kimura's inept. His battalion is intended as a permanent garrison, and they're no better than you'd expect. Lieutenant-Colonel Higuchi has a provisional battalion out of the Thirteenth Rifles. Two of his companies will be available out of brigade reserve on Landing Day plus one. The heavy stuff, Lieutenant-Colonel Ebyl's light attack battalion, isn't scheduled to come down until after we won't need it any more. For fire support we have the four warships for two days to shoot up aircraft and interdict communications."

Vereshchagin interrupted. "Matti will be working fire coordination, the usual thing. Go on, Matti."

"One thing I didn't say, buildings are stone or cement with steel reinforcement. There's no hardwood, and cement is cheap. Remind everybody about ricochet casualties. As far as tactics, reaction category four. We don't want bodies. When that changes, we'll be sure to mention it."

"So who are we shooting?" Henke asked with some asperity. If he'd had epicanthic folds and the ability to hold his opinions to himself, Matti Harjalo would have been at least a colonel. "Dear me, the admiral must have forgot to mention that. I don't know. Acting Major Rettaglia, the task group intelligence officer, doesn't know. Admiral Lee declined intelligence gathering prior to landing to preserve strategic and tactical surprise, which is supposed to be our most priceless asset. A few people down there don't like USS or each other. They may not like us. The admiral doesn't expect to see anyone shoot at us, but his data is falsified or stale. The paper says we establish an Imperial presence. Beyond that, your guess as to what we're supposed to do is better than mine, Paul, yes?"

The Hangman desisted.

"One thing more," Harjalo said. "They tell me it's September down there." The ship's calendar read January. Time for colonial battalions was idiosyncratic; it commenced with L-day—Landing Day—of Week 1.

Harjalo twisted around. "Anton, it's your turn. They know what we want. Tell them how we want it."

The key objective was Complex, which, essentially, made everything the planet used. Vereshchagin bent to lay a plan.

Lieutenant Yevtushenko would insert as soon as Kimura's first echelon secured the spaceport. Complex had several hectares of flat roof. A couple of ultralight Sparrow aircraft could put a team in place to cut through the roof and greet the USS planetary director when he arrived for work.

"We'll ask His Excellency for the time of day and whatever else comes to mind," Yevtushenko observed.

"Ja, take your little toy planes and go play while the rest of us are working," Harjalo said, which drew a laugh and failed to obscure the fact that having the director under lock and key during the landing might be an exceedingly desirable thing.

Lead elements of the battalion would shuttle down and split into assault groups, one for the ocean tap and a second to move by road to Complex.

Vereshchagin preferred to drop a rifle company on top of Complex in the middle of the graveyard shift, but Admiral Lee had ruled that out. Vereshchagin would have also liked a few main battle tanks as road-openers, but that was a purer fantasy. For reasons of cost, there was not a single main battle tank available to the task group or, indeed, on any of the colonial worlds.

With logistical cost factored in, for each main battle tank, two companies of light infantry or two light attack platoons could be transported and supported. Given the amount of money the Diet was willing to authorize and the nature of wars fought against colonial insurgents, units actually sent to fight colonial wars bore an unsurprising resemblance to old-style paratroop formations.

The spaceport had a single shuttle runway. Constrained by this, Vereshchagin based his plan on speed and surprise. No. 14 light attack platoon from Major Henke's D Company and No. 9 rifle platoon from Captain Sanmartin's C Company would form the lead element for the assault on the Complex, Raul Sanmartin leading the combined battlegroup. No. 3 platoon from Major Kolomeitsev's A Company would buccaneer down the Blood River on rigid assault craft to seize the ocean tap.

A second light attack platoon, No. 15, and the remaining platoons from A and C Companies would follow, bit by bit. Overnight, if all went well, Captain Yoshida's B Company, the battalion reserve, would be landed.

Vereshchagin did not intend to waste sleep over imponderables. "Raul, Piotr, you two decide what you want to do. Then the rest of us will knock holes in it."

As they recessed, he gathered up his battalion sergeant.

"Yuri, the spaceport will be sticky. We'll be alternating trips with Kimura's soldiers. The brigade commander, Colonel Lynch, has a few flower boys officiating. None of them have done a combat landing and they do not seem to know what is combat loaded and what is not." The schedule the flower boys had contrived was preposterous. Lieutenant-Colonel Kimura's companies would be fortunate to off-load in twice the time allotted, and the shuttle crews were green as well. "I suspect we shall have to improvise a bit."

Sanmartin paused at the door to listen. In a few hours, the intermingled companies would link arms in the gymnasium— before the focus narrowed to a single instant in time and the men who could provide covering fire—to listen to the Variag say things he had said before, in a quiet voice from atop an ammunition box. Vereshchagin was a talisman, their icon perhaps.

Whenever Raul Sanmartin stepped outside himself to look back in, he was awed by the Variag's merry men, himself included. So long as they thought they could take on the known universe and win, they might very well be right.

Quiddities(1)

ALTHOUGH NO BIRDS FLEW BELOW ITS FIRMAMENT, IT WAS ON the morning of the sixth day of Genesis that man came to that world he later named Suid-Afrika.

Despite its potential, it did not initially appear that the planet, then called Musashi, would ever be colonized. Even with the devastation of the crack-up, Earth is a rich planet. For its few needs, better planets were closer.

The laws of supply and demand being what they are, gold, silver and precious gems scattered like sand on a beach would not bring men so far into space. Rare earth metals like gadolinium and dysprosium are not rare; the demand for these is easily filled from terrestrial sources. The platinum group metals—platinum, ruthenium, rhodium, palladium, osmium, and iridium—are essential tools of the metallurgist in catalysts and alloys. Yet the thought of occupying Musashi/Suid-Afrika solely to supply them was ludicrous, and the notion of mining chip metals such as germanium and indium there no less so.

Only the least common of the industrial metals, the fusion group metals, could drive men to open up a virgin colony nine months ship-time into space. Because it absorbs neutrons readily, hafnium is necessary as a flux-suppressor; zirconium is invaluable because it has a low neutron cross-section and does not. The refractory metals, niobium and tantalum, are even more irreplaceable in space applications. In a rare jest by an unknown god, the only Earthlike planet where these metals were discovered in relative abundance was Musashi/Suid-Afrika, the irony being that the need for these metals is slight apart from their use in fusion bottles and other space technology. Man needed fusion metals to leap into space and needed to leap into space to acquire fusion metals, which is an interesting application of the principle illustrated by the dilemma of the chicken and the egg.

Sunday(1)

OBSCURED BY THICKETS OF HEAD-HIGH FALSE CLUB MOSSES, Fripp gave Sanmartin a quick thumb and let his weapon swing free. Fripp had traded in his assault rifle for a scatterchoked shotgun. His partner, de Kantzow, had not, retaining his own battered piece with forty rounds visible in the clear magazine and a forty-first chambered.

Moisture pouring down the sides of his neck, Sanmartin nodded and double-pumped his arm to speed them up, not trusting himself to speak. The rest of No. 9 platoon's second section trailed. Miinalainen moved behind him effortlessly, the big 88mm recoilless gun hooked to his belt with a shotgun round chambered and flimsy plastic wrap over the openings at either end to keep out the drizzle. Kirponos hovered at Miinalainen's heels like a big bird, sweltering under the weight of twenty rounds for the 88, his submachine gun, two throwaway rockets, and enough water to drown a small horse.

The remainder of the main body—Section Sergeant Beregov, the general purpose machine gun team, and three riflemen—was well behind, partly because good soldiers don't bunch and partly because nobody in his right mind wanted to be behind the venturi if Miinalainen cut loose. Beregov himself carried an s-mortar with one round chambered and five more in the magazine under the firing tube; on either flank and to the rear he had paired riflemen with light machine gunners festooned with fat coils of caseless 5mm × 40mm ammunition in plastic pouches.

The spaceport had presented no difficulty. Lieutenant-Colonel Kimura's lead company had met with no resistance and managed to organize sufficiently to get out of Sanmartin's way. Either the corvettes tasked to degrade communications had done their work well or the inhabitants had kept their gunmen well away; Kimura *had* gotten involved in a pitched battle, with a half company in rancher livery, which was turning Kaapstad riverport into ashes.

The immediate objective for the second of No. 9 was the alcohol farm at Complex, which had to be taken before the other two sections of No. 9 cracked open the main works. The other two sections were waiting where Sanmartin had left them, perched on Sergei Okladnikov's four overarmed type 97 cadillac armored cars and a "school bus"—a massive eight-wheel 160mm mortar carrier from Henke's mechanized mortar platoon—proudly painted with the white gallows insignia that the Hangman affected not to notice.

Scattered in pairs on the roads north and south, Lieutenant Okladnikov also had four well-armed slicks, two-man scout vehicles with noses and sides acutely angled to enhance thin protective armor. Okladnikov had been waiting nearly an hour.

Sanmartin halted to twitch a signal to *Graf Spee* overhead to assure their position, since an error in navigation would likely disrupt the operation beyond redemption. The confirmation placed them less than a hundred meters from where they thought they were. Sanmartin sucked his lungs full, flashed four fingers to Fripp, and willed his rubbery legs forward. Fripp caught the gesture and screwed up the pace.

The battalion sergeant was busy straightening up the confusion at the port so as to bring in No. 15 light attack platoon. No. 3 rifle and Major Kolomeitsev were on their way to the ocean tap. Coldewe and Vereshchagin were pushing pieces of No. 11 up the road in freight trucks to link with Okladnikov before Colonel Lynch, the brigade commander, tired of meddling with the firefight in Kaapstad. Everything else was piling up in orbit.

In Okladnikov's words, never have so few been led by so many.

A WIDE SWING PAST THE GATE BROUGHT THEM ALONG THE thin fringe of scrub separating the cleared area on the high ground from a precipitous drop into the coastal marshes. Twenty or thirty local Boer militiamen were nervously manning a check point at the factory gates while the rest of the workers who had shown up for shift were off trying to organize themselves. Sanmartin intended to sugar their tea, but the alcohol farm came first.

According to Lev Yevtushenko, who had a recon team sitting in the director's office with the director smoking the director's cigars, confusion was something close to total.

Three hundred meters from the first line of storage tanks, Sanmartin pulled up to contact Okladnikov. "Nine point one zero one. Break," he said, hitting the contact on his wrist mount. "Sergei, we're ready to start. Is number eleven up?"

The radio synchronized itself with the other radios it was speaking to, "shook hands," and shifted wavelengths every few hundredths of a second. Okladnikov's reply crept up Sanmartin's back and under his cap before registering through the bone induction plates over his temples. "Lieutenant-Colonel Vereshchagin extends his compliments and wishes to know what kept you."

"There was the small matter of a forested swamp approximately ten hectares in size, to which maps and words do no justice. Give us seven minutes. Let Lev know. What's in the building that isn't on the plat?"

"Lev said it's two hectares of die, stamping, molding, and imaging equipment. We take it out, the populace had best start chipping hand axes. I wonder if anyone on Earth knows it's here. Luck to you.''

"I wonder if anyone on Earth knows we're here. The same, Sergei. Out.''

The high, featureless reinforced concrete face of the alcohol farm loomed like a castle wall. Beyond it was the main building, its smooth surface marred by a single door.

Sanmartin touched the contact and squeezed his fingers together. "Nine two point Akita. Break. We're set. Fix bayonets so they'll know we're not selling brushes. The door's out front, you can see the path leading from the main building, so that's where we go. Remember, don't shoot unless you see a weapon and can hit what you're shooting at. The last thing we want is a few thousand liters of alcohol spilled on the floor. Who's in charge of prisoners?'' His slight nervousness was mostly hidden.

"Fripp and DeKe,'' the section sergeant replied with commendable patience.

"Aksel, you drop off with the gp as we go in. Cover the main building and be ready to move up. Don't blow anybody away unless you have to. Any suggestions? Is there anything I left out?''

If there was, they failed to mention it. Like wraiths, they moved into position in front of the door to the alcohol plant. Sanmartin poised his foot to kick it in.

Section Sergeant Beregov halted him with a hand signal.

He turned the knob and walked in. Sanmartin slowed just enough to get trampled.

Beregov fanned four men out on either side among the vast yeast tanks. Two more stayed to watch the door. Feeling slightly useless, Sanmartin watched Roy de Kantzow, Filthy DeKe, grab the only man in sight by the shoulder and slam him to the floor, flipping him neatly on to his stomach.

"Goede morgen. Wij zijn keizerlijk soldaaten,'' de Kantzow emphasized in what was evidently intended to be the bastard Dutch they'd learned aboard ship. He was holding his bayonet lightly against the side of the man's head. It was the longest continuous sequence of clean words Sanmartin had heard from the Deacon's mouth.

Fripp picked up the man's clipboard and patted him down. "The Deacon is not a linguist. He does better with the ladies when he uses sign language,'' Fripp explained sagely.

Sanmartin, no better linguist than the Deacon, watched the

little robots scuttle about on their appointed rounds. "Where's everybody else?" he asked the fellow on the floor.

"In the cafeteria," the bearded Boer blurted out in strongly accented English.

"Where's the cafeteria?"

The man looked up at de Kantzow and pointed out the door toward the section of the main building where sugarcane bagasse was converted into paper. Beregov appeared from behind one of the massive cane presses with a light machine gunner and half a dozen prisoners in tow.

"Berry, give me Fripp's team while I run next door. I'll take Miinalainen and the gp. If you find a window, cover me," Sanmartin said, knowing Fripp to be the superior private Beregov trusted most to keep his company commander out of trouble.

Beregov tugged on his mustache and nodded.

Running out the door with Fripp at his heels, Sanmartin pointed to the entrance for Miinalainen and the gp machine gun to shift fire lanes. He reached the door. Waving up the 88 and the gp, he put an ear to listen.

He couldn't hear a thing.

He thumbed his radio. "C for Chiba point two. Break. Sanmartin. Hans, what is your progress?" he asked his executive officer.

"Raul. What kept you? We're almost through cleaning up the north side."

Sanmartin fought down an urge to blaspheme. "We're just outside what I think is the cafeteria. The workers are supposed to be concentrating there."

"I wouldn't doubt. Check with Lev. Shall I send someone by to give you a hand?"

"Miserable lump."

Coldewe laughed and closed the circuit. Sanmartin tapped out another.

"Recon point one. Break. Sanmartin. Lev? We're outside the main door on the southwest side. Is that the entrance to the cafeteria?"

Two clicks, which meant yes. It also meant Yevtushenko was too close to someone unfriendly to speak aloud.

"Are all the workers gathered there?"

Three clicks, which meant, "who knows?"

"I'm going in. In thirty seconds, I want you on the loudspeakers. Can you do it?"

Two more clicks. Sanmartin turned and nodded. "I'm first,

Fripp, DeKe, the light, then the gp. Aksel, you're last, set?'' he said, fingering the wooden singlestick he had tucked into his webbing. ''Now.''

Fripp shrugged. He flung open the door and adrenaline pushed Sanmartin through. He found himself behind someone who was shouting from a tabletop and gave the man a helpful shove. De Kantzow lightly butt-stroked a very short man carelessly holding a rifle. The rifle hit the floor first. The light and the gp moved to cover the crowd from either side.

Sanmartin said the first thing that came into his head. ''His Imperial Majesty sent us. You can all go home for lunch.''

At the other end of the cafeteria, a knock sounded on the interior door. It opened, and Lieutenant-Colonel Vereshchagin stepped in followed by a half section out of the first of No. 9.

''Hello, Raul. We were wondering when you would make an appearance,'' Vereshchagin said.

At that moment, the planetary director came on the broadcast system to call upon his employees to assist the Imperial forces in their peaceful occupation of the facility.

Sanmartin shook his head and sat down on top of the table to watch his men police up weapons. De Kantzow gingerly plucked the orator from somebody's soup to dust for iron.

THE RUNWAY STRETCHED ALMOST TO THE HORIZON. SMALL ARMS fire issued faintly from the south where Kimura's battalion was still in action. A little white dot appeared at the far end and grew in stature until it merged into the long black ribbon. As it continued to lose speed and increase in size, the delta wings showed themselves as thin white lines. Rolling thunder, the shuttle finally braked to a halt with a roar that shook the soil.

The clamshell door opened at the back as a ramp even before the nose cone stopped glowing. Even in the semitropical summer, the heat emanating from the shuttle struck the men who were running up. An armored car poised itself at the head of the ramp. Inexplicably, it did not move.

Malinov, a vine cane in his hand, stood at the foot of the ramp and waved the vehicle on. There was no response. Finally, he strode up to the top and rapped on its side.

''Move. What are you waiting for?''

The driver's hatch opened, and the driver stuck his head out. ''We can't, Battalion Sergeant. She won't start.'' The vehicle commander popped out of the turret and would have said something had he not seen the look in Malinov's eyes.

"Move it!" Malinov barked. He looked to the other vehicles crammed into the shuttle. Slicks were hung from the roof and wired to the sides like flies in a spider's web. Poised behind three other armored cars, the big mortar carrier trembled as its engine turned over in confined space, bare centimeters to spare on either side. A little utility vehicle burdened with a Hummingbird reconnaissance drone was almost hidden. Muravyov, the No. 15 platoon commander, stood in the turret of the second Cadillac trying to levitate his lead vehicle by sheer power of will.

The lead driver continued to shake his head. "She won't go. She was fine on the transport, but she just won't go!"

Malinov leaned very close. "I will say this in simple terms that your simple mind will understand. There is only one runway on this whole frosty planet. It has a frosty shuttle sitting on it that can't unload half of the only ten frosting armored vehicles the battalion is going to get to invade this whole frosty planet because THAT FROSTY PIECE OF JUNK OF YOURS IS BLOCKING THE FROSTING DOOR."

Malinov kicked the offending Cadillac as hard as he could.

The engine roared into life.

"Many thanks, Battalion Sergeant. Many thanks!" the driver yelled over staccato machine gun fire as he drove down the ramp.

Malinov continued to stand at the head of the ramp as the rest of the vehicles filed past. "Dumb, frosting Prigal," he finally said, shaking his head.

ON A DIFFERENT ARMORED CAR TRAVELING THE PRETORIA ROAD, Sanmartin unglued his hands slightly from the handholds affixed to the back of the turret, choking on the dust. He found himself asking Vereshchagin, "Did you really drive up to the gate four armored cars abreast and every mother's son whistling *The Little Tin Soldier*?"

"No, nothing quite like that, Raul. We have it on tape. As Matti says . . ."

"I know, ammunition is expensive. What did we do with the other two slicks?" Along the side of the road there was a torn-up area where a missile from *Graf Spee* had rooted up and shredded a telephone cable.

"I sent them farther north with a few of your riflemen to screen the Johannesburg traffic."

"Sir, are we really going to take over Pretoria with two platoons, less detachments?"

"Raul, sometimes you worry too much."

"I worry too much?"

"Think of it in this way: Lieutenant-Colonel Kimura, who commands the Baluchi battalion, imagines that he is fighting a war. However confused the inhabitants are, when he shoots, they shoot back. Admiral Lee does not believe anyone is supposed to be shooting at us. If we tell the militiamen this, they may assume the admiral knows what he is talking about." He snapped at the waist like a jackknife to avoid being decapitated by a hanging vine.

"In theory, all these fine folk are Imperial subjects. Their quarrels are not with *us*, but with USS and each other. They never expected to see Imperial infantry in a thousand years. We may, perhaps, even get away with this. Smile a lot, and wave."

They came up to a bend in the road where the two scout vehicles were stopped.

"What is up there?" Vereshchagin shouted through cupped hands.

The gunner spat upon the ground. "Ambush. Light stuff and a machine gun." He jerked his head upward, where Lieutenant Okladnikov's Hummingbird flew overhead. "The bird took their picture."

The gunner stuck his finger in a hole and wiggled it. "They were pretty nervous. We circled back for you." He added significantly, "No armor-piercing stuff, or they'd have been firing that, too."

"Did you fire back?"

"No, sir."

"Good boys." He rapped on the turret. "Sergei, leave the hatch open and stop the car when I start pounding. Please do not shoot unless I so request. Start up with *The Little Tin Soldier* and see if you can point the 90mm so that they will be looking down the barrel, that ought to help, do you think? Where is the flag?"

Okladnikov handed out a cased Imperial ensign on a collapsible staff. Vereshchagin began fitting it together. He paused briefly.

"Raul, you must keep an open mind on the advantages of the unexpected in warfare."

Just past the turn, Vereshchagin rapped on the hatch. Okladnikov stopped his armored car dead and killed the engine. To the strains of *The Little Tin Soldier*, the other three Cadillacs whipped to a stop facing to either side. Behind them, for moral support, the 160mm mortar halted within the view of the Boer militiamen.

"Sergei, kill the music," Vereshchagin hissed. He waved, leaning on the flag which was itself precariously planted. "Hello! I need to see the burgemeester in Pretoria. May I offer you a lift in exchange for directions?"

Badly out-gunned, a few nervous Boers stuck their heads out from the thick growth alongside the road.

Vereshchagin turned to Sanmartin. "Lev thinks they may have telephone service restored within the town limits. When we get to the outskirts, we will stop and give the mayor a ring."

AFTER THEY ARRIVED AT THE STAATSAMP AND DROPPED THEIR escort off in front, His Excellency, the lord mayor of Pretoria— sleeves rolled up—was shredding every document from tax assessments to vital statistics. The squat, stolid building was marred by the gash of a strike from corvette *Ajax* that had torn the transmitter tower from its moorings and flung it to the street. The Boer provisional council, which functioned as a district government, had fled the city almost an hour before. Borrowing an interpreter of sorts, Vereshchagin managed to calm the burgemeester enough to function.

Vereshchagin pulled Sanmartin close with the hand that wasn't wrapped around the burgemeester's shoulder. "Raul, I am going to stay here and kiss babies. Paul Henke has borrowed a few trucks to send me one of Piotr's platoons. I would like to keep Karaev and one of his sections. Please double back and head for Johannesburg." He clapped Sanmartin on the shoulder. "There are only ten or fifteen thousand people in the whole town, so you should not have any trouble."

Sanmartin stepped outside. "Sergei!"

Okladnikov stuck his head out.

"Scrounge some fuel. Save what's in the trailer, the mayor says there's a tank out back and I wrote out a promissory note. We leave in ten minutes."

"For where?"

"Johannesburg." He noticed some riflemen standing around. "Go inside and scarf up all the shredded paper. We're going to do this in style."

* * *

HENDRIK PIENAAR HEARD SOMEONE POUND ON HIS DOOR. "THE door is open," he said without looking up.

Olivier turned the handle. The Pretoria businessman headed up the informal committee Pienaar had come to see to discuss the situation with the cowboys. "Heer Pienaar, there is a matter of greatest urgency," he said, red-faced and out of breath. Curiosity got the better of him. "What are you doing?"

"Cooking. The hotel restaurant is closed." Pienaar had improvised a frypan out of metal foil and wire.

"The Imperials have landed!"

"Oh?"

"They have taken the burgemeester prisoner!"

"We should make them keep him," Pienaar answered absently, trying to flip the eggs without breaking the yolks.

"We must fight them!"

"Why?"

"Why?" Olivier repeated. He sounded puzzled.

Pienaar had heard that Olivier was a straightforward, zealous man. He had also heard that Olivier drank too much and beat his wife, not that Pienaar believed everything he heard. "You and I and who else?" he asked instead.

"Be serious!"

"Oh. How many men do the Imperials have? What weapons? Space-borne fire support? What do they intend?" Pienaar pulled the eggs off the flame gingerly. "What have they done to us?"

"I don't know."

For all the talk that the Afrikaner nation stood shoulder to shoulder, the fat city men had been less than eager when it was merely a matter of Chalker's cowboys claiming Steyndorp lands. They all had bigger schemes to fry. Now someone else's shoe pinched. "Would you care for an egg?" Pienaar said dryly as he glanced out the window at the armored cars in the street.

OKLADNIKOV HALTED HIS CADILLAC ON A CAUSEWAY BRIDGE over the backed-up waters of a billabong. The two slicks were already on the other side waving them across.

"If this is the best road on the continent, I'd hate to see the others," Sanmartin commented, spitting out some dust. "What's up there, Sergei?"

Okladnikov replied by gunning the engine.

On the other side, his missing slicks were operating a parking lot. Twenty vehicles, from horse-drawn wagons to a huge road train with forty-four wheels, were sited off the road, hidden from the on-coming traffic. Okladnikov pulled up, and Sanmartin hopped off.

"So this is where you've been. Any problems?"

The lance-corporal pulled off his cap and scratched his head. "One truckload of militia. They're over there playing cards. We dumped their weapons in the swamp."

"Good enough. We're going through to Johannesburg. Give us about an hour, then get these people on their way."

The lance replied by flipping an ignition coil in the air and catching it smartly on the way down. "These things are a lot harder to put back."

Sanmartin laughed. He turned to climb back and was almost run over by a bakkie truck—on some worlds they called them pickups—with a load of chickens on the flatbed. Speeding by, it veered around Okladnikov straight into the mire.

Listening to the chickens, Sanmartin watched the truck settle in over the wheelwells. The lance looked at him expectantly.

"Try and clean up the area a bit before you go," Sanmartin directed. "It's untidy."

On a knoll overlooking Johannesburg, he left a rifle section to commandeer a stone house and planted the mortar carrier to fire star shells and colored parachute flares. With the riflemen on top of the armored cars throwing confetti, they rode into the town to the strains of *The Little Tin Soldier* about the time Major Piotr Ilyich Kolomeitsev started up the road to Bloemfontein on a farm tractor.

Sanmartin pounded on Okladnikov's back as they waved to the stupefied inhabitants. "Sergei, isn't this the craziest war you ever saw?"

The casualties the battalion suffered were remarkably light. Heat exhaustion knocked down a double handful. Kolomeitsev had four men lightly wounded securing the militia armory in Bloemfontein, and in C Company, F. N. Nikitin managed to break his leg in two places walking off the back of a moving Cadillac.

In Pretoria, there was one task which Vereshchagin reserved for himself. In the courtyard hard by the town hall stood a flagpole. He slid the small bayonet from his belt and slashed the halyard through, to watch the *Vierkleur* flag come drifting down.

Monday(1)

KIRK HUNSLEY, SECRETARY PRO TEM FOR THE READING DIS-
trict Council, paced the floor of what was called the District
Courts Building. Most of the wits in town—there were many—
called it "the Arsenal," which accurately described its appearance and function. Although the Reading Council was the
closest thing to a government the big ranchers acknowledged,
the significance of the fact that the council found it desirable to
conduct its activities in a concrete blockhouse was not lost upon
many.

For once, however, the petty bushwhacking endemic to the
politics of inland ranchers was eclipsed. The arrival of Imperial
forces had caught everyone off guard. Most of the council members were waiting to see what would transpire before commit-
ting themselves to anything that might diminish their wealth or
be construed as treason. To Hunsley's orderly mind came un-
bidden the thought that everything that the council had done
could be construed as treason in strict legal terms, everything
since the day that Big Jim McClausland and Janine Joh had
extorted the transfer of governmental functions from the director
at Complex—who had had no authority to grant anything of the
sort.

It was a thought that the secretary pro tem of that unauthorized
council did not relish. Even if someone as smooth as Kirk Hunsley could explain to Imperial satisfaction the usurpation of governmental functions, some of the ranchers and their mercenaries
were shooting at Imperial troops. In theory, those mercs were
council armed forces, and Imperials didn't take kindly to colonial armed resistance. It was slight consolation that Kirk Hunsley wasn't the only one who could feel a noose around his
throat.

It was ironic that the arrival of the Imperials put Kirk Hunsley
on a level with the big cats inside. Occupation of a council seat
differentiated the men who squeezed from the men who were
squeezed, although the council's lack of legal authority was
matched only by its lack of actual authority over the big landowners it ostensibly governed.

A greater irony would be if the Imperials infused enough
authority into the council to make it an acceptable puppet.

There lay a glimmering of hope. Hizzoner Jeff Newcombe
was already running down that rainbow as fast as his short little
legs would carry him. Newcombe's witless assertion that he

intended to force the Imperials to recognize the council was widely held to be proof positive that Jeff intended to sell himself and anything else if the Imperials were buying.

Hunsley grinned mirthlessly. After seven months as president of the council, pudgy Jeff Newcombe still didn't realize that the day heavyweights like the Joh or McClausland could agree on the time of day was his last in office.

Of course, if Newcombe's ploy succeeded, Hunsley was out of a job and maybe a lot more. Kirk Hunsley had played one rancher faction off against another so he owned none of them master. That was something Newcombe had never appreciated, and Jeff was enough of a fool to make his likes and dislikes apparent.

And being an ass, he planned a surprise for Vice-Admiral Robert E. Lee. The admiral had directed the council to await his pleasure for "discussions," which was the first demand of many, and one the admiral hadn't tried to phrase politely. For once, Hunsley didn't know what Newcombe was up to, which was one reason why Hunsley was pacing around the back of the council chamber in a stiff collar with sweat pouring down the back of his neck.

Newcombe was fool enough to do anything. Hunsley had done what he could by warning the Joh. If she landed feet first, Hunsley hoped she'd remember.

He looked at his formal watch. Opening the stiff, metal door, he walked out onto the soft carpeting that covered the stark concrete reality of the council hall and looked from face to face: thirteen heads out of twenty-five, a bare quorum. McClausland and Chalker were not present, nor was Tsai. Fat Joos was already seated, an angelic smile between his two red little cheeks. Anyone who didn't know what Joos had done to the jungle bunnies might think he was the chaplain's choir boy.

Heaven alone knew where Newcombe was. Andrassy, the closest thing Newcombe had to a creature of his own, was standing at one end of the big table. Several men were smiling, which was hopeful. Andrassy never told the truth unnecessarily, and if they still saw fit to smile, there was light at the end of a tunnel and it wasn't Andrassy holding a lamp.

The Joh was at the far end wearing a thin, black dress. Hunsley tried to catch her eye. Instead, she caught his and gave him a radiant smile that never touched her hard, washed-out eyes. Hunsley sighed deeply and waited, cursing Newcombe under his breath.

A full two minutes passed. The door flung open and New-combe made his appearance. Hunsley almost rubbed his eyes. Newcombe was wearing antique dress, a gray, vaguely military outfit complete with a sword and topped off by a wide hat with a feather in it. Watching people stare, Hunsley had to stifle an impulse to giggle before the computer between his ears re-minded him that Newcombe was a historico-drama buff. And if play-acting in historical costume could persuade Admiral Lee that black was white, there was a sudden sickening feeling in Hunsley's belly that sad, stupid Jeff had out-smarted them all.

As one thought followed another, four Imperial security po-licemen marched in wearing tailored battle dress with long black stripes extending down the sides. They cradled assault rifles and formed in pairs on either side.

Even fat Joos was standing. Mechanically, Hunsley took his place to Newcombe's left, eyeing eleven empty places. New-combe's white lace gloves irritated him beyond measure.

Newcombe lifted one of them in a theatrical gesture. Re-corded music filled the room. Hunsley saw Newcombe looking at him malevolently out of the corner of his eye. "It's called *Dixie*," Newcombe whispered as two Imperial aides walked between the blacklegs, tall and blond in white dress.

At the point of retching, Hunsley saw a hidden, unmistakable gleam of triumph in Janine Joh's eyes as a short oriental officer entered dressed plainly in blue, flanked by two more blacklegs. The officer stopped and smiled slowly like a shark.

"Ah, a historical scholar," Admiral Lee remarked blandly. Newcombe jerked as if he had been shot.

"My father was such, fascinated by the last of the gay cava-liers of Virginia." The short yellow man dressed in plain blue stopped smiling. "I wish I could say I shared his interests, Mr. Newcombe. Instead, I have important things to discuss." He added as an afterthought, "Lee is a common name in many countries."

Kirk Hunsley began making mental notes as always. Admiral Lee's council would need a good secretary pro tem. Hunsley had precious little to sell, but he didn't intend to be the last rat on the good ship Council Reading.

Tuesday(1)

WHILE EYBL'S AND KIMURA'S BATTALIONS DROVE SOUTH TO smash Tsai's cowboys in the delta, Vereshchagin split his battalion to control Johannesburg, Pretoria, and Bloemfontein. Higuchi's troops occupied Complex, the ocean tap, and the spaceport.

The first brigade assets to land were construction engineers. They converted a warehouse for themselves and started work on the rest of the spaceport. Other brigade assets were billeted in the big USS terminal as they arrived: the security police platoon, the tiny biochem section, signals, and the heavy transport companies. The support battalion remained in orbit, Lieutenant-Colonel Moore having made her views on unsecure lodgings scathingly clear. The Border Police set up a recruiting booth; neither soldiers nor blacklegs, they were the men who would handle domestic strife and petty subversion with placid arrests and soft words.

Medical went over to Complex as a need for their services developed.

Wednesday(1)

PARTLY LOST, SANMARTIN WHISTLED THROUGH HIS TEETH AS he passed each of the buildings clustered at the east end of the runway in turn. The Variag had not scheduled any sightseeing the first time through, and Rettaglia had Task Group Intelligence in the old customshouse, which looked like sixteen other structures. The cheerful Gurkha riflemen guarding the port gave bad directions; they weren't especially good with numbers to begin with, and the silly bastard had already amused himself painting them out for security reasons.

Counting down the second row of buildings, Sanmartin rapped smartly at the door of yet another concrete block. Metal echoed under his fist. A tiny sergeant with a thin mustache opened up. He was clutching a wave pistol.

Before Sanmartin could stammer out an explanation, he was enveloped in a bear hug. "Raul!" Rettaglia said, holding him by the shoulders. "It's about time you got here. Another eleven hours and I would have owed the senior sergeant some money. Raul, this is Senior Intelligence Sergeant Shimazu."

Shimazu bowed slightly, pocketing his pistol.

"Our exec, Major Harjalo, let slip that the intelligence officer was named Rettaglia and seemed to know what he was about. There can't be two IOs who fit that description. It took me a day or so to manufacture an excuse."

"And?"

"Somebody misplaced a bergan coming off the ship. I gave mine away and got out of my company sergeant's way rapidly."

"Your company sergeant is Steel Rudi Scheel?"

"You've heard. This really isn't worthy of his talents, but it'll do until something better comes along. Acting major, now?"

"On the voyage over, Major Randriamahazoman kept finding reasons why the admiral couldn't do what the admiral obviously wanted to do. When the admiral called me in, I didn't know whether he was going to let me kiss his ring or feed me to sharks," Rettaglia explained, leading Sanmartin back.

"And Randriamahazoman?" Sanmartin asked, stumbling slightly on the unfamiliar name as he folded onto the tatamis.

"Rejoined his ancestors."

"Did you undercut him? You sound sincere."

"Believe as you will, I played him straight. He deserved that much. What about you with a company?"

"The Variag can spot talent. What did you age on me, a year?" He peered down his nose, trying to read what Rettaglia had screened up.

"About two years relative. More gray is showing." Rettaglia flicked off the screen from force of habit. "I kept track of you. Your people did a good job."

"We did, didn't we? Thank heaven we didn't need any reserve." Sanmartin laughed ruefully, remembering Beregov and the Complex. "But I had the Variag along to hold my jacket."

"Interested in moving on? I have something lined up."

"Staff? Thank you but no, Rhett. I like where I am."

"You'd love Admiral Lee's staff. If you can count to twenty with your shoes on, you're the proverbial one-eyed man. Want to rub noses with the clouds, former roommate?"

"I hope you haven't forgotten what I think of rubbing up clouds."

"Here I am, poised to hand you creation . . ." Rettaglia said in mock lamentation.

"C'est dommage, n'est pas? Es tut mir leid."

"Sanfairyann. You'd have finished sixteen places higher at the academy if you'd bothered to learn a third expression in a classical language. Well, if your choice is the Variag, my blessing. Did he let you see the materials I had Colonel Lynch send over?''

"He gave me the briefing materials. I'd hate to tell you what he does with everything else Colonel Lynch sends over."

"The Variag is a man of many talents. What kind of time have you got?"

"Another hour before the transport's loaded."

"Then we'll waste it on business. When I come down to Jo'burg, I'll buy you dinner so we can trade stories about Ashcroft, Earth, and points in between."

"Done, if there's a dive on this mudball worth eating in."

"Live, learn, and prosper. The dive is Die Koffiehuis on Krugerstraat, the owner is a Greek married to a local girl. That was Shimazu's first assignment. I must have sent 70,000 k of briefing materials, did you read all that junk?"

"I don't know how to play mah-jongg, and it's been a dull week, so far."

Rettaglia allowed his face to assume a serious aspect. "There are a number of burning facts about this mudball that don't fit, but one particularly perplexes me."

"Ha! You want my keen insight, you've got to pay for it."

"Reach into the bottom drawer behind you. The amaretto's for me, and the arak is for you."

"You brought arak?" Sanmartin said, opening the cabinet and handling the bottle reverently.

"Staff officers don't have weight allowances. Why don't you switch to drinking something healthy, like metal polish?"

Sanmartin cradled the bottle against his chest. "Rhett, I did training on the isle of Kalimantan three times." He took the bottle by its neck left-handed and swirled the liquid inside. "This is the only thing that'll even slow thread-leeches and crotch-rot."

"Internal or external application?" Rettaglia asked, taking the bottle from Sanmartin's hand to open.

"Just pour. What is it you want to know, what killed the sects?"

Rettaglia looked at him narrowly as he filled little glasses. "You're a little unwashed to run a company, but maybe the Variag does know what he's about. Yes, the sects. The jungle bunnies. The strandloopers. They were dying in swarms even before the nice people began using them for target practice, yet the nice people weren't."

Sanmartin poised his head in an exaggerated parody of studiousness. "You want to spot the snake in this lovely Eden. Well, no snakes yet. Limbless amphibian types perform the same function. The ecosystem is about a quarter- or a half-billion years behind Sol III, roughly equivalent to early Permian. Amphtiles are roughly equivalent to labyrinthodont amphibians. Did Mayor Randuia . . . whatever-his-name-was ask your scientists for an answer?"

"Raul, this expedition orbited seventy-seven days after the Diet voted final funds. Scientists take that long to decide which urinal to use," Rettaglia explained, doling out liquor. "Mind you don't spill any, it'll eat the furniture. What say you?"

"No diseases. Anything that does adapt will probably manifest itself by spreading like plague. Animal life is no problem. The big newts are dumb enough to try and eat anything that moves, but they're not agile. What about normal human contrariness?"

"As an answer, the scientists love it. I think it's putrid. Sect villages were falling apart and starving long before their inhabitants were spearing each other and getting shot by pleasant strangers," Rettaglia answered after a pause.

"Well?"

"Well, now that you've bored me to tears with your erudition, what's the answer you smug little lump?"

"A studious smug little lump," Sanmartin corrected with relish.

"Speak friend, and enter."

"Exhibit one: my biochem is stale, but the amino acids this planet uses are different, they almost look to be three-quarters reversed. The sugars and the carbohydrate chains look almost as funny. There's nothing there you and I could live on, the proteins and sugars wouldn't process."

Rettaglia stared at him for a minute, then nodded.

"Exhibit two: the soil's infertile. Histosols with scattered oxisols and ultisols. Call it muck and mire with outcroppings of low-grade dirt. There isn't much useful organic matter, and the fern things don't aerate. I notice it takes a fairish amount of time and effort to turn the best of it around. If the cults expected to bring the crops in and live off the bounty of Allah the Almighty, well, the first few years they'd have been lucky to get their seed back, resulting in malnutrition, kwashiorkor, and cannibalism."

Rettaglia nodded slowly.

"The clue is the cow dung. When the cowboys got here, they

had most everything figured except cow dung. Nothing native can touch a cow patty. By the time they shipped in dung beetles and tailored bacteria, they had five meter manure piles.''

Rettaglia laughed aloud. ''I should know better than to leave you an opening.''

''Ex parvis saepe magnarum momenta rerum pendant.''

''Which means, 'events of great moment often hang on trifles.' When did you start that?''

''The Latin? Serving with the Eleventh Shock Battalion on Kalimantan. When I asked for a colonial posting, they were very happy to let me go.''

''I won't ask.'' Rettaglia let his smile fade.

Sanmartin swirled the liquor in his glass. ''So tell me, Rhett, when does the excitement start and have you figured out who we're supposed to be shooting?''

''We're shooting ranchers and their mercenaries to start with,'' Rettaglia said grimly. ''Some of them are making cooperative noises, but Tsai and his neighbors aren't. They all had relatives in the riverport Lieutenant Colonel Kimura slagged. They have rice cached all through the swamps in the Vaal delta, and they're leading him a merry chase. Until Kimura gets a handle on that mess, we are spread so thin it isn't funny. The factions Chalker and McClausland head up are sitting on the fence.''

''I'm not going to ask what the ranchers do for government.''

''Call it creative anarchy.''

''What about everyone else?''

''Let me try and explain,'' Rettaglia answered. He reached over and took hold of Sanmartin's arak. Thinking clearer, he tipped a little amaretto onto the smooth surface of the table instead. With the little finger on his left hand, he traced a tiny pinpoint of liquor.

''Think of it as concentric rings. A few surviving jungle bunnies who don't matter at all, various sets of ranchers, Boers, and USS,'' he said tracing rings in the liquid.

''Start with USS.''

''USS is reorganizing. The new director is Yugo Tuge. He brought his own people with him into exile. He's a toppled tree. Interestingly enough, it was originally his idea to ship mercenaries to the cowboys here.''

''A former throne and power?''

Rettaglia nodded. ''The local USS people were singularly short on illusions and reacted accordingly. Most everyone except

USS did exceedingly well out of anarchy and had enough of a sense of humor to blame everything on the mercs. Eventually, friend Tuge found himself on the platform apologizing to the assembled shareholders' reps.''

"So now he's sipping the sweet wine of Elba."

"I'm not sure he realizes it, yet. He acts like he's still in the boardroom with his dossiers. He's even got one on you, not that the information in it is worth anything. The old director cut his belly publicly. As near as I can tell, the man played the local factions like a musical instrument for years to maintain a semblance of USS control. Tuge has a talent for making his errors egregious, and I suspect that one will cost us dearly."

Sanmartin grunted. "What about the Boers, I have a city full of them I'm sitting on."

"They did a job on USS and the bunnies, and they held their own with the ranchers. Your people did well to nail them up. They'll probably stay quiet, at least as long as we're shooting cowboys, but they'll be trouble. A lot of them would prefer expressing their political opinions with bullets rather than black sashes."

Sanmartin missed the historical allusion. "What do they do for government? We've shut down the district councils and the landrosts' courts, which were a cross between a debating society and a carnival. Did I mention that my burgemeester in Johannesburg objected to my taking away his police? His replacement is a man named Beyers."

Rettaglia stretched, as if debating whether or not to answer. "It's obvious your specialty is mollusks and not people. Beyers should work out well. Just between us, your Boers have been leaning on USS for seventeen years, local. They could have set up their own central government at any time over the last six."

Sanmartin looked startled. "Why didn't they?"

"I have two notions. If the Boers had set up a government themselves, they'd have frightened USS and the ranchers into some awfully stupid things, but USS needs to stop the chaos. If we weren't here, somebody like Tuge might be dumb enough to ask the Boers to form one. And the Boer thrones and powers might not think they need one just yet, at least out in the open."

"That's a wonderful thought. It means we've got a real mess to police up. Wonderful."

"Isn't it? Spend a minute considering the possibilities as you ruin your body with more thread-leech specific, then I have an even better idea for you to consider. There are also the ranchers' mercenaries, who are going to start thinking for themselves in the near future. The admiral has decided to make an example of them. He wants them exterminated; they're going to gravitate toward the people shooting at us.''

Sanmartin looked at him and carefully set his glass down.

''Did you say things were dull?'' Rettaglia continued with relish. ''Until Kimura finishes fooling around in the delta, things could get interesting for you people.''

Thursday(1)

TIMO HAERKOENNEN COUGHED EXPECTANTLY, POISED TO COMplete the morning ritual. Solemnly, Vereshchagin unpocketed his little black book and handed it over.

Senior Communications Sergeant Haerkoennen lightly flipped to a page at random, scanned it with a light pencil, and recorded an encryption code for the battalion radio net. That portion of his task completed, he returned the book to Vereshchagin, who solemnly stuffed the ruined page in his pipe and flashed it.

Ease of communication from level to level was one of the fundamental strengths an Imperial battalion possessed.

Haerkoennen turned away, and Saki Bukanov took his place with a sheaf of requisitions to present. The intendance officer was buying up construction materials. Reinikka, who commanded the engineer platoon, had drawn up a detailed list of requirements before going off to Bloemfontein to help the Iceman make life miserable and brief for a few cowboys. With a single question, Vereshchagin initialed off. Bukanov called up a spreadsheet and bounced it off his assistant quartermaster.

Bukanov had a deputy quartermaster and a quartermaster sergeant named Redzup, but his ''assistant quartermaster'' was the little computer that lived in his lap. The battalion had a standing jest that if the assistant quartermaster ever bought it, they'd have to call off the war. A short, swarthy man with pronounced lines under his eyes, Bukanov was, in Harjalo's quaint phrase, ''a walking contradiction,'' an honest intendance officer. Bukanov was one of a handful of roses Vereshchagin had plucked from the soil of Ashcroft; Purnamo had given him away freely since an honest intendance officer was the very last thing Purnamo had a use for.

Although his quartermaster element had long ago been stripped bare to fill out the rifle companies, Bukanov somehow contrived to make do. His computer and vehicle mechanics, clerks, communications specialists, and armorers were the slender, truncated "tail" Vereshchagin's battalion needed to survive. A third of them were "straphangers," women who had attached themselves to the battalion on one world or another. Bukanov's also were the "extras," the hewers of wood and drawers of water who handled ammunition resupply and miscellaneous tasks until they replaced casualties in the rifle companies.

Bukanov discovered an answer that pleased him and walked away in Haerkoennen's footsteps. Vereshchagin dusted his hands, carefully reflecting that looking after communications and supply might be the most important tasks he accomplished in the course of the day. He was diverted by the sight of Matti Harjalo sliding through the cellar door with a twinkle in his eyes.

Intending to liberate anything not firmly nailed down, Harjalo had left for the spaceport in Yuri Malinov's company. Without doubt he and the battalion sergeant had done precisely that.

"There were a lot of combat rations and ammunition just lying around, so we signed for them and brought them back," Harjalo replied to the unasked question. "Electronics, too."

"That is very good," Vereshchagin commented noncommittally, wondering what name Matti had chosen to sign. "Anything else?"

"They were unloading machine guns for the volunteer battalions they plan to form, and we may have picked up a half dozen or so by accident." Vereshchagin's executive officer made little secret of his view on putting real weapons in the hands of cardboard commandos. "We swapped for two light trucks and an extra fuel lighter to carry it all back."

Past experience with centralized supply had immunized Vereshchagin to excessive solicitude for the welfare of the supply functionaries Matti had driven to distraction. He asked about replacements, which was uppermost in his mind.

That did bring a smile to Harjalo's broken face. "We have nineteen of our own from Helsinki, one a sublieutenant, Tikhon Degtyarev's son. From the replacement pool, I pried another four and a sublieutenant out from under Colonel Lynch's fingernails, but that's all we'll get. Kimura's taken a fair number of casualties, and Ebyl will need the rest."

"Did you actually sign for them?" Vereshchagin asked in a resigned tone of voice.

"Why no. It must have slipped my mind. The battalion sergeant has them for the time being. He dragged them off to teach them who the first commander of the battalion was and so forth. I don't suppose it will hurt for them to stay on Colonel Lynch's books for a while.''

Vereshchagin rapped his pipe against his thigh pensively.

"I looked them over thoroughly," Harjalo continued, using a euphemism for setting aside trash. "Our sister battalion seems to have done a fair job this time." In the past, their sister battalion, the 2nd Battalion, 35th Imperial Rifles, had not been overly scrupulous in selecting men to send to the stars.

"And Degtyarev the second?"

"He's fresh as daisies, of course, but he'll do very well, I think. He's twice as big as Tikhon, and if he's half as mean he'll do very well indeed." By some fluke in the measurement of time, so far as the battalion was concerned it had only been a few years since the elder Degtyarev had taken his medical retirement.

"How do you wish to divide the spoils?"

"I'll put Degtyarev and nine to Piotr to bring him up to strength. If Chalker's cowboys start acting up, he'll need them. We can give the spare sublieutenant to Raul, and he and Yoshida can split the rest.''

"Agreed. Good enough, but not enough." Vereshchagin noted his commo personnel eavesdropping shamelessly. "I will ask the admiral if we may recruit a few locals. He will not like it, I think, but he will not forbid it. We can give them to Paul to whip into shape. What about the officer?"

"His file looks promising."

Vereshchagin wondered how much that had cost. "What did Yuri say?"

"Our esteemed battalion sergeant thinks he'll shape nicely. See for yourself!" Harjalo looked up through the open cellar door and a slight, coffee-colored sublieutenant dropped through like a cat. "Edmund Muslar. They had him running the replacement pool."

Vereshchagin walked over and carefully shook hands. "What lies did Matti tell you?"

Muslar smiled, exposing even white teeth. "Sir, I was kidnapped."

Vereshchagin laughed. "You will do well."

"I am honored, sir," Muslar said. "I know that this is a Russian battalion with unexcelled reputation . . ." He stopped when he saw that Vereshchagin was walking away and followed him back into the partitioned space that served as both office and living quarters.

"This is not a Russian battalion," Vereshchagin said, closing the door and irreverently conjuring up a vision of *pukkas*, troikas, and artificial snow. "We recruit from Suomi, the sons and grandsons of refugees from the former RSFSR and native Finns like Matti. Over that kernel is an Imperial glaze. Still more of us are colonials or chance accretions like yourself."

He maneuvered Muslar into an empty chair like a slender plastic spider. "As for our reputation, it is what they have made it. Our men generally complete a double term of service and take their muster pay to the colony on Esdraelon. The Battalion Association becomes a second home for many of them. We have second generation soldiers from there."

For many of them, the battalion was a first home. Suomi—Finland—was a poor, cold, overpopulated land with forests dying, still slowly poisoned by the radioactive plague spots at either end of the old Karelian border. Esdraelon might be Suomi reborn some day, but it would not come for free. Although a large measure of the pay and entitlements flowing through the battalion ended up there, Esdraelon was still another ragged colonial world starved for capital.

"Tea?" he inquired politely.

Muslar politely declined.

"In some ways we are much like a family, as unusual as that may seem. The battalion has been on active colonial service for sixteen years continuously, which is forty years relative to Earth. As you might imagine, discipline here is very different than it is back there."

Muslar made no reply, knowing enough not to speak merely to hear himself talk.

Vereshchagin paused to contemplate Muslar. On Ashcroft there had been the desert to sort out mistakes. He reached over and tossed one of the tiny backported radios to Muslar, who examined it carefully.

"This has been modified. I see a disk mount and two ports," Muslar exclaimed.

"Quite correct. As you may recall, there is a tiny but powerful computer inside that does little apart from scrambling and unscrambling messages. We use them for quite a bit more. Some of the academy courses are popular with our noncommissioned officers. Men in this battalion can be trusted to do whatever is necessary without a great deal of nonsense. They are, however, unlikely to tolerate a great deal of nonsense from you. Have I said enough?''

"Yes, sir. Quite enough," Muslar said thoughtfully.

"I will be sending you to Captain Sanmartin's C Company. Please excuse me while I make Raul Sanmartin aware of your existence." With a word of thanks, Vereshchagin accepted the receiver Timo Haerkoennen handed through the doorway.

As Muslar executed a stiff salute and departed, Harjalo plopped himself in the empty seat with undisguised enthusiasm. "How gently were you planning to break the news to Raul about his new job?"

"I had anticipated that you would provide me with a carrot to offer him first. Do we have a connection? Hello, Raul? How is everything? . . . Yes, I know that you are bored, but I have been working on that. . . . No, there is no reason for you to worry. Excuse me for a second, there is some background interference." He waved Harjalo to silence.

"First off, you are getting a new sublieutenant. . . . No, you do not have to kill anybody to keep him. His name is Edmund Muslar. Put him in number eleven and put him through the usual. You are also getting five riflemen and two more bodies that Matti scraped from under rocks. . . . The battalion sergeant has them in hand, and I expect that he will release them in a day or two. . . . You are most welcome, Raul. . . . Oh, by the way, Acting Major Rettaglia gave me a call, I believe that you and he knew each other at the academy. . . . He spoke very highly of you. . . ."

Vereshchagin looked over at Harjalo, who was beaming with undisguised glee. "We have worked out an arrangement so that you can be the assistant intelligence officer for the brigade. . . . Raul? Are you there? . . ."

IT TOOK SANMARTIN APPROXIMATELY SIX MINUTES TO GET through to brigade intelligence. He would have done it in two had he been able to speak coherently.

"Rhett? Rhett, you slimy, slinking lump!"

"Calm down, Raul. Don't shout so. You'll give yourself an ulcer. The connection is very good. I hear you perfectly. I told you you'd make a perfect IO. Lieutenant-Colonel Vereshchagin was very understanding when I explained what an opportunity this was for you," the voice said on the other end.

"I'll shoot him. No, first I'll shoot you. What about my company, you idiot!"

"That's part of our understanding, you keep your company and double up to learn the business," Rettaglia answered in a syrupy voice that somehow failed to soothe.

"Are you trying to tell me I've been saddled with two jobs?"

"I worry about you, Raul. Lieutenant-Colonel Vereshchagin was just telling me how bored you were; he assured me that your exec would help you with everything."

"Rettaglia, if this is your idea of a joke . . ."

"You'll enjoy every minute. Shimazu will be up with an interpreter the day after tomorrow to set up. Just don't say your old roommate didn't do his best for you."

"Rettaglia, when I get my hands on you . . ."

"I have to get moving, Raul. It was fun talking to you. Ciao."

"Rettaglia! You long-beaked buzzard, I'll trash your Verdi for this, do you hear me?" Sanmartin shouted into the dead line. He stared at the receiver as if it had bitten him.

"You sound upset," Hans Coldewe observed with a touching show of concern.

Friday(1)

ONE ROTATION OF THE PLANET WAS A LITTLE MORE THAN 70,000 standard seconds, which made for a twenty-hour day. A ten degree axial tilt made for fairly long nights on the southern rim of Akashi Continent. Long nights encourage troop movements. The Iceman's platoons had taken considerable pains to discourage that sort of thing on several planets. They referred to themselves as "the night shift."

Section Sergeant Suslov was a charter member of the night shift. On three worlds, he had alternately frozen or fried. Cleaning his rifle in the gray light of dawn, he felt his mind snap to instant awareness. His hands moved to snap the pieces of his weapon together effortlessly as his mind registered what the radio had to say.

"Hardin. Small group of cowboys, platoon-size maybe. Maybe mercs. Don't know enough to stay off the trails. They're coming up the red river road to play with the Afrikaners," the outpost said.

"All right. They've been warned," Suslov replied. He switched off to ring up the mortar team. "One point five zero one. Break. Suslov. Koskela, we have flies on the web. Have a marker to drop onto killing-zone Bryansk."

"Only a marker? If you like," Koskela replied.

Lieutenant Jankowskie would be disappointed, Suslov decided. Jankowskie was a good platoon leader, as was anyone who aspired to command one of the Iceman's platoons for more than a very brief time, but he had categorically refused to believe anyone would be silly enough to cross at the loop in the Vaal where Suslov was.

Heaven knew, the cowboys had been warned. The area between Bloemfontein and Chalkton between the rivers was the heart of the shooting war between the cowboys and the Boers. Major Kolomeitsev had declared it no-man's-land and given both sides twenty hours to get out.

The Steyndorp Boers had taken the Iceman's measure. Ian Chalker's cowboys apparently hadn't. Instead of helping the Tsai's bunch tie Kimura in knots, they were coming through to maul the Boers. Kolomeitsev had two of his own rifle platoons and Yevtushenko's reconnaissance platoon. He couldn't keep them all out indefinitely, but apparently the Chalkton cowboys had even less patience than good sense.

Sery, Suslov's general purpose machine gunner, swung his gun to cover the partially cleared area that was killing-zone Bryansk. Suslov tapped him on the shoulder. "Don't fool around. Just knock them down and keep them there."

They waited.

Two men dressed in civs came strolling. After seventeen hours in the swamp, Suslov's nose twitched. The thin pretense wore thinner when the second man began sweeping with a portable imager. Suslov's nose twitched again. As hot as it was, even a calibrated thermal imager was worthless on reflective clothing.

The main body appeared in a clump, mercenaries and cowboys mixed. There were perhaps thirty of them, understrength for a platoon. Their clothing looked new. They knew enough to keep a point, but they'd detailed neither flank nor rear security. The first two came across. The remainder on the far shore knelt on one knee, in perfect view.

Suslov rubbed his chin reflexively. That was the trouble with mercs, even the ones who acted like soldiers weren't. Another few minutes would serve to teach these fancy boys that.

"One point, Akita. Break. Suslov. Sery will initiate," he said as a few men from the main body reached the near shore.

Suslov took a craftsman's pride in his work. When the point men approached to forty meters, he finished counting down and impersonally tapped Sery.

The ambush was laid as a Saint Andrew's cross to place mutually supporting fire on any portion of the curve of the bank. The point team had no chance. As shrill coughing from the light machine guns erupted from either side, it disintegrated in the deep roar of the fire from Sery's seven-seven.

From behind Sery came a single round from the 88 and an arching sheaf of projectiles from the s-mortar that exploded among the bunched main body with devastating effect. S-mortars were most effective firing triplets: one short, long for luck, and the third up someone's trousers.

The fire pinned the survivors where they stood, huddled behind a slight depression a few meters from the river's edge. Whether they charged the ambush or ran, flanking fire would take them from at least one of the arms. "One point five zero one. Break. Give me the marker," Suslov called. Obediently, a single 105mm mortar round exploded in a cloud of red smoke.

Suslov squinted at the billowing smoke and juggled numbers on the calculator on his wrist. "Sloppy. If I tell you I want live rounds, bring it in twelve and seven to the right," he told the mortar before closing the contact.

A few of the cowboys trapped by the river bed returned unaimed rounds at the machine gunners who were stripping the forest ferns ankle high. The rest hugged the earth for security it could not give.

"One point A for Akita. Break. Vladimir, Martti, everyone, that's enough!" Suslov shouted, slapping Sery on the back. A silence drifted over the disturbed forest as the last of the red smoke played out.

Suslov cupped his hands. "Okay, cowboys, give up!"

One man dropped his weapon and stood, to be shot down by another. Hesitantly, rifle shots punctuated the silence. Suslov slapped Sery, and immediately the machine gun fire resumed in earnest. He punched Sery lightly. "I've forgotten. Did the Iceman say he particularly wanted prisoners?" His loader shook his head from side to side and continued to guide the linked rounds.

"One point five zero one. Break. Give me one, wait five, then dump it," Suslov told the mortar crew. Almost immediately, a single round spun overhead to explode almost on top of the cowboys. Five seconds passed. Suslov made no correction, then two and ten more rained down, high explosive and white phosphorus fused for near-surface bursts at precise two second intervals from the short-barreled 105mm mortar.

Before the last round dropped, the shrieking of the wounded stopped. Suslov tapped Sery and spoke distinctly into his mount, "Hold up! That should do it."

The rifles and the light machine gunners darted forward from either flank one by one. Suslov nodded to Sery and moved off crabwise. Sery, a faint golden down on his pallid cheeks, watched for movement until the first of the leaping riflemen strayed across his line of fire. Then he cleared his weapon and looked at his loader.

"Amateurs," Sery said, blinking his young-old eyes.

One of the riflemen got close enough to see into the little depression. Abruptly, he turned his head and vomited.

There were half a dozen prisoners after all, but four of them were so badly wounded that Suslov called in one of the big tilt-props to get them out. Sery walked over uncertainly. "They look so stiff. Shouldn't we bury them or something?"

Suslov looked at the curious, buzzing "insects" and spat. He thought for a moment and shook his head. "We'll tell the cowboys where they are. Or the river will rise and save them the trouble." He spat again.

The hum of alcohol engines contrasted with the buzzing. A stubby, four-wheel utility vehicle climbed up over the goat path that passed for the Red River Road to halt behind a fern-topped mound. The long mortar tube stuck out over the downward-sloping hood. With the baseplate and ammo stowed in the center, the two men sitting facing each other in back gave it a gap-toothed silhouette. It was followed by a second loaded with ammunition.

Suslov grinned. "You packed it in quick. If I'd put in another mission?"

"Told you to find another mortar," burly Koskela shouted back, his face split wide.

"Need help," Suslov shouted as the first rays of golden sunlight appeared. He jerked his head toward the cowboys his men were slinging into hammocks, a thin, telescopic pole resting beside each of them.

Koskela shrugged. Burdened with their submachine guns, he and two of his men hopped out.

The mortar platoons were invariably split. One of the short tubes was normally attached to each platoon, although the Iceman had instead given a mortar to each of Jankowskie's three sections in prepared ambush positions. A fourth tube was with the company headquarters in Bloemfontein under the direction of the sergeant platoon commander.

The short fellows could dump a fairly massive amount of steel a limited distance with superb accuracy. Beside the shallow Vaal, Suslov watched Koskela appraise his work critically. Mortarmen had a variety of rounds to choose from. Each gun layer had a preference, as ''WP''—white phosphorus—Koskela had his.

With a grunt, Koskela went to the river's edge and filled his hat with water. He walked back and poured it over the leg of one of the twitching cowboys so that a fingernail-sized chunk of the white phosphorus wouldn't burn its way out the other side. Almost before he finished, Suslov heard the drone of engines and stood up straight.

The stubby tilt-rotor drifted in and slid to the right to spill lift with a fast, practiced ease. The four rotors, mounted front and back on either wing, seemed to overlap as they moved from horizontal to vertical. Suslov held his arms over his head and crossed them to guide the big bird down. The ramp between the tall, twin booms opened out even before the wheels touched. With a gentle hand, the pilot kept the rotors spinning without lifting free.

Koskela's drivers wasted no time in maneuvering on board. Grunting under the weight of his bergean, Suslov picked up one of the poles with Koskela and kicked his only relatively un-scathed prisoner, a dazed bearded man, toward the open ramp. The gp and the eighty-eight moved in through the forward doors along with the s-mortarman, almost buried under an array of captured weaponry.

With the massive, counter-rotating front and back rotors swung out and pointing toward the sky, it never ceased to amaze Suslov that they never tangled even when they seemed to overlap moving from horizontal to vertical. Although Suslov's mind accepted the fact that a tilt was safer than a helicopter, his heart was slow to follow. In actuality, whatever advantage the tilt-props gave away to true helicopters during vertical lift, they more than made up in sustained flight with the pusher engines in back feathering to lessen fuel consumption. Although inferior in over-all performance to normal planes, like the ''jump-jets'' of an earlier era, their ability to take off and land vertically more than compensated for this disadvantage.

After the first three wounded cowboys were loaded, Suslov pulled in his teams on perimeter security while the mortarmen went back for the last two. "One point Akita. Break. Vladimir, Martti! If you don't come in, we won't hold dinner."

They appeared almost immediately at a disciplined quickstep from either side. Between the time the tilt-prop first appeared and the time the doors closed, six minutes passed.

James McClausland rode in that evening from the lake country to discuss terms with Admiral Lee and Janine Joh. On balance, Admiral Lee considered the operation extremely successful.

Saturday(1)

DR. A. DE R. BEYERS, BURGEMEESTER OF JOHANNESBURG, folded his hands calmly, looking across to young Captain Sanmartin.

The demand for the food that the farmers could market had increased, and so had the demand for the products the workers at Complex could turn out. The Volk were already more divided. One attempt at a boycott had failed miserably when the Imperials hinted that they would shift their purchasing to the *uitlanders*. With a commendable sense of the absurd, the populace had nicknamed the Imperial garrisons from the captain's battalion the *suikslapers*, which translates best as "squatters."

The Imperials were a fact. Since announcing the abrogation of the United Steel-Standard charter, they were almost popular, but Albert Beyers had little doubt the captain's vehicles merited the gallows insignia they bore.

Beyers's predecessor had chosen to treat Captain Sanmartin's politeness as an absense of resolve. In lieu of names and addresses which had failed to materialize, Captain Sanmartin had appeared in his predecessor's office with a few light machine gunners to accept a letter of resignation, printed in impeccable Afrikaans. Albert Beyers had his job.

Peering across the glass-topped table, Beyers was mildly surprised that his predecessor, for whom he had no great regard, had found a proper estimation so difficult. Beyers could recall the faces of the old men who had passed through the fires of the Bantu Wars. The young captain had a measure of that; their present inability to communicate was mildly irritating.

Beyers had already spent most of a day attempting to locate a suitable interpreter, du Toit's interpreter having failed to realize that guileless Captain Sanmartin would record discussions for later review by someone who spoke Afrikaans. However, if Beyers understood the captain correctly, the Imperials would send one out in a few days. Beyers looked forward to his arrival.

Beyers intended to arrange acceptable accommodations with the Imperials. He was desperately afraid of what would occur if he did not.

Far away, on the north bank of the Vaal, kindly hands grasped the rancher Ian Chalker as he methodically tried to match severed legs to the bodies of two of his sons. The bloated, blackened corpses were difficult to distinguish one from another.

Sunday(2)

ON THE EIGHTH DAY, MOSTLY THEY RESTED. MATTI HARJALO observed that it made good sense to sleep in on a day when the Boers were in church praying for God to afflict the minions of Pharaoh.

Along the line of the Vaal, the Iceman, Major Kolomeitsev, left one rifle platoon to man a screen of outposts and threw in two light attack platoons, his own and the one allotted to Yoshida, to cover the minefields which Reinikka's engineers had laid from opposite Chalkton to Little Lizard Swamp.

He calculated a further lesson to the cowboys was in order.

Quiddities(2)

FOR FIRST WEEK THE IMPERIALS WERE DOWNSIDE, OPPOSITION was scattered and uncoordinated. Apart from Tsai and Chalker, the rancher lords adopted a policy of accommodation. The existing power structures in the Afrikaner communities likewise adopted no radical measures. They were far too concerned with immediate needs to bother with politics, for several reasons.

Electric power from the ocean tap was easily produced and well suited for most home and industrial uses. Most of all, it was cheap. The fixed rail system that brought ore from the mines to the refineries and raw materials from the refineries to Complex ran on electric power. Many of the trucks, buses, and automobiles ran on electric power. The telecommunication system degraded by *Graf Spee* and her consorts on L-day ran on electric power. From appliances to refrigeration, in one way or another, quite a few things were dependent upon the ocean tap, and backup systems do not command a high priority in a pioneer society.

When Admiral Lee turned out the lights at the ocean tap "for a limited time pending the restoration of full services," lights went out. They came back on gradually for selected industrial operations and selected, pacified communities.

Admiral Lee also suspended deliveries of alcohol from Complex. The expected panic set in, with widespread hoarding of available stocks. Although alcohol stills are much easier to cobble together than are power plants, the shortfall was not one that was made up in a day. Apart from the delivery of essential items such as foodstuffs, movement in and between communities virtually ceased.

Those few areas that took steps to expand home guard formations with an eye toward resistance immediately encountered difficulties. Lured both by tradition and the lack of practical alternatives, both ranchers and Boers turned to the horse as a means of transport and transportation. In areas such as Dewetsdorp District where the number of experienced horsemen was not large, efforts collapsed even before the Imperials applied gentle pressure. The Dewetsdorp home guards convinced themselves that their beasts could be fed on a steady diet of ferns and other native plants. They were nicknamed "the horse-breakers" before they disbanded.

With the imposition of martial law and curfew, it was nine days before a full meeting of the executive council of the Afrikaner Bond could be arranged to decide what the response of the organization would be. In the interim, local cells, largely left without direction, avoided incidents, and the Afrikaner "provisional" district councils were permitted to fade into obscurity.

Of course, even Admiral Lee's detractors were willing to concede he was very smart, for a Korean. However, grasping control of the situation is merely the first step undertaken by an Imperial task force.

Monday(2)

COLDEWE TOED SANMARTIN AWAKE. "RISE AND SHINE, BRIGHT eyes. The sun shines, the birds sing. You have guests, and your presence is desired," Hans hissed in a sugary stage whisper.

"Stretch forth your hands and touch the new rays of the morning," he added, presumably quoting something or other.

It had been a bad night and a worse morning. Sanmartin rubbed his eyes. A patrol and a court-martial had not improved his disposition. "What birds?" he croaked. Thinking better of this, he added, "Hans, I'm going to stake you out on an anthill."

"Honored sir, I believe Lieutenant Coldewe is no longer able to hear you," said an unfamiliar voice.

Sanmartin bolted upright, reaching for the assault rifle that Coldewe had thoughtfully slipped from his grasp.

"I am, however, most pleased to understand that you will be learning matters of intelligence from me. I trust that our association will be a pleasing one," Senior Intelligence Sergeant Shimazu continued crisply. He snapped to attention and offered a brisk salute.

Sanmartin staggered to his feet and returned the salute with something less than a flourish. He noticed a civilian behind Shimazu blushing.

"Juffrou Bruwer will be our interpreter," Shimazu said.

"Honored to meet you, Juffrou Bruwer," Sanmartin said, conscious of the fact he was wearing the emperor's new clothes.

"I am most pleased to meet you, heer captain. If you could please excuse me . . ." She scurried out of the bunker.

"Honored captain, is there anything you would require of me before I begin to set up?" Shimazu interjected.

"No. Nothing. We're happy to have you as our guest, senior intelligence sergeant, and I look forward to learning something about intelligence."

Sticking his head into a bucket of water, he hastily climbed into mottled fatigues. He failed to locate Coldewe. Finally he sighed and walked out to the remodeled farmhouse where Kasha the cook had her field establishment.

Habitually split off to function independently, Vereshchagin's rifle companies were not overwhelmingly endowed with dead weight. Sanmartin had a clerk, two communications men, an armorer, something euphemistically called an acquisitions clerk, and two cooks. The rest filled spaces in the platoon perimeters. While combatant companies were intended to be exclusively male, one made exception for genius. "Kasha" Vladimirovna was arguably the most important person in the company. Her understudy existed solely in case she bought herself an urn.

As for the rest, Rytov, the armorer, had joined the battalion at sixteen straight from the orphanage in Lappeenranta to which he had been evacuated at the age of three from Leningrad. He had refused promotion thrice, retirement twice, and claimed to have seen the paintings destroyed with the Hermitage. The company clerk was an utterly efficient cipher who split watches with the commo men, fed the computer, and kept the books reasonably crooked. Grigorenko was the company scrounger.

Normally, two or three of them were present in Kasha's mess at any given time. Entering, Sanmartin saw only Shimazu's new interpreter seated with her shoulders slumped, untouched sausages and duck eggs in front of her on a plate. He altered course. She saw him and rose disjointedly, bowing.

Slowing, he waved her down. "Please, Juffrou Bruwer, please sit."

"Heer captain?"

He flipped a chair around and settled in, resting his elbows on its back. "Welcome. First, I must apologize for inadvertently embarrassing you. My executive officer usually organizes his practical jokes with more discretion." He glanced down at her untouched meal. "Aren't you going to eat that?"

"Well . . ." she stammered.

He pulled her platter over. "Please, may I? If Kasha even suspects you don't like her food . . . You don't actually dislike food, do you?"

"Nothing like that. I just did not feel like eating," she replied distractedly.

"Good. That's very good. If Kasha thinks you don't like it, she will weep and relay messages through canaries. How did Rhett talk you into this, anyway?"

"Rhett?"

"I'm sorry, Acting Major Rettaglia, our intelligence officer, who can sell snow to polar bears." Cutting into the sausages, Sanmartin watched for Kasha Vladimirovna out of the corner of his right eye. Kasha had a soft spot—either in her heart or in her head—for stray nestlings which her present husband took in stride.

"I am not certain what you mean, Heer Captain."

"Please forget it."

Sanmartin wondered what normal people did for conversation. He examined her face between forkfuls, studying it and her. Bruwer had high, broad, even cheekbones that swept down into a pointed chin. Her mouth was not wide, and it turned down naturally at either corner. Her hair was a fine gold-blond, cut straight across the front and hanging down straight with some sort of flare at the sides that he supposed was a style. She was neither thin or fat. The overall effect was not unattractive in a brittle way.

"When did you get here?" he asked, mopping up the last of the shell eggs. When she made no response, he laid down his fork and studied her closely. "Do you always look this pale, or is there something in particular bothering you?"

"There was a man here. They lined up and shot him."

"That. Just so. I'm sorry, it's not as though we greet every guest with a field execution. *Justitia suum cuique distribuit.*"

"I am very sorry, I do not recognize the words. Are they Japanese?"

"It's a Latin tag. 'Justice renders to everyone what is due him' is an acceptable translation. Our newest and least distinguished replacement committed forcible rape. Bardiyev was fool enough to let him off at a checkpoint to empty his trousers. I suppose I'll need you to translate the sentence of the court for the benefit of the townsfolk. After we put a few holes in the wall where former Recruit Private Novelo was standing, I ripped a stripe from Bardiyev for general stupidity."

Bruwer blinked back in concern. "Are you then so very strict?"

"Not I. Somebody strict like the Iceman would have had Bardi standing next to Novelo for even thinking about trying to cover up a mess like that. He should have shot Novelo on the spot and saved us the bother. I gave his job to Beregov." He saw her dazed expression. "*Bonis nocet quisquis pepercerit malis.* 'In all things, whoever spares the bad injures the good.' The truth is, we don't shoot people very often. Our own, that is. This was my first." He dabbed at his mouth. "We are pleased to have you. How is it that you came to work for us?"

"Some friends, they called. They seemed to think it would be a good idea. I spoke to my grandfather, and he agreed. I had no job." She hesitated. "How is it that you came?"

"I wasn't asked, I can tell you that."

"No, I meant why did you Imperials come."

"The usual, I suppose," he said, lightly. "To make ourselves a peace."

"If we do not care for your peace?"

"We'll make ourselves a solitude and call it peace, as Galgacus said of the Romans, I suppose."

She looked at him wide-eyed.

"Sometimes that's what we do," he said.

She looked down, then she looked up again. "You are spilling your tea," she observed hesitantly.

"Oh, just so." He set the cup down with an effort. "Considering it's tea, I'm not sure I mind. My hand seems to be shaking."

She stared at him. "Then it does bother you."

"As I said, this is my first."

She thought for a second. "I almost left. I would have."

He smiled, a little. "Juffrou Bruwer, I have a request. I came to apologize and have a polite, friendly conversation. Are there any polite, friendly questions I can answer?"

She sat very still for a moment, then she dimpled very slightly. "Yes, I have two, Heer Captain. What is that song that you were playing when you drove into Johannesburg? Everyone has been asking."

"Fame at last. That was *The Little Tin Soldier*, which is nearly as popular as *The Whistling Pig*. We save it for very special martial occasions. It's the battalion drinking song. And?"

"Heer Captain, is there a room . . ."

He coughed politely. "That we're working on. I noticed Hans put a couple of men on it. And please stop calling me 'Heer Captain.' I keep turning around. 'Sanmartin' is fine. 'Raul, you idiot' is probably better." He waved his hand airily. "They used to call me *'Tak Tochno,'* which is Russian for 'Just so.' "

"Oh."

He picked up the teacup, cradled it with both hands, and then set it back down. It was a wonderful way to start off. Sanmartin wondered what else he could foul up. He bowed politely and began to rise.

"Captain Sanmartin!"

"Yes?"

"Please call me Hanna."

He continued feeling only half-dead and slightly foolish.

Tuesday(2)

VERESHCHAGIN HAD ATTENDED MANY STAFF MEETINGS. UNFORtunately, Colonel Lynch's weekly staff meetings placed futility on a new footing. Uwe Eybl, the light attack battalion commander, had openly displayed his disenchantment, both with his brigade commander and with the infantrymen of Kimura's that his vehicles were supporting.

After the meeting, before Vereshchagin could slip away, Lynch had called Vereshchagin aside, crushing out his cigarette with obvious irritation.

"Vereshchagin, I wish to inspect your command."

Vereshchagin wrinkled his nose. His antipathy to burnt tobacco was legendary, which might have had something to do with this. "As you desire, Colonel. When would you care to come by?"

"Right now. There is no time like the present. I want to see C Company in Johannesburg."

"Most of C Company is standing down from night patrols," Vereshchagin explained patiently, as if to a small child.

"All the better. I want to impress upon all my units that instant readiness is expected in my command. They should be prepared every second of every day. Little police actions like Ashcroft take the edge off soldiers. They get slovenly. I will not tolerate this."

"As you wish. Do you have your own transportation?" Vereshchagin's eyes fixed on Lynch's protruding gut. Lynch's aide, Captain Dong, stood in silent witness.

"You came in on the supply flight, didn't you? My staff and I will do the same."

Vereshchagin mentally flipped a coin to see whether food or ammunition suffered. Colonel's Lynch's reluctance to approve direct resupply from space had prompted Uwe's original outburst. Food won the toss but lost the space anyway.

"As you wish, Colonel."

"We'll be leaving at 1300 local time. No communications, now, Vereshchagin. I want to surprise them."

"As you wish, Colonel." Vereshchagin saluted, walked out, and tried to decide where he could best twiddle his thumbs for three hours. To cadge a meal, he walked into the bunker that served as a mess for the headquarters detachment. He discovered an old friend in ambush.

"Buy a girl a cup of coffee, soldier?" Eva Moore croaked raucously.

Vereshchagin winced. "Tea."

"Done!"

Graying hair and lieutenant-colonel's rank had hardly changed her. Vereshchagin walked over to the samovar and came away with a mug in either hand and a few lumps of sugar. He squeezed behind the rickety plastic table. "Hello, Eva. You seem to have expected me. It's been a long time since Cyclade."

"Six years. Plus a few extra months for time dilation for me. Have you been avoiding me?"

"Stop teasing, little dove." Vereshchagin gestured toward a table of suddenly silent lieutenants. "The children don't know any better."

"It would only help my reputation."

"Eva?"

"Truce."

"Truce." He placed a sugar cube between his teeth and took a sip of the hot tea. "The metal fragments are still in there, you know. I have never had them removed. They make cold weather uncomfortable. I was expected?"

"My sources on Colonel Lynch's staff are impeccable."

"How have you managed to avoid attendance at staff meetings?"

"I had Molly bribe Dong. Do you know him?"

"The little catamite? When I buy a man, I prefer one who will stay bought."

"That's him. Did you warn your battalion that the white typhoon was on his way?"

"Colonel Lynch directed me not to do so."

"And?"

"Fifteen minutes after the supply run is overdue, Matti Harjalo is going to ask what in the name of heaven is going on. Matti is perfectly capable of counting to two on his fingers. Do you know Matti?"

"No, I don't remember him."

"I will introduce you at the first opportunity. Matti is a true gemstone, the pearl of great price."

"Congratulations. Congratulations on your battalion."

"And you as well. Six years ago, who would have thought it?"

"Don't fool yourself, Anton. They need us out here on the fringes where the golden boys won't go."

"Perhaps. How is Miriam?"

"Dead. A contact mine on Albuera."

"I am sorry."

"Don't be. It's been two years. The wound is healing."

"Are you seeing anyone now?"

"No, the girls all seem much too young. They're like the daughters I never had. I hold them at arm's length."

"You never worried about that before."

"It is not tactful for you to point that out. How about yourself, Anton?"

"There is no one, of course. How could it be otherwise? And who would have me?"

"You should meet my orthopedic surgeon."

"Slender? Brown eyes and short dark hair? I saw her when I went to see the two of mine you still have lying around shirking. Thank you, no."

"At least you're still alert enough to look. She'd be perfect for you."

"Eva, stop playing matchmaker. It does not suit you."

"I should think I'd be perfect. Neither one of you is my type, and I like you both."

"Oh, stop it, Eva."

"No, I'm serious this time, Anton. My little Natashenka is a very nice girl from Tyumen. I truly think you and she should know each other better."

"Eva, the woman must be a meter eighty. How can you possibly call her little?"

"Stop quibbling."

"Eva, this is neither the time nor the place. Even if the inland cowboys do not explode into revolt in the next ten minutes . . ."

"Anton Aleksandrovich," she said in a firm, quiet voice, "cease this nonsense immediately!"

Years of discipline had left their mark on Vereshchagin.

"Look at who they've sent here. You and I and Eybl are expendable. Kimura has a father-in-law, so it would have been impolitic to shoot him outright. Higuchi couldn't keep his mouth shut and made old Kajitani look like a fool. Colonel Lynch is a fool, and Rear-Admiral Irie, who hasn't set foot off *Graf Spee*, makes Lynch look smart. Admiral Lee is too smart to be Korean and too Korean to be left near the thrones and powers. I could go on if you like. A merry band of brothers, are we not? Just how long do you think we're going to be camped out on this mudball?"

Vereshchagin blinked.

"Anton, I'm going to be a nice girl. When you come to see Colonel Lynch next Tuesday, don't plan on flying out. Instead, bring along your manners. Now, how long do you have before you go?"

"About two hours."

"Get me lunch and we'll talk old times."

They did, and Vereshchagin still had an hour's delay on the runway.

AS THE AIRCRAFT APPROACHED THE CASERNE, VERESHCHAGIN noted the sea change in the knoll C Company tenanted. Makeshift bunkers had been formed from long, stone sheds reinforced with concrete, steel, and a meter of earth tamped and impregnated with a chemical solvent to give the resulting mass elasticity. The farmhouse itself had been radically transformed with the addition of steel cribs packed with fill and faced with tough plastic foam. Work had begun on other structures, including a sauna.

To the fury of the dispossessed farmer and adjoining landowners, outside the perimeter, the waist-high wheat was laced with feathery vaalbush and laid with cleared fields of fire. Warning wire delineated devil's gardens a half kilometer in depth.

Vereshchagin saw Colonel Lynch's mouth tighten. He recollected that Kimura's caserne at Reading was laid to a different pattern, cropped as smooth and orderly as a parade ground.

Like matchstick figures, sentinels stood smartly in front of the bunkers, not sprawled in the fighting positions on top. Idly, Vereshchagin wondered how much prompting Matti Harjalo had found necessary. He set the thought aside as the transport touched down.

They stepped off into the sunlight. A sentinel in a freshly pressed uniform presented a rifle salute which Colonel Lynch returned, open-eyed.

Hans Coldewe emerged immaculate from a bunker and snapped off a hand salute. This Colonel Lynch returned brusquely. "Are you in command?"

"I am at present in command of the company, sir!" Coldewe replied, only the faintest trace of a smile on his face.

"Lieutenant Coldewe is the executive officer for C Company," Vereshchagin explained helpfully.

"All right, Lieutenant. Shall we start with the mortar pits? The *unmanned* mortar pits I spotted during the approach?"

Coldewe coughed. "Not those two mortars, sir. They're sheet aluminum which we polish up for the locals to admire. We'll have to go through the downstairs. If the Colonel would permit?"

Colonel Lynch started inside the bunker and stopped. A platoon was sitting around in sections in pressed battledress with hammocks slung and equipment laid out. They were sipping tea with elaborate unconcern. It was a little much, even for Colonel Lynch. Vereshchagin ruefully conceded that it was a little much, even for Raul and Matti.

"Where is Captain Sanmartin?" Colonel Lynch hissed, eyeing Coldewe as if he'd sprouted wings and begun singing chorus parts from *Die Walküre*.

"Captain Sanmartin is in his quarters, sir. He left orders that he was not to be disturbed." Coldewe inclined his head toward a partitioned space at the far end.

"He did what?" Colonel Lynch asked, astonished.

"He left orders that he was not to be disturbed," Coldewe said, carefully accenting each syllable. "I believe he is working on his monograph, sir."

"His monograph?" the colonel replied, nonplussed.

"Yes, sir. I believe he's working on the distribution and interrelationships of the *Erosaria*."

"Shall we go inside?" Vereshchagin inquired.

"Lieutenant, would you please be so kind as to tell me what in the depths of hell the *Erosaria* might be?" Lynch demanded.

"One of the most widespread subgenera of the *Cypraeidae*. They are widely spread throughout the Indo-Pacific region," Coldewe replied blandly.

"Cowrie shells," Vereshchagin interjected firmly.

"Cowrie shells?" Colonel Lynch questioned.

Vereshchagin decided that greater clarification was in order. "Sea shells," he stated.

"Sea shells?" Colonel Lynch repeated in evident disbelief.

"Captain Sanmartin is an amateur authority on cowrie shells. His company has taken a great deal of interest in his hobby," Vereshchagin offered dryly. "Lieutenant Coldewe, would you please be so good as to convey my respects to Captain Sanmartin."

"At once, sir!" Coldewe saluted again and departed. Lynch and Vereshchagin were left standing in the bright sunshine.

"Vereshchagin, I have never seen a company with such an obvious lack of discipline and fighting spirit," Lynch began.

Sanmartin appeared with suspicious alacrity. "As directed, sir," he said, saluting. "I have been told the colonel has expressed interest in my monograph."

"Captain Sanmartin, your command could be involved in desperate combat at any instant. Am I to understand that you squander your time on a monograph concerning *Erosaria*?"

Lynch rolled the unfamiliar word around on his tongue and fairly spat it out.

"I regret to say, sir, that you appear to have been misinformed," Sanmartin replied.

Colonel Lynch halted in midtantrum.

"My current monograph concerns the shells of the *fimbriata* complex, specifically the position of *serrulifera* Schilder and Schilder. I concluded my monograph on the *Erosaria* in the course of an extended firefight on Ashcroft."

Colonel Lynch opened his mouth, but no words came out.

"Would the colonel care to inspect my specimens?" Sanmartin asked politely.

"I seemed to recall in an afteraction report the part played by, what was it, the thick-sided cowrie?" Vereshchagin commented.

"The *caurica*, sir. While we were waiting for *Glowworm* to interdict their retreat, the cakes seemed to take my discourse on the species as a personal affront, which exacerbated their problems with fire discipline."

"Raul, we should like to inspect your unit," Vereshchagin said pleasantly. "You have five minutes to prepare. Colonel Lynch and I are going to take a short walk and have a nice, quiet chat about the nice medal Admiral Nakamura gave you for that bit of inspired lunacy."

He led the unresisting Colonel Lynch, waving the colonel's entourage to the manor house. "Why don't you all go inside and ask Kasha for a cup of tea?"

"Well, Hans," Sanmartin said, rubbing his hands together briskly, "shall we prepare for inspection?"

"Raul, would you please tell Kasha that Colonel Lynch is going to want a nice hot cup of tea when he comes over to check the menu," Vereshchagin added over his shoulder, watching little warning lights go off in Sanmartin's eyes.

Sanmartin sidled over to Coldewe. "Hans, what are we eating?"

Coldewe shook his head. Drops of morning rain began to fall.

"Send Rudi, I'm on my way." Taking advantage of a momentary hesitation, Sanmartin vaulted past the huddle of staff hangers-on, darted inside the farmhouse, and shut the door behind him.

"Kasha! *Zdraste!*"

Kasha laughed, the muscles rippling under her apron. "You do that good, Captain. What do we got?"

"What are we eating? I'm supposed to be inspecting."

"That stuff again. They must think you don't trust me."

"We got a colonel, and the Variag's going to bring him here as soon as he's off the can."

"Hokay. We got no fish, and that battalion sergeant, Malinov, says we use local produce because we're short of rations. So *bitochki* for supper and *blinchiki* for dinner. Maybe *shashlik* tomorrow, we got a lot of meat."

"Wonderful. You ready for inspection?" Sanmartin found himself saying, acutely aware of the presence of Hanna Bruwer, lured from her work station by the commotion.

Kasha bellowed with mirth.

"Hokay, there are five staff officers and some aides who'll be here in a minute. Feed them some tea and keep them from mischief." Outside, he grabbed his company sergeant by the arm. "What in hell are *bitochki* and *blinchiki*, Rudi?" he whispered.

"I just eat them," Scheel admitted, eyeing the bewildered staff officers, "but *bitochki* are like meat patties, and *blinchiki* are pancakes with stuff on them."

"Well, Colonel Lynch won't know either. Please, get the computer to spit it out and post it."

"Posted. The Variag eyed it on his way through."

"Oh."

Sanmartin watched his brigade commander's flower boys walk past with sidelong looks. "Do you know, Rudi," he said with finality, "after all that time chasing cakes, I forgot what being in the military was like."

At length, departing with Lynch in tow, Vereshchagin noticed the word "helicoprolite" circumspectly stenciled on to the high split tail of the tilt-prop. He considered it painting the lily.

THAT NIGHT, VERESHCHAGIN HEARD A RESPECTFUL KNOCK AT the door to his quarters. He unlocked and opened.

Standing at the threshold was Matti Harjalo, bending a piece of wire into a picklock with short, powerful fingers. "Hello, Anton. I figured this would be less messy than breaking down the door," Harjalo said cheerfully in a soft voice.

"Please, join me. Is this you or a delegation?" Vereshchagin asked.

"Nobody here but Haerkoennen manning the com, and he's silent as death and snow. The battalion sergeant and I cut cards to see who would have the privilege of stopping by. We used my deck.'' Harjalo sat and took out a bottle and two glasses, pouring out some of the raw spirit. He lifted his glass, waiting, as Vereshchagin shut the door.

Vereshchagin lowered himself slowly into his spider chair. Inclining his head, he tapped the other glass with a thumbnail.

"Kippis."

"Skoal!" Harjalo replied with morbid good humor, and downed the liquor. He reached into yet another pocket to extract a small container and shook it.

"Chicken?"

The unfortunate chicken in question had been skinned and boned, cut and quick-steamed with spice and vegetables. Vereshchagin extended his curled fingers slightly in a gesture of negation. Harjalo shrugged slightly. He pulled out his pocket-knife and began spearing pieces rapidly with the point. Vereshchagin absently watched the play of the tendons in his hand. Ashcroft's desert sun had burned away the fat, leaving muscle and tendon sharply defined.

"That mewling Ivan never uses enough salt," Harjalo complained.

"With salt, as with many things, too much is ultimately as fatal as too little," Vereshchagin observed.

"Well?" Harjalo asked, setting aside his knife.

"So it begins."

"It never changes."

Vereshchagin sipped the liquor in his glass and made a face. "I sometimes think that we kill men with the same callous indifference that we chop at trees, a word of regret and it is done."

"I won't argue poetry with you, you'll have to get Coldewe," Harjalo said with a smile. "What is it, Anton? Premonitions?"

"Perhaps. Recruit Private Novelo, today."

"Novelo deserved it."

"No one deserves it, Matti. To train a man and send him all this way to put a bullet in his head? I deplore the waste."

"Waste of five good bullets. Did Raul have trouble putting together a firing squad?"

"He had to turn away volunteers, I believe. This is the fourth we have had to execute in what, five years?"

"Four it is. Just relax and talk, tomorrow you can go back to being infallible. Did I tell you that little cretin, Dong, called up to express outrage on behalf of Colonel Lynch? It seems that when we shot him, Novelo was still assigned to brigade."

"I am aware. What did you say?"

"I offered to send Novelo back, only slightly used and almost as good as new. While Dong was puzzling that one over, I had Timo cut the circuit."

Vereshchagin laughed. He set his glass aside. "Did I mention Claude to you?"

"Dapper Doctor Devoucoux? He's already telling me this place is 'unutterably' tedious. Labrador without snowshoes."

Vereshchagin idly reached for his pipe and tapped it against his knee. "Despite appearances, Claude is a sensitive soul." He meditated briefly. "This planet troubles him, as well. He recalled to me a phrase which Jacques Cartier committed to his journal to describe the New Found Land."

"Which was?"

" 'This is a land God gave to Cain.' That skirmish with the cowboys, we will have trouble with them."

Harjalo nodded.

"Did I ever tell you that I wanted to teach?" Vereshchagin said, settling back into his chair.

"Yes, several times."

"I wanted to teach."

"You mentioned that."

"I hate sending them out, Matti. It has barely started, this time. I feel a goose walking across my grave."

"What's this about a goose? That's one I've never heard before."

"An English premonition. How little the language changes."

"Can I offer you more of this?" Harjalo said, shaking the bottle.

"Like Latin, a language for business and soldiers, belonging to every man and to none. Thank you, no," Vereshchagin answered, staring at the tiny light.

"Your choice. And if you think English doesn't change, go listen to the cowboys."

"Eddies swirl in and out of the main current; the current runs true. The cowboys, Chalker's cowboys, are going to hit Piotr. I feel it. I demanded fire support from the warships since Lieutenant-Colonel Kimura does not seem inclined to use them. The admiral agreed."

"Good job. What else?" Harjalo asked.

"I saw Eva Moore today."

"How is she?"

"Miriam is dead."

"Her girlfriend? I'm sorry for her. And for you."

"She has walled away her grief and set it aside. It has given her a sense of mortality. She was playing matchmaker."

"The devil! What, is she seeing gooses, too?" Harjalo asked with a faraway look.

"Geese. She told me the pigs will be building their nests in trees before we get off this mudball."

"Gods." Harjalo shook his head. "If this world were normal, we'd have people eating off our fingers. Another Ashcroft?"

"Worse, perhaps. We have yet to finish with the cowboys and their mercenaries, and Admiral Lee is already formulating plans to rework the Boers."

"It sounds insane."

"It might be necessary. What do you know of the Afrikaner Bond? The Brothers."

"Not one thing."

"Nor had I."

"A nucleus for guerrilla resistance?"

"Possibly. Rettaglia pulled me aside to discuss covert operations. Before they pull themselves together, he intends to snatch them up."

"So we're collecting documentation."

"Correct. We should move up weapons collection. Tomorrow?"

"Can be accomplished. I'll be on it tonight. You were expecting me to show, weren't you?"

"I would have been astonished if you had not."

Harjalo laughed. Vereshchagin smiled. "To tomorrow? One day more on the volcano?"

"Tomorrow!" Harjalo rejoined, touching his glass to Vereshchagin's.

Wednesday(2)

DANNY MEAGHER SQUEEZED THE JUICES FROM A LUMP OF DELTA mud. They ran like warm blood down the side of his hand.

Meagher was a merc, a real merc, he reflected savagely. Rotting in the mud, he had a bare dozen more to stiffen the three bleeding companies the Imperials were chasing. Mercenaries weren't cannon fodder, they trained cannon fodder for little dustups. For all that Meagher tried to convince his young charges of their own battle worthiness, it bothered him sometimes that the little squirts—and his employers—sometimes thought they were real.

Fools like Whiteman had encouraged that sort of sloppy thinking. Old Tsai had been hotter than a torch with Whiteman at his elbow. The Imps were shooting off-planet mercenaries after Whiteman's stupidity at the filthy riverport. Well, Whiteman was gone, dropping his mess in Meagher's lap. Shooting him was the best thing the damned Imps had done since they'd hit planet.

A squirt had actually asked whether they would avenge him, the sorry sot. Meagher had laughed in his face. By all accounts, it was Kolomeitsev's company of the Imp 35th Rifle who did him, and those boyos were nasty. Whiteman's heirs and assigns could have that job. Danny Meagher had problems of his own.

Fortunately, the lot combing the swamps wasn't Kolomeitsev's. Kimura's 64th Imp Rifles were parade ground johnnies, and Meagher had run the filthy sons of Allah.

But the net was closing on Meagher's employer. Tsai's trousers were hanging in the breeze, but Danny Meagher had played the game. The old rancher would have a tiny surprise the day he decided to hand over his pet mercenary's head to buy himself a pardon.

Unfortunately, that wouldn't go far toward resolving whether Meagher would be bringing his skin off this particular ball of mud. Brooding, Meagher caressed his precious assault rifle.

USS had screwed them, well and truly. They'd hired up mercs with the moon and the stars, then they'd lost their nerve and whistled for the Imps. A right bleeding bunch USS were, even in small things.

What the Imps didn't know is that they'd shot down Chalker's sons when Kolomeitsev ambushed Whiteman. Meagher grinned mirthlessly. Chalker was hiring all the squirts the other ranchers had let go. The rancher lord wasn't very bright, but he ought to manage something for himself with half the Imp army combing the delta for Meagher and Tsai. Having Chalker massacre all the Imps and Boers he could lay hands on would be just the diversion Mother Meagher's little son needed, and if Chalker jumped, some of the other ranchers might jump as well.

Danny Meagher intended a good several innings before he'd be toasting toes in hell, and he was marking himself a little list. There was even a bit of a war to keep idle hands busy.

* * *

IN READING'S TOWN SQUARE, ULRICH OHLROGGE SPAT OVER THE right side of his vehicle. Lieutenant Ohlrogge was not pleased.

He was not pleased at being shunted from a war front on one planet to a war front on another. He was less pleased with his new armored car, which had broken down before it was broken in, or the fair city of Reading, the dump that called itself the capital of the cowboy country. And he was especially not pleased with Colonel Lynch, who was hosting his little soiree in the sun.

Temporarily embarrassed by a lack of troops, Admiral Lee had accepted the offer Newcombe made as President *pro tem* of the Reading Council to assist in putting down the Chalker's rebellion before it spread to the rest of the upland ranchers. Colonel Lynch was here to muster Newcombe's four hundred into Imperial service, and from his vantage point as an unwilling honor guard, Ohlrogge was having trouble deciding which of the two was the bigger idiot. Between them, they'd kept Ohlrogge out for an hour while Newcombe's "soldiers" were diddling themselves.

To Ohlrogge's right was a section of blacklegs commanded by a lieutenant. A platoon of Kimura's geeks was lined up to his left, mostly in splints. He spat, to his left.

Kimura had dropped the geeks to seize the Reading runway. Drops can't be practiced shipboard. When the shuttle dutifully slowed to stalling speed to bounce them out, they'd come falling out of the sky like sacks of sand, and the runway itself was soft as concrete. Stupid gesture. Ohlrogge had been waiting there three hours for the geeks to show.

He cast a surreptitious glance for Hunsley. Hunsley was a slimy civ, but he was the only thing with brains south of the Vaal, except for Janine Joh, who was the only thing with balls. He didn't see either. Another one of Newcombe's uniforms came dancing about, and Ohlrogge used the diversion to steal a glance back at the cowboy barracks.

Newcombe's cowboys were waving homemade red, blue, and white flags out the windows. Ohlrogge spat, this time to his right.

As it turned out, Newcombe had a democratic army. After holding a democratic meeting, they had struck for better working conditions. They didn't like the food, saluting, or becoming Imperials, and Ian Chalker was offering double what they were getting. Newcombe democratically spent an hour haranguing them, and they assuredly didn't like Newcombe. Their officers had "democratically" left the barracks.

After a few hours, Ohlrogge found himself becoming slightly concerned. Against four hundred of Newcombe's best, there was one Cadillac with a busted engine and a geek platoon—blacklegs didn't count. Kimura had ordered up a company out from the swamps, but it would be hours before they showed, assuming they found the way. In the meantime, Newcombe's four hundred were having a wonderful time shooting out windows and singing.

Of greater moment, Ohlrogge was tired of sitting in the sun. After democratically looking around for Colonel Lynch, he turned to his gunner. "Chicken! You remember anyone actually giving us orders?"

The gunner, Hicken, shook his head from side to side solemnly. "I'd remember a thing like that."

"Just be sure and remember it when Uwe Eybl asks. Put a 90mm smoke through the front door. I want to see those silly flags come jumping out the windows." He heard the whip-crack of the shell almost before he looked up. Ohlrogge decided it was worth his chance for a pension. Afterward, he was never sure whether it was flags or cowboys who came jumping out first.

Newcombe's cowboys formed up pretty well after all. While they were obviously unfit even to take on Chalker, at least they weren't on the other side. Hicken won the vehicle pool, correctly wagering that they'd get a medal without getting court-martialed.

THAT NIGHT, IAN CHALKER'S MESSENGERS RETURNED.

Two days before, they had gone forth to swell the muster at Chalkton, calling for riders and captains of war. Ian Chalker had buried his sons, they said. He had dipped his hands in their blood; their blood cried out for blood.

It was truth few were eager to raise hand against the Imperials. Nine and twenty men of Chalker's own had set out and gone to red ruin with Chalker's sons. Only Henderson answered the plea.

Grim of face and manner, Chalker took up a bloodstained rag in his withered hand. He had bought up every free man, every unattached merc on the planet. He prepared to lead out his own men and those of his sister's son. Across the Vaal they would ride, in magnificence, where Kolomeitsev's platoons awaited.

Thursday(2)

SAVICHEV STUDIED KETLINSKY'S FACE IN THE DIM LIGHT AS THE engineer corporal scratched his head. Other than the delta, the only "hot" sector was between the rivers. If the little engineer's face was any guide, someone had relit the fire.

Ketlinsky finally shook his head over his instruments. He commented, "We've lost the mines at EC 34-4689, the path there."

Kolomeitsev had nowhere near enough men to cover between the rivers, but mines and sensors come cheaper than men, and Reinikka's engineers had supervised the sowing of enough to make the entry fee prohibitive. The path in question had deliberately been seeded lightly, and someone was about to find out why.

Muravyov's No. 15 light attack was to the west, Savichev's No. 16 to the east. No. 15 was out of position. No. 16 was not.

Studying his map, Savichev quickly concluded that the cowboys were heading toward the Red River Road. Two of his slicks were best left on the picket line. A third could trail the cowboys without any great difficulty, the fourth could head them off. Savichev placed his finger on a stream crossing.

"Get the little bird up," he told the two men on his amphibian curtly. He turned to Ketlinsky. "Men or vehicles?"

The little engineer thought for a moment. "From the pickup, I'd guess they ran cattle. After that, who knows? Could be horses or horsemen. Could be a lot of them," he added quietly.

"We'll be back," Savichev shouted down from the top of his Cadillac as he pounded on the hatch to awaken his driver.

"Watch yourself, Sergeant Platoon Commander, I'd hate to have to break in a new man," Ketlinsky said.

Savichev made a rude gesture Ketlinsky could not see. He lurched in his seat as his driver gunned the engine into life and negotiated one of the larger chuckholes in the road. Three more armored cars followed in single file, with a half section of Kolomeitsev's No. 3 platoon clinging uncomfortably to the handholds. Counterattack, sudden and savage, is the heart to a mobile defense. No. 16 platoon was small in numbers, but a military unit is measured by its capacity to generate violence.

Savichev put his finger on the map overlay and began to tap it softly as the vehicle built up speed. The mortar would go to firing-point Ista, he decided. Turning to his gunner he said, "Como, you take the Hummingbird for now." His gunner looked at the map and nodded, reaching across to take the controls.

Savichev keyed his headset to alert the mortar, the slicks, Kolomeitsev, and No. 15, and to vector in a Sparrow. The Iceman had left for No. 15's sector three hours ago; he was out of position as well.

The Iceman left Savichev to devise his own tactics.

Ten minutes later, a succinct message came in from a prowling slick. "Skramsted. There are horse shits and candy wrappers all the way up path Chiba seven. We are following. Out."

Savichev set the map aside. Chiba seven meant the stream crossing. Kolpakchi's slick would be the trigger.

"Sixteen point seven. Savichev. Kolpakchi, get yourself to the crossing marked five. We will ambush with support from thirteen two, you will initiate. Repeat back what I just said. . . ."

Kolpakchi did. When he stopped his driver, the stream crossing was the center of a sunlit amphitheater, flanked by high, narrow walls of jade-green moss and lichen that choked off the streambed in both directions. Where the path crossed, the right-hand bank was broken down into a gentle grade. A small spit of land from the southern side projected out gradually into the water, where it broadened into a mat of round stones in the shallows. On the other side, a line of sunshine overhead marked where the path broke up the trees.

Touched by the serenity, he paused for a few seconds before switching on his radio. "Sixteen point one. Break. Kolpakchi. We're in position."

Minutes passed. Savichev slowed his column to avoid running into contact. The cowboys hadn't moved off into the forest. There were tire tracks from at least two dozen bakkies. There was precious little room on path Chiba seven. He thumbed the radio for the net the Sparrow was working from.

"Aviation point six. Break. Savichev here. Where are they?"

"I'm drifting over the column now," the pilot responded. With two forward stabilizers sprouting from the fuselage like an extra pair of wings and the eight curving scimitar blades of the prop, a Sparrow looked more like a translucent butterfly than a military aircraft. "The center is about three tenths of a kilometer from your stream crossing. Gods! Lots of cowboys. Too bloody many. Looks like half the cowboys in the bloody jungle."

Savichev grunted, immediately slowing the little Hummingbird under his control. What he had wasn't enough. He grabbed the radio.

"Big Brothers. Break. Savichev. Linear mission Gifu Oita five one seven, down the axis," he said into his wrist mount. He repeated it twice, hoping that the relay wouldn't foul it up.

Far overhead, corvette *Exeter* acknowledged. The computer-assisted optics of the warship could plot fire to within twenty centimeters on a clear day. *Exeter* was little more than a manned fusion bottle with stacked, layered mirrors to turn bottled hell into lasered light. Ian Chalker had chosen to move on a day without dust and precipitation.

"Good job. Savichev out," Savichev said. He grunted again as he looked through the eyes of the little Hummingbird at the cowboys spread out below. "Gods! Andrei, please be in position," he whispered. "Thirteen point two. Break. Savichev. Guns, we got lots of company. Give me sixteen shells for luck when I'm ready."

"Bushchin here. Acknowledged. Out," was the answer from the mortar.

Savichev took a deep breath to clear his mind. "Sixteen point seven. Break. Savichev. Kolpakchi, are you sure you're where you're supposed to be? If the cowboys slip through, we haven't got an ambush closer than Steyndorp. The bird says they're right on top of you, and the horse dung is fresh."

Kolpakchi's reply was emphatic. "We're in position. I went up this trail twice, day before yesterday, and I still see ruts."

Before Savichev registered the thought, Kolpakchi opened up an A for Akita line to all of No. 16. "Kolpakchi here. There's a bunch of cows coming up the road."

"Akita. Break. Savichev here. Hit them, guns!"

"Shot. Bushchin out."

A signal to *Graf Spee* had enabled the mortar carrier to fix its position to within ten centimeters, firing off a map that was only eight days old. The big, rifled 160mms on the school buses were the battalion's heaviest firepower.

The first warning the cowboys received was the booming crash of a 160mm round blowing down ferntrees in a series of concentric rings. Horses and bawling cattle bolted away into the jungle in terror. The screaming of wounded horses and the noise of the big shell panicked mounts the shrapnel missed.

Seeing through the Hummingbird's eyes, Savichev called out, "Shift left four and you're right on the first bend south of the stream, guns! Shift left four and walk them down!"

Corrected by a hair, the second round blew a crater a half-meter deep directly on the path, expanding a geyser of flesh and mud. Fourteen more rounds followed in quick succession. The second and last groups of four shells were napalm airbursts that exploded almost simultaneously. They dropped thick, suffocating sheets of fire over the men and animals lucky enough to be directly underneath and hideously burned the ones on the fringes.

Kolpakchi knew the routine well. The seven-seven on his slick was a gyrostabilized extension of his seat and moved with his body. As soon as the noise of the big gun ceased, from the far back he broke the almost silence by directing unaimed machine-gun fire down the road.

The surviving cowboys in front responded by opening up with every weapon. Inexperienced soldiers fire high; their return fire raked the treetops. Unfortunately, the comforting noise served only to blind the cowboys to the real danger.

"Big Brothers. Break. Savichev. Fire linear mission Gifu Oita five one seven, down the axis, two minutes worth," Savichev said, signaling *Exeter*.

A quarter of a kilometer of the road erupted in a moving sheet of flame as all four warships in the sky dipped low into the upper atmosphere and fired in a series of incredibly rapid pulses. The whine of touched-off rifle ammunition, punctuated by the deeper sound of grenades and other ammunition exploding, turned the day into a Chinese New Year.

After their first quick pass, *Exeter* and her comrades back-tracked, dusting the sides of the road thoroughly with chicken-seed, two-gram composite particles that absorbed fusion and kinetic energy during their passage and released it on impact. In hissing implosions the particles struck. Much of the screaming stopped. Within the ten-meter kill zone, fires were spreading.

Savichev didn't stay to watch. He was already moving before the light show closed. Timing himself, he moved his Cadillacs up to strike just after the 160mms and the warships had turned most of Chalker's column into hamburger. They roared in, hit the tail end hard.

A Cadillac gunner has four video screens to give him 120 degrees of arc from side to side, with an idiot switch to shift from sight to thermal/infrared; leaning forward or back raises or lowers the field. Under his left foot are three pedals to spin the turret left or right and brake it. Under his right, another set focuses aiming circles. His right hand rides the joystick for the big gun, either a 90mm gun or a 30mm automatic cannon. His left controls the 7.7mm gatling. His right index finger controls ammunition type on the 90mm and rate of fire on the 30mm. Firing buttons are under his thumbs.

Exceedingly agile, in theory the Cadillacs were too lightly armored, although a fine network of hard-alloy wire over vulnerable angles gave them additional protection at minimal cost in weight. In practice, with good crews, people seldom stayed around long enough to test the theory.

Savichev's Cadillac was first in line. A single impact-fused 30mm shell will briefly turn a man into a pretty red flower and shatter a ferntree into lethal fragments; 7.7mm is less dramatic but equally effective. His gunner could discharge the twelve hundred 30mm rounds in the linkless feed system at one round, six rounds, or twelve rounds a second, and the 7.7mm even faster. After four seconds, having run short of better targets, Savichev's gunner twisted the turret to hose down the dismounted cowboys who had taken shelter on either side of the path.

Skramsted stopped his slick beside the first of the corpses as Savichev's vehicle finished with the cowboy rear guard. Armed with a continuous-feed s-mortar instead of a seven-seven, Skramsted paused to shower the trees ahead with rounds. Composite shards from the airbursts ripped into the cowboys. The 90mm on the second Cadillac spat thrice to add to the carnage.

As the Cadillacs rode aside two shattered bakkies and plunged ahead into the thin smoke of the burned-out area, the tiny half section of infantry rolled off the side to engage cowboys cowering to either flank. Dropping second, Orlov whipped an egg grenade into the brush on the right. Necdet Aykac followed and bounced to his feet, shrieking with delight.

Superior Private Aykac had a predilection for hand-to-hand combat. He was expected to enjoy a short and illustrious career. Emptying five shots to drop one man firing a long-barreled handgun, Aykac went for the man beside him with his bayonet.

The cowboy stood, fumbling with his safety. Aykac speared him in the chest, adjusted his weight, and slammed his guide hand on the foresight. The blade eviscerated the cowboy from sternum to groin.

Two other cowboys took to their heels. Orlov fired and missed them both. Crouching, he paused to listen to the sounds of battle moving up the road. With the tail of the column smashed, its middle and head obliterated, survivors were vanishing in the forest to either side. Aykac wiped the blood and intestines from his hands on his trousers and then reached up to wipe his face.

"Even for a Turk, you're a sick one," Corporal Orlov commented. He sprinted up the path and knelt. "Tibor, poor kid. Through the head," he said rolling a body over. "Find his partner before he does something stupid."

"Poor kid," Aykac repeated mechanically, trotting toward the occasional sounds of gunfire.

Within minutes, it was over. Savichev stood up in his turret and watched his handful of riflemen drift a short distance into the forest in pursuit until it was clear the cowboys were too disordered or disheartened to reform. He spilled fuel from the Hummingbird and brought it low into the wind, altering the elevation of the flaps and the pitch of the blades until it hovered and touched down. Two men jumped down from his number two vehicle to retrieve it.

Along the trail, a half-grown boy was leaning against the stump of a ferntree holding tight a ruined shoulder. Beside him was the luminescent skeleton of a pickup, the plastic of the body melting off in tiny rivulets on to the road. What might have once been an arm hung out the side of the cab. A pall of smoke overlay the forest.

A fair number of cowboys had been in the road when the Cadillacs had come through. Savichev hoped that most of them had been dead. He leaned over to examine a scar on the left side of the turret, where a rocket had scored a glancing hit, then straightened as Orlov walked from one wounded horse to the next.

Savichev shook his head sadly. He loved horses a lot more than he loved people. The horseboys should have had enough sense to stay off the trails. Nothing ever went according to plan, but people who made predictable plans diminished their chance of living long enough to change them. He cupped his hands and bellowed. "Hey! We can't stay here all day." Light-attack men never felt comfortable halted. Mobility was their chief asset in offense and defense.

A few cowboys were emerging from the forest with their hands held high. "Take the prisoners we've already got. Leave me the slicks to pick up a few more," Orlov shouted.

"Good enough." Savichev reached into his pockets and pulled out a timed charge, which he tossed to Orlov. "When you get enough weapons, touch them off. Save anything that looks unusual."

Orlov gave him the thumbs-up. The column of armored cars wheeled in parade order and disappeared.

Forty kilometers to the north and east, Chiharu Yoshida was already loading sections of Kiritinitis's platoon aboard three of the battalion's four light transport aircraft to effect mop-up. The commander of B Company had picked up a mouthful of alloy teeth and a scar on either cheek from a projectile weapon on Ashcroft. He'd refused to let Devoucoux remove the scars. Captain Yoshida was capable, as it is said, of "driving nails into a stone wall with his head." His troops called him "Tingrin" behind his back and allegedly found it strange the shot had caught him with his mouth closed.

Most of the survivors of Chalker's men escaped his net. Although nearly a quarter of the cowboy force would straggle out of the forest in ones and twos over the next few days, few of them would have the stomach for more fighting. Ian Chalker's body was never found. Kolomeitsev correctly concluded he would have no further trouble from the cowboy side of no-man's land and decreed a time for mourning. It was left to Fripp and DeKe de Kantzow, of C for Chiba fame, to pronounce a fitting epitaph.

"That man, Chalker," Fripp said conversationally as details filtered in, "bringing cows to the Cattle Raid of Cooley."

De Kantzow, honing his bayonet, yawned elaborately.

"Filthy DeKe!" Fripp jabbed a finger at his erstwhile Boswell. "You're holding an anachronism! An obsolescent oddity! An emancipated penis for a castrated capon with staff epaulets to fondle as he whistles martial airs!"

"Frosty straight?" de Kantzow queried.

Vereshchagin discouraged profanity. Filthy DeKe, who was somewhat aberrant even for the Variag's hardened collection of misfits, found this a trial and a hardship in light of his inability to string three words together without at least one descriptive adjective, adverb, or noun. By arrangement with Raul Sanmartin, he worked six punishment hours on the first day of every month to atone for blasphemies of the previous thirty.

Fripp waved his hand dramatically. "Verily! Hospital reports show that not a tenth of a percent of battle wounds are caused by the bayonet."

The Variag's men, the Finns in particular, equipped themselves with an astonishing variety of edged and pointed weapons. Mizoguchi in B Company carried the two swords, the

Hangman's exec Willem Schwinge a short axe, and Karaev of No. 9 a battered black umbrella.

"Maybe," de Kantzow conceded calmly, judiciously eyeing his edge. "But if you're close enough to use the frosting thing, the froster's not going to a hospital." He gave the straight blade a few more strokes. "This'll do it for the frosting cowboys. What's it the frosty Japanese say, Frippie? Three strikes and you're out?"

"Assuredly," Fripp said. "Then they say, 'Next batter.' "

Friday(2)

HAERKOENNEN RAPPED ON VERESHCHAGIN'S DOOR SOFTLY. "Message traffic."

Vereshchagin nodded from his familiar spider chair. Harjalo was seated on the floor cleaning his weapon. "What do we have, Timo?" he asked.

"Message from Colonel Lynch. He wants a copy of our battalion roster."

"Dong?" Vereshchagin questioned.

"More likely the political officer, Gamliel," Harjalo reflected.

"Pass it to the battalion sergeant. Ask him if he would be so kind as to fake something up," Vereshchagin directed.

Haerkoennen nodded and pulled out another flimsy. "Message from Colonel Lynch. He wants to know why our medics aren't wearing cross armbands."

"He noticed that?" Harjalo inquired.

"The cakes used the cross and crescent for a bull's-eye. The medics we have left tend to shoot first. Should I mention this?" Haerkoennen asked.

"No, I have an aversion to casting truth before staff. A thought is coming to me. Matti, who do we have certified as medics?" Vereshchagin asked thoughtfully.

"Damn all. Vincente for sure. I'd have to ask the battalion sergeant. Gods, Anton, you know as well as I do how long it's been since we've been anywhere near a certification course. As for the replacement system, hah! I still think you should have shot Pritcher four years ago. Selling drugs is like selling weapons." Harjalo looked down the barrel as if sighting on a multitude of Pritchers.

Vereshchagin tapped his pipe against the side of his leg for a moment. Recognizing this, both Harjalo and Haerkoennen held silent. Vereshchagin opened his eyes.

"Matti, we are authorized one medic per rifle platoon on our table of organization. We have two certified, I think. Count them carefully and request seven more."

Vereshchagin tapped his leg a few more times. Harjalo waited for the thought to finish itself.

"Please delay on that for a few days. I would not care to be with Eva when the document arrives on her desk." Vereshchagin discovered the pipe in his hand and replaced it in a pocket.

Haerkoennen nodded and pulled out yet another flimsy. "One more. Message from Colonel Lynch. He wants to know why C Company patrols haven't been carrying flak launchers."

"Is that Dong's style? Please say something snide."

"This is ridiculous, Anton," Harjalo observed. "How many high performance aircraft do they think the locals have? We're going to have to do something. Raul's little stunt kept the flower boys quiet for a couple days, but we're beginning to get two and three of these things every morning. Look at the time Higuchi's companies spend shuffling paper. It's a toss-up whether Colonel Lynch or the Boers is going to be a bigger problem."

Vereshchagin nodded, pulling out his pipe. He walked away lost in thought.

Haerkoennen looked at Harjalo and shrugged. "One more. The admiral congratulated us on our weapons collection."

Harjalo burst out laughing.

The admiral had sent his blacklegs up to speed up weapons collection. In Johannesburg, Albert Beyers had turned white as milk when the Variag broke the news. Even on the fringes of settled space, Imperial security police had an unwholesome reputation. Raul Sanmartin's interpreter had done yeoman work getting him to cooperate.

After Battalion Sergeant Malinov had a heart-to-heart talk with a blackleg platoon sergeant, Sanmartin's officers had gone along with the search parties to avoid any excessive zeal on their part. They picked up three hundred forty-seven weapons without incident, and the collection had set the tone for the other towns.

Senior Communications Sergeant Haerkoennen wrinkled his nose and left.

A few moments later, Harjalo heard another soft rap at the door. Looking up, he saw Edmund Muslar.

Muslar had made himself very popular around the headquarters in the space of a few days, assisting Bukanov. His nickname was "Midnight."

"Door's open," Harjalo observed, squeezing over.

"Sir, I wish to speak with Lieutenant-Colonel Vereshchagin," Muslar said hesitantly. "I do not think I should be sent to one of the line companies. I believe that under prevailing conditions, it would be better if I remained in this headquarters, sir."

Harjalo glued the rifle barrel to his eye. "Why?" he asked.

"I believe that it would be detrimental to our relations with the local populace, sir."

"Oh," was Harjalo's reply. He ran another lubricated patch through the bore and held the barrel up to the light. "Edmund, dig yourself a rock and chat with me," he said, running a dry patch through to sop up any remaining fluid. He collapsed his cleaning rod. "Higuchi's and Kimura's last saw action with Noah and the Flood. Eybl's have been at it so long they don't really care who they shoot anymore. Modesty forbids me from characterizing this battalion, but someone obviously went to a great deal of trouble to yoke mustangs and cart-horses to the same plow."

Muslar smiled, flashing teeth. "It was determined that consistent with available assets, care would be taken to avoid inflaming local prejudices."

"I thought it was something silly like that."

"When I boarded, I was understandably concerned when Captain Dong decided that I would not be assigned to a battalion because of my skin coloring. I am gratified not to be relegated to administering the replacement pool. However, I understand Captain Dong's reasoning and do not wish to be a liability."

Harjalo made a noise in his throat that might have been a chuckle. Raul Sanmartin had gotten the information secondhand from Bruwer that after one look at Kimura's Baluchis, the Afrikaners were saying, "better *Kosake* than *Keffers*," better Cossacks than Kaffirs.

"Edmund, I wish I were as young," he said.

Muslar exhibited puzzlement. "I am not certain I understand you, sir."

Harjalo laughed softly. "Never you mind, Edmund. How did you get orders?"

"I received orders two days before lift, sir. I suspect they were rushed."

"Edmund, I would like to point out a few truths before you

try your line of reasoning on the Variag.'' Harjalo snapped his bolt assembly home with a click.

"First, Dong is a cretin. If you go around quoting Dong, you'll be back in that replacement pool so fast your eyes will spin in their sockets.

"Second, we've got about twenty soldiers we recruited on Ashcroft that make you look like a snowflake. The people here are not going to like us all that very much, so we don't much intend to spend time pandering to their prejudices.

"Third and last, if you go in and tell the Variag what you just told me, he is going to politely and quietly clean you out up one side, down the other, and around the back until he runs out of breath. Comprehend?''

"Yes, sir.''

"And stop saying 'sir.' The children are in bed.''

"Yes, sir.''

Harjalo finished reassembling the bolt. "Edmund, you either have ingrained reflexes or a very bad memory. My name's Matti. Family? Brothers? Sisters?''

"One of each—Matti. A brother and a half sister actually.''

"A corporation family?''

"We are middle level in a Mitsubishi supply subsidiary. That is where my brother is.''

"So you're the younger son in a one-position family. So tell me where we start with the Boers.''

"Without experience, it is very difficult for me to properly form an opinion. However, I think that we ought to try to gain their confidence.''

"We'll have to shoot at them just to gain their attention. Suggestions?''

"I will consider the problem, sir. I am certain that something will occur to me.''

"It had better,'' Harjalo said only half-humorously. "All right, run along. Some day you're going to have to explain to me about this prejudice business.''

Muslar smiled broadly. "I am not sure that I can, sir. You could perhaps ask some of the Boers to explain, they would be much better qualified than I.''

BECAUSE OF THE DARKNESS OF THE NIGHT, SENIOR SERGEANT Shimazu checked the street address with great care. He then rapped respectfully on the front door.

Citizen Jannie Theron padded to the door and opened it,

grumbling loudly. He found himself stunned and bundled into a restraining sack. He never heard his wife calling him back to bed.

Awake in the same city, Senior Censor Ssu was momentarily irresolute, something he despised in himself and others. He allowed his hand to pause over the receiver.

The function of an Imperial Censorate has not altered appreciably since the days of the First Emperor and the Roman Caesars: to maintain public morality, to reward virtue, and to punish iniquity in a manner consistent with the survival of the state.

On Suid-Afrika, overseeing print media was not difficult. Although printed broadsides would circulate, papers enjoying advertising revenue had already found the firm but gentle hand of the Imperial censorship unavoidable. The penalties for evasion were draconian, as Ssu had politely explained. Most of the publishers had understood. A few had not; only nine papers were permitted editions this week. Broadcast media presented more difficulty, but Ssu had himself written the programs to gauge Afrikaans content and connotation. None of this explained the feeling in Ssu's belly.

Die Afrikaner had wanted to run a less than subtle editorial espousing the principle that it was immoral for Afrikaner to buy from non-Afrikaner. The author, Dominee W. K. Strijdom, had argued, unsuccessfully, that the opinion expressed was purely theological.

The Afrikaners were a difficult people; in response to the statement that white was white, they could argue that white was black or at least gray, and further discussion encouraged the elaboration, ''You must understand the Afrikaner in the national-political context. . . .'' But something in Strijdom was different.

Ssu punched out Rettaglia's number. The senior censor had served in his arcane field for thirty-one of his forty-nine years; uncorrupted by puling modesty, he placed trust in his intuition.

Something in Strijdom's soul frightened him very badly.

''SO THIS IS INTELL,'' SANMARTIN COMMENTED, WALKING across the runway beside Rettaglia. ''I'm not so sure I like the hours.''

Rettaglia smiled, his uniform precise. ''It's easier to pull frogs from the pond with a flashlight. Less fuss. You'll be back in Jo'burg by morning, a little wiser. What did you think of Die Koffiehuis?''

"Bland."

"Raul, you couldn't touch a piece of beef like that in Tokyo for a week's pay!" Rettaglia said in a hurt tone of voice. He flipped a pack of cigarettes, which Sanmartin plucked neatly out of the air.

"What's this?"

"Change."

"I don't smoke." Sanmartin examined the pack.

"As cigarettes, I'm told they're pretty awful. However, the people had to use something when USS started monkeying with the currency and the currency went to hell."

"You paid in real money," Sanmartin said.

"So I did. The admiral will make the changeover public in a week."

Sanmartin made a scissors motion with the first two fingers of his right hand. "About three minutes after that, USS stuff isn't going to be worth cold spit. In my city, that'll chop a lot of people off about ten centimeters short."

"It's a fact I'd like you and the Variag to consider if you make any friends between now and then."

As they reached the step, Rettaglia cautioned, "Keep quiet unless you're behind the sound buffer. It may take a few hours, so you may want to get a cup of tea and come back."

Sanmartin shuddered. "Anything but tea." He followed Rettaglia in and down a level. "I'd think you'd get claustrophobia down here in the dungeon," he commented.

"It's an advantage." Rettaglia stopped in front of a massive metal door. "Welcome, and abandon hope all ye who enter here, or words to that effect," he said, allowing Sanmartin to pass in front.

Inside, a man was slumped over in the narrow chair to which he was strapped. His head was covered by a black hood. Rettaglia nodded. "His name is Theron. He's a schoolteacher, a low-echelon Brother," he said, turning away. "Intelligence Sergeant Menzies, may I impose to the extent of discovering whether the injection has taken hold?"

"Should it please the major, the client should begin to attain partial consciousness at any moment," Menzies replied with an eye to Shimazu, who was in charge.

"Most excellent. Please keep me informed of your progress," Rettaglia said as he stopped to read the life monitors. He straightened immediately. "To my concern, it would appear that the client's respiration is disagreeably shallow, do you agree, senior sergeant?''

"I quite agree, honored major. However, I would respectfully suggest that it is well within tolerances. It would perhaps be counterproductive to introduce any stimulant at this time, if I may suggest," Shimazu said deferentially.

"I quite agree, senior sergeant. No stimulants. However, please give appropriate consideration to fitting the client with an oxygen hood. It would be most unfortunate if he were to rejoin the company of his ancestors," Rettaglia directed.

"The major's suggestion is worthy, and it shall be as he desires. I also must state that the senior censor has asked you to return a call."

Rettaglia nodded and turned back to Sanmartin. "I should have gone to medical school. What do you think?"

"It looks like an old movie set," Sanmartin replied. "What is that you injected him with?"

Rettaglia looked crestfallen. "Mostly serotonin and scopolamine. There's probably ibotenic acid and a few other things as well, but the composition is classified beyond my level. I can tell you it's effective."

"I thought the mad scientist always told the victim what he's being injected with."

"Wrong movie. Sometimes we'll say something, but you don't seriously expect us to release classified information to a client, do you?"

"I hadn't thought of it that way."

"It's a complicated dance, Raul. Truth is such a fragile thing. In the course of our little dialog, a client will try and tell us only what he thinks he wants us to know. We try and do the same. In coming to a common understanding, tiny deceptions lubricate the process just as they do in normal social intercourse." Rettaglia smiled and ran a hand through his thinning hair. "Without a few deceptions, there would hardly be a need for intelligence officers, would there?"

"Probably not. No whips and thumbscrews?"

"Hardly. We try to be professional."

Shimazu interjected himself without a hint of impoliteness. "Honored major, if I may suggest, our client is beginning to regain consciousness. I would say that the optimum moment for commencing is imminent."

"Commence, senior intelligence sergeant. Raul?"

"I'll be back in an hour or so."

"Superb. Ciao."

"Ciao."

FOUR HOURS LATER, RETTAGLIA CAME UP TO FIND SANMARTIN asleep on his futons. He prodded him awake.

"Raul, are you alive? It's time to pack you off."

Sanmartin stirred. "If I died, you're an awfully ugly angel. How did it go?"

"Very well. We have nineteen names and three or four more that are questionable. Theron has a lisp of sorts. We have his local pretty well tagged, and we think we have the head of the district watch committee, a businessman's preacher named Snyman."

"I wish I understood what that meant. What line did you feed Citizen Jannie to get him to open up?"

"Neck injury in a vehicle wreck. His 'Friends' needed to know who to contact."

"And he believed it?"

"Why shouldn't he? With that dosage, Shimazu could have convinced him he was the Mahdi."

"And?"

"We'll put him back in his bed for his Friends to find."

"This is obviously not charity on your part."

"Obviously. Clever of you. For us to succeed here, we'll eventually have to dispose of the Bond."

"That's another thing. What's the Bond?"

"Call it a secret society. The Brothers ran the Second South African Republic for nearly a century, placing or co-opting people in the political parties, the government, the military, police, media, cultural entities, churches, universities, corporations, and so on. They suffered during the Bantu Wars when hardliners and soft-liners started chopping at each other, but they've rebounded. USS has been spectacularly unsuccessful in keeping them down. Who did you think was running this planet?"

"We have a problem."

"We do. They aim to preserve the Afrikaner people and culture, and they're not overly concerned with who gets trampled. They organize by cells on a regional basis with a parliament called the Bondsraad, a judiciary in the watch committees, and an executive council of twelve known as 'The Twelve Apostles.' For a while now, the Brothers have been happy eating up the pie. Now that we're here, I suspect they're a trifle unhappy."

"Are you going to let us rip them out, root and branch? Cheaper in the long run."

"My predecessor argued that option to the admiral past the point of prudence. No, we'll go with careful surgery. Comatose Brother Jannie will be the thinnest of wedges."

"I assume you laid on something elaborate."

"Sergeant Menzies is quite an actor, and at a distance he bears a passable resemblance to our friend. Theron has a neighbor who saw everything he was supposed to see."

"I assume there's more."

"Shimazu is very good at prying open information storage systems. The Pretoria Volkskas has a few accounts it didn't have before. Jannie has one hundred thirty thousand sen in there now, and he'll have another two hundred thousand sen tomorrow."

"That should get their attention. So tell me how this disintegrates the Bond. I'm a little dense, you see."

"We'll pull in frogs twenty or thirty at a time. The Brothers are going to rave when they start finding Therons. We'll let them execute a few while we keep pulling them in."

"That's a lot of bodies."

"We'll work the ones we want, and return the rest to the street as a screen."

"Looking to find a few real traitors."

"They will have Theron's example to profit from. After the Brothers start purging each other, we'll start weeding the survivors until we have something useful."

"In the interests of a higher cause, Schoolmaster Theron will have to take his chances."

"Uncharacteristically tactful of you."

"I hope he'll have a decent burial if you happen to find him dumped in a swamp somewhere."

"The best money can buy. After all, in a manner of speaking, he is on the Imperial payroll. You sound soured."

"I suppose. After Recruit Private Novelo raped a citizen and we shot him for it, I had a woman wonder aloud that there was precious little difference between the two acts. I think I take her point."

"Juffrou Bruwer, I take it. So tell me truth."

"Rhett, as much as it grieves me, I will tell truth. You are better wired than is plausible in an intelligence officer, far better than certain persons I would not name who have sushi for brains. Yours is a fine circus; I love the dancing dogs and prancing ponies, but military intelligence is a contradiction in terms and a little bird is telling me that there's something fundamental you haven't factored. We're going to eat stones and drink gall before this is over.''

"First Ssu, now you. With you, it must be the Celtic blood. Well, as Admiral Lee is fond of pointing out, we have four combat battalions and ships in the sky,'' Rettaglia replied.

"Couldn't we could play this one straight up and put the ones who are going to cause trouble on a ship now that we've finished shooting cowboys?''

"Not an option, roommate. The admiral won't consider it, and on paper he has a good case. But between you and me and the Variag, do not wear your pants down around your ankles or we'll really have a problem.''

Sanmartin thought for a moment. "When we get hit, what have they got? Tanks and nukes?''

To Sanmartin's surprise, Rettaglia slammed shut the door. "Of course, they have nukes,'' he whispered fiercely, "but the admiral doesn't believe it. Shut up and don't joke about it. Just don't bunch up outside populated areas or they may tip their hand. Now get out of my sight. Next time you're down, we'll crack a bottle.'' He slapped Sanmartin on the shoulder. "Menzies is waiting in the car for you. Next week, I'll drop by and let you lose some money at chess.''

"I may surprise you.'' Sanmartin managed a faint smile. "Let me know when you turn the Twelve.''

"I'll consider it. Ciao, little brother.'' Rettaglia heard the door latch itself shut. "And one of the Twelve was Judas,'' he murmured so softly that not even the walls heard.

AS BARRACKS-ROT ABOUT THE AFRIKANER BOND BEGAN TO CIR-culate, the Imperial soldiers rechristened the Afrikaners "Bros.'' For obscure but obvious reasons, the cowboys were immediately renamed "Cons.'' This resulted in stiff protests—after the cowboys told the Boers what a "Bro'' was—which resulted in a stiffly worded directive from Colonel Lynch to desist, where-upon the Imperial soldiery began calling them all "Stills'' because they were still Bros and Cons.

Saturday(2)

AGING SENTRIES, THE TWO PIANOS WERE NEWLY POSTED IN THE rear of the mess. Like Cadillacs, the pianos were built to a purpose with solid electronics, to do a job and do it well. While he waited for the Ice Maiden to appear, Coldewe watched Letsukov pick away at one.

Bruwer had not found herself an apartment. She tended to take her meals at odd hours when no one else was around, which said much about her personality and went far toward explaining why she and Sanmartin got along. Almost before Coldewe completed the thought, he spotted her edging into the room.

"Good morning, Miss Bruwer!"

She blinked. "Good morning to you, as well, Heer Coldewe." Her eyes brightened a bit. "Business for me?"

Like virtually everything else Major Rettaglia had a hand in, her employment description was deceptive. Her only real intelligence job was to rewrite documents the computer translated so that they made sense. She got along famously with Mayor Beyers, who knew her grandfather and had a son and a daughter nearly her age, and she spent most of her time on community matters for the Variag's casernes.

"I strive for transparency," Coldewe admitted. "Company Armorer Rytov has formally requested your presence at the launching of the still. Eleven hours thirty, tomorrow?"

Not that Rytov had spent a great deal of time in the deliberative process—Bukanov had all the straphangers working long hours. Locally, choices for the honor were limited.

She knit her eyebrows together. "Please?"

"The price of vodka in town has gone up, and Rytov was tasked with contingency planning. The battalion sergeant passed word for the time being, we might as well drink and be merry. After Preacher Erixon—occasionally Superior Private Erixon—finishes sprinkling holy water over the thing, I say a few words of wisdom and you smash a bottle over the prow."

"Oh." She digested this momentarily. "Captain Sanmartin?"

"Oh, he'll be there, wearing the traditional hoodwink and smile. He'll also kick the silly thing to pieces if the need arises."

Coldewe couldn't help smiling. The key to Hanna Bruwer's quarters had gone with the farmer. When she'd raised the subject, Raul, with his usual aplomb, had confidently assured her that not a soul would get through the company perimeter at night.

That was the first time Coldewe had ever seen Steel Rudi Scheel's poker face crack away entirely. A beet-red Raul had tossed her his pistol without another word, and Rudi had managed to subdue his levity just long enough to clear the weapon and explain the safety. Raul still hadn't gotten it back. For all Coldewe knew, she was the only armed Afrikaner in Johannesburg.

Bruwer knit her brows again. Then she smiled, changing the entire aspect of her face. "I will be happy to do so."

"Many thanks!" he called out as she skipped toward a beaming Kasha without a backward look.

Although Raul Sanmartin liked virtually everyone, Coldewe could number the people he genuinely felt comfortable with on two hands. The Ice Maiden seemed to have made the list.

Letsukov was still picking away, waiting for his partner to come off duty so they could work on the 1812 Overture together. "They're playing our song," Coldewe said to himself inconsequentially.

Sunday(3)

JAN SNYMAN WAITED UNTIL 6 HOURS 30 BEFORE HE ENTERED, walking the street with his hands in his pockets. Inside, he went past the sign for the Border Police to the sign that read "Imperial Recruiting Station" in three languages, pausing in front of the door. Before his mind was completely made up, a voice said, "Come in," in strongly accented Afrikaans.

After an instant's hesitation, Snyman did. A wiry soldier in combat uniform sat behind a small, metal desk. Had Snyman been able to read his rank tabs, he would have recognized the man as a senior quartermaster sergeant. The man spared him this difficulty.

"Good day to you. I am Senior Quartermaster Sergeant Redzup. I assume that you are here to see me. Do you speak English, and would you care for a cup of tea?"

Shyly, Snyman nodded his head twice and received a cup of tea for his troubles.

"What is your name, please?"

"J. N. Snyman. Jan Nicolaus, sir. Of number fourteen Vilshoferstraat."

Senior Quartermaster Sergeant Redzup smiled like a wolf. "Snyman, a senior quartermaster sergeant is a noncommissioned officer in His Imperial Majesty's service. A noncommissioned officer is not referred to as 'sir.' Do not refer to me as 'sir.' I know who both of my parents are. I work for a living. You may refer to me as 'quartermaster sergeant.' Have you eaten?"

"Yes, sir, I mean quartermaster sergeant. I mean, no, quartermaster sergeant, I have not eaten breakfast."

"Excellent, you express yourself clearly. Please go in the back room. You will find four green boxes fifteen centimeters by ten centimeters by five centimeters in size. The contents of each will be listed on the side panel. They will be sitting on top of the desk. After selecting one, pull the red tab and wait two minutes. Shake the box thoroughly before you open it. The box will open at the top corner, which will peel back. You will find tableware in the drawer. After you have eaten, we will talk. Do you have questions about what I have just said?"

"No, quartermaster sergeant. No."

Jan Snyman got up in some confusion.

"Meneer Snyman." Redzup smiled again. "Please take your tea with you."

After Snyman had eaten, he returned to find Redzup screening records.

"You are the son of L. P. Snyman, the dominee of the Paulskerk, Pretoria. Is that correct?"

"Yes, quartermaster sergeant."

"A determined man and no friend of ours. Your school records are very good. Your English is particularly good."

"Thank you, quartermaster sergeant. My mother's mother was English-speaking, and my mother and I often used the language when my father was not present, quartermaster sergeant."

"I see. Your age is given as sixteen and seven months in Earth-style dating. Do you wish to enter Imperial service?"

"I think so, quartermaster sergeant, I do," Snyman stammered, not having anticipated such a flat question. "That is why I came."

"Very good. Sit down, here. We shall talk. I first will explain what Imperial service entails. I will not sweet-sell you. I will instead make clear to you what life as a soldier is, which is often short and miserable, and make clear to you what will be expected of you. Do you follow what I have said?"

"Yes, quartermaster sergeant."

"Good. I have already turned away one lad this morning. I am recruiting for Lieutenant-Colonel Vereshchagin's battalion, which is the First Battalion, Thirty-fifth Imperial Rifles. The battalion is stationed among the caserne outside this city and in the casernes outside Bloemfontein and Johannesburg. If you join this battalion, you will be a rifleman. If your heart is set on something different, I will redirect you elsewhere. Is this clear?"

"Yes, quartermaster sergeant."

"We have time. Tell me a little about yourself."

Perched with his cup of tea on his knee, Snyman found himself telling the quartermaster sergeant more than he ever expected. The quartermaster sergeant was patient and spoke Afrikaans well enough to smooth over rough spots. Just as Snyman was becoming uncomfortably aware of just how much he had said, Senior Quartermaster Sergeant Redzup smiled grimly.

"Ours is a combat battalion, a very proud battalion. We kill people under unpleasant conditions, men like you and I. In doing so, we sometimes die." He leaned very close.

"We do not make 'men' out of 'boys' or any such puerile nonsense. A seven-year term of service is a long period of time."

Having broken away from the pattern of his presentation, he examined Snyman intently. "Now tell me, Meneer Snyman, does your father know you have come here to sign up?"

Snyman sucked in his breath. For a short moment, he did not speak and did not attempt to meet Redzup's eyes.

When he did speak, it was in a dull voice very much unlike his own. "No, he does not, quartermaster sergeant. If he knew that I was here, he would disown me—if he has not done so already. Does he have to sign papers or something, quartermaster sergeant?"

Redzup smiled his wolf smile, all incisors. "Not for Vereshchagin's battalion, he doesn't, Meneer Snyman. We are more concerned with what you are than with how old you are. Had you lied to me, however, I would have thrown you out. Whatever else may be said about Vereshchagin's, we do not lie to each other. What age would you prefer to be? I suggest nineteen."

Snyman exhaled. "Nineteen is fine, quartermaster sergeant," he said quietly. Although there was a great deal more to be said, he was suddenly very tired. "I think that I would like to become a soldier."

* * *

HANS COLDEWE SAT UP WITH HIS FEET IN A BUCKET OF MEDI-cated water, reading Karl May. While medicated water may have been Vincente's prescription for badly blistered feet, Karl May was Coldewe's.

For some silly reason, his boot lining had developed a crease about thirty kilometers out, and while Coldewe was wringing out the blood, Rudi Scheel had happened by. Scheel, who occasionally delighted in antique idiom, had pointed out with some degree of accuracy that lieutenants are expected to exercise at least as much sense as green recruits and observed that Coldewe could either soak his feet or his head.

Unabashed, Coldewe had his reader out. While disks of Thomas Mann and Goethe occupied prominent places in his box, Karl May and James Fenimore Cooper were well worn.

He sighed and set aside the untamed frontier, reflecting that the enforced rest was an unusually good opportunity for reflection. He found himself mildly surprised at how well the Afri-kaners were taking the Imperial presence. So far, even the one percent that had some genuine interest in how things were run had been fairly quiet. In Jo'burg in particular, Beyers had things under control. Certainly he had handled the search very well, as had the Ice Maiden.

Still domiciled in the farmhouse's back bedroom, Bruwer would say the things she'd been taught to say, but she was unpredictable. She had her own mind and listened more than she spoke, which evidently pleased Shimazu to no end. The hostility of the towns-people had evidently been a jolting experience for her. Coldewe looked to see little doors in her personality open up.

By coincidence, Steel Rudi interrupted Coldewe's musings. "There you are, Lieutenant Hans. I've been looking for you."

Coldewe grimaced. Company Sergeant Scheel had first put on his uniform as a callow youth to see out the tail end of the *uchikowashi* after the crack-up, nuclear firestorms, and the plagues. Anything that Rudi thought was funny wasn't.

"You know, Hans, for eighteen months you've been tipping the horse dung in my lap. Today, I light one small candle," Scheel said by way of conversation; he had no religion worth mentioning. "You remember the translator that came with Shi-mazu, Bruwer her name is?"

"What about her?" Coldewe replied cautiously.

"She just had some kind of argument with Raul, and she's packing her bags to leave. Her religious beliefs, I think. Raul's wandering about with some kind of funny look on his face, and she's up there crying.''

Coldewe said something sulfurous that didn't come from Karl May.

Scheel laughed. ''The way I read human beings, you'd think I was one. You, go knock sense in his head.''

Coldewe put on his shoes. He left to find Sanmartin in quarters, morosely stirring sugar into a mug of hot water and studying the mail that had been emptied out of the computer.

''Hello, Hans. Sit down. Whatever you want to talk about, this comes first,'' he said sharply as he began skimming and summarizing for Coldewe's benefit.

''Ebyl's boys have their vehicles out of their wrappers, and they've captured the spot where Chalkton used to be. Also, number five platoon was out to Dewetsdorp to back up the Border Police. A retired civil engineer stood up in the middle of a sermon and starting preaching jihad. The hospital has him for evaluation.''

''It sounds like your friend Rettaglia has nets in place already.''

''I wouldn't doubt it. One bit of humor, there was a mutiny in Reading a few days back. The cowboys who were supposed to go to the volunteer battalions went on a tear and ran out the red banner. One of Eybl's officers handled it.''

''It's nice to know there's another battalion on this stupid ball of mud,'' Coldewe said agreeably.

''Just so. This is for you. USS had decided to run a convoy from the mines to the spaceport Wednesday. Gold, niobium, palladium, tantalum, and so forth—the usual. Seven and twenty trucks, maybe thirty billion yen or so. We provide the escort. Two Cadillacs, two slicks, and an infantry section, commanded by an officer of suitable rank, which is you. Signed by Vereshchagin, commanding.''

''Is the Variag dipping powder?''

''I'll mention your concerns to Admiral Lee. That's where this one originated. Take a section out of number ten and rendezvous at Boksburg thirteen hours Wednesday.''

Coldewe wrinkled his nose.

''And last, the admiral has officially accepted our assessment of the area as pacified.''

''Ha! It took him long enough. Which means when?'' Coldewe said rubbing his hands together.

''Friday. The shuttle's going to dump off six one-ton pallets:

ammo, rations, wire, matting. Redzup's coming up to handle the joystick himself.''

Paradropping was a cheap and effective means of resupply. A skilled operator could bring a load within meters of a mark without even cracking the breakaway plastic that absorbed the shock of impact. Redzup had been pulling pallets from the sky as long as anyone could remember, having handled in excess of two hundred live drops and uncounted thousands of computer simulations.

"It's still a stupid regulation." Coldewe stopped rubbing his hands. "We don't get bulk supply until we demonstrate we don't need it.''

"It would be a little embarrassing to have one of the happy natives put a rocket into fifty cases of mortar rounds.''

"In the middle of the perimeter. Agreed. Now, is that all for overnight message traffic?''

"All right, go ahead.''

"What's between you and Bruwer?''

Sanmartin looked down at the flimsies uncomfortably. "I don't know, Hans. We were up late, so I took her down for breakfast at a reasonable hour for a change.''

"Everything fell through to the substrata?''

"Number ten was in there. Little tin gods, Hans, she stopped, she turned white, she pointed to Isaac, and she asked me, 'You let them eat with people?' Then she said something about Bantus which could have come straight out of that thing about the Mad Hatter's Tea Party which you have a habit of quoting *sotto voce* on ceremonial occasions. What's a Bantu?''

Isaac Wanjau was the biggest, blackest man Coldewe knew. "That must have been one of the things they covered while you were dozing through Political Theory," Coldewe said agreeably. "What then?''

"When Isaac turned and waved, she went up the steps two at a time. Well, I followed her.''

"Of course.''

"When I got up there, all she could say was, 'He was right there! He waved at me! The big, black one!' Waving her arms.''

Isaac was a former cake from Ashcroft. Sanmartin had jumped him two grades for time spent shooting at Imperials.

"And then?''

"Well, after ten minutes of that, I finally lost my temper and told her that Isaac was worth about ten mop-headed civilians on any scale of relative values.''

"Tactful."

"And she quit. She said, 'I never wanted to be part of this precious battalion of yours.' So I said, 'Quit!' I don't know what I did wrong."

"She's packing her things to leave," Coldewe told him, folding his arms.

Bruwer was still getting over one disastrous love affair she refused to talk about, a fact known to everyone except Sanmartin, who had clearly spent too much time with slugs and bugs in his youth.

"Does Shimazu know?" Sanmartin asked uncomfortably.

"Shimazu knows everything about everything. Rudi said she was crying," Coldewe added unnecessarily. "If she goes we'll be short an interpreter. Also, think of Rettaglia's feelings."

"He doesn't have any. Damn it, Hans! Has she been on the same planet with the rest of us?"

"That's ninety percent of the problem. Don't shout."

"I'm not shouting!"

Coldewe examined him with exaggerated compassion. "Well?"

"Well what?"

"Well, apologize to her!"

"Hans, she's wrong!" Sanmartin found himself shouting.

"You're shouting. Of course she is. That's an even better reason for apologizing."

"Hans, you're not making sense. Besides, all I've done since I met the woman is apologize."

"Consider it good practice."

"Hans?!"

"Raul, you're shouting. How much do you know about women?"

"Damn all. How do you think I got this job?"

"Sometimes I wonder."

"Hans, just forget it. Anyway, I've got to go running with number ten in fifteen minutes."

"Raul, you're pretty well done with the fimbriatid monograph, and you definitely need a new hobby. Look, we've got ten minutes to rehearse before we go meet Rudi, who is having the same conversation with Hanna, undoubtedly with more success."

"All right, Hans. I'll try." Sanmartin sighed, wondering how his exec could make the dumbest ideas sound plausible.

Fifteen minutes later, Coldewe, relapsing in the mess with

No. 10, saw his company commander saunter in. With a polite smile, Coldewe turned to Wanjau, who was big, black, and shaking his head in disbelief. Coldewe accepted his custard with a polite comment on the evils of gambling and assumed an unusually angelic look as Sanmartin slung his weapon and mounted a chair.

No. 10 quieted expectantly.

"I am told the seventh day is a day of rest, and last Sunday, some of you commenced by resting through His Excellency the chaplain's sermon." His remarks were greeted by a scattering of polite laughter.

His Excellency, Superior Private Erixon of No. 11 platoon, was a Lutheran lay deacon, a pleasant, towheaded man who found the call to arms not incompatible with his calling to God or vice versa. He was deeply wounded by the callousness of his compatriots.

"In order to permit all of you to rest up for tomorrow's sermon, we will run short route number two today." Turning to Gavrilov, the sergeant platoon commander of No. 10, he said, "My turn to lead. Four columns." Gavrilov nodded. Sanmartin hopped off his chair and headed for the door.

A few groans percolated upward along with laughter. Short route number two crossed two dongas and went up one side of a towering kopje and down the other.

As he came out, he saw Bruwer at her window. She waved. He took his rifle up in his left hand and waved back just as No. 10 came pouring out to form up.

In four columns, Platoon No. 10 moved out at a quick pace behind their mortified company commander. Carrying weapons and full gear, they ran through the streets of Johannesburg and out into the rain.

Monday(3)

SCHEEL'S BODY BLOCKED THE SUNSHINE IN FRONT OF HIS DOOR. "Company for you," he announced gently.

Seated behind a desk borrowed for the occasion, Sanmartin sighed and looked up. "Last one, Rudi?" he asked in a despairing tone.

Rudi Scheel shook his head. Sanmartin sighed again. "Father or husband, this time."

"Father. A dominee named Snyman, Louis Pretorius."

"The name sounds familiar, I think Rhett mentioned it. Well, as the Variag is fond of pointing out, an infantry battalion is an inherently unnatural arrangement. How many does that make?"

"Four this week. Ours are making up for lost time."

"Just so. I suppose the Boers are afraid of miscegenation. In nine months, the population of this town would double if holding hands were all it took. It may do that anyway; ours seem more appreciative than the local males. If this keeps up, we'll have sections volunteering to man checkpoints."

"The honeymoon will be over soon enough."

"All too true. Does this dominee have any English?"

"Not a word. Bruwer will escort him up."

"That will seriously restrict what I can say. I wish I could do what the Iceman does."

Scheel laughed and attempted to mimic Kolomeitsev's even baritone voice. "Good afternoon to you. I have been informed that you have come to discuss your daughter's relationship with Superior Private Ivan Ivanovich Ivanov. Superior Private Ivanov requires authorization in order to marry. He has not been so authorized. Company Sergeant Leonov? How many years has Superior Private Ivanov? Four years, one hundred seventy days? In two years, one hundred ninety-five days he will be free to consider the notion. I will not attend the ceremony. If you will excuse me, I have duties to which I must attend."

Sanmartin laughed. "The Hangman's worse, though. He has them out in two minutes, and they actually thank him for it."

"This one will take longer. It's not the daughter, it's the son. He enlisted yesterday. The Hangman has him out training on the island."

"Damnable," Sanmartin said with a touch of clairvoyance. "If this dominee didn't hate us poisonously before, he will now." He looked at Scheel and his eyebrows wrinkled. "Hold on, Rudi, you just reminded me of something. When Colonel Lynch was here, he complimented me on overfulfilling our training schedule. What was that about?" He looked out the window to where the engineers were laying steel-reinforced sidewalks, to the evident puzzlement of the local inhabitants who were in a position to observe.

"The battalion training officer said that we met or exceeded all objectives of our unit training program," Scheel said with a placid expression.

"We don't have unit training objectives. I didn't even know

we had a battalion training officer,'' Sanmartin said with a puzzled look.

Scheel held a finger to his lips. "Little colonels have big ears. The holy Table of Organization still has a place for one somewhere.''

Sanmartin managed a shocked but dignified expression. "And Colonel Lynch thinks that . . .''

"And demands appropriate reports on a daily basis,'' Scheel replied. "If he found out the Variag cannibalized things like that to fill out the rifle platoons years ago, he might be distressed.''

"I imagine he would." Sanmartin was trying to maintain an expression that would be consistent with the dignity of a bereft dominee. "Think up some names so we can get them right if we're asked.''

"Already I asked our resident intellectual to make them up. We now have a Sergeant Felsen, a Sergeant Roche, and a Sergeant Peña.''

"I can't put my finger on it, but something is suspicious.''

"When you know what the joke is, tell me so I can kill him.''

"Count upon it." Sanmartin grimaced. "Ship in the dominee. If he's not gone in ten minutes, come in and bail out the ship. When will this foolishness end?''

Scheel brayed loudly through his nose. "About the same time you get your pistol back!''

ON THE HANGMAN'S ISLAND, THE DOMINEE'S SON WAS RECEIVing firsthand exposure to the Hangman's mode of discourse.

Henke glanced over the recruits mustered into four uneven ranks. "Good morning, gentlemen. I am Major Paul Henke. I will be your chief instructor. Please take a moment and look at the man on either side of you,'' he added. "One of the two will not be here when you complete training.''

In the front rank, Jan Snyman, standing rigid in the manner demonstrated by Corporal Orlov, echoed the major's comments in Afrikaans for the Afrikaners whose English was not yet up to standard.

"The standards you are expected to meet are high, perhaps higher than you can imagine. Each of you will require assistance at some time during training. If you fail to request assistance from me, from your other instructors, or from your comrades, you will be terminated, for stupidity, and rightly so.''

Even on Ashcroft, where potential recruits had been scarce, the Variag's officers had been a little careful about trying to make over garbage into soldiers. Henke waited for some comment to make itself apparent from the staggered ranks. None was forthcoming.

Snyman found himself comparing Major Henke's laconic style to Corporal Orlov's. Corporal Orlov's introduction had been equally unpromising.

"If the answer to any of my questions is 'yes,' please raise your right hand," the Hangman continued. "Are any of you practicing homosexuals?"

They looked at each other uncertainly.

"Are any of you practicing heterosexuals?"

Most cautiously raised their hands.

"Are the rest of you out of practice, unsure, or undecided?" This last question was greeted by a nervous laugh.

"Plus, minus, or alternating current, we have one simple rule: on leave with consenting adults. In uniform, on duty, keep it in your trousers. If you wish to play around in the bunkers at night, please feel free to join Lieutenant-Colonel Kimura's battalion."

In addition to battle dress, Henke wore a small, flat pack that looked unconscionably heavy, as did Orlov and the rest of the cadre. Snyman did not, as yet, know why.

"Do any of you use alcoholic beverages, tobacco, or other drugs, excepting coffee, tea, or maté?"

All of the cowboys and many of the Boers raised their hands.

"Occasional social use is acceptable. Dependence or drunkenness is not. Use in the field is not. If any of you believe you will have difficulty with this, see me. Any habit of yours which would endanger your comrades we will eradicate, or we will eradicate you. We have few rules. We do not expect you to break the ones we have."

Henke was smiling. At least, Henke thought he was smiling, and no one contradicted him.

"Muster for allegiance parade, ten minutes," Orlov whispered under his breath.

THE TOWN OF VENTERSTAD WAS A CRUCIFORM, THE LONG AXIS running along a length of the road and the short axis extending on either side toward the fields. Alerted by two dogs, its citizens peering out windows saw eighty-eight teams set themselves on the rooftops for unobstructed fire and gp machine guns align at the north and east arms as the first of Jankowskie's sections began filtering in.

Venterstad was Jankowskie's third village for the day, and he was not inclined to Christian forbearance. Before his men began rousting the inhabitants with brief and courteous explanations, two of Wojcek's helicopters cracked the sound barrier at an altitude of thirty meters then alighted at the far end of the village.

Wojcek's choppers were not troop-carrying aircraft by any stretch of the imagination; a 30mm gun mounted in a chin turret like a dragonfly's labium, semirecessed hard-points for ordnance, and a narrow stinger tail made this apparent at a glance. Nevertheless, they could carry four persons easily if not comfortably in catwalk seats located on either side of the engine. Wojcek's disgorged a tiny, disconcerted group of technicians from civil and a slightly larger mound of equipment to process identity cards. Kokovtsov's discharged a team of Reinikka's engineers.

Jankowskie's men knew the drill. As the search teams moved the locals out to have their fingerprints scanned, Reinikka's engineers began examining walls, floors, and ceilings for characteristic traces of weapons and explosives. Out in the street, Jankowskie's platoon sergeant, Peresypkin, stood controlling the supporting weapons, fidgeting as the piles of contraband began to grow.

Peresypkin, "Pertsovka," was almost as annoyed as Jankowskie. In the previous village, they'd spent the better part of two hours tearing up cement where the density meter had picked out a cavity. Instead of explosives, the cavity had turned out to be stuffed with the corpse of somebody's missing wife, slightly the worse for wear. That had made a stink, and it had been still another hour to get things straightened up after that.

His attention was diverted by the approach of a solid civilian in a straw hat with a weathered face and a young woman clinging desperately to his wrist. The man brushed aside one of the Border policemen who were along. The light transport aircraft the platoon had ridden in on were sitting in a field, and Peresypkin had a shrewd idea who owned it.

The girl—Daniela Kotze was her name—ended up talking. Her father was too mad, but that was what the terrified little sublieutenant from civil had a box of money for. His Imperial Majesty's military government made enough from indirect taxes to spread incidental losses equitably. Peresypkin made sure the man got his.

Kotze was attractive. He told her so, which didn't stop him from making a note of her number.

Tuesday(3)

VERESHCHAGIN GLANCED DOWN AT HIS WRIST MOUNT. He closed his eyes, waiting for a knock. If Saki Bukanov had a single flaw, it was the precision that made the intendance officer's actions unerringly predictable.

A few moments later. Bukanov knocked respectfully. A perplexed look was evident on his face. Vereshchagin guided him to a chair.

"Sir, there is a problem."

"What might that be?" Vereshchagin asked innocently.

"Sir, we are only authorized ten recruits over strength. We have seventeen."

Vereshchagin tapped his chin thoughtfully. "By the time Paul finishes, we will not. Please pay the extras out of the flower fund and bring me the authorization to sign."

Bukanov assumed the expression of a bishop who has just seen the Pope spit in the baptismal font. Vereschagin took him gently by the arm.

"We have been doing this for ages. Thirty-eight is actually a very small draft for Paul to work with. Please see if you can find him a few more in the next few days."

His task completed, Vereschagin sailed off majestically before Bukanov had an opportunity to develop his expression further. Matti Harjalo trapped him outside the door.

"Is that the morning traffic, Matti?"

Harjalo smiled. "Message from Colonel Lynch," he commenced, flipping through another of the innumerable computer-generated flimsies. "Logistics section on the staff is questioning our vehicle requisitions."

"What did we take, twenty-seven?"

"We did. I'll grease that over. Staff stole more vehicles than that."

"Good enough. What else."

"Message from Colonel Lynch. Someone remembered that Chiharu Yoshida didn't have his General Maintenance Manuals updated."

"Please don't say it, Matti. Do I need to see any of the others?"

"No," Harjalo replied, glancing at the last.

"Thank you, Matti. Please, say nothing more. I know." He looked up. "I have been directed to report to his office in three hours time. I must see to the flight."

* * *

ON ONE WALL OF COLONEL LYNCH'S OFFICE, A GOLF CLUB HUNG in a place of honor, as a sword might have done in an earlier century. The hand-tooled leather binding was obviously of more recent vintage than the metal shaft. It was a mute reminder that Colonel Lynch's stylized pursuit of excellence was inherited.

An interview between Colonel Lynch and a subordinate was tedious, Vereshchagin reflected. At least the carpet was soft.

Lynch came to the point rapidly. "Vereshchagin, this is unacceptable! Am I to understand this Captain Sanmartin of yours carried out an execution on the basis of some allegation without any sort of official inquiry?"

"Colonel Lynch, I am not certain what you may or may not understand. I have rendered my report. The matter is closed," Vereshchagin replied carefully.

The Boer communities collectively possessed an almost pathological fear of rape dating to the Bantu Wars and perhaps beyond. Sanmartin had acted with the diligence Vereshchagin expected. The issue was whether the incident could be made into an excuse for a court of inquiry. Like any man risen to rank through staff duty, Lynch affected to perceive a distinction between minutia and trivia.

"Vereshchagin, explain yourself!"

"Colonel Lynch, I have reduced the incident to writing. I will not have my officers subjected to harassment under any guise. I will not have my unit tampered with under any pretext. The matter is closed."

A troublesome tic developed on the side of Lynch's face. He moderated his voice. "Perhaps you are too close to the matter to adequately assess it."

"Colonel Lynch, if you wish to inquire into the conduct of my battalion generally, I suggest that you find a more plausible excuse. The matter is closed."

Vereshchagin did not invest in insubordination lightly. Lynch left the cup where it lay. He began pacing back and forth. "These reports you're sending to me are rubbish!" he remarked inconsequentially.

No question was asked. Vereshchagin made no reply.

"I will have Captain Dong get to the bottom of these things!" Lynch said finally, slamming his palms down on the polished teakwood desk.

"Please ensure that Dong remains away from my battalion area," Vereshchagin requested mildly.

"Why do you say this?" Lynch asked suspiciously.

Vereshchagin smiled a wintery smile. "My battalion sergeant is likely to shoot him."

All the blood drained from Lynch's florid face. For a moment, Vereshchagin looked beneath the kurago's mask and saw a tired, frightened man grasping for some semblance of order and discipline. Vereshchagin was not disposed to be generous. The universe begrudged order and discipline most unwillingly.

"Request permission to depart."

Lynch did not trust himself to speak, nodding instead. Something implacable had settled in his eyes when the mask had settled back into place. Vereshchagin saluted and left without waiting for his salute to be returned, aware that Lynch showed entirely different facets of his character to persons identifiable as rivals.

That evening, in deference to custom, Vereshchagin held a chair. Surgeon Solchava managed to assume her seat in any case. Eva Moore, who enjoyed her role of benevolent despot, had placed the two of them at the long end of the table she had liberated for the occasion.

"Anton Aleksandrovich Vereshchagin," he said by way of introduction. "I believe we have met."

"Natasha Alevtinovna Solchava. We have. You danced in my wardroom."

Vereshchagin twinkled and shook his head. "Mikhail will lose the knee," he stated quietly.

"Your man Remmar? Perhaps. There is very little left to save."

"I suppose we will have to make a turret gunner of him."

Solchava blinked in surprise. "With a prosthetic?"

Vereshchagin smiled mischievously. "A man named Bader once fought with two. I mention this so that it will not come quite so much as a shock when we ask you to certify him as fit for duty."

"I had not realized he was quite so special."

"No," Vereshchagin said absently, "Mikhail is not special, but he is a soldier, and they are sometimes difficult to come by." Unfamiliar with the other personnel from the medical company, he allowed an awkward silence.

"I see the wine being passed, colonel. Would you care for a glass?" Solchava replied.

"No, thank you. I might mention that I have not been invited to attend in an official capacity. The only colonel present is Lieutenant-Colonel Moore."

"I stand corrected, Anton. However, Colonel Moore will insist that you try the wine."

"In that case, a small glass." He allowed her to pour. The wine was a local product, fruity and very sweet. "Is this your first duty off Earth?"

"It is."

"You should enjoy it. As worlds on the edge of nowhere go, this one is rather nice," he said, and allowed the dinner to pass with his thoughts elsewhere.

As plates were cleared, he saw a glance directed his way from the far end of the table. He turned and made an effort to converse.

"The meal was splendid. Eva surprises me."

"Lieutenant-Colonel Moore is not a strict vegetarian. She does allow fish on occasions. I am sure we are grateful for your presence."

"And I for yours," Vereshchagin responded. "What was the fish?"

"The fish?" Solchava's eyes expressed surprise. "It was trout. They raise it."

"Thank you." He bore a curious expression. "One forgets."

"How do you know Colonel Moore," Solchava asked, studying him cautiously.

"We met on Cyclade," he commented with a slight smile. "She was the commander of the hospital company, and I had an infantry company. She tells the tale much better than I. In the highlands, the man behind me had the misfortune of straying from the cleared path onto a mine. My kidneys were protected and no further, and when I permitted myself to be flown out, I found it necessary to rest in the stretcher facedown."

He ruefully fingered his high-collared tunic. He had lost a kilo or two since it had last been worn.

"As I was in a hurry, Eva was kind enough to minister to me. She administered a local anesthesia of moderate effectiveness, took a scan, and set to work with a magnet and tweezers. The insurgents had made do with pins and bits of wire, and the operation took a considerable amount of time. It was, in its own way, a most interesting introduction."

"I see," Solchava said, biting her lip.

"She has been known to say that I was pompous until she let out the air. Has she . . . ?"

Solchava shook her head emphatically.

Vereshchagin chuckled. "Eva and I, we do very well. It is sometimes very difficult to retain a sense of humor when you have been in this profession as long as we." He stopped speaking.

Off-balanced, Solchava fumbled for a topic. "I understand Colonel Lynch was displeased with you," she said.

"Somewhat." He looked at her wistfully.

To this, Solchava had no immediate reply. "Will you have coffee?" she asked. "There is no tea, I am afraid."

"If I must, I must." He smiled. "I have steeled myself for any sacrifice this evening."

"White or black?" Solchava asked, bemused.

Vereshchagin shrugged, a gesture curiously out of character. "Black. There is no point in sweetening a bitter cup." This struck her as a most peculiar statement to make about coffee.

Wednesday(3)

DAWN IS AN ENCOUNTER BETWEEN DAY AND NIGHT. SHE FOUND him when she came down to the mess for an early breakfast, the weariness of a long patrol written into his face and a kind of despair.

"Hello, Hanna." Sanmartin automatically glanced at his wrist. "I'm waiting for Hans to return. I didn't expect you." He reached out for his coffee cup.

Bruwer stopped him from spooning salt into it and pursed her lips. "They tell me Hans is escorting a convoy. . . ." she began. She read his face. "It was a bad patrol."

"It was a good patrol. Exploring without expecting to get gun-shot every five steps. Even when your legs hurt." He closed his eyes and opened them. When he saw that she didn't believe him, he told her, "Up by the mines at Mariental, they're putting in Earth grasses, running sheep, overgrazing." He added dreamily, "Furry suction cleaners. It's stupid."

"I don't understand."

He made an effort to think clearly. "The ferntrees aren't wood, they can't stand drought. Osmotic pressure holds them up. When the water fails, they come down. Where they've broken up the forest canopy, the water doesn't recycle. The plants, the animals, they go away. The sheep are turning what replaced them into waste." He opened his eyes. "Have you done something to your hair?"

"No," she told him, and filled the space by saying, "I am sorry, I never thought about it carefully. I supposed plants and animals here were very much like ones on Earth."

He opened his eyes. "Some ways," he conceded. "Convergent evolution. You don't have coral and stony sponges build your reefs, but reefs are reefs. What works on Earth works here. Overgrazing sheep doesn't."

"It hurts you," she said.

Teaching small children had given Bruwer a directness that Sanmartin found reassuring in contrast to the evasions of other civs. He opened his eyes, balancing the hot cup of coffee on his knees, and looked for words. "The mines are the worst. They're tearing up the mountain and sucking it dry. The ore grades out at two and half a percent niobium. The rest goes into slag heaps and tailings ponds."

He absently found her hand on his shoulder and took it into one of his own. "The mine effluents blow off the surface of the ponds. Everything stripped, kilometer after kilometer."

He tried to make his mind work. "The worst of it is the silence," he said. "Just the sounds of blowing dust and water."

"I think that people try to fit themselves into patterns they understand," she said, deliberately misunderstanding.

He closed his eyes. "We also went past what's left of New Zion, the Incorporated Successor Church of the New Zion, where the Bothaville kommando anointed them with alcohol in a steel shed and tossed in a torch."

She caught him gently by the wrist and held on, knowing it was when he was nearest exhaustion that his pretense at cynicism wore thinnest. "Raul, please go sleep," she told him gently. "I will tell Hans."

Behind the partition, Kasha contrived to look away.

COLDEWE'S CONVOY HAD LEFT BOKSBURG ON SCHEDULE. RIDING the seat beside him, Uborevich shook his head. "Cat-A security for metal," he wondered aloud as he attempted—true to his infantry calling—to squeeze a little more effort from the vehicle's air conditioner.

"I suppose this is better than working for a living," Coldewe answered dejectedly. He looked out the window to watch the ammonia plant slide by, replacing fields sown in grain amaranths and pervasive sugarcane.

By combining hydrogen gas and nitrogen in the presence of a catalyst, the plant had produced immense quantities of anhydrous ammonia for the farmers prior to L-day, most of which was wasted by the leaching rains. Because it is almost as easy to turn anhydrous ammonia into nitric acid as it is to turn it into fertilizer—nitric acid being the base material for any number of wonderful explosives—it would likely be a warm day on the back side of the moon before the place reopened.

"How far are they behind us do you think?" he asked.

Uborevich thought for a second. "Two kilometers. Even two and a half."

On the other side of the road, euphorbia was being grown to the horizon for hydrocarbons that went into synthetics and plastics. Fuel petroleum in quantity was still years away; although ethyl alcohol only produces about seven-tenths the kilocalories per gram that benzene does, double-burned it was efficient enough.

Normally, even in Vereshchagin's battalion, Coldewe would have been back with the convoy instead of on point. With Okladnikov along, however, Coldewe's presence, while doubtless reassuring to Director Tuge, was also unnecessary.

"Three would be better. Can you move this thing faster?"

"If you like speed, let *me* requisition next time," Uborevich suggested. Coldewe ignored the comment.

After a few minutes, Uborevich—once again true to his infantry calling—began recounting the story of his adventures in Johannesburg. As audiences had been quick to observe, the tale had grown in improbability with each retelling.

"We've got to move a bakkie off," Coldewe interrupted, spotting a white pickup on the road ahead. "Go on, you're almost to the point where she comes out with the rose between her teeth."

Uborevich remained strangely silent for some reason. His preoccupation reflected in his driving.

"Watch the road," Coldewe remarked as their vehicle bounced along the shoulder. "And stop staring like that. It's rude." He took a better look. "We'll split this up," he directed. "You watch the road, and I'll stare."

The driver of the bakkie was a slender woman with red-gold hair, expensively dressed. Striking blue eyes shone in her rear reflector.

"Perhaps she has a radio that works," Uborevich offered.

"One way to find out. Obverse or reverse?"

"Obverse or what?"

"Chrysanthemum or crowns?" Coldewe asked, holding up the coin.

"Crowns, it is."

"Crowns, it is," Coldewe said, spinning the coin where Uborevich could pluck it out of the air and slam it on the dash.

"Chrysanthemum," Uborevich observed dejectedly.

"Sorry. Always use your own coin. Besides, I speak Afrikaans." Coldewe switched on the line-of-sight radio built in. "Come in, please, white pickup with Jo'burg ID, come in, please."

A lilting feminine voice answered in English. "Hello, is that you back there?"

"Yes it is, dear one. Hans Coldewe, lieutenant, late of Tuebingen. I'm dreadfully sorry, but I'm running a convoy through and I'm going to have to move you off the road. Sensitive materials and all that. Dreadfully sorry, and what is your name, dear?"

The woman had a laugh like bells of silver. "You are one of the Imps, then. My name is Brigitte. I hadn't thought a lieutenant would be out directing traffic."

Her voice was piercingly sweet, which the radio amplified well. "I think that it's the lilt that does it," Uborevich observed.

"Well, dear one, someone has to do it, and it gets very lonely sitting around the caserne doing nothing," Coldewe called back.

"Sir, with all due respect, you need to work on your technique," Uborevich added dispassionately.

Coldewe snorted. "There's a side road about a kilometer down. Please be so kind as to pull off on that," he suggested.

"I place myself in your hands, Lieutenant Coldewe," was the reply.

"Please, call me Hans." He held his hand over the mike. "Do you think you could let me off? I could catch a ride when the convoy comes through."

Before Uborevich could interject, the woman asked, "Did you say that you were from Tuebingen?"

"There was I born and passed sixteen years of my life. Do you know of the city?"

"Tuebingen? Of course! My son took his degree there before we emigrated. I am sure that he would like to meet you, he has such fond memories."

Uborevich refrained from comment to his eternal credit.

* * *

SANMARTIN WAS PEACEABLY DOZING, NOT PRECISELY A FIGURE of grace when Coldewe entered. Resting his hands on his hips, Coldewe announced generally, "Raul, you are one lucky idiot!" He colored his voice with amazement and envy.

Sanmartin awoke with a start.

"Hans," he inquired as he put his weapon back on safety, "have you been sniffing exhaust fumes?"

Thursday(3)

THIN SHAFTS OF SUNLIGHT PENETRATING THE TREES, AND THE mist caused the air to shimmer. Suspended motes of dust sparkled in the shifting columns of light. Caught in light, Meagher blinked. He was damp and desperately tired from the clinging mire. The tangled, choked delta was fit for neither man nor beast, but it kept away Imp armor, which was more than could be said for many things more pleasant.

At his back were forty men. Three were real mercs.

Meagher had broken his force into pieces two days previously when Kimura's lot had given way to Lieutenant-Colonel Ebyl's lads. Meagher had sent out two company-sized columns that delta mud had swallowed up. Tsai had tried to make a deal with the Imps; Meagher had kept the old rancher with a rope around his neck until the man's heart had given out. Ebyl's choppers were still somewhere overhead.

With the river to one side, the sea to the other, and the armor boyos behind, things were not promising for Mother Meagher's little lad. The mercenary couldn't rid himself of the feeling his were being herded like cattle to a pen. Their last evasion had cost them fifteen men. Little flying tanks the choppers were. They had a trick of firing blind into the canopy; an hour ago and a silly squirt had fired back. They'd saved Meagher the trouble of shooting the man dead, but a sweet mess it was.

He held his hand for a halt, tilting his head to listen. The hand signal was one familiar to his squirts. Without bothering to remove gear, they flopped, panting, onto the sodden muck. Meagher grinned mirthlessly. With Ebyl's lads combing the delta, straggling was self-correcting. No one did it twice.

He suddenly swiveled his head at a sound, that of fixed-wing aircraft. A pair of short-takeoff Shiden ground-attack aircraft were flying side by side. Meagher's mind tried to encompass what that meant.

With a touch of real fear, Meagher turned to hurry on his tired cannon fodder. He heard instead a series of pops and knew that with only four of forty men wearing protective gear, his men were as good as dead. "Down, all of you, down!" he shouted. Throwing himself into the ground, he huddled with his knees up, his neck pulled in.

Hell came in a series of spaced bursts, the tolling of a knell. One group of sticks exploded, followed by the popping of the next.

Dropped in pairs, sticks opened to spill sixty-four individual whirligigs, whose casings split and sailed them toward the ground like winged seeds, rotation carrying each of them to a proper place in the grid. At five meters, the charge in each whirligig's tail drove down an iron rain that came from the bomblets as sheaves of slivers, well packed.

Noise and air assailed Meagher's ears. A hot poker went through his arm. Other fragments tore at his vest. The impact stunned him as the concussive wave passed him by.

Meagher shook his head to clear it. Two more sticks exploded. Looking up, he saw the sun through the ragged gaps where ferntrees had been sawed away. Two planes meant a pattern five hundred twelve meters by two hundred fifty-six meters. Sowing fields, they called it. There were far more elaborate things with delayed detonations and sensors and optical pickups. On terrain like this, the simple things worked as well as any and better than some.

Ripping his sleeve with a practiced care, he wrapped his arm carefully in plastic as another set of sticks exploded, and then a sixth and seventh. For some reason they didn't use an eighth, and Meagher felt somehow disgruntled. He tested the arm before rising to his feet.

Zhou was on the ground, the great hole in his leg being bandaged by Patrick. The younger mercenary was ignoring a scratch of his own. Meagher's third merc was moving not at all.

All told, there were eight or nine dead or nearly so, perhaps twenty-seven or twenty-eight wounded of sorts; a fine strike, indeed.

"Well, it looks like I won't be seeing you," Meagher said slowly.

Zhou made as if to rise. Patrick held him softly.

"Don't be a fool, man. You're bleeding like your throat's slit, and you can't walk on that. Hold a moment." Meagher reached down and took up a light machine gun and a canteen nearly full from one boy who surely wouldn't be needing it. Gently cradling the boy's curly head, he removed the boy's hand-stamped identity disk of copper and threw it to Zhou, who caught it up in his good hand.

"Get rid of the vest, and you've a fair chance of sliding through," he said. The mercenary nodded.

Meagher turned to Chapman, the levelest and most nearly unwounded of his noncommissioned officers. "They're yours, Jimmie. We'll be going, now. They'd chop us for sure, but you they won't. Take the lightly wounded and bandage the rest. It's a hard thing I'm asking of you, but when the Imps show, surrender quietly. They've likely eaten our dust for days, so don't give them any excuse to shoot you."

He nodded toward Zhou. "If him they should ask about, he's your brother-in-law, and you've known him for years." He shook hands with Chapman and then with Zhou. "Will you be coming today, Pat?" he said softly.

With one man out of forty, the mercenary moved through the forest without a backward glance to his stricken squirts.

THAT EVENING, ONE OF LIEUTENANT-COLONEL HIGUCHI'S VE-hicles lost its brakes on the Kitzbuettal road and slammed into the back of a bakkie full of children, cracking the spine of the only niece of a minister of religion named Strijdom. It was a significant datum Major Rettaglia's computers missed. It altered a pattern.

ASCENT _____

The pig put on his webbing, and they marched him up and
  down
   He did it with a whistle, so they gave him sand to pound
 He crossed the burning desert, and he trekked the arctic night
   And they made him do it over so he'd learn to do it right

Sunday(11)

SANMARTIN POURED OUT THE LAST OF RETTAGLIA'S BOTTLE OF arak and downed it. Letting it warm his insides, he rolled the glass between his fingers. Rettaglia waited him out.

"Rhett, I'm serious. It's been a long three months. I want out of intelligence. Knight to B4, check."

Rettaglia moved the piece for him, then his own. "King to F3. Did I mention there's a general strike in eight days time?"

"What?"

"They want it to last a week. They'll want demonstrations. I'll give you times and places. Be assured, Admiral Lee will provide orders. I assume you want to play knight takes pawn."

"The Admiral wants it discouraged?" Sanmartin asked, studying the board.

"He does. There won't be a great deal of support for it, and we don't want to give people the impression the Brothers control the streets."

"Wish them luck. Is the word out?"

Rettaglia smiled broadly. "No. Our Friends are going to wait until very nearly the last minute to make it appear spontaneous."

"That's asinine."

"Quite."

"*Hakkaa Päälle,*" Sanmartin chanted softly.

"Pardon?"

"It means, 'Cut them down.' The Finnish cavalry of Gustavus Adolphus used it in battle a half millennium ago. We use it ourselves now and again."

"No martyrs," Rettaglia cautioned. "I'll tell you now, you're going to be wearing leg irons. Reaction category eight."

"Cat eight? *Eight*?"

"Designated snipers, only, will fire at armed men not in crowds if fire is taken."

Sanmartin expelled air from his lungs in a hiss. "That's even more asinine. Well, we'll manage. We've done riots."

"How do you plan on handling it?"

"I don't know, but I'll have a week to think of something suitably silly. Yes, I'll take the pawn. Were you trying to distract me?"

"I don't need to, the arak has been doing your thinking for the last six moves. Bishop takes knight."

"Rook takes bishop."

"Rook to H8. Concede?"

Sanmartin studied the pieces for several minutes. "You can force the exchange in two and march the little clowns down, can't you?"

"With my king in front to shepherd the little lambs, your pawn advantage goes for naught."

"Concede." Sanmartin stood up from the mats and stretched. "Rhett, I'm serious. Apart from the fact that I haven't got any aptitude for intelligence, I don't much like it."

"Shimazu says that you're doing fine."

"It must be the drugs he's on. Does he sleep?"

Rettaglia chuckled. "Shimazu has the Brothers panicked. He keeps allowing them to follow him to the houses of other Brothers."

"The Brothers are going to shoot him one of these days."

"I have a great deal of confidence in Shimazu, Raul. I think he'll surprise you. He has fine things to say about both you and Bruwer."

"He's doing a better job of making an intelligence officer out of her."

"He did say something to that effect," Rettaglia mentioned diffidently as he cleared off the board and folded it away. "He really is very good at diverting attention from Menzies. Did I tell you he got four thousand sen for a map of your defenses?"

"That map is such an obvious fake I'm surprised he got four hundred. I just hope he gets a better funeral than Schoolmaster Theron did when they fished him out of the muck. Are you going to tell me why you want me in intell so badly? Otherwise the Variag and I are going to have a long, long talk."

"Promise you'll give serious consideration to sticking with it," Rettaglia replied.

"Agreed."

"Then sit and relax yourself. Talk about life in general." Rettaglia started to place the intricately carved pieces in their soft swaddling of velvet.

"You realize Matti Harjalo is still breathing fire from his nose over the weapons the blacklegs carted away."

"Any possibility of convincing him it was a mistake?"

"Not the slightest. We record serial numbers with a light pen, and when Matti found out we'd dug up the same rifle twice, you could actually see smoke."

"Can't be helped, Raul. If blacklegs were honest, they wouldn't be blacklegs. Speaking seriously, it serves a very useful purpose, which is why I turn a blind eye. You've been turning up a fair number of caches, and I don't want the Brothers panicking, which they'll do if they think they're running out of guns."

"You try telling that to an irate major named Harjalo."

"I value my skin. You're holding back most everything you find anyway, so why worry?"

"I refrain from comment. What else is there I should know at Landing plus eleven weeks?"

"We've pretty much hunted down the last of Tsai and Chalker's remnants. That reminds me to ask, most of the cowboys are Amies, does that bother your lads?"

"No, not really. The crack-up was a long time ago. National rivalries died with it. North America got plastered almost as bad as the Soviet Union, so most of ours figure it was a fair exchange."

"Have I mentioned you're getting a new surgeon?"

"No, that's new to me. Who?"

"Natasha Solchava. I don't know if you know her. Keep it a secret between you and your confessor."

"No, I don't know her. If this is supposed to be a surprise, how do you know?"

Rettaglia gave a very hurt look. Sanmartin laughed aloud and sloshed his drink in his glass. "I swear you must spend half your life spying on the staff."

"Raul, how do you think people get ahead? There are intelligence officers who spend their whole life spying on the staff."

"I thought political officers were supposed to do that."

"Naïveté becomes you. Raul, political officers who aren't ditherers are dabblers, they aren't happy unless they have a finger in three or four pies, like Gamliel. Speaking of political officers, how did you manage to steer clear of the PO at your last station?"

"Ashcroft? Purnamo had his eyes set upon retiring rich rather than famous. He got his hooks into the logistics company, had Nakamura kick us out of town into the *bled*—the deep desert—and concentrated on career goals. When it came to our internal matters, if the Variag told him it was sleeting dung outside, he'd put his head out the door and stick out his tongue."

"Aptly put. Was he repaid?"

"A few of mine paid their respects to his place of business before we departed. I understand they got four meters of lift out of the roof when it blew. The Variag was most displeased. He had me give them each at least a thirty-second oral reprimand on the sins of ostentatious display."

Rettaglia chuckled. "I wish Gamliel were as easily handled.

I've had to arrange for Lieutenant-Colonel Moore to shift biochem to Complex to keep it out of his hands."

"That's a wonderful setup, the hospital and biochem together. The Florence Nightingales barely tolerate *us*; I can imagine what they think of biochem's wizards."

"Oh, the hospital company loves it. 'Biochem' is still a dirtier word than 'nuclear' ever was."

"What I can't imagine is why Gamliel would want biochem."

"Because it's there, I suppose. There's no better explanation. People don't exactly trip over themselves to associate with them."

"What do we have in biochem, anyway?" Sanmartin asked.

"Two biochemists, two chemists, a dozen or so technicians and things. Some equipment."

"Anything much?"

"Only a little real wizard stuff and nothing much in the way of dispersal systems. They have some nerve agents—two gases and a toxin, I'm sure of—an incapacitant, a vesicant, and some irritants. On the live bio side, they mostly have tailored strains of old stand-bys: QF^8, EM^{13}, and PS^{37} for certain, and I've forgotten what else. Token amounts."

"Encephalomyelitis[13], psittacosis[37]?"

"The EM is a primary infectant, the PS is an epidemic. Both are long-term debilitants."

"A debilitant is five-percent lethality or less, correct?"

"Correct. With treatment, of course. They didn't bring any of the real killers they let loose during the crack-up."

"Good thing. People wouldn't stand for it. The problem with live biologicals, the dispersal systems are always too random to do any good in a tactical environment. Even primary infectants spread themselves unexpectedly. You can't very well dribble out wildfire in measured doses," Sanmartin said, diverting his mind to consider the problem. "What's the latest on the Afrikaner Bond?"

"Nothing shattering to report. They're quiescent for the present. The long-term picture still distresses me."

"In what way?" Sanmartin asked absently, still engrossed in biologicals.

"A thousand words are worth a picture." Rettaglia turned to his computer and punched up a passage, keying the computer for voice.

A member of the Bond must subscribe to the ideal of a never-ending existence of a separate Afrikaans nation with its own culture. In order to achieve this ideal, our goal is *baaskap*, and the *verafrikaansing* of this planet in all aspects. . . .

The computer's voice was low and feminine, strangely devoid of harmonics. Sanmartin reached over and tapped out a pause. *"Baaskap?"* he queried.

"It doesn't translate well, but 'domination' conveys the overall effect. *Verafrikaansing* means what you think it does," Rettaglia replied.

"The Japanese are at least subtle."

"The Brothers aren't," Rettaglia stated. "The concept of Afrikanerdom lives and breathes. The document is entitled, *'Ons Taak.'* One of the Menzies's contacts supplied a copy." He sped through the file until he found another passage he liked.

Against the background of our current situation, it is clear that we Afrikaners, especially as members of our organization, must once again fill our people with enthusiasm for our exceptionally important national-political action, and in this way demonstrate our own maximum political and cultural unity to internal and external underminers and enemies of our nation. Our task must include the following:

One. We must unfailingly and systematically inculcate in every member, every Afrikaner, and especially every young Afrikaner, the national-political responsibility and duty to achieve our own national and separate development as a nation on the basis of united Afrikaner resources.

Two. We must inspire the Christian-national Afrikaner to give himself a positive Christian-national role, and to desist from the hairsplitting search for reasons for the birth of the present situation. Our present Christian-national leaders know better what shortcomings must be rectified on an organized national-political level.

Three. As a cultural organization, it is our particular task to start now to immediately plan and organize unifying and inspirational cultural functions on a large scale to imbue the Volk with a sense of historical mission utilizing functions such as the Oxwagon Trek, the Star Trek, the Monument Meetings, the language festivals, and other large volk festivals to prepare the Volk for the struggles ahead.

Four. We must marshal in a positive manner all our communications media to unite and to not divide the Afrikaner's national-political power for the struggle of survival. In this, our leaders must take the initiative. We must give constant attention to a greater historical-Afrikaans content in order to duplicate the achievements of the years of fusion and combat divisions, and thereby ensure that the Afrikaner's cultural struggle is politically assured.

Five. We must fight with all our might and power and completely eradicate all old-womanish slander about each other and all underhand criticism of our leaders. To speak frankly to each other means to understand each other and to pool our strengths rather than to divide and weaken with personalities. . . .

Sanmartin hit the pause sharply. "It sounds like kokutai trash," he observed sourly.

"Not so loud, roommate. If you'll recall, you almost flunked out because of your lack of proper appreciation for the unique characteristics of the Japanese national-political heritage."

"Kokutai is nauseating, and so is this stuff. Do the Boers have their own kokugaku history, too?"

"You don't know the half of it. They keep telling Ssu the English put ground glass in the porridge of Boer children in the concentration camps."

"Is there more?"

"Thirty pages, close-spaced," Rettaglia murmured.

"Spare me. Did they write that drivel before or after we arrived?"

"Before we came and gave them cause to be upset, but they've taken time to update it since. Their goals are the same, there merely seems to be some uncertainty as to how to accomplish them. Some of them wish to cooperate with us. Others don't."

Among the Twelve, the current deadlock was five to five with the chairman and one other undecided, which Rettaglia did not mention.

"Huh," Sanmartin said. He thought for a moment. "So now that you've led me all the way around the potato patch, why do I stay in intell?"

"You already know the answer. Politics. The war's begun for us, and we've lost it," Rettaglia said bluntly. "The mice in plans and the frogs in operations fought it out. The rats have won. Both sections have forfeited any influence they had with the Admiral."

Sanmartin just stared at him.

"Colonel Lynch wants to see the Variag burn. Gamliel in political is coaxing him on. Gamliel wants to see me burn, and he wants his Zone of Administration quadrupled. With the mice and frogs out, Admiral Lee will pitch us over. He's not exactly a fool, but he's convinced himself the Boers won't rise, which diminishes our value."

"Is Rear-Admiral Irie of any use?" Sanmartin asked.

"Irie hasn't set foot off *Graf Spee*, and he's senile when he's sober," Rettaglia said.

If Gamliel's Zone of Administration quadrupled, only Major Kolomeitsev's semi-independent fiefdom would remain untainted by his administrators. And Vereshchagin would be vulnerable. Through extended colonial service and a great deal of jugglery, the battalion had managed to defer a decade's worth of changes to the Table of Organization. One change would lop the third section from each rifle platoon. This would reduce the battalion's authorized strength by nearly a hundred fifty men and its effectiveness by a great deal more.

Reading Sanmartin's face, Rettaglia said, "I know, it's a hell of a thing when you have to hope your enemies will save you from your friends. And we will have trouble. Unfortunately, Admiral Lee doesn't believe it, not with four combat battalions on the ground and ships in the sky. Gamliel and Lynch are telling him precisely what he expects to hear." Rettaglia poured himself another slug of amaretto and downed it.

"Some of the Boers will hit us. They may not hit us soon enough. The admiral is getting awfully tired of hearing me predict disaster." Rettaglia began putting bottles and glasses away in an unhurried fashion, speaking all the while.

"If I go, Raul, I'll need someone to pick up the pieces or Lynch will stick one of his pretty boys in and you'll all be dangling with your toes in the wind. And I know you better than I know the back of my hand. You'll do the job. You won't like it, but you will. And you'd better. As of yesterday, the freighters are gone and so are the transports except for *Shokaku*. Construe, my friend."

Sanmartin filled in the missing piece. *"Aut vincere aut mori."*

"Precisely. We win or we die."

For a long moment, neither of them said anything.

Sanmartin shook his head. "I have a patrol, and I want to be back before Hans goes on a rampage."

"That's one thing I haven't kept abreast of."

"Hans is the last of the Romantics."

"I won't ask."

"Don't. You would have to observe firsthand."

"Accepted. Oh, I'd like to borrow that little interpreter back for a spell. I've thought of a way I can use her."

"Rhett, she's one of two people on this battered ball of slime who doesn't genuinely hate our guts, and she's too pretty to start measuring for a coffin."

Rettaglia laughed and slapped Sanmartin's wrist deftly. "Thought I'd catch you!"

"You weren't serious," Sanmartin said slowly.

"Not really."

"Rhett, I've been meaning to ask you if you would transfer her to another caserne. Truth is, I like her too much."

"Raul, consider her a humanizing influence you sometimes lack. I'm playing a hunch I'll want her near to hand when things get sour, and her liking you is a bonus I truthfully hadn't expected. Just watch yourself. She's as honest and apolitical as any person on this mudball, but she's still not ours. How's bug hunting?"

Sanmartin considered his reply. Even in immature state, the Suid-Afrikan rain forests showed promise of a diversity that could hardly be matched by forests alternately iced or flooded on Earth. It made the ruin of those forests even more poignant.

"That's something else I want to talk about sometime," he said. "I don't like what I'm seeing. This place could be a paradise if the inhabitants running it applied half the intensity they spend trying to seduce each other's wives."

"I can truthfully say that the more I see of this planet and its inhabitants, the less I like it and them. Next time?"

"Good enough. Ciao!"

"Ciao, Raul. Enjoy your patrol."

As Sanmartin vanished through the doorway into the twilight, Rettaglia paused to consider the anomaly of soldiers and of Vereshchagin's battalion in particular. It was something the brigade political officer, Major Gamliel, had touched upon. Gamliel, "Lying Louis" to his friends, was beginning to become the power behind Lynch and even more than a painful nuisance.

Happiness and joy didn't keep Vereshchagin's men in line of battle; they'd seen most of the slimy sticks in the known universe, and they figured on seeing the rest before too very long. It wasn't glory. Heaven and the devil as witness, it wasn't loyalty to His Imperial Highness or confidence in superior commissioned officers.

Piotr Kolomeitsev was a case in point. The Iceman had no family, no friends, no discernible interest in anything outside his company. Ambition didn't drive him; over the years he'd torched bridges so thoroughly it was difficult to recall a clique he hadn't stung. His opinion on fighting for His Imperial Dryness and the Disquiet had been made known so often and so publicly that his political reliability index made Raul Sanmartin's positively sparkle.

The lack of an explanation for Kolomeitsev's motivation, and that of the rest of the Variag's men, was obvious enough to bother Gamliel. That made it a problem.

Monday(11)

IN FOURTEEN HOURS, BEREGOV'S TEAM HAD COVERED FORTY kilometers, but if they objected to watching Sanmartin observe a herd of witkops cavort, they made no mention. Small familiarization patrols were the staff of life to Vereshchagin, who wanted his soldiers to know the country better than its inhabitants. For Raul Sanmartin, they were that and much more.

Like other large amphtiles, witkops had little or no fear of man and were scarce in settled areas. Although the booming trade in amphtile leather had managed to work itself into a state of collapse after depleting stocks and saturating markets, armed inhabitants were still prone to use amphtiles of whatever size for target practice. Semigregarious herbivores, the witkops limited their retaliation to an occasional bulldozing of a maize field.

Early in the planet's history, one species of proto-amphtile had sidestepped Earth's evolutionary history by retaining unshelled eggs inside the body until the young had completed metamorphosis into a land-going form. With reproduction no longer dependent on ancestral waters swimming with ichthyoid predators, that species had adaptively radiated into several orders and dozens of genera. To Sanmartin, that startling innovation appeared to have turned into an evolutionary dead end, at least for the larger species, because the locals had a penchant for shooting gravid females.

In witkops, the crosspiece of bone between the forelimbs, which passed under the vertebral column in most amphtiles, was lowered away from the column and thickened, with the forelimbs and the neck vertebra themselves lengthened. Amphtilian giraffids, the ugly, ungainly creatures were able to crop foliage a full two and a half meters from the ground.

Sanmartin recorded a few more observations before Beregov coughed discreetly, a sound that caused the nearest of the browsing witkops to lift her head. The sun shone full on the patch of weathered gray behind her ear from which the name "witkop" came.

To Sanmartin they were lovely beyond any telling of it.

He nodded to Beregov. They moved off.

When they returned, a few of Gavrilov's could be glimpsed outside Bruwer's window in the predawn, flinging cutlery at an outsize target. The scoring system to the game was elaborate. They called it "Sentry."

Sanmartin mounted the steps to the farmhouse, shrugging off his field webbing. When he settled into a chair, Bruwer already had water heating on the hot plate Rytov had put together with spare tungsten wire. She dropped in a coffee bag as the wire began to glow.

He enjoyed coffee, and Bruwer was pleased to make it for him. He was unusually unreceptive to puns on the subject. Drinking tea was a unit tradition he would have cheerfully allowed to expire in a damp hole. On Java serving with the 11th Shock Battalion, he had once pointed out in the palatial serenity of the officer's mess that the inferiority of green teas was occasioned by the relative absence of mouse droppings. The comment materially speeded his transfer off Earth.

Bruwer asked, "Was this another patrol?"

"Beregov's and I," he answered.

"Another chance to spy out the secrets of the land," she said calmly.

He nodded. "We saw a herd of witkops and stopped two farmers. I have forty k of notes."

"On the witkops or the farmers?" she asked, knowing his weakness. She handed him the glass.

He watched her eyes as she sat on the edge of the bed, the morning breeze brushing the blond hair over her face. She listened far better than anyone he knew, not even excepting Vereshchagin. Underneath her shyness, she sometimes had strong opinions. It had occurred to him that if the Boers ever wanted a spy, they had one spectacularly placed. The coffee was burning holes in his free hand, so he drank some.

"You told me that Major Rettaglia was your roommate at the

academy. I would have thought him so much older," she said to divert him.

"He is, by almost five years. I sat at seventeen. Rhett had six years in before they gave him the chance." He allowed the coffee to settle out his insides and paused to reminisce.

"They called us 'Tweedledum and Tweedledee.' We got even by pretending we were even crazier than we really were."

"I might imagine," Bruwer said, laughing. She settled back and thought about him, about what he had said.

"Just think how much you owe USS for bringing us here," he said to needle her.

"Those of us who weren't chained with contracts they called concessionaires, concessions they could revoke. Salary men is what they would make of us." It was not a topic she found humorous.

"Your people trimmed them."

"In the city, some are saying that you have come to forge new chains," she said quietly.

He looked around the room. She had contrived to give her furnishings an aspect Sanmartin vaguely considered feminine. The walls were tinted blue, and a painted ceramic kylix occupied a prominent place on a low table. The curve of the kylix's base swept up gracefully into a shallow bowl and then into handsomely curved ears on either side. It gave the room an aspect of permanence.

"They won't rent you a place to live," he said.

"There are few places. I have decided to stay here," she answered. She lifted her hands and let them drop, a small gesture. "The best people, they are afraid. They don't want trouble. Some of the others say things. No," she said as if reading his mind, "there is nothing you can do. You, they fear. They are very polite. For me it is different."

He nodded. "Your family," he asked, "could they help? Or are they part of the problem?"

"My grandfather, my mother's father, he would never criticize me."

"The one who can't farm."

She nodded. "But he cannot help. He has always been as much a lone person as I. I think that he could have been an influential person if he had wanted, but he did not. He told them all they were crack-brained. My stepmother?" She shook her head. "When she came to tell me how happy she was that I would be working for the Imperials, it was like rain falling out of a clear sky. She must have been very, very frightened then. Since then, to her I have not spoken. Nor to her children.''

''Friends?'' he asked.

''There were people I knew, but I think that like my step-mother, they would not want to become involved.''

''Why were you up and about so early?'' he asked, changing the subject.

''This is the most beautiful time of the day. I was thinking about that Hans, he called me 'Ettarre' all of yesterday.''

Sanmartin smiled, the ugliness that was Johannesburg momentarily forgotten. ''It's out of another one of his books. From *Men Who Loved Alison*, I think. I'm Horvendile or somebody else this week.''

She sniffed.

''He says all the prose worth reading was written between 1830 and 1930. Sometimes it starts to creep out and affect his sanity. When Rudi shot a cake with that hand cannon of his once, for a solid month he was Old Shatterhand. That made me Winnetou. Rudi nearly died laughing.''

''Oh,'' Hanna said, contemplating this. ''Oh, I remember!'' She took Sanmartin's pistol from a drawer and handed it to him solemnly.

''Thank you!'' he said with evident gratitude, examining the magazine and the chamber. Satisfied, he pointed it toward the floor and pulled the trigger with an audible click.

''It didn't shoot!'' she observed.

''Of course not. It has to be loaded,'' Sanmartin explained as he tucked it away.

''It wasn't loaded?''

''I don't have any ammunition for it. Colonel Lynch only said I had to have a pistol.''

''You knew it wasn't loaded?!''

''You might have hurt yourself with it,'' he explained, stepping hurriedly into the hall and closing the door behind him. From the sudden and violent hammering that postern bore, he concluded that it might be wisest to seek counsel.

Unfortunately, instead he found Coldewe, regaling Kasha in the mess. ''Morning, Hans. How are you?'' he asked cautiously.

Kasha tapped her temple in response to the question.

''Ah, des Rocques! Enter, enter!'' Coldewe said with a wave of his hand. ''I am lamentably bored, des Rocques! Bored, I tell you!'' he insisted, stretching out his feet. ''The paynim are quiescent, the solemn rites of peace enshroud the land.''

''I was just speaking with Hanna . . .''

''Ah, La Beale Ettarre! How does she fare?''

''I got my pistol back.''

''Comprehension within me rejoices! You flee for your life.''

Sanmartin cast his eyes skyward and pulled up a chair. ''What is this 'Ettarre' business? Is this your jumping frog man again?''

''Ah, Guiron, this fixation with the most estimable Clemens of yours! Nay, it is the glorious Cabell whose works I have again embraced.''

''Make up your mind, des Rocques or Guiron. Cabell?''

''Guiron, you are one and the same. Cabell! Greatest of the fantasists! The dragonfly in amber, whose belles lettres marked the passing of the last flowering of the glorious South! My blessed confrere, your unacquaintance does you little credit.''

''What happened to Horvendile?''

''You are he only in a manner, as the shadow of a shade,'' Coldewe hinted darkly.

Sanmartin shook his head from side to side.

''I observe little complaint when Letsukov sings *Boris Godunov* in the showers,'' Coldewe observed coldly. ''You yourself remit leisured hours on slugs and bugs.''

Sanmartin dropped this unprofitable line of discussion. ''Hans, if you're really bored, why don't you come learn something about intelligence?''

''Nay, Guiron. Shimazu has a class of two souls. The triangle isosceles is the most unstable of figures,'' Coldewe replied firmly. ''You shall face the unquenched wrath of Ettarre La Beale alone and unchampioned.''

''Of all the lunatics . . . You were normal when we got you,'' Sanmartin lamented.

''A mere bud, I flowered. Truly, Sidvrar Vafudir himself, or someone, guided the Variag's hand when our two destinies were paired,'' Coldewe replied. He added reflexively, ''That is the cream of the jest.''

''There you are!'' said the voice of Hanna Bruwer.

''You are discovered!'' said Hans.

''You knew it wasn't loaded!'' said Hanna.

Kasha tapped her temple, again. Tomi, the other cook, nodded in solemn agreement.

* * *

THE FILLED, ORNATE ROOM WAS STICKY, SILENT BUT FOR AN-
drassy. With a convert's zeal, Andrassy had turned a five-minute
speech into twenty, detailing Newcombe's crimes for the edification of the multitude. Tactfully, he failed to mention other
names, which made it convenient for others to overlook his own.
After Andrassy finished, the rest of the jackals would tear at the
corpse.

Caught up in the dock, Newcombe looked disheveled, even
wild. Hunsley pursed his full lips. The last three months had
not been kind to "President" Newcombe.

Kirk Hunsley almost regretted using Andrassy for the final
twist of the knife, but Newcombe's erstwhile protégé was exceedingly contrite and too slippery for words. Using Andrassy
to strip Newcombe of his presidency and his council seat would
serve to nail the son of a she-ass as well as the mother.

In leisured moments, Hunsley freely admitted to himself that
Newcombe could have been eased aside a month ago. Although
Hunsley had needed the time to solidify his position, he could
not deny taking a certain pleasure in seeing Newcombe sway
this way and that.

However, every good thing must give way to something better. Hunsley had worked hard to clear away loose threads for
Admiral Lee, who had no desire to bind the mouths of the kine
that milled his grain, and Director Tuge had advanced an exceedingly generous line of credit. When Newcombe's forfeited
properties came onto a depressed market, there was no reason
why Hunsley might not discreetly fill his cheeks. Indeed, with
Admiral Lee's tacit approval, there was no reason why Kirk
Hunsley couldn't enjoy a council seat in his own right. And if
Janine Joh somehow managed to stumble, perhaps the council
president might someday be more than a figurehead.

In the flush of the moment, he almost felt sorry for Newcombe. Newcombe had tried so hard. Unfortunately Admiral
Lee preferred useful tools.

He caught Newcombe's eye and smiled sweetly. As stupid as he
was, Newcombe should know who guided the thrust. Yes, Newcombe knew. Hunsley could see knowledge burning in his face.

Then Newcombe did something that surprised Hunsley. He
stepped away from his seat and came close. Hunsley leaned
forward to hear what it was he had to say. Instead, Newcombe
pulled out an antique handgun. He fired it at Hunsley's chest six
times at very close range. Hunsley felt hammers break his ribs.

He slipped to the floor slowly, each instant lasting a lifetime.

It seemed to rise to meet him. As he lay, he touched his white shirt being stained crimson by the blood. "It's ruined," he thought aloud.

AT COMPLEX, THE DUTY SURGEON, SOLCHAVA, PULLED THE sheet over Hunsley's face.

Solchava then returned her attention to Mikhail Remmar's damaged knee. Dissatisfied with her initial scan, Solchava shifted angles and resectioned, searching her screen for the incomplete burgundy that would mark a break. Knitting damaged and destroyed nerves was a delicate task, inexplicable in its successes and failures.

Although personal success had eluded her, Solchava was both technically proficient and single-minded; she accepted that these were interrelated. Goaded by Anton Vereshchagin, she had privately decided that Mikhail Remmar would walk.

Remmar understood her intensity. If Solchava said so, he would damned well walk. Most especially because Company Sergeant Leonov, the Iceman's alter ego, disliked excuses including impossibility.

As Solchava set her results for analysis and methodically began putting instruments away, a messenger arrived with orders to pack.

She entered Moore's office with her face full of expression, however hard she attempted to contain it. "Lieutenant-Colonel Moore, I am a surgeon. . . . Please be so kind as to explain why I am going to a battalion," she asked.

"Devoucoux spent thirty months with Vereshchagin. He should be rotated out," Moore said, trotting out reasons. Before he forgets which end of a scalpel is which, she couldn't help thinking. She added cryptically, "Since Mohammed won't go to the mountain, we'll see about moving the mountain."

"Did Lieutenant-Colonel Vereshchagin request this in some manner?" Solchava asked harshly.

"Natasha, the Variag won't even know Devoucoux is being replaced until you step off the plane."

"I find it difficult to believe you have engineered this transfer for this reason."

"You're right, of course, Natasha. Now tell me what you think of Anton."

The tall surgeon hesitated, disarmed. "I cannot say. I have seen him only twice, when he danced the Cossack dance in my wardroom and again when you embarrassed him beyond belief.''

Moore pounced on the criticism the words implied. ''It wouldn't be the first time,'' she crowed, her features animated by hidden delight. ''Pliers. He had the most pained expression.'' Her voice abruptly lost its grating quality; it became almost humble. ''Please tell me, Natashenka.''

Solchava thought for a moment. ''He seemed like a very nice man. He seemed distracted, very quiet, very Russian. He dances well.''

Moore snorted. ''Nice is not a quality people usually ascribe to Anton. And his mother was a Karelian Finn. If you can get him drunk enough, he'll recite the Kalevala.''

''Cossack dances?'' Solchava questioned.

''Unit tradition. If you want to be on Anton's good side, find him seven hundred red roses for May Day. You'll understand.'' She laughed to herself gently.

''Have you ever seen Higuchi in a kilt and sporran? Something both rare and wonderful is a Japanese field officer commanding a Gurkha battalion dressed as a Highland Scot.''

Solchava made no reply. Moore saw fit to amplify her remark. ''Natashenka, there's something you need to understand if you're going to stay. Battalions have personalities. Look at Kimura's, they couldn't find water while standing in the sea. Anton's has been savagely successful for as long as I've known them, which is a long, long time.''

Unconsciously, she touched the strands of her hair. ''You know he was relieved on NovySibir during the riots. Well no, I suppose you wouldn't.''

''No, I had not.''

''One of His Imperial Majesty's worst kept secrets. Stupid to send him to NovySibir. Stupider still to expect him to obey orders. Anton's sins are many, but he won't sacrifice men to no purpose.'' She made a bridge of her hands and let her chin rest on top of it.

''He didn't stay fired for long, of course. Ishizu appointed a staff officer who had an accident with a pistol four hours later. Anton's exec went into Ishizu's office, shut the door, and told Ishizu the battalion had more pistol ammunition than Ishizu had staff.''

Vereshchagin's battalion owed precious little allegiance to Diets and admirals. The battalion fought because Vereshchagin told it to fight. Moore idly wondered what Lynch would find to say the morning of the day Vereshchagin told it to stop. She allowed her bridge to collapse, laughing as if it were the funniest thing in the world, quietly, until tears coursed down her cheeks.

Sensing some weakness, Solchava returned adamantly to the attack. "Lieutenant-Colonel Moore . . ." she began carefully, as if her voice might chip and shatter.

Moore straightened her back, once more erect, her eyes dry. She interrupted, grinning, as if she were letting the younger woman into some wondrous secret.

"You need exposure, Solchava. Besides, I like Anton. I like you. It's one of my many vices. And we're going to be here a long time. A long, long time."

Solchava began a sentence she never finished.

"I've told Anton much the same," Moore continued impersonally. "Devoucoux has a very good kit up there, all you'll need are personal effects. Pick up a copy of your orders from Molly and hop a lift tomorrow. There's one oral amendment: memorize every word out of Anton's mouth when he finds out you've replaced Devoucoux. I'd pay money to see him goggle-eyed."

She paused, and the side of her mouth twisted sharply. "I have fifty daughters in this battalion, and you're the only one I can provide for, when things fall apart. And I expect they will."

Tuesday (11)

IF VERESHCHAGIN WAS THE HEAD OF THE BATTALION, A DUBIOUS analogy, Malinov was its heart. Sipping tea in the early dawn with his battalion sergeant was a ritual that Vereshchagin could not forgo; osmosis was often the only way to extract information from him. Hearing a rap on the door, Vereshchagin raised one eyebrow. The interruption was not precedented.

Entering, Timo Haerkoennen hissed a terse summary before going to find Harjalo and Yevtushenko. Vereshchagin narrowed his eyes, carefully lowering his glass. Malinov's expression was unreadable.

"Do you know where this school is? Go there. Keep Yoshida under control and begin organizing the civilians. I wish to get hold of Raul and Rettaglia," Vereshchagin enunciated swiftly and clearly. Malinov nodded and rose, his face still unreadable.

* * *

MOMENTS LATER, IN JOHANNESBURG, SHIMAZU ASKED, "JUF-
frou Bruwer, is this perhaps your coat?" even though it was the
only such item within the confines of the perimeter.

This fact was not one Bruwer was prepared to deny. She accepted the light overjacket.

"Please come with me. A helicopter is approaching from
Pretoria, and it is necessary that you and I board it in company
with Captain Sanmartin. I have been informed that a group of
mercenaries has seized a primary school in order to hold the
staff and students as hostages. It is necessary to prevent the
indignation of the local inhabitants from interfering with
the conduct of operations. You at one time were a member
of the faculty there. Your assistance will be required."

Numbly, Bruwer allowed herself to be steered to the landing
pad in front of the C Company bunker.

HARJALO SPIED YEVTUSHENKO SPREAD OUT IN THE CORNER AS
he entered. "What's the problem, Anton? Fire, flood, or foes?"

"The latter. Stray mercenaries formerly belonging to Chalker
have taken over the Louis Trigardt primary school. They hold
forty-seven children and eight staff hostage. They have been out
in the forest starving. Their sources of information are not good.
They wish passage out and some ridiculous amount of money.
Apart from the warships and *Shokaku*, there is nothing in orbit,
and I am told that it is a very long walk to Earth."

"Is this connected with the assassination down in cowboy
country?"

"Doubtful. I will need you to take charge of negotiations."

"You'll stay and square the admiral before Colonel Lynch
gets involved?"

Vereshchagin nodded.

"Who's manning the barricades?"

"Chiharu is moving Per Kiritinitis's platoon in place. Yuri
will be on site. Use Chiharu as you see fit and keep your eye on
him. He wants to go in sword in hand. I had the devil's time
dissuading him."

"Literally?"

"I expect the order I gave to be obeyed."

"So you told Yuri to shoot him if he can't keep his trousers
buttoned, and you're telling me the same. Who's massaging the
bruised Boer egos? They must be panicking."

"They are, and Yuri is attending to it for the moment."

"Gods, that's smothering a fire in benzine. Drag Raul down,

he can be appallingly smooth when he puts his mind to it. It must come from associating with Coldewe.''

"He is on his way. Shimazu and Bruwer as well. Bruwer is familiar with the school.''

"I'm on my way. How?''

"Thomas is waiting for you outside. Bukanov threw together what you will need. Negotiate.''

"I bore them to tears.'' As Harjalo turned toward the door where Thomas and a Sparrow were waiting, Raul Sanmartin almost ran him down.

"Raul, you have been briefed?'' Vereshchagin inquired. Sanmartin nodded.

Vereshchagin turned his attention to Yevtushenko, huddled in the corner over a building diagram and oblivious to the conversation that had taken place over his head. Unhurriedly, Yevtushenko looked up and outlined a plan based on Malinov's assessment of the ground.

Vereshchagin listened patiently. "One thought,'' he said, "I dislike our inability to see what is occurring inside the classrooms. Do either of you have suggestions?''

A light brightened in Sanmartin's eyes as he realized why he had been asked to be present. "How about an optical fiber shoved under the door?''

"Could work,'' Yevtushenko said slowly, "but we don't have one, at least one that would do the job.''

"Rhett does.''

"Quite possible,'' Vereshchagin agreed. "He undoubtedly has a few doors for you to practice upon. Will an hour be sufficient? Raul, I need you and Juffrou Bruwer to help Timo in communications.'' He watched Yevtushenko and Sanmartin disappear in different directions.

Three hours later, Vereshchagin was back on the radio, "How does it go, Matti?''

As far as Harjalo was concerned, it had been a very long three hours, and from the sound of Vereshchagin's voice, it had been an even longer period of time for him.

"Not well, but not poorly. The man I'm talking to is a professional. He knows the game's up, but he'll play it to the end. He's holding out for passage, but I think he'll settle for not having a bullet in the back of the neck,'' Harjalo replied.

"The roof?''

"We can't land on the slant. Yuri's right, there simply isn't an acceptable way for us to preposition people there.''

The Afrikaners preferred their public buildings like castles with the surrounding land manicured. There was no cover and no dead ground worth mentioning. The mercs had picked their target well.

"Tactical?"

"Lev dropped the sensors himself, Ketlinsky is interpreting. Ten mercs all together, with two more possible but unlikely. From the noise, my friend on the radio is in the administrative office with one other. Hostages are split between adjoining classrooms marked four and three on your plat. My friend on the radio made a point of assuring me they're closeted with men wearing enough explosives to blow them all to another life if we try anything. I see no reason to disbelieve him. The other mercs are scattered about. We've confirmed four locations with visual sightings. Do you want me to run them down?"

"Not necessary. Can you conclude unconditionally? The admiral is unwilling to offer terms."

Harjalo couldn't tell whether Vereshchagin sounded tired or merely disgusted. "Six hours, maybe."

"Is that a definite maybe?"

Harjalo briefly considered the personality of his opposite number. "No," he admitted.

"It is just as well. The admiral strongly prefers a military solution, and we have a deadline of two hours. What does Lev say?"

Harjalo glanced over at Yevtushenko and held up two fingers. Yevtushenko nodded gravely. "Lev thinks he can do it," Harjalo replied.

"I am on my way," Vereshchagin said as he broke the connection.

He stopped to check in on the com room.

For about the tenth time since the first call came in, Sanmartin was thanking the creator of the universe for Ssu the censor. Suspension of live coverage had kept the situation within tolerable limits. With Shimazu to manipulate the media, Bruwer handled distraught parents, leaving Sanmartin to field the occasional concerned personage.

One such was His Excellency, the lord mayor of Pretoria. As Vereshchagin watched fascinated, it seeped into Sanmartin's conscious that His Excellency knew just enough English to be offensive. The board belonged to Timo Haerkoennen, and Sanmartin made a sweeping chopping motion for Timo to cut the volume while he contemplated turning His Excellency over to the Hangman, of whom His Excellency was justly terrified.

Haerkoennen stopped trying to rub life into Bruwer's whitened hands and reached over to adjust his dials. The situation was toughest on Bruwer, who knew the children and the staff and even some of the parents.

Vereshchagin spoke for the first time. "Timo, I have asked Mayor Beyers down. When he appears, please have him assist." Then he left.

Sanmartin waited until Bruwer closed the circuit she was on, then grabbed an arm and held on grimly. He thought back to that first week, remembered sitting on the mats spinning out to all who would listen one of those wildly implausible, mixed-together tales the people of the Islands love so well, the story of Momotaro, the Peach Boy. Bruwer had been in one corner, very silent.

The daughter of a king found a boy child in a peach floating in a wondrous chest among the reeds, once upon a time. Lifting him, she kissed him thrice and called him Momotaro.

Pharaoh the king had a mortal enemy, the frost giant Marhaus who laid truage on him for seven years and seven. Accompanied by a cat and a cock, a dog and a donkey, Momotaro sailed off in his chest.

There were adventures with robbers, an ogre or two, a wardrobe, a lion, and a witch. Three times, the giant told Momotaro to grow tall. With the cock on his head, Momotaro stood in turn on top of the donkey, the dog and the donkey, and finally on the both of them and the cat as well, before an unwilling Marhaus came forth. Momotaro hit him in the center of the forehead with a peach stone of gold coughed up by the cock and cut away his head with the enchanted sword Gram. Leaving the cat and the cock, the dog and the donkey to govern the land, Momotaro sailed back to the king with the giant's treasure.

When it ended, Bruwer had said, "The poor giant."

EARLY MORNING WAS YEVTUSHENKO'S LEAST FAVORITE TIME FOR a stealthy assault. It offered advantage only in being unexpected.

Getting to the window had been the hard part. Even with covering noise unwittingly provided by the horde of media types on hand, it had taken Yevtushenko nearly an hour to negotiate the final fifty meters. Crouched under the sill on his back he stared at the ugly little pistol in his hand as he let his ears do his thinking.

Holding aloft a pebble in his free hand, he jerked it twenty meters, where it bounced away with a sharp sound. When he saw the reflection in the glass over his head, he reached up and discharged the energy weapon soundlessly into the merc's face four times at a range of seven centimeters through the unbroken glass.

"Recon point two. Break. Thomas, let's go," he whispered in a soft, bored voice. Then he broke the connection and exhaled, noiselessly and deeply.

Reaching up with a suction cup, he attached it to the window which he slashed free of its frame with his cutting bar. Placing the window aside, he entered and used the cutting bar in his hand to make certain the merc corpse on the floor stayed a corpse. Thomas and two other shadows made their appearance out of the semidarkness. The four of them paused by the door to the room and tested it gently, as a second and a third of Yevtushenko's teams made their own stealthy approach.

Thomas was the best shot in the battalion, as Lev Yevtushenko was the worst. His task was the sentinel atop the school's atrium. He stopped by the door. Yevtushenko moved silently past him toward the end of the south corridor, the knife in his hand lightly poised to throw or thrust. The merc at the end of the south corridor continued to stare out the window into the dimming light, peering outward.

Crouched by the wall, Thomas watched him, conscious of the submachine gun in his hands, the two mercs, and of little else. He concentrated on the submachine gun, to do anything in his power to make the few seconds pass quickly.

Behind the cylindrical silencer, the submachine gun was a simple blow-back weapon up through the breach. Behind the breach, the weapon came up over the wrist and ended in an elaborate buffer arrangement butted up against the crook of the firer's arm.

It was not intended to be shoulder-fired. Overengineered and somewhat delicate, it was popular with rear echelon troops; Life Guards officers had particularly favored it. On Cyclade they'd left enough lying around for Lev and his Forty Thieves that Koryagin had two on hand for every serial number authorized. It was not a bad weapon. Still, Thomas figured the Ordinance Procurement Commission had let the contract on a particularly busy day, in one of those deals that usually involved somebody's brother-in-law.

Out of the corner of one eye, he tracked Yevtushenko's progress. The other never left his assigned target. As the corridor sentry watched the camera crews cavort on the lawn, Yevtushenko covered the last two meters in a quick bound, and his left arm tightened.

The knife punched twice into the right kidney and spleen and then glided across the man's throat. Yevtushenko ushered the merc and his weapon tenderly to the floor.

Thomas then ripped three quick bursts that flattened the merc in the atrium against the wall. The other three team members relaxed their weapons slightly. The second team passed them to cover the top level. The third team headed for the second level, pausing momentarily to practice fitting keys to the locks in the empty ground-level classrooms.

He smiled slightly as Yevtushenko sat down heavily and allowed his eyes to close. The next phase was for the third team and the supporting weapons. Zerebtsov, the corporal commanding the third team, slapped him lightly on the shoulder as he went by.

As Zerebtsov mounted the stairs, he spoke crisply into his wrist mount. "Battalion point two. Break. Zerebtsov. Phase two complete. Fire, three minutes. Fire on my signal."

Behind and to his left, his partner, "Abdullah" Salchow, was panting inaudibly. The heavy goggles over his mask lent him an unreal appearance. Zerebtsov made a fist and tapped him reassuringly. Salchow bent and pushed his face up against Major Rettaglia's magic box, maneuvering the fiber under the door of classroom number four with his fingers as Zerebtsov covered him. He jerked his thumb and a forefinger into the air, signifying he saw two mercs with a clear shot and no obstacles.

Zerebtsov inserted a janitor's passkey into the lock and wiped his hand on his trousers as if it were slippery, even through gloves. Turning slightly, he checked the progress of the riflemen doing the same to the door to classroom number three.

The door to the administrative office suddenly swung open. A merc stepped out, letting the door shut behind him as he fumbled with his trousers.

With three quick bursts, Thomas spun him around and dropped him. The merc slumped down with his mouth open and the assault rifle still strapped to his back. Visibly sweating around the edges of his mask, Zerebtsov whispered over the radio, "Zerebtsov. On three. Supporting fires on five. Out," and heard the echo of his voice as his team and the support team confirmed.

On "one," Salchow brought himself erect and poised. On "two," Zerebtsov turned the key and flung himself against the door with a grunt to clear it from Salchow's field of fire; a popper trickled from his fingers into the room to explode with the first of a dozen blinding flashes and shattering retorts. As Zerebtsov reached three, Salchow took apart the back of one merc's head and removed the face from a second for the edification of twenty-four school children. Twenty-three more were similarly entertained across the hall. Light machine gun fire blew out the windows in the administrative office for s-mortar rounds to enter and spatter the remaining occupant across the walls on five.

The rest was mopping up.

Zerebtsov paused to rub his sore shoulder and punched Salchow lightly. Apart from a protruding lip and a neck like a camel's, there was nothing remarkable about Abdullah, but without a few Abdullahs, the battalion wouldn't have been worth much.

Outside, Albert Beyers, armored with hope and the kind of faith that moves mountains, listened to what was coming in and began dancing a jig with a flustered Timo Haerkoennen. Chiharu Yoshida was caught by the gunfire in the middle of an interview he did not finish.

RAUL SANMARTIN PULLED THE HEADSET AWAY FROM BRUWER'S temples and took one last call. He listened for a moment in mounting incredulity and then flung the headset down. He announced to no one in particular, "His Excellency, the lord mayor of Pretoria, is on. He wants to know who's going to pay for the damage."

The admiral was only mildly displeased. In the Tuesday editorials, the Boer media were only mildly critical. The city of Johannesburg, in the person of its lord mayor, Albert Beyers, made a point of paying for the extra keys.

AWAKENED FROM DEEP SLUMBER AT MIDDAY, VERESHCHAGIN felt rather than heard the slight rap on his door. "Matti?"

"Malinov," was the reply.

"Come in, Yuri."

Malinov entered in combat harness, sparing his words. "From Rettaglia. Caverns near Bloemfontein. Major arms cache, munitions depot, maybe."

The task group intelligence officer paused for channels and

ceremony only when he thought it advantageous. He was not prone to overstatement.

"Matti?" Vereshchagin questioned.

"Went to grab Wojcek out of his hammock. Reinikka is on his way to close up the city's relay switching, and Piotr has the phone system shut down for purported repairs already. He has number one and a ground section on the recon waiting for the transports."

The battalion's four light transport aircraft could carry four sections. In a pinch, the four attack helicopters could crowd in one more.

"Shall we try brigade for a heavy transport or two?"

"It would take them at least two hours," Malinov stated carefully.

The light transports would suffice. "How long until contact?" Vereshchagin asked.

"Piotr says one hour twenty."

"Thank you, Yuri," Vereshchagin said.

"Matti said to tell you the little kid who caught the ricochet will be okay," Malinov added.

"Thank you again, Yuri," Vereshchagin replied, and Malinov made his departure.

In choosing twenty thousand families to migrate across the void, the Afrikaners had seemingly selected for intransigence. Vereshchagin was not one to assume that every effect had an obvious cause, but it appeared possible that in at least one case, intransigence had been tempered by something akin to gratitude.

"An interesting day," he murmured.

When Solchava entered, hours later, he was still seated in his spider chair, although he appeared awake, tapping a pipe against his knee. There was a hammock strung in the room and a second chair, but there seemed to be no desk. Another officer, a moon-faced major with high cheekbones, was standing beside him.

"Lieutenant-Colonel Vereshchagin?" she asked timidly.

Vereshchagin gave no sign he had heard. The major held a finger to his lip.

"Matti Harjalo, battalion executive officer," the officer said quietly by way of introduction. "Anton will be with you momentarily."

Vereshchagin let his eyes open slowly. "Matti, the cavern Piotr blew was twenty-three kilometers from the town limits of Bloemfontein, was it not? Let us see how predictable the Broth-

ers are. Lay hands on a geological map. Ask the navy to help.
It occurs to me that there might be equally large dumps em-
placed within twenty-five kilometers of the other cities. I must
attend Colonel Lynch's staff meeting.'' Harjalo nodded and left.

"Did someone else say something a moment ago?'' Vereshchagin asked with the pipe held in his two hands lengthwise in
front of his body. ''Surgeon Solchava, this is indeed a surprise.
What brings you up to Pretoria? Please, be seated.'' He gestured
toward the other chair.

"Lieutenant-Colonel Vereshchagin, I have been ordered to
report in place of Dr. Devoucoux,'' she said stiffly.

For a moment, there was a faint flicker of movement across
Vereshchagin's eyes.

"Indeed. Welcome. I must say we are quite pleased to have
you. I would ask you to excuse me for one second.''

He turned his body slightly and called out the door, ''Matti,
I must leave for the staff meeting, and there is a personal matter
that wants arranging. Call Raul, and ask him if he still has that
pipe. I seem to have broken the stem on mine.''

THE STAFF MEETING DID NOT GO WELL. EVA MOORE BIT BACK A
sharp comment at the drawn lines in Vereshchagin's face when
he came over to see her before returning. Admiral Lee had been
present, and despite the success at the school, the admiral was
still in an unusually foul mood. The Hunsley assassination was
an auspice that his efforts to control the Suid-Afrikan dynamic
would not move to plan.

"How went it?'' she asked. ''I don't suppose they fired you.''

"It was a near thing. Eva, heaven preserve me from my
friends. My enemies, I will manage.''

"Uwe?''

"Uwe has no sense. He brought up the munitions dump we
eliminated just as the admiral finished castigating me for failing
to keep Colonel Lynch informed of my operations. It appears
that Colonel Lynch neglected to brief the admiral because the
admiral tore Colonel Lynch into small pieces.''

"So Lynch is doubly furious with you.''

"At least. He believes Uwe and I arranged it between us.
There was also the soap yesterday morning.''

"The soap?''

"Several sacks of soap were transferred from a warehouse to
the courtyard in front of Colonel Lynch's residence in time for
the morning rain to simulate the onset of winter.''

Moore threw back her head joyfully. "Lord of heaven, I thought it was a rumor! And he just stood there while the bubbles crawled up his legs and filled his shoes? Anton, that was priceless. However did you manage it?"

"Soldiers used to the exigencies of combat tend to find garrison tedious," he rejoined mildly. "Unfortunately, yesterday he also sent Dong to Reading to investigate Hunsley's murder. You are aware of the pride that Dong takes in his physique? Uwe subsidized a small corps of talented street children and deployed them to strut about like miniature fighting cocks. One of my lieutenants christened them the Baker Street Irregulars."

He sighed. "Three incidents was excessive."

"You'd prefer Lynch off-balanced rather than rabid."

Vereshchagin nodded. "Uwe has no sense," he repeated. He paused momentarily. "If you are waiting for me to raise the question of Surgeon Solchava, I will not."

Moore laughed even louder, harsh and grating. "Then I won't either. Here's something to fortify your tea. You look as though you could use it. It's been a long day."

BLOEMFONTEIN WAS A PRETTY TOWN AT DUSK. THE HOUSES were plaster or stucco, colored in pastel hues of every shade.

Section Sergeant Suslov slapped the top of Savichev's hatch. Savichev slowed to let a few pedestrians cross in front, one of them with an infant walker. Four men could crowd onto the back of a Cadillac comfortably, four men was what each Cadillac had.

Pretty towns were dangerous. Behind beautiful facades, sometimes houses were thin-walled plaster, sometimes miniature fortresses of steel and concrete that had to be blasted apart, floor by floor, room by room. Then the town wasn't so pretty.

Having inflicted a fictitious "fire survey" on inhabitants of yet another world, Kolomeitsev had a master map of Bloemfontein and the surrounding communities showing the construction of each edifice and the names of occupants. Still, the thought of taking apart a town the size of Bloemfontein was not one Suslov relished. Patrolling it was bad enough. Light attack commanders were positively paranoid surrounded by tall buildings, and Sergeant Platoon Commander Savichev was one of the worst.

Suslov had brought Sery and his seven-seven machine gun solely to calm his friend's nerves. Sery, for one, was enjoying the ride. With the gp mounted into the ringbolt on the armored car's turret, he had the lightest load and the best seat. He grinned, pointing to the shipsbottle Suslov had hooked to his belt.

Suslov smirked. The polished steel tea urn Savichev had yoked to his engine with liberated copper tubing was a marvel of precision engineering, but Savichev made lousy tea.

In some respects, city runs were a waste of time, but C Company was running some sort of operation in a local tavern they didn't want disturbed. Since the Imperials were almost popular for the moment, the advantage of acclimating the townspeople to the sight of Imperial armor in the streets at odd intervals far outweighed the risks.

Hardly one blinked as they drove through, which made Suslov's task easier. While some like Yevtushenko worked best in the forest or the desert, reading odors and the flight of what passed for insects, Suslov was at home in a city, interpreting faces and movements, looking for differences in the streets and on the rooftops that he could rarely quantify. Only little things out of place gave men away, eye expressions and the cut of clothing, like a black frock coat.

He vaulted to the pavement suddenly, almost knocking aside one startled woman with an armful of parcels. Locking eyes with the gray-bearded man standing with his arms folded, he heard the sharp click of Sery's seven-seven locking a round. The Cadillac slowed, training its turret to cover the length of the street.

The gray-bearded man raised both his hands slowly. He dropped his wide-brimmed hat on the ground and opened the heavy coat. A thin smile danced about his lips.

Heedless of men and women milling about in confusion, Suslov stepped quickly toward him, taking care not to obstruct Sery's field of fire. Hooking his rifle in the man's belt, Suslov patted him down, a matter of a few seconds. He found nothing.

Unhooking his rifle, his eyes still locked, Suslov said, "Not this time, old man?" Hendrik Pienaar nodded agreement. Not this time. He bent to pick up his hat from where it lay.

As Suslov regained his handhold on top of Savichev's Cadillac, Pienaar looked up at him. He nodded again slowly and emphatically. Suslov tipped him a salute. Then he cast a glance over to the guest house where C Company was operating.

Inside the guest house, Fripp and Muslar sat together on a low-backed bench. They were ignored by the other patrons until well after the darkness had fallen. Around them was the Springboks football club, which had ended its league season successfully by defeating the Pretoria-Wes team by the honorable score of six goals to two. Most recent heirs to that ancient and honorable name, they were duly getting stinking drunk.

Fripp hummed an old tune under his breath.

> With their guns and drums, and drums and guns,
>> the enemy nearly slew ye,
> Me darlin' dear, you look so queer,
>> why, Johnnie, we hardly knew ye.

Fripp had once been recommended for academy. He might have been accepted if his political reliability index had not been lower than mite dung.

He was also obnoxious. In the distant past, it had occurred to Muslar that shared recreational activity was an excellent vehicle for breaking down Boer hostility. He had suggested as much to Major Harjalo, who had said neither yea nor nay. The engineer lieutenant, Reinikka, had dutifully issued challenges, to which the Boer club sides had also said neither yea nor nay.

After a suitable vigil, Harjalo had intimated that shared recreational activity was dead and buried in hell like al-Mansur, the Ever-Victorious. Muslar, wise beyond his years, had taken counsel with Rudi Scheel. Scheel had roped in Fripp.

Accordingly, Fripp sprung the ambush.

"Oh, come now, Edmund, gods and little red devils, it's small wonder the girls chase after uniforms. When have you ever seen such insipid play?" he said, opting for the crudest of the three approaches he'd rehearsed.

If Fripp's comments failed to cause windows to rattle, they nevertheless carried to Springboks who knew enough English to be offended. At least one man jerked as if he'd been struck with an ice pick.

Muslar gave a sickly grin that was only half feigned. If his reply was inaudible, Fripp's rejoinder was not.

"I've seen better passing from Little Sisters of Charity. Clown routines belong in a circus."

Were truth to be told, Pretoria-Wes had played aggressively, if not skillfully, and the Springbok's captain, le Grange, had bruises to prove it. Like Zeus from his throne, he rose slowly.

"May I do something for you gentlemen?" le Grange said slowly in English. Some of the remaining fire of combat glowed in his eyes.

"I don't believe we've been introduced," Fripp said coldly, turning his back.

Muslar manifested the palm of his hand in token of peace and another sickly grin that was not at all feigned. "Fripp, the man is trying to be polite."

Fripp turned. "Your pardon, sir," he said with obvious, icy distain. "I did not realize. My name is Fripp, Charles James Edward Fripp. At your service. And what might I do for you?"

"Le Grange. Are you perhaps speaking of today's game?" the burly Springbok inquired with his teeth clenched.

"Oh, yes. I recognize you, now. Sit down, it'll be my pleasure to buy you a beer. You were the one who blew the coverage on the wing when they scored their second goal," he said, hanging his cape on the bull's horns.

Muslar winced.

As anticipated, some lingering sense of fair play stayed le Grange's hand momentarily. To match his height and weight, Fripp needed an anvil to stand on. "I don't drink with Imperials," le Grange said distinctly.

"Take it to your own table, then. Myself, I was never much for converting the heathen. But it's pure coincidence you happened by. I was just remarking to Edmund here that it's a shame you can't scrimmage with his team, I'm sure they could teach you something."

"He has a team?" le Grange asked, again deflected from anticipated mayhem.

"You can imagine how difficult it is to keep them sharp on a mudball like this. If you were politely asking, I'm sure they might even give you a game to remember them by," Fripp announced to the establishment at large.

Muslar grabbed his arm. "Fripp, we are guests. We do not want to embarrass the gentlemen."

Fripp grinned hugely. "Not good enough for you, are they?"

The veins on either side of le Grange's square head seemed about to pop. "You want to play a game, you say so! We will be the ones to show you!" the Springbok captain shouted, to a muted roar of approval from his inebriated teammates.

"I would not dream of abusing your hospitality," Muslar answered awkwardly.

While le Grange was momentarily unsure who he wanted to punch first, Fripp sprang to the assault. "If you do talk him into it, I'll wager a week's beer your clumsy apes lose by two goals. While I wouldn't rob a drunken man . . ."

"Fripp!" Muslar murmured.

Fripp finished his sentence. ". . . if you're serious, just pick a time and place!"

Le Grange's response was forceful and conditioned. "I say to you, any time, any place!"

Fripp turned to Muslar. "Well, sir, you have a game."

Muslar nodded. "A game it is." He reached down to his wrist mount. "Chiba point base. Break. Muslar. Patch me through to Major Harjalo, please. Hello, Major Harjalo? Muslar. I have the captain of the Springboks standing here. He has just challenged us to a game and asked us to name a time and a place. . . . Any time, any place, he said distinctly. Quite fine, sir. Muslar out."

Le Grange had forgotten to close his mouth, which gave him a distinctly slack-jawed appearance.

"Major Harjalo says your field, eleven hours tomorrow. Standard international rules. You supply one referee and we supply another. He suggests you bring your own fans. An acceptance will be delivered to your residence, and Major Harjalo will personally notify Mayor Beyers," Muslar said, sinking his barb. He rose, grasped le Grange's unresisting hand and pumped it solemnly. "May the best team win."

Le Grange's father was an old schoolmate of Albert Beyers. They entertained a healthy dislike for one another. Whether the engineers had a game now or not, they'd have one by eleven tomorrow. Leaving Fripp to fight a rearguard action, Muslar stepped carefully over le Grange's net keeper on his way out.

Wednesday(11)

FOLLOWING THE FLOW OF PLAY WITH HIS EYES AND HIS IN-stincts, Muslar momentarily keyed on le Grange about to launch himself downfield for a breakaway pass.

The score was three to zero, engineers, before the Springboks had quite realized it. Now they were fighting grimly to cut the deficit, with a pride and ferocity only partly sapped by the evening's excesses.

Before unfamiliarity with the engineers' style of play had put him on the bench, Muslar had cleared for both Harjalo and Moushegian. Fripp had cautioned him, "First couple of times down the field, run quick as a gazelle and cut in front. I mentioned that you like to knock headers in from there." To Muslar's mild rejoinder that such was not his shot, Fripp had responded, "Then there's all the more reason for you to run quick and have them think you will, isn't there?"

As Muslar watched, le Grange took one long stride and his feet disappeared, Moushegian deftly stripping the ball handler and dropping the ball off. Harjalo stopped it with his foot and smiled at the indecisive little Afrikaner referee. He whistled through his teeth until Yevtushenko turned. Grinning, Harjalo held up three fingers.

Yevtushenko nodded and blew his whistle, stopping play. He took the ball from Harjalo and flipped it to le Grange for a free kick. Le Grange rose unsteadily to his feet and dropped his jaw.

Yevtushenko shrugged. "We let Matti have about three concealed fouls and then we make him call his own," he explained, pumping his arm. Le Grange stood rooted until a couple of his battered teammates came over to pull him away.

A swarming defense took back the ball.

Harjalo accepted it from the keeper holding up four fingers, and suddenly the crowd began chanting, sensing. With a quick pivot and a head fake, Harjalo split a seam and careened downfield side by side with Ketlinsky.

Slowed by dissipation and the pummeling at the hands of Pretoria-Wes, the strength was beginning to ebb from their legs, but the Springboks were not ready to quit. The keeper came out to cut the angle, and two defenders converged. They followed Harjalo's eyes to the upper right corner of the net as his foot plowed forward.

Unexpectedly, the ball flicked off directly to Ketlinsky, who made a quick left-footed stop. Reacting, the keeper made a sudden lunge to his left to block the shot that never came. Instead, Ketlinsky passed off to Moushegian on the post. Screened, the Sniper dropped the ball softly into the open, empty net.

When the Springboks pulled their keeper, the engineers held them and scored twice more.

LE GRANGE TOOK FRIPP TO FOUR DIFFERENT BARS, WHERE FRIPP initiated the unenlightened into the mysteries of the game of two-up. He returned with three newly minted Afrikaans verses to *The Whistling Pig*, having promised to introduce le Grange to Matti Harjalo at the first opportunity.

On balance, Matti Harjalo considered the operation extremely successful.

* * *

ON THE HANGMAN'S ISLAND, JAN SNYMAN WAS INVOLVED IN A different game.

In four and a half weeks of the Six Weeks War, Jan Snyman had been killed five times, wounded five times, and captured once—an average crucifixion. He had also become inured, if not sympathetic, to Corporal Orlov's oft-repeated assertion, "A couple grams brain, a little heart, I make soldiers. Instead I get thimble-wits! Always thimble-wits!"

Harris's seventh trip to the land of the shades daunted even Orlovian descriptive powers. Harris had mistimed his progress with a stick grenade so that it had gone off roughly between his thighs. The energized clothing fibers of Harris's trousers were stained red down both sides where the light energy had been absorbed, and two more bright spots on his chest marked where a thoughtful rifleman from No. 10 had scored while he had been distracted. The harsh fact was that he and anyone relying on him would have been dead three times over.

Snyman had originally objected to being paired with the cocky young cowboy. It was only after a week of listening to Harris's loud mouth that Snyman realized the noisy little *bekdrywer*—backseat driver—was really a bright and lonely lad.

Harris crawled over, his face as red as his pants, as Orlov ran out of breath. Snyman looked down at the boxes he'd fished out of his bergan. "Your choice. Monkey meat or old donkey."

"Donkey." Monkey meat was almost as bad as goldfish or, God forbid, diced squid.

Pulling the tab to heat the meal, Harris ate quickly, using the biscuit on the side to sop up the sauce. Finishing almost before Snyman had begun, he crumbled up the box and cocked his arm to throw it.

Orlov jerked his head around. "What do you think you are doing with that, thimble-wit?"

"I forgot," Harris mumbled.

"Not in my forest you will not. Corpse or no corpse, you flatten it out and tuck it away," Orlov commanded in a terse, flat whisper.

Although Orlov wept crocodile's tears every time one of his protégés got snuffed, he was as genuinely angry as Snyman had ever seen him. In fact, Snyman didn't realized quite how angry Orlov was until he saw Orlov put his hand right through his glove trying to put it on. Even Harris noticed.

"What's with Boris Karloff there?" he complained. "You'd think he was the flaming Queen of Hearts!"

He was still grumbling when Orlov shipped him off to see the Hangman. Snyman let Kobus relieve him and stretched out with his eyes shut. Despite the heat and weight, he made no effort to remove his cap or his jacket. The Hangman had conducted that demonstration just once. The cap was double-layered, the inner layer convex. At five hundred meters a 5mm round went in the front and came out the top, the outer layer having absorbed a small portion of the impact and disabled the bullet's flight path so the inner layer guided the projectile away from where the wearer's head would be. Of course, at four hundred meters, the bullet went through both layers and out the back.

Moments later, he heard Orlov's voice almost at his ear. He opened his eyes and let Kobus pull him into a sitting position. However much of a lump Kobus had been as a farmer's son, he had taken to soldiering with a frightening intensity.

Orlov squatted low with his elbows resting on his knees. "It's just the three of us, now, so we get started. The Hangman is interrupting the normal cycle. Instead of another week and a half of pretend war, we do it real. It's only jungle bunnies, but remind yourselves that being dead is real, too," he said gruffly.

Snyman interrupted. "Shouldn't we wait for Harris?"

"I spoke to the Hangman, he needs another idiot around like he needs a hole through his head. Harris goes to the volunteers, they probably make him a corporal with all his brains."

Snyman persisted. "He really is trying. Couldn't we—"

"Your buddy, Harris, he's so smart he doesn't think. He keeps doing the same stupid things. He got you shot twice, he even got me shot. I got no objection he gets himself killed, I got plenty objections he gets me killed." Orlov spat on the ground. He caught Snyman looking at Kobus just for a minute and reached over to ruffle Kobus's hair.

"Harris? I make better soldiers out of tin." He reached over and took Snyman's rifle from him. He snapped the telescopic sight out into a carrying handle and removed the attachment from the laser ranging.

"Try not to embarrass me by getting killed. It's only a couple jungle bunnies, but you get hit on the head with a stone club, you're just as dead. I'd sooner use Kimura's geeks, but the admiral would object we shoot his geeks." He began handing Snyman ammunition magazines, then stopped and wrapped his arm around the two of them to give them a quick squeeze.

* * *

NAUDE WAS J09 SLASH 03. HE HAD A LAST NAME, BOTHA, BUT Menzies used the number, never the name, running nets.

J09/03 arranged his contacts for Wednesday nights, when his wife had a *Helpmekaar* meeting. On Earth, he had been a tired, little man; here he was a tired, little, old man. Wisps of his gray hair stuck straight up. He wore a dirty synthetic nightshirt that had a hole somewhere, always, as if that were a requirement for Wednesday's nightshirt. He never offered Menzies tea. He made a point to mention, always, that he was afraid to have to explain a second dirty teacup to his wife.

Intelligence Sergeant Menzies didn't like face-to-face meetings with curtains drawn in shabby, little rooms. Drops were more reliable for transferring cash money one way and physical documents the other; electronic devices were infinitely more reliable for transmitting information. J09/03 could have stayed in his bedroom and spooled off anything he liked to the big dish at the Jo'burg caserne for Rettaglia's computers to screen and winnow, but efficiency was one thing, the human factor another. Operatives were guilt-ridden bundles of anxieties who needed handling.

"They are burning witches!" the old man fulminated as he drank down the tea he'd fortified for the evening's ordeal. "They are unhinged entirely, all of them. They rush about this way and that, and no one knows what is happening. They have canceled the yearly meeting. We elected one who spoke adamantly for peace, and the next thing he is speaking for war! I see documents passed with limited circulations, 'Do not show to Brother so-and-so.' Heer Snyman and the watchdog committees listen everywhere, they touch everything. They execute persons who I know to be perfectly loyal to the ideals of the Bond. It is crazy! Have you Imperials infiltrated men into our very midst?"

Menzies didn't answer directly. J09/03 didn't need prompting. Words were tripping over themselves out of his mouth.

"My son is in the *Ruiters* as you know. . . ."

Information passed from the son about the Bond's junior league was almost more valuable than information about the Bond itself.

"The agenda of cell meetings is now fixed by order from above. Unscheduled initiatives are not permitted. The lieutenant of the cell must determine the content of speeches and single out who is to be criticized. Each meeting, one is 'flogged' and everyone must participate. Is this is what we have raised up? It is as if inimical forces have seized hold of the bastions of our cause and driven followers of Christ into the desert. My son is made a field cornet, and he had no choice, none at all!''

J09/03's hands were shaking so hard that he could barely hold the cup. He set it down with an effort. J09/03 was scared, and not merely at the thought of being found out. That in turn scared Menzies, because J09/03 was an idealist of sorts. The Bond was being destabilized, but the scenario was not playing itself out.

''I know my Brothers, I know the Executive,'' J09/03 continued more calmly. ''These are patient men, they know how our people have suffered. They would not willingly lead us to destruction. What is being done? Why are voices of moderation silenced?''

Almost as he finished his remonstrance, there was a violent pounding on the door. J09/03 stood hesitantly, trembling as someone shouted, *''Oopmaak!''*

Menzies slipped to the back window. He undid the latch and nodded for J09/03 to go to the door.

Before J09/03 had a chance to comply, the thin plastic of the door melted away, and four armed men spilled inside. Menzies waited no longer. As the first of the four gunned Botha down, Menzies was already out the window, into a roll, and onto his feet to run. He gripped the wave pistol in his pocket, calculating odds.

One of the weapon's advantages was accuracy. At middle aperture it was almost impossible to miss a man at five meters. The other was silence. The charge that collapsed the induction field was muffled by the baffles, and the microwave radiations themselves were totally noiseless. The weapon's disadvantage was its almost nonexistent range.

Menzies made up his mind abruptly. Jumping a low hedge of hibiscus, he crashed on to someone's lawn and rolled to the wall, crouching in the shadows, flattening himself against the cool cement. Absently, he noticed that the fancy ruffles of his shirt were torn. He brushed his fingers against them.

In the street he had left, three men were running. Holding his gun tightly, Menzies tried to organize his mind to think whether he could drop all three. They continued down the street. Crouching in the darkness, he was suddenly aware of a window opening. He heard an unfamiliar voice.

''Sniffing around my wife, eh? I told you!'' the voice said in Afrikaans, and there was a noise like thunder.

Turning, Menzies felt the terrible pain in his chest and opened his mouth to explain what a terrible mistake was being made. It filled with blood. His last thought was that Major Rettaglia would never know the crystal-clear deduction that occupied his mind. It was really so simple, not complex at all.

Thursday(11)

WHEN VERESHCHAGIN RETURNED FROM BLOEMFONTEIN, HE found Malinov waiting.

"Greetings, Yuri. Is Matti here?" Vereshchagin asked, seating himself.

"Shortly," his battalion sergeant responded.

Vereshchagin recognized Harjalo's quick steps in the hall outside, and he heard him pause to rub the battalion crest for luck before walking through.

"You're back. How was Bloemfontein?" Harjalo asked, leaning against the doorjamb.

"Bloemfontein is a lovely town. As always, Piotr has matters well in hand. I mellowed him." Even the Iceman was better for a little human contact occasionally. "I also found occasion to chat with a gentleman named Hendrik Pienaar, who is quite an engaging old cutthroat."

"Another one of Rettaglia's inspirations?" Harjalo asked pointedly.

"Quite. I think you'd like Heer Pienaar. An exuberant man. He still wears his medals from the Bantu Wars."

"Oh?"

"He says it annoys the devil out of his contemporaries and allows young fools to know what sort of idiot he was when he was younger."

Harjalo laughed. "You're right, I would. And I don't doubt he'll be shooting at us with the rest of them when the time comes. How is Tikhon doing with our berserkers?"

"Very well. Surpassingly well. With number two, one always worries. I am quite pleased with both him and Muslar."

Even in a universe of disturbed personalities, killers were few and far between, but Vereshchagin did have a double handful of dragon's teeth concentrated where the Iceman could direct their energies. Although No. 2 was not normally a place for a callow sublieutenant, Degtyarev the younger had essentially been in training for his present position since the age of three. With luck, Tikhon the second might rival Tikhon the first.

Vereshchagin inclined his head. "I understand Colonel Lynch passed through during my absence."

"Ja, he gave me hell for not being here and Paul hell for not effecting better rapport with the elected officials. Then he went down to rapport with our friend, Laurens."

"So I feared."

Unlike his colleagues in Johannesburg and Bloemfontein—the latter was afraid to set foot outside his office for fear of offending the Iceman—the mayor of Pretoria, "Laurens of Arabia," would have stolen a hot stove and come back to steal the smoke, at least until he became certain that the Hangman would shoot his lights out if he so much as spit on the sidewalk, an acute observation.

"After rapporting with Lynch, Laurens decided that as a colonel's friend he was too busy to talk to mere majors. We owe the city for a new door. Paul put his hand through it. He's dealt with the matter for the time being, but after Gamliel's little toads start filtering in, it'll come undealt. I'd let the Boers have their strike if it would keep Gamliel out another week."

"Patience, Matti. What else resulted from Colonel Lynch's visit?"

Harjalo's gray-in-blue eyes glinted, flecked with an unholy light.

"We did get a delicately phrased request from a Lieutenant Fuwa in admin. He's been directed to ask what a "helicoprolite" is. "Heli" I know, and Raul tells me a coprolite is fossilized what-you-don't-want-to-step-in. Dinosaur dung."

Malinov altered his expression very slightly.

"Any other news?" Vereshchagin asked.

Harjalo arched his back and grinned, catlike. "Do you remember the tinned beer we borrowed—"

"Stole," Vereshchagin amplified.

"Tingrin told Mizoguchi not to issue more than a tin to a man at a time. . . ."

Vereshchagin sighed.

"So Mizoguchi passed it out and rang Tingrin every ten minutes to ask if everybody could have another sip."

Vereshchagin briefly studied Harjalo's face. "You are making this up. Matti, have you no respect for my graying hairs?"

"Seriously, Anton." Harjalo looked at Malinov, who had remained silent throughout. "In garrison, Chiharu Tingrin Yoshida is an ambitious ass. In the field, I shudder."

"Matti, let me refresh your memory. We shopped Chiharu to

Admiral Nakamura's staff. Admiral Nakamura gave him back and made us give him a company. I know what you are thinking, Matti. The answer is no.''

"Anton, don't go limp on me.''

"Patience, Matti. As Colonel Lynch would say, you fail to see the broad picture.''

"I see enough to know that you can't make a nail out of leather.''

"Matti, if we shopped Chiharu right now, he would be back in a month as a major, possibly in your place.''

"It's as bad as that, isn't it? Anton, we may not have a month. And who said anything about shopping him?''

"No, Matti," Vereshchagin said judiciously, "do nothing precipitate. Patience. We might as well play soldier with the rest of them for a little longer. Chiharu has even shown signs of improving.''

"I know. We only shoot the ones we can't reform. I think you're making a mistake, Anton, but I'll play along. Nonsense aside, I respect the Boers more than I do Lynch, and they're heading for some sort of eruption. I don't doubt you've been laying brickwork for some massive chicanery on the slight chance Admiral Lee is going to give us some space to maneuver in.''

"I will not deny making modest preparations.''

"I suppose we're going to have to do this the way we did with Ishizu on NovySibir and trust to luck and your aura of omniscience to fill the holes," Harjalo said.

"And do you recall what you wanted me to do about Admiral Ishizu?''

Harjalo laughed, commenting, "Nothing is new under the sun, stars, or sky. Everything changes and ends up the same.''

"No, I think that you are wrong, Matti. Even people change, occasionally," Vereshchagin replied philosophically. He watched him depart.

In actuality, Matti had touched his finger on several sore points. Yoshida was a superb officer for an Earth battalion, but nothing he possessed to lend to B Company could match the quiet fanaticism of the Iceman, the professionalism of the Hangman, or even the calm insanity Sanmartin occasionally displayed. Despite some exposure to combat and even a wound stripe, Yoshida inspired neither zeal nor confidence, and there was a tangible difference between B Company and the others.

As for Lynch, he was dangerous if only because he lacked the experience to understand his environment.

Vereshchagin looked at Malinov. "The defect is latent. We wait, Yuri. And you? Is our other weakness Raul?"

Malinov nodded.

Vereshchagin folded his hands. "Raul's passions are inherited, Yuri, as we have inherited passions of our own. His father served ten years solitary on the Malvinas when the Argentines purged the Ecologists."

Malinov nodded again.

"Is it the girl that bothers you?"

"Bruwer," Malinov said, "is her name."

"I know, Yuri," Vereshchagin said softly. "We let ourselves in for some very hard choices, do we not? I may have made a mistake. It is perhaps a small one."

Malinov nodded. Unhurriedly, he rose and left, closing the door softly behind him. Small mistakes took so very long to show themselves.

Seated, Vereshchagin recalled a story he had read as a child, about an Earth under siege and a lone pilot flying interception for the beleaguered planet.

For years on end, he beat back wave after wave. The parts of his body were replaced by gleaming metal, part by part, and time dilation changed the very surface of the world below. A final friend died, a last link severed. He flew into the void, escorted by phantom ships and the ghosts of dead pilots.

Vereshchagin had spent two years of his last fourteen on Earth, and those cloistered with other misfits at the war collegium. The battalion had moved from one colonial world to the next, refilling its ranks with whatever came to hand.

In a way, this was his fault. The battalion had never undergone a savage bloodletting, there had never been shattered scraps to be cost-effectively returned to reform and recruit. Instead from Odawara to Cyclade to NovySibir to Ashcroft, there had only been a gradual attrition and an overwhelming lassitude as the ones who were attached to worlds left behind disappeared or lost interest. Uwe Ebyl's unit was no better, a floating foreign legion that had left its old vehicles and every memory with burnt embers on the savannahs of Canisius.

As for Yoshida, he was blind to many things, but not all. His career had gone spinning into an ash heap when the battalion went nine months ship-time from thrones and powers and influential in-laws. Only a startling coup would put him on a fast track.

One such coup would be for Yoshida to become acting battalion commander, and it was undoubtedly possible that Colonel Lynch had thought that far ahead. Still, on Ashcroft, Admiral Nakamura, more perceptive than wise, had called Vereshchagin his Quintus Sertorius. Lynch did not know, and Yoshida had never thought to ask why.

It was Independence Day. Checking the time, Vereshchagin reached for a candle and went out in Malinov's company.

ON A HILL OUTSIDE THE CASERNE, HANNES VAN DER MERWE swallowed bile at the unfairness of having to pull secret duty with less than three weeks until Christmas. Orders were orders, but a lot of fellows who turned in reports never left their beds.

Watching the Imperial casernes was a waste of time, anyway. Nothing ever happened. Bored and a little frightened, he doodled sixes on his notepad. Suddenly, he gasped as the Pretoria caserne was lit by a circle of fireflies.

"Jacobus!" He prodded his partner awake.

For an hour the candles flickered, then extinguished, one by one, leaving the two young Boers mystified. On this world, December sixth was but a mark on a calendar, but in some fashion, this day Suomi celebrated its independence and mourned its war dead. Yuri Malinov, oldest of them all, left the last candle burning on Szigety's crypt.

Friday(11)

ON FRIDAY, THE RABBI SLEPT LATE. SO SAID HANS COLDEWE, who was known to occasionally dip his bill in literature from eras earlier and later than the love of his life. Kolomeitsev's preacher, who possessed the longest chin beard that could be stuffed into a protective mask, flew in at noon for those devoutly Orthodox souls who couldn't decide whether the Lutheran Erixon was the Antichrist or just another godless atheist. Rudi Scheel, who was still trying to puzzle out the significance of Sergeants Felsen, Roche, and Peña, was not amused.

Unfortunately, as his bearded excellency noted with asperity, the arrival of twenty-four sides of freeze-dried steer scrounged by Grigorenko occasioned more interest. Vereshchagin's companies had quietly begun to scale back their purchases from Boer areas. Poison is a weapon of war.

Saturday(11)

THE REVEREND DOCTOR WILLEM KLAUS STRIJDOM SPOKE QUI-etly, as befit his stature, in attempting to persuade waverers of the fitness of his course of action. The softness of his voice belied the fire in his eyes, in his belly.

Four of his fellows on the Executive of the Bond shone with the light of God: five more spoke with Satan's voice. The chairman and one other vacillated between heaven and hell, as they had for weeks. They would only approve the mildest of gestures, such as the forthcoming general strike. Its failure would weaken his voice in council and paradoxically strengthen it, for he knew that he could count on the Executive no longer.

Strijdom felt it unfair; where Jesus had had but one Judas and one Peter, he need contend with five and two. Addressing his words to the latter, he spoke casually, but formally, hiding the light of God that was within him so as not to burn away their fragile faith. Not yet, not yet.

"Thesis is countered by antithesis, becomes synthesis. That is the human condition. The political-cultural-historical tide grinds to sand and chips away the great rocks. In order to surmount this degradation, we must destroy the middle, deny this hateful synthesis which erodes all that we believe. We are the forge upon which the Imperials must cast their antithesis. We must provoke Satan's host to repression, and each man who does not choose to cleave to us must recognize that he clings to the antithesis to God's Law. Each traitor who would alter one word, one line, must be cast out and destroyed ruthlessly. It is thus that the laws of history push us forward on our sacred path."

That imp of Satan, de Roux, openly sniggered. For all his fair words, since the day he had been selected to the Executive he and his had deflected all Willem Strijdom's efforts, or so he thought. It was all Strijdom could do to hold his voice in check; although the time for reckoning was near to hand, it would not do for those accursed by the Lord to suspect that the Lord's host would rise in spite of their treason, that the fabric of the Bond was to become stainless and white.

Then would the faithless, the Imps and Imp-lovers, have their comeuppance. The Imperials must rule by the consent of the governed. What must be eradicated was the possibility of such a consent, of such compromise in the minds of the people.

The blandishments of Satan were hearkened to. The martyrdom that had befallen the small band of the Elect who had died in the caverns outside Bloemfontein to preserve their sacred trust had already caused more of the halfhearted to wobble, and Strijdom was not so ignorant of matters practical to think that the loss of so many weapons of war was anything less than a tribulation that the faithful must strive mightily to overcome.

Yet blind, ignorant fools stubbornly refused to see that such setbacks only showed that the Lord was abroad and actively choosing His own for the new Covenant. Their eyes would be opened for them. The Imperials were the anvil upon which God's Chosen would be hammered out, the fire in which His instrument was to be forged and His will be done. Strijdom let his mouth subtly betray the pleasure he would take in transforming, with fire and the sword, the implements of Satan into tools of the Lord. The memory of the humiliations he had undergone at the hands of that yellow-skinned Bantu-lover Ssu burned at his very soul, and more so the memory of his niece in her wheelchair.

Still the time of the Lord's vengeance was not yet at hand, and Strijdom cloaked his faith. His was the path of history. He who would not compromise must dominate those who would, Jacobins must annihilate the Mountain until they are eaten in turn.

Quiddities(reprise)

"VAN DER MERWE" IN THE QUINTESSENTIAL AFRIKANER. HIS name has the same prominence among Afrikaners as does Smith among Amies or Holub among Czechs. For two hundred years and more, Irishmen have told Irish jokes about Pat O'Reilly; Afrikaners have told jokes about Van der Merwe.

At the spaceport, one of the ground crew invited Van der Merwe to see the robots charge fusion bottles. He watched the robots work through the remote hookup and watched the technicians at their dials. Finally, somebody asked him what he thought. Van der Merwe pulled on his beard for a minute. Finally, he said, "Too many workmen. Give me half a dozen blacks, and I'll do the job myself."

* * *

"ARE THEY ALL THAT BAD?" IS THE QUESTION. THE ANSWER is, "No, because some are worse."

The customs officer asked Van der Merwe, "Did you just come from Earth?" Van der Merwe told him, "What do you mean, did I just come from Earth? This is Earth!" The customs officer said, "Don't you even know what planet you're on?" Van der Merwe replied, "There aren't any other planets." Then he held up his Bible. "And this one's flat."

IT IS SAID THAT THE ONLY FORM OF HUMOR LOWER THAN A VAN der Merwe joke is a pun. However, a pun is not a form of humor.

Listening to the war news during the Bantu Wars, Van der Merwe heard the announcer say a heavy Bantu assault had been stemmed with nerve gas. For every Afrikaner casualty there were five dead terrorists. A little later, the announcer came on again. A second assault had been ground into the dirt by tactical nukes. For every brave boy dead, ten kaffirs had been vaporized. A little after that, the announcer spoke a third time. A third Bantu thrust had been stemmed with plague. Twenty Bantus had died writhing in agony for every Boer slain. Van der Merwe turned off the radio and put his head in his hands. "They're winning," he moaned. "Pretty soon there won't be any of us left."

THE SUCCESS OF A VAN DER MERWE JOKE CAN BE MEASURED BY the reaction. A good Van der Merwe joke will draw a smile. A better one will draw a laugh. The best Van der Merwe joke will cause a man to run away screaming with his hands over his ears.

Van der Merwe was cutting wood. Out of a clear sky, lightning struck the axe-head and knocked him spinning into the well. Bouncing from the axe-head, the bolt of lightning fired the barn. The livestock burned. A gust of wind lifted up the burning roof and dropped it on the house. Running from the kitchen, Van der Merwe's wife fell and broke her leg. Van der Merwe pulled himself from the well. Surveying the desolation, he weakly lifted his fist to heaven, saying, "Those damned Bantus!"

IN ANY SOCIETY IN WHICH THE HEADS OF GRAIN THAT STICK out from the rest are lopped, self-depreciating humor is a safety valve. Even during the worst days of the Afrikaner Second Republic, the thought police made no arrests for telling jokes.

Sunday(12)

BRUWER SPIED SANMARTIN SPRAWLED ON A PONCHO, ALL BUT hidden by small horsetails. He appeared strange to her, then she realized he was wearing civ clothing, a tunic and pants in pale blue-gray. His hair was grown out a little, and had begun to curl.

She stopped the pickup and waved. Shading his eyes, he waved back with his singlestick. She left the vehicle beside the surf and came across holding out a rucksack. "Hans asked me to bring this to you. He gave directions. I was only lost twice. Why are you sitting here? Shouldn't you be back telling your soldiers what to do?"

"Kind, thoughtful Hans. I never tell my soldiers what to do. Rudi tells my soldiers what to do. I tell Rudi what it is I think I would like my soldiers to do, and sometimes he arranges it."

He flung a pebble in the direction of the ocean. "My beloved lieutenant-colonel told me to take the day off and I can't go sailing, therefore I sit. Did I mention that one can go sailing in Chubut?" He poked the rucksack with his stick. "What have we here?"

She opened it and discovered it contained a field table and a picnic lunch.

"What kind of cheese do you like?" he said.

"That Hans!"

"That isn't kind. Hans has good qualities, I will have you know. I can't think of any, but something will come, by and by."

"You're as bad as he is."

"Not really. He has a knack for it. I have to practice."

She sat down beside him and smiled. "Actually, Katrina told me about the basket."

"Who?"

"Katrina! Your cook!"

Not even Kasha's husband referred to her by her given name, and he laughed aloud.

"Did Lieutenant-Colonel Vereshchagin really tell you to take today off?" she asked.

"Just so. Lieutenant-Colonel Vereshchagin watches his officers very carefully." Sanmartin carefully set aside his quebracho singlestick and selected a mango. "Every few months or so, he sends Major Henke off with a fishing pole. There ought to be some symbolism in that, but I've never figured out what it is.

"The Iceman, Major Kolomeitsev," he continued, "never lets go of the reins for an instant, seven days a week, forty-eight hours a day, until you begin to believe he's some sort of machine. Then he'll disappear only the Variag knows where."

"And you?"

"I'll wake up in the morning and look out and say to Hans, 'Hans, it's Saturday in Chubut.' Hans will say something profound in German, from Thomas Mann or Schopenhauer, and off I'll go. Of course, the Variag knows when it's Saturday in Chubut three days before I do.

"There is also Hans to consider," he said presently. From his pocket he took an embroidered handkerchief she had given him and wiped his chin. "He's going to be a very fine company commander if I don't shoot him first. He needs to get practice in. Is that enough of an explanation or shall I think of something more?"

She laughed. "It will suffice. You look well."

"I feel naked."

She laughed. "Why did you come here of all places?"

"The sea, the sky, the breeze, I suppose. It reminds me of Java," he answered lazily.

"Java?"

"Java, a wonderful island, the richest and most densely populated of the *Sunda Besar*. South of Kalimantan, northwest of Australia, southeast of Asia." He smiled at some memory.

"What amuses you?"

"We had a beach like this one. We wrote out six-part warning orders and seven-part operations orders to move platoons down to count coconuts. They'd bring their wives." He laughed softly to himself. "The Variag cured me of that bad habit quickly enough."

"And what of your other bad habits?"

He coughed. "To tell the tale, I first caught up with the Variag off in the middle of nowhere. As prescribed for such occasions, I jumped down from my vehicle, snapped off a salute, and requested orders in my best parade ground manner."

"Oh, no."

"Oh, yes. He tapped that pipe of his for no less than five minutes. Then took me by the arm over to the third of number nine. They were sitting around in the sand looking like pirates, and he said to them, 'All right, children, gather. This is your new executive officer, Lieutenant Sanmartin. Take him up the Wadi Fahed Alrasheed'—a wadi is a kind of donga—'and I would like him back on Wednesday, so I would ask you to please try not to lose him.' I must have just stood there like a sheared sheep because the next thing he said was, 'Lieutenant, paper is expensive. I will see you on Wednesday.' Ten minutes later, I was wearing ten kilos of sand and cursing his ancestors for seven generations. Of course, I did the same to Hans.''

"Oh, no.''

"Oh, yes. When he got back, the whites of his eyes were brown. Dust and all, he gave me one of those academy salutes and said, 'Number eleven platoon patrol returning as ordered, sir!' I'd borrowed a pipe for the occasion, so I banged the bowl of it against my knee, and said, 'Hello, Hans, did you have a nice trip?' He was so mad, he couldn't see.''

"Wasn't that dangerous?''

"Dear one, we ran patrols up that wadi for seven solid months and never made a contact. That was part of the reason Hans was so mad. War on Ashcroft was usually very dull.'' He pointed at the field table. "The legs there fold out and down.''

"Tell me more about Ashcroft,'' she said, ignoring his instructions.

He stared up at the sky and held up his hands to examine them minutely in the sunlight. "Ashcroft is hell,'' he commented matter-of-factly. "The days are hotter than Hades, the nights colder than the devil's kiss. I had a watch my mother gave me. The second day out, the crystal cracked across. The highest forms of native life are single-celled algae that my friend the marine biologist wasn't sure were native.''

She held aloft a wrapped delicacy.

"Kasha made it. Don't ask,'' he replied to her unspoken question. "Before the crack-up, they seeded the seas swimming with diatoms, copepods, coccolithophores, dinoflagellates, radiolarians, and I forget what else.''

She set aside the wine and opened two bottles of the lager, one of which he took.

"We lived in respirators. You could watch plastic melt and be frostbitten by midnight. I saw a man with sunburned retinas, green herring straight off the ship. He never looked up, the sun reflecting off the rocks got him.'' He drank some of the warm beer.

She closed her eyes and opened them. "When I think of desert, I think of heat and sand, palm trees. Camels.''

"There were four different deserts, really, stone deserts to break axles, ice deserts so bad even the cakes stayed away, sand deserts, dust deserts. The sand deserts ate paint and glass when the khamsin blew. The winds couldn't lift the sand grains well. We'd find a hill and watch the wind blow the sand like wheat rippling in a windstorm. The dust deserts . . ."

He stopped and touched her hand momentarily to watch the skin flush, the deadened white springing back to life. "The dust storms killed. The big ones were ten meters tall and a hundred kilometers across. We couldn't run. We couldn't hide. The fine particles ate our respirators. Finer still, and they'd seep through and eat our lungs. That and the static electricity murdered our engines. Every day we'd think, today we'll do something wrong and not come out. We always did, though."

"Why would anyone live there?"

"Why does anyone live anywhere? It's close to Earth, even short-haul freighters can make it. Shipping lanes run past. One of the companies lured fifteen thousand people there with pretty brochures and built a city on men's bones. I know your people don't like blacks, and maybe you've reason, but if men ever had a reason to run riot, the cakes did. They were charged for the food they ate, the air they breathed, and spaces where they slept in shifts. The overseers and the other parasites kept the thumb-screws tight. Do I sound prejudiced?"

She nodded.

"I am. For a pin we'd have cleaned that city out and given it to the cakes."

"They fought."

He nodded. "They figured out that it wouldn't be their children who inherited the promised land. *Adde parvum parvo magnus acervus erit*. Add little to little and there will be a great heap, said Ovid. One of their number with a classical education called himself Spartacus. He taught them to feed the labor guards their guns and whips, and the concern's pet legislators convinced the Diet there was a revolt to be put down. The whole time, ships to Dai Nippon were landing without the slightest idea anything was happening."

"What did he do?"

"It was what he didn't do. He didn't massacre the parasites, and he didn't surrender when we showed at his door and rang the bell. *Bis peccare in bello non licet*, to blunder twice in war is not permitted," he quoted, picking up his assault rifle from where it lay and running his hands absently down over the trigger mechanism and the mirrored safeties on either side. "We blew them out of the city. The survivors took to the hills with the food, and we played at stabbing water until Admiral Nakamura decided who he wanted to shoot in what order. We did end up hanging five directors for enslavement. Of course, the fact that the cakes took up arms had already finished the parasites."

"Survival of the fittest?" she said with a slight smile.

He grimaced. "No, that's not really what Darwin said. Creatures multiply and specialize to fill all the little niches. Then the environment changes. A grass uses silica to protect itself or an ice sheet comes, and the niches aren't there any more. Species who find new niches live and proliferate. The rest disappear."

He dusted his hands and examined his singlestick minutely, tracing the fine grain before he slashed out at the horsetails suddenly.

"People are just the same, they proliferate, they stratify and modify their behavior to fit a particular niche. Then the tide comes in to wash the sand castles away. We're good at that. Soldiers, I mean."

She looked through his eyes as he tried to pin a fragment of a memory and classify it.

"The managing director there, I saw him, a little wizened man," he said to complete the thought, "carrying his possessions out of his big office in a little sack. I don't suppose anyone ever told him there were people outside he was killing."

He stared out at the sea. "I saw a land turtle patterned red-brown and brown like a lacquered box, up at West Point on Hudson, north of the corridor of fire. It had the director's skin and eyes. It was lying off the side of a road with a cracked shell. The universe had trucks, and it never understood."

"I've read about the corridor of fire," she remarked, reading into his silence.

"They were the lucky ones," he responded. "The ones caught up in the plagues of the wizards' war didn't have it so easy."

"What is the swearword that Heer de Kantzow always uses?"

"You mean 'Frosty'? Just so, that came out of the plague years. They let loose one unusually virulent sexually transmitted disease that left its victims looking like albino lepers." He paused for a second to collect his thoughts. "It's strange, but the crack-up was the best thing that could have happened. It gave us a chance to breathe, some of us. Like the Black Death, it gave succeeding generations something to propel themselves forward.''

''Four billion dead?'' she asked.

''Is a small price to pay for survival and the stars. We would have paid something, sooner or later. We poisoned the forests and the rivers and the pitifully few productive areas of the sea, and we crowded ourselves until we couldn't breathe. If the crack-up hadn't come when it did, we might not have left enough to build on.''

He picked up the horsetail he'd destroyed and handled it tenderly. ''I know,'' he said, not looking at her. ''Maybe it would have been better if we'd all stayed home loving each other until Malthus and the rats laughed. Lord and heaven, we've tried to wreck every other world we've been on, this one included.''

As he was speaking, fluffy clouds touched the tops of the forested mountains and gathered, turning black. Thunderbolts split the sky and then a torrent of water turned the dust of the road into a sea of mud.

''Help me get everything into the pickup,'' Sanmartin said, sweeping up his stick, the rucksack, and his rifle.

''Nonsense,'' said Bruwer firmly. ''We put it all under the table and eat it here.''

She began speaking as they finished fruit and satay, watching the rain pour over the sides of their shelter and around, via the little trench he'd scratched into the soil. She told him a parable, what she remembered of her years on Earth.

''I was nineteen when I began teaching in the camps. They still have camps, you know, filled with Afrikaners who have never been permitted to find a place after all these years. In autumn, I said to the children, 'Let's have a rugby team.' They said that was splendid, but they asked why they couldn't have two teams, so that the teams could play each other. I said that that was all right. The two best boys were the team captains, and I let them choose up sides.

''Their first practice was on a Saturday. I asked them what the names of their teams would be, the Springboks or the Impalas or whatever they liked. They told me they hadn't really thought about names, but one team was for the Potgieterites and the other for the Malanites. The ones whose families supported Potgieter were on one side. The ones whose families supported Malan were on the other. I had to excuse myself so that I could go to the girl's room and be sick.

''Later, much later, my father called me,'' she said, as if

recounting the tale someone else had told her. "My father re-married after my mother died. We were never close, especially after I went away to school, but he called one day and said that he had received permission for the five of us, my stepmother, her children, I and he, to emigrate. It was not that he was unkind or uncaring, but he ordered. I told him that I would have to think. And he pleaded for me to come. And so I went. He never pleaded except that one time."

"And he died when he got here," Sanmartin said.

"Yes, it was his heart. But there was the ship, you see. The ship was packed with Afrikaners, filled with families. It was almost like a reunion, because it seemed that half of my class was traveling. It was days before I realized that only the Potgie-terites were on board, none of the little Malanites. It was then that I understood my father."

"I always meant to ask you why you threw your lot in with us," he said.

She laughed softly. "I didn't really. It was so strange. When they decided to stop teaching English to the lower classes, there was no job for me. The next week the same people were begging me to interview with an Imperial major."

Sanmartin remembered the time Rettaglia had spent that first week rooting out people the thrones and powers had squeezed out of a normal existence. Once you eliminated the obvious misfits, he had said, it was like holding Diogenes's lamp.

"They were disappointed with me; it was unusual for a woman not to marry and leave," Bruwer explained, as if what she said was perfectly natural. "I don't know what I would have done. I did not want to understand. I wanted to go through and not see what was around me. A lot of people do; it isn't always easy to look at the unpleasant things."

"No," he said slowly, "it isn't always easy."

"The people are asking themselves, you know."

He nodded.

"You have governed us by martial law. Well and good, but it has been three months. Sober, responsible people ask them-selves what it is you will do when you decide to stop governing us by martial law. That man, Andrassy, who was appointed as landrost, they see him, they see who appointed him."

He nodded.

"It's growing, like one of your ice sheets, to sweep us all away." Her grandfather had himself asked, several times. Fear was like contagion, like the great infections of the crack-up, sparing neither adult nor child.

"You never say anything about your homeland," she stated after a while.

The muscles around his mouth tightened. "I don't have a home." He stroked his singlestick. "When I left, there wasn't much I had to bring away."

It was her turn to have no answer.

"I took some months off, once," he said, "sailing around the Great Barrier Reef and north to the Solomons and beyond, to see the reef fish and watch the crowns of thorns scour coral heads white through the boat's crystal bottom. The locals thought I was crazy to take a small boat over the reefs at night. They were right, I suppose. Some day, I'll do the same here, to see what there is to see. I don't think anyone has yet. They're too busy grubbing for metals."

"You tell me what it is that you find."

"I will." He stuck his hand out in the rain and cupped it, letting it fill with water. He let a few minutes pass. "We had a firefight once, out in the *bled*—out in the desert. Five of us and a half-dozen cakes. Then right in the middle of it, the clouds came low and they started baling out heaven with buckets. Most rain on Ashcroft was ghost rain that never reached the ground, but that day it hit like the wrath of God, lightning spears and the wadis filled with water shooting by like surf in a tidal bore. We ended up together on one little hill, cold and wet and miserable, and we went back together—cakes and everyone."

"That was Isaac, wasn't it?" she asked.

"Just so. If it hadn't been for a rain like this, I would have killed him or he would have killed me. It wouldn't have meant a thing to either one of us."

"No, that is not so," she said frowning.

"I loved the sandy desert," he said after a while. "The shifting dunes like tides in the sea. The big ones last for centuries, growing a little and shrinking a little, serpentine like beautiful women stretched out against the sky, with plumes of sand leaping from the crescents of the *barchans* into space."

"What of colors?" she asked.

"Yellowed sands. Dust in reds of every shade from pink as fine as the skin on your hand to red like the blood of oxen. Brown takyrs, clay patches smooth as glass that sand slides over, where floods run into depressions so shallow they can't be seen and die, century by century, measure by measure, polished by the dust and the wind. Black stones, iron and manganese oxides. Sometimes blues and grays on the horizons along eroded rock faces, streaked and carved. There were other colors, I suppose; I remember those.''

He stopped speaking, and it was as if a door had shut itself, never to reopen. He let the water that had trickled from the sky spill out of his palm. ''On Ashcroft, I didn't know there were colonial worlds like this one.'' He put his arm around her shoulder.

''It bothers you.''

''You have everything the cakes didn't have.''

''And we throw it all away.''

''Some of you want a little more.'' They watched the rain. ''Every one of these colonial worlds festers until it rots. The Diet's too frugal to stop it before it starts, but they can afford whole battalions to sweep the litter.'' He slashed at the horsetails. ''Half of me says everything here is going to pop, the other half says, 'the Variag has *keramat*. Fate enfolds him with her wings.' Somehow . . .'' He slashed out at the rain, adding, ''The Variag is as tense as I've seen him, and I'd be lying if I said I think I'll take that boat out to sea. Why did Rhett send you?''

She stopped his mouth with her hand. ''Hush!'' she said, and he made no protest. After a span of time, she said, ''The rain is stopping. Would you like to go back?''

''Yes,'' he said, looking out at the waves.

ORLOV SEEMED TO DISAPPEAR INTO THE PARTIAL SUNLIGHT AS Snyman watched. The charcoal and green splotches of the battle dress seemed to change color as the light melted into them, individual threads standing out against different backgrounds, subtly allowing the whole to blend. Dark shadings high, and lighter shadings low, made shadowing disappear, and the irregular patterns swallowed him whole.

All around, the tall, majestic spires of the spiketrees rose straight from the broken fragments of their toppled brethren, filling interstices between soft, rotting trunks, compacted one upon another. In a few places, jet-black pools of water could be seen swirling in sudden movement far below. Spiketrees were shallow-rooted and deserved their reputation as widow-makers. The living forest grew to its towering height between the corpses of fallen giants.

As Snyman moved, the surface seemed to quiver. There was

another rustling noise underfoot. Snyman tensed, then relaxed as he recognized the amphtile scuttling away.

Where drainage was good, ferntrees crowded the spiketrees out. Where farmers dug their ditches, induced drought disrupted the fluid pressure in the cells that held the weight of the trees aloft and brought them crashing down. Where it was worth the effort, loggers cleared them for short-fiber paper.

Here, every hollow was filled with standing water and partly decayed vegetation, and the spiketrees flourished. Snyman imagined them stretching for a thousand kilometers unbroken. The rain forest was a splendid and frightening thing. Neither cowboys nor Boers remained long in the shadow of the big trees. The Imperials, now including one Jan Nicolaus Snyman, adapted.

Thought drifted through his mind as he felt his way forward carefully, gazing from left to right in his allotted arc then over his shoulder to the man behind. For three days, they'd crawled through the swamp forests, patiently following almost imperceptible traces. The pace had quickened as the trail freshened and habits of their alerted quarry became recognizable. Horizons had narrowed.

It was less a test of weaponry than a test of skills, of endurance, of half rations in the rain.

"Ten minutes, even numbers," Snyman heard Orlov echo, which brought him to a different plane of reality. They halted abruptly with security out. Snyman had lost count in the heat, it was the fifth or sixth time they had stopped. Even numbers were first on, odd numbers first off, if such a thing mattered. Snyman felt a reassuring hand on his shoulder and gave Orlov a weak smile.

The sections were mixed, twenty-three recruits, eleven cadre, a dozen men from Earth, even a double handful of medics sweating to master the unwelcome skills of the infantry. Snyman was paired with Kobus, Orlov with a cowboy named Nelson Bolaños from a defunct team.

Bolaños was all right. Week One, after the second run, they'd retched their guts up, side by side. During the Six Weeks War, he'd been the first actually to hit one of those arrogant streetsweepers from No. 10. That day he'd been practically crowned and anointed.

From three directions, jungle bunnies exploded from the fern thickets waving clubs and spears.

The first shots rang out. Snyman fumbled desperately at his

safety, confronted by the brown man charging directly at him. Incredibly, no fire seemed to touch him, and Snyman's focus diminished. Pulling up his rifle, he aimed. And froze.

The brown man stopped. And smiled. Snyman had to blink twice before he recognized Isaac Wanjau wiping away makeup and leaning on his spear. Others, also recognizable from No. 10, were doing the same.

Orlov gently took the rifle from Snyman's hands.

"It wasn't real. The rounds were blank," Snyman said to himself, over and over, softly.

"For you, it was real," Orlov said gently, supporting him with his shoulder. Looking on with incomprehension, Kobus cleared his weapon standing next to Bolaños, who trembled as he tried to remove the magazine from which he had fired forty rounds.

Snyman went next to see the Hangman.

"Many men are incapable of assimilating the reflexes of a soldier," Henke said. "Some like your friend Harris never learn to stay alive. Others cannot bring themselves to kill." The Hangman turned to Orlov with cold, cold eyes.

"We keep him," Orlov said emphatically.

Henke looked Snyman up and down remorselessly, balancing sides on an unseen scale. He made up his mind abruptly.

"The people you will be shooting are likely to be your own. Let us therefore try you with something different, Jan Nicolaus. Would you care to be a medic's aide?" he asked as Snyman found that his hands had stopped shaking.

LATER THAT EVENING, PIOTR KOLOMEITSEV HEARD VOICES FROM inside his mess. Preparations for the strike completed, he glided unerring to the source of the sounds.

Two of his officers and one of his platoon sergeants were engaged in discussion. "What are you youngsters up to?" he asked genially. "Who is running the war?"

The Iceman's face was smooth and rounded, unmarked except for the slight thickening of a scar that extended in an arc from his lower lip and rendered his infrequent smiles sardonic. The iris of each of his eyes was of the palest gray imaginable so that they seemed to lose all semblance of color in the light. Physically, there was nothing very extraordinary about him save the fingers of his hands, which were very long and very fine. They seemed to move independent of the rest of his body, which persons found disconcerting.

Malyshev, his executive officer, flushed and stood. "Company Sergeant Leonov politely requested that we depart so he could address number one privately."

"We were discussing military theory," Jankowskie added defensively. He was still slightly deaf from having unintentionally blown the top off a mountain attending to Major Rettaglia's arms cache, and had taken a good deal of kidding.

"I will not inquire among you as to why the Company Sergeant felt it necessary to run you off," Kolomeitsev commented, knowing his company sergeant was polite by accident rather than design. "When does he want you back?"

"Thirty-nine more minutes, sir," Malyshev said. "Local time midnight," he added unnecessarily, listening to the nightingales of platoon No. 3.

The noise from the night was one of song. No. 3 platoon had no duty, and they knew dozens, each with dozens of verses, each more indecent than the last. Their ribald good humor was infectious.

The fingers of Kolomeitsev's left hand curled reflexively around Peresypkin's shoulder. "Well, military theory it is," he said, eyeing the half-empty bottle on the table. "Are any of you going to invite your commander to join your discussion?"

Their shock at seeing the Iceman unbend warmed Kolomeitsev's heart. Malyshev hastily surrendered his own seat and handed Kolomeitsev a plastic canteen cup filled with vodka.

"Please join us, sir! How thoughtless of me!"

The gods of war winked. "What aspect of the vast panorama of military futility has captured your interest?" Kolomeitsev asked.

"Arkadi was discussing why soldiers fight," Malyshev imparted, nodding toward Peresypkin.

"Defend your proposition, Platoon Sergeant Peresypkin. What insight have you to offer?" Kolomeitsev said, sipping the warm vodka. He suddenly stared at the canteen cup decorated in rich swaths of greens, sand, and chocolate brown as if it were a snake. "Have you been draining this from the armored cars?" he asked.

"No, sir," Malyshev and Peresypkin echoed in chorus.

"Major Henke adulterates his fuel stocks, you know," Kolomeitsev commented by way of conversation as he studied the offending canteen cup. "I have been told that he prefers an additive which turns one's urine a bright blue."

Malyshev and Peresypkin immediately looked to Jankowskie, who protested weakly that he had purchased it in town.

"I am, however, more alarmed at finding my soldiers drinking vodka quite so, so tepid," Kolomeitsev continued, having searched for and discovered a suitably ignominious adjective.

Malyshev coughed discreetly. "We do have a little ice," he announced.

"In vodka?" Kolomeitsev shook his head.

As Jankowskie reached for the refrigerator, Kolomeitsev took another sip and motioned for Peresypkin to continue.

"We were just discussing why soldiers fight, sir," Peresypkin said uncomfortably.

"Tell me, gentlemen, why does a soldier fight? Lieutenant Malyshev?" Kolomeitsev asked.

Malyshev looked at Jankowskie. The Iceman rarely philosophized. "Not for honor, glory, or remuneration," Malyshev admitted. "Rolled up in a ball, what trickles down wouldn't buy a pot of tea. Loyalty and duty?"

"To whom? His Imperial Majesty, who reigns but does not rule? The leeches in the Diet? Lieutenant Jankowskie, what are your views?" Kolomeitsev inquired inexorably.

Detlef Jankowskie's Baltic ancestors had been successively Polonized, Germanized, and Russified before being discarded on the ash heaps of history.

"The philosopher Clausewitz is credited with originating the doctrine that war is an extension of politics by other means. Of course the most serious flaw in his works is his inexplicable omission of the corollary that politics is an extension of economics by other means. Repetition of this error seriously degraded much early historical analysis, but even in Clausewitz's own lifetime, the political impact of the economic concerns of strategically placed firms and individuals on, for example, the 'Sugar Wars' of the eighteenth century or the 'Opium Wars' of the nineteenth must have been unmistakable," Jankowskie recollected from dimly remembered political training while he attempted to fathom the objective toward which the Iceman's sudden flanking movements were directed.

Kolomeitsev smiled chillingly. "I recall asking you why soldiers fight, Lieutenant. I do not recall asking you why wars are fought. Economics bears the same relationship to combat as does the craft of the swordsmith to the art of fencing.

"In our own context, United Steel-Standard owns the mines, the spaceport, the transportation network, most of the secondary industrial output, and almost everything else. An honest government would clean them out in a heartbeat, not that I recall an honest government. The cost of buying a government evidently would have increased the cost of doing business. The Diet in its infinite wisdom decreed that this was a shameful thing, and so we are here. Why then do we fight? Platoon Sergeant Peresypkin,'' he inquired in order.

"Soldiers fight because it is their profession?'' Peresypkin offered uncertainly.

"That, Platoon Sergeant Peresypkin, is suspiciously close to tautology,'' Kolomeitsev responded coldly.

"I mean, if you're a craftsman, you put your soul into it. Part of it is the Variag and everyone else, but if you don't believe in doing the job right . . .'' Peresypkin ventured uncertainly, unpleasantly aware the Iceman had singled him from the herd to stalk. "That's not to say we don't have private lives, but after a certain point what you do is your private life, and everybody dies sometime. Is this the point we are to draw, sir?''

"It resembles the truth sufficiently,'' the Iceman said with a trace of deception. "The Variag tells us to fight. He went troppo years ago and has the soul of a poet. We fight and do it well. What else might we do?'' the Iceman said, asking a question rather than answering one. "There are two types of war, gentlemen. Limited war for limited purposes by limited means, and war to the knife, whose goal is nothing less than the recrafting of a society. We soldiers are seldom asked which we would choose.'' He glanced around the table. "Platoon Sergeant Peresypkin, have you ever visited the prostitutes in the *bordel mobile de campagne* which Colonel Lynch has installed for our pleasure and his profit?''

Peresypkin blushed faintly.

Jankowskie almost started to laugh, the effect was so comical on Peresypkin's ruddy face. "Pertsovka'' had broken hearts on three worlds, including one on Ashcroft, which serious students claimed could not be done.

The Iceman was patient when sinking a barb. He fixed Jankowskie with a look and returned his attention to Peresypkin. "I am aware of the Miss Kotze you have been seeing,'' Kolomeitsev continued, "I will give you one word of advice. If you are apprenticed to the butcher, do not befriend the pigs.''

The Iceman had left his wife in her cold barrow on Earth to seek the stars. He had gone on, as they said.

"Drink up, gentlemen, we have a strike to break in the morning.'' Break it they would, easily or otherwise.

Monday(12)

"TODAY IS THE DAY, IS IT NOT?" COLDEWE ASKED, RUBBING HIS palms together.

"A few hours. Boers like to sleep in," Scheel answered.

"I suppose they'll show. The idea ought to be fresh in their minds. Did you know that the length of the average sermon last week was nearly two hours?"

"It would be very nice to have a few of the noisy preachers off the sidewalks."

"Raul said Ssu the censor was so flamed that he tried to submit his resignation. He's right. What's the point in sucking venom out of the newscasts if the Boers spend all day Sunday hearing it in church? And category eight? If they upped it to cat seven we could at least throw mud pies at them." Coldewe shifted gears. "Anything from battalion?"

"I spoke to Malinov. He told me to kick the still to pieces and I did. He also says the medics on the island are shaping up nice. If Major Henke doesn't wash them, we'll get two or three."

"That's good." Coldewe stretched and yawned.

"Did we ever figure out what happened to Menzies?"

"An accident, intelligence seems to think, strange as that may seem."

"Then who were the people waving pistols that number eleven shot down?"

Scheel shook his head. "Is Raul awake?" he asked.

"I let him sleep in. He looked tired. Do you think—" Coldewe asked suddenly and stopped.

Scheel laughed. "If you're asking me whether God's innocents have figured out how it goes in"—

Coldewe threw up his hands.

—"If my right hand knew, it wouldn't tell my left," Scheel finished. "We have decided as a company not to intrude." Sensing an opportunity to turn tables, he added cagily, "I took an opinion poll."

"How many opinions did you take?" Coldewe asked.

"Two, yours and mine."

"Rudi, did anyone ever tell you you're an old fraud?"

"Malinov. With regularity. They were arguing about melanistic New Caledonian cowries last night."

"What do you think?"

"Sometimes I think she lets him win."

"I'm glad he took my advice and found himself a different

hobby,'' Coldewe said. "Let's let him sleep until eight, and then we'll get started.''

AT EIGHT HOURS THIRTY, OKLADNIKOV STOOD STRAIGHT UP IN the turret of his Cadillac. "How do you want us to start?" he asked Sanmartin, who was surveying the silent streets of Johannesburg.

"The shops. Why don't you start with that bookstore over there and move up the street.''

The Brothers wanted a show of unity among the Volk, into which the battalion was about to start poking holes. Shimazu, with his usual efficiency, had spread the word like manure on a field that the bells were going to be ripped off any place that wasn't open for business. In addition to Boer reprobates, the town was full of cowboys from Reading, and a bigger bunch of thieves Sanmartin had yet to see. The Border Police, scattered in pairs throughout the city, had things other than petty larceny to occupy themselves with.

Riflemen attached the tow chains to the steel doorframe. On a jewelry store adjacent, the door opened and the shopkeeper came out wringing his hands.

"Good to see you this morning, sir. Please see you don't close early,'' Okladnikov said. The jewelry man feigned incomprehension. Okladnikov's driver gunned his engine and wrenched the door off the bookstore.

The jewelry man vanished. A moment later the shutters on his shop vanished like mist. Okladnikov moved on to a tobacco shop. Sanmartin hopped off.

"Sergei, I'll leave you here to carry on. The schoolteachers should be forming up in about ten minutes.''

"Later!'' Okladnikov shouted. "Luck!'' he added.

Sanmartin walked the street briskly. A few people were beginning to open their windows furtively, which was a positive sign. On the Boulevard Die Taal, he hitched a ride on one of the little utility vehicles, conspicuously devoid of its mortar and mounting instead a large, round tank with a pressure hose attached amidships. Mekhlis had the hose clutched in his hand and wasn't about to let go.

At the Jacobus Uys school, the demonstrators were already beginning to heat up. Three speakers were leading them in staccato chants of *"Imperialiste uit! Imperialiste uit!"* Two of the three wore business suits. The third was a woman in a fur coat and raised heels. Sanmartin let the corner of his mouth twitch, wondering what they'd done with the brass band. One of Mekhlis's crew began calmly shooting stills for posterity.

Muslar was present with a half section of rifles. He looked apprehensive. Sanmartin hopped down, patting him on the shoulder.

"Ever done this before, Edmund?"

Muslar shook his head. The chanting changed. *"Staan vas?!"* yelled a man with an amplifier. *"Die toets deurstaan!"* returned the crowd.

" 'Imperials out,' and 'stand fast.' Not very imaginative. Don't worry. Take my word for it, this will be joy and laughter compared to doing cakes. Now, *they* were a hardheaded bunch."

"Staan vas?!"

"Die spit afbyt!"

Sanmartin began putting his mask on unhurriedly. He looked at Mekhlis. "Let the speakers have it first." Mekhlis nodded.

Then he turned back to Muslar. "Edmund, your people know the drill. You'd better get your mask on."

Already, the first stones were being thrown from the middle of the crowd. One bounced off Sanmartin's chest as he stepped forward with a hand amplifier. Whistling *The Little Tin Soldier*, Sanmartin pulled out a nail file and began ostentatiously cleaning his nails. Curiosity overcame activism.

Sanmartin winked. "I saw Matti do this to a crowd of cakes."

"Did it work?" Muslar asked, his voice distorted.

"No," Mekhlis said with obvious delight.

Sanmartin threw away the nail file. "I am authorized by His Imperial Majesty's representative to permit you a peaceful, orderly march to the staatsamp with no deviations in route," he said. This, he repeated in carefully memorized Afrikaans.

One of the speakers, a corpulent man Sanmartin recognized from Rettaglia's files, seized a sign from a thin woman and waved it. What he said did not require translation.

Sanmartin let the electronic marvel in his hand float his voice over the babble. "It does not appear you can be trusted to conduct yourselves in a peaceful manner. I direct you to disperse. Anyone wishing to conduct an orderly march may assemble by the rear entrance. The rest of you are directed to return to your homes. You have one minute to comply." This he repeated in Afrikaans and stepped back before a shower of projectiles.

As a large rock sailed past his head, Sanmartin turned to Muslar who was trying to count the crowd and had given up at three hundred. Only a few souls near the back were slipping away.

"We'll want to shake them up before they pull in ash and trash from around the town," Sanmartin murmured calmly to Muslar.

The chanted slogan had become a crisp, *"Imperialiste! Uit! Staan! Vas!"* A few in front of the crowd ran several paces forward to hurl their missiles before retreating to the relative safety of the mass.

As a cluster of zealots from the front rank began to surge, Sanmartin finished counting down. "Five, four, three, two, one," he said to Mekhlis, jerking his arm downward.

Mekhlis needed no urging. Under heavy pressure, a jet of liquid played over the mob, which melted away with a shriek. Playfully, Mekhlis pulled the spray down to squirt the civil servant and platform speakers. Signs began falling like leaves.

Sanmartin turned around, satisfied. "Edmund, move your teams out, column marching and all that. And don't hang your mouth open like that. You'll break the seal of your mask and wish you hadn't. They have skunks where you come from? Little black and white mustelids? Well, this is homemade skunk oil. Reinikka and I had a chat with a little man in biochem."

"I hope the fat one doesn't have a heart attack," Mekhlis commented as he doused laggards.

"Those poor, wasted suckers are going to wish we'd used bullets," Sanmartin explained for Muslar's benefit. "It'll bind with their skin, and they'll pretty much have to let it wear off. I'll bet it's hell on contact lenses, too."

"So much for 'stand fast.' If the ones we tag want to march, they'll clear the streets. For the next few days, they'll be about as popular as social disease," Mekhlis said.

"Chiba point two. Break. How's it coming, Hans?"

Coldewe was in the Stellenboschstraat. "Not bad. We have one peaceful march with about thirty people. Two other groups of would-be rioters have called it a day. About a dozen Border Policemen called in sick, local recruits. The commandant is out making them wish they were. One major incident so far. Sniper."

"Sniper?" Sanmartin queried sharply. The Variag's companies had little liking for urban guerrillas.

"One bright boy took two shots at Karaev from a rooftop. Winged him, too. Karaev's annoyed. His arm's in a sling, but he's all right. The bright boy is hanging from a light pole with his weapon tied around his neck. I've posted a guard to make sure he stays there awhile. We'll want whoever sent him.''

"I can't argue that. How are we doing on identifications?''

"We should have more than enough to please your roommate.''

Rettaglia wanted pictures for identifications. It was always a little shock for would-be activists to receive a polite morning-after letter from Imperial intelligence. It made it easier to screen would-be martyrs from the faceless masses before they caused problems and got themselves killed.

"Oh, and do you know that silly handgun Rudi has?''

"The one that looks like a cannon?'' Sanmartin asked.

"Right. A group of teens got unruly looting one of the shops Sergei's lads did up with their tin-opener. Rudi held up that peacemaker of his, and shot out a light pole. Quietest bunch of looters you ever saw. Any problems on your end?''

"The teacher's union has gone home to scrub off and burn their clothes. Good, bourgeois burghers don't make good rioters. They called their general strike for a week. A dinner in town says it's over by tomorrow afternoon.''

" 'Son, some day a man will come up to you with a deck of cards upon which the seal has not yet been broken . . .' ''

"Is this Sky Masterson with the cider again?''

"From Damon Runyon. You've heard it.''

"I swear, you make these names up. Is he your jumping frog man or the Yankee clock peddler fellow?''

Coldewe shook his head, a gesture that Sanmartin was in no position to observe. "Stick to seashells.''

"All right, Hans, you've had your fun for the morning. I've got to go find Beyers. Out.''

Reaching the staatsamp, he looked up at Beyers's wide windows with a mental note to have them sandbagged before he had to elect himself a new mayor. Beyers was in his office in a patched cardigan sweater, munching a croissant absently. He wiped away the crumbs and rose to pump Sanmartin's hand. The Bond had tried to enlist Beyers immediately after he assumed office. With considerable courage, Beyers had refused.

Most of the shops were open and enough public maintenance workers were being dragged out of beds to make the town function. The young man swaying in the Vryheidsplein was an inducement to good order.

Beyers's comments in the English he'd learned over the past several months were cutting. Johannesburg would not have struck if it had not been for Landrost Andrassy's heavy-handed attempts to enforce the conversion laws and Director Tuge's arbitrary revision of the price schedules.

Far below, a ball sailed by on the cobbled stones of the Vryheidsplein. The huge form of Rudi Scheel seized it and flung it back in one graceful motion. Sanmartin and Beyers both leaned out the window as Scheel walked over to the knot of young Afrikaners. There were five or six, boys of about eight years by Earth's standards and little hellions by any. Beyers looked at Sanmartin.

"That's Company Sergeant Scheel. You should remember Rudi. Rudi is fond of children," Sanmartin said.

"Many of my people dislike Imperials. I am distressed their children this attitude may share," Beyers said stiffly.

"Company Sergeant Scheel has nineteen years' service in the battalion," explained Sanmartin cryptically.

Before the mayor could comment further, Scheel bent to the little rats. As he did, one of them spat in his face and began running.

For an instant, Beyers thought Scheel would chase the boy. Instead, Scheel's left hand darted inside his jacket almost faster than the eye could follow and whipped out a small pistol.

Beyers gasped. Leveling the pistol, Scheel fired a stream of water into the back of the hoodlum's head that sent him sliding on his belly into a trash can. Rudi smiled at the others and blew imaginary smoke off the end of his gun. Pushing back his cap with the barrel, he rubbed his bald, bullet head.

Beyers was clutching his chest. He looked at Sanmartin beseechingly.

"Rudi is right-handed," Sanmartin explained.

Rudi walked over and picked up the little toad like a sack of sand. Making a few ineffectual passes to dust the boy off, Rudi held him at arm's length and stuffed him headfirst into the trash can.

"Rudi carries a real pistol on his left side. It's much bigger," Sanmartin commented. He looked over at Beyers, who was panting hoarsely. "The first time I saw him do that, I nearly had a heart attack myself."

LEFT IN THE ALMOST DESERTED CASERNE, BRUWER LOOKED OUT her window into sunshine, feeling the hours of her life passing away. She did not dare go into town, not today of all days, and she felt pent up, as if she were back in the camps.

Her grandfather remembered the camps as places to die.

In some ways, he had been a father to her. Like other men who had spent a double span of years trying to grow maize on peaty soil, he knew how thin was the taproot that supported the pretty, bourgeois life the Afrikaners had made for themselves.

She had not mentioned to Raul Sanmartin that he suspected the pseudoblast that had destroyed the strandloopers' rice was alien. "The strandloopers," she recalled him chuckling grimly. "What is it your new friends call them? Jungle bunnies! I think some one of us murdered them, Little Princess," a name she had long outgrown.

In the company of Vereshchagin's men, Bruwer's differences made no difference. Bruwer felt herself free as she could remember being nowhere else.

But she was not, and she knew she was afraid.

Tuesday(12)

HENDRIK PIENAAR HAD COME TO SEE THE *HUURLING IER*, SO HE couldn't very well leave without doing so. Pushing the door open with distaste, he walked into the room.

"Good day to you, my name is Meagher," the mercenary said, squatting on the cold, concrete floor with a deck of playing cards in his hand. "And who might you be?"

"Hendrik Pienaar."

"Well, Hendrik Pienaar, I'm pleased to have met you." Meagher pushed two rounds of machine gun ammunition into a center pile and dealt himself two cards. "What brings you here?"

"A few influential Friends asked for me to come. They wish for me to command you and your mercenaries."

"Very interesting, it is." Meagher threw in a few cards and added a few more bullets to the heap.

To Pienaar's eyes, Meagher seemed to be playing some variant of poker solitaire. "What religion have you?" Pienaar asked out of curiosity.

"Didn't you know, General Hendrik Pienaar? All the Irish are Christian. It's just that some of them remember it in a more timely fashion than others."

Pienaar coughed. "What would you say the status of your men is?" he asked.

"Not good, not good at all. They're what remains of Chalker's lot, you know. They were even less keen on coming over to you Afrikaners than I was, but there was nowhere for them to go." Meagher studied his cards. "I can hold them together for another two weeks, maybe three. After that, I could shoot a few if you like, but they won't stay. They don't think much of this business of no war and peace for everyone except themselves, and they flat don't like camping out here in the jungle with not a thing to do."

"Are they any good for an attack?"

"They might be. Mind you, for love or money they won't like going up against Ebyl's armor again without better antitank weaponry than they've seen, and you Afrikaners have shown them precious little of one or the other, General Hendrik Pienaar." The mocking insolence in the mercenary's voice transferred itself well. "Are you perhaps thinking of an attack, now? If so, you'd best give me a few days to plan for it."

"You mercenaries have not become popular."

"Ah, it's poor Hughie you're thinking of, rather than mercenaries in general. The man was daft to think of going back to school at his age. Still, you needn't be so harsh. We all do what we must, and I understand they had a rare time scraping up enough of him to bury." He looked directly at Pienaar for the first time. "Do you know, General Hendrik Pienaar, since the Imps have refused us amnesty, there aren't very many of us hirelings left. Sometimes we have to stick up, one for another."

"You haven't been playing very long," Pienaar interjected.

"Why no, that I haven't. I didn't start until we saw you coming."

"Why was this?" Pienaar asked.

"Well, General Hendrik Pienaar, some of the young squirts your masters have sent from time to time to keep an eye or two on me these last few weeks were pious, God-fearing folk who didn't hold with gambling and playing cards and suchlike. They didn't stay. However, it occurs to me now that you took your fair time getting into this rattrap of a building to see me, did you not?"

"I did. I wanted to find out whether your sentries knew how to shoot those pretty guns of theirs before I stuck my head in this rattrap of a building of yours."

"Is that so, now?" Meagher said, sweeping up all of the cards into a single stack in his left hand. "Tell me, general, about this attack you mentioned."

"The spaceport. In and out." The weather forecast for the week was for light rain through Saturday, with showers and thunderstorms following on Sunday and Monday. The worst of it would partially nullify the Imperial space-borne fire support.

"Indeed," Meagher commented. "How many people know your plan?"

"One. Me. If you keep your mouth shut long enough, you might know, too." Pienaar took the deck of paying cards from Meagher's hand. He began dealing them out.

Meagher looked at him thoughtfully. "Do you know, Hendrik? You'll do, I think."

Wednesday(12)

ON THE SOFT WOODEN BOARD, LIGHT AND DARK ONYX PIECES mingled in confusion. Sanmartin swapped a knight for a knight with a savage glee, intending to simplify, to push the game to a resolution.

"Rhett, be honest. It ruins your concentration. Whose idea was it to dissolve the Bond? I mean, I was touched by the proclamation."

Rettaglia's nostrils twitched as he studied his position. "Colonel Lynch. He seemed quite taken with the idea." His hair was graying noticeably.

"And when do we enforce it?"

Rettaglia's lip curled.

"That's what I thought. Did the admiral tell Lynch they have an ordinance prohibiting fornication in Johannesburg, too?"

"He might have. Although the admiral is singularly lacking in humor, he possesses a well-developed sense of whimsy. How is Hanna?"

Sanmartin made a grimace.

"She figured out about the mercenaries at the school?"

"Wanjau, of all people, let slip that we planned and executed a stupid idea flawlessly, which is a nice way of saying we should have been sweeping up toasted tots with a shovel."

"The Variag said as much to the admiral, which did not greatly please him." Rettaglia pushed his queen's knight pawn to open a long diagonal. "Kimura's battalion will be switching over to a depot establishment. They will be the permanent garrison. We'll be up to our knees in Baluchi wives, livestock, and children. Higuchi's battalion will ship back when the goats arrive."

"Where will that leave us?"

"Here for the present."

Sanmartin pushed forward a pawn. "A bunch of itinerant killers, that's what we are."

Rettaglia stared at him curiously. "Where did you pick up that notion?"

Sanmartin grimaced again. "Probably chatting with Solchava."

"I understand that you and Albert Beyers got her into the hospital in Pretoria."

"It's the closest thing there is to an advanced medical facility on this mudball. Our beloved Dr. Devoucoux asked me to help her out before he left. Albert and Hanna finally smoothed it over between them, but for a while I thought I was going to send a half section of rifles. You can imagine what Solchava thought of that idea."

"The Brothers on Earth handpicked their doctors the same way they selected predikants. How is she working out?"

"The Variag's helping to ease her integration, but she's a strange one." The Variag had charm. He remembered her saying almost wistfully, "Lieutenant-Colonel Vereshchagin is a very unusual officer, is he not?" before staring away.

"She transferred from the civil side. It shows."

That made sense. Dapper Claude had come the same route. Medical specialists who desired passage to the new worlds often found that only the military was hiring.

Sanmartin smiled. "She doesn't understand why we need to rely upon rifles."

"Rifles command obedience. And they're not too expensive. We'll have them as long as they can do that," Rettaglia said complacently.

"I suppose. What's the latest on the politics on this orb of slime?"

"I can tell you that we are ready to come to a conclusion with the Bond. The first salvos have been made. A committee of 'well-disposed citizens' has presented itself." Rettaglia countered his move with a knight. "Rear-Admiral Irie, Gamliel, and I will present them with nonnegotiable demands."

"I suppose Lynch's proclamation reduced them to quivering fear and trepidation. Is this what you expected?"

"In truth, no." Strijdom's proposal had flabbergasted half the Executive. The move smacked of some subtle plot on the part of the old fanatic, and Strijdom was not a subtle man.

"This might be legitimate. Three-percent probability?"

"Cut by a factor of five."

Sanmartin lifted his eyes. "Is this why you're wearing a face I expect to wear at my funeral?"

"In part. As a result, the admiral made the decision to give the blacklegs to Acting Major Dong." Reading the lack of comprehension in his friend's face, he added, "Dong's stupefying ineptitude aside, I will be required to clear detentions through him and Gamliel. Lying Louis suggests that further detentions will destabilize negotiations. Effectively, there won't be any."

Sanmartin let his jaw swing free. "Has everybody up there in Cloud Cuckoo Land gone collectively silly? Brandfuhrer Snyman, at least?"

"Snyman least of all. He's untouchable, even for you and the Variag. Gamliel thinks he's running Snyman and several others I might name."

"Rhett, are you saying the ones stirring up the ants with sticks are working for our side? The son's a good trooper, but his father is poison."

"I didn't say that. I said Gamliel thinks he's running them. Half of the people I want are on his payroll, feeding him feathers."

Sanmartin slouched, obviously and visibly disgruntled.

Rettaglia calmly adjusted his rook. "Charity. The holiday season is upon us. The sixth was sort of a Finnish O-Bon festival for you, the Boers celebrate the sixteenth, and Christmas is next."

"It's still unconscionable to have thirty-four days in December," Sanmartin growled. He thought for a moment. "Rhett, for the last six weeks, you've been touching all the right wires and the frog is kicking every which way. Why? Is there somebody else I don't know about making the puppets dance?"

Rettaglia paused, suspending his surviving bishop, asking himself whether there was another layer of secrecy to the Bond, men possessed of "secret knowledge" not vouchsafed to the little frogs, or perhaps a rump secret society within the Bond trying to wag the dog. The thought had occurred, more than once. A man named Hertzog once tried something similar.

There was no evidence, nothing to put a pin to. There was still the feeling that instead of chopping the heart out of the Bond, his covert war had only served to clear away brush so that something unhallowed could blossom.

"Raul, we've done two hundred interrogations," he said aloud to give himself time.

"*Alitur vitium vivitque tegendo.* Seriously, Rhett, for the last few weeks, when I listen to you I tell myself it's just Lying Louis muddling the waters, but it doesn't feel right."

"Vice is nurtured by secrecy. Virgilius, I think. And you're correct, it doesn't feel right." Rettaglia pushed aside the board. "Raul, come back on Friday?"

"What?"

"Call it a whim. I want you back to talk with after I get a feel for this delegation."

"You're getting almost as strange as Hans. Friday, then." He clapped Rettaglia on the shoulder and made his way out, leaving Rettaglia nestled amidst the tatamis and the empty glasses, lost in meditation.

Thursday(12)

"BUT CONSIDER," COLDEWE SAID, OBVIOUSLY ENJOYING HIS role as advocate of the devil, "a handful of flak launchers—"

"Aren't worth spit if the pilot's good. As for guns, you show me the gunner who can hit without radar. You turn the radar on"—Beregov made a chopping motion with his left hand. "But you string satellite strong points all over, you got to keep paths open between them."

Coldewe held court in the estaminet of the Fortunate Rabbit, as he had renamed the mess, and Beregov made a good foil. Beregov was fitting well into his role as platoon sergeant of No. 9, vice Bardiyev.

A company cannot occupy enough ground for a secure airhead. The choice between evils was to pack the platoons in tightly as Sanmartin had done, or to scatter them so that they could only support each other by fire. The point was never resolved as Bruwer diverted Coldewe's attention.

"I'll be back," Beregov said, relinquishing his seat quickly.

Coldewe nodded and turned. "Hello Hanna, where is Raul hiding?"

"He will come. I asked Isaac, and he said he would. Is this bean curd? I can never tell," Bruwer replied in an offhand fashion.

"In one of its many permutations," Coldewe replied, looking at her intently. Most people stopped growing mentally at twenty years standard, and the rest stopped growing emotionally at twelve years standard, but the Ice Maiden had surely given them a few surprises.

Actually, he grumbled silently to himself, so had Raul, which left the question of Hans Coldewe.

"Why do you ask? Is everything all right?" she questioned.

Coldewe altered his face slightly. "Mere envy, I suppose. Your fine friend is bouncing about with springs in his legs. There's something the cowboys call a supplejack which is a real and alive seed fern, whatever that might be."

"Yes, he mentioned it to me. He was very excited."

Coldewe made an untranslatable noise in his throat. "This planet isn't alien enough."

"Yes, you also have noticed the convergent evolution."

Coldewe gave her a mystified look.

"The convergent evolution," she repeated. She absorbed his blank expression. "It is when creatures of different heritages develop in similar ways to meet environmental challenges. Deep infaunal bivalves on Earth, *Mactridae*, *Solecurtidae*, and *Solenidae*, all show the same progression of characteristics from rounded, ribbed shallow burrowers to sleek, knifelike deep burrowers with a pronounced gap between the two shells. And world continent felids developed the same saber-teeth displayed by the South American marsupial borhyaenids . . ."

Coldewe found himself lost in the technical discussion that followed as she trotted out further examples, but he did gather that while Equidae—horses—had developed toward placing all their weight on a single toe, South American Proterotheriidae—one family of litopterns, whatever litopterns were—had done the same and progressed even farther before dying out.

"While natural development always proceeds within the limitations imposed by ancestral structure, it is remarkable how living things on this world have developed so similarly, however incompletely, to those on Earth," Bruwer concluded.

"Is that unadulterated Raul?" Coldewe asked.

"We have libraries," she responded coldly.

"Hanna, repeat what you said, about the litopterns or whatever they are."

"Please?"

"It's a mnemonic trick. I keep forgetting that you're smarter than I am."

Sanmartin spared him further embarrassment by making an appearance holding a stiff envelope of paper. "Oh, there you are."

"What about me?" Coldewe queried.

"Morning, Hans."

"What news? Good or bad."

"Both in measure. Ssu the censor has finished sparring with *Dagbreek*. He told the admiral to either let him shut it down or send him home, and the admiral agreed. The new ownership put out their first issue this morning." He pulled a copy out of one of his side pockets. "They sold out twice."

"You would have thought the former ownership would have muted the toxin they were peddling after Ssu had *Die Afrikaner* clean off fourteen staffers," Coldewe observed.

"What did they say?" Bruwer asked.

"You tell me. I can't read it. All I know is that it's the first good press Albert's gotten since the 'responsible citizens' took a hand," Sanmartin, replied handing it to her.

"The lead editorial is by Prinsloo Adriaan Smith. I know of him slightly," she said, scanning the thin sheets. "It is entitled, 'Yes or No, Johannesburg?' There is a very nice paragraph describing how Heer Beyers helped us when the children were rescued." She gave Sanmartin a sharp look which he evaded.

"I suppose the Brothers are annoyed?" Coldewe said.

"Half the brothers are hopping up and down on one foot, and Gamliel has a stone in his belly."

Coldewe digressed. "Why only half?"

"Some of the Brothers are quietly supporting Heer Beyers, although to the people, it is Heer Beyers against the Bond," Bruwer injected unequivocally.

"We need it. A couple of responsible citizens laid an action in the landrost's court claiming Beyers was improperly admitted to office, and Andrassy is giving Albert fits."

"It's a shame the admiral needed a crumb to toss Tuge in exchange for the metal taxes," Coldewe commented. "The cowboys wanted him gone, and Tuge probably didn't think the Boers deserved any better. But even if Andrassy is silly enough to throw sand in Beyers's teeth, the admiral will stomp the thing flat. The admiral will, won't he?"

"I wish I knew. If Andrassy decides against him and Beyers has to step down pending action by the admiral, Tuge can step in and persuade the admiral that he's damaged goods."

"But what's the point?" Coldewe continued, monopolizing the conversation. "Albert's a cracking good mayor, and he's not even making money at it."

"Too many persons have reasons not to have an honest mayor," Bruwer said.

"Rhett didn't say much, but he seemed willing to bet that

Gamliel was somewhere in back of this. Our reach with the admiral is very, very short.''

Coldewe gave vent to a thoroughly German exclamation of distain. ''Dear Lying Louis, he is useless on top of the ground; he ought to be under it, inspiring the cabbages.''

Bruwer eyed Coldewe speculatively. ''Is Hans bored?''

''Your jumping frog man,'' Sanmartin said with marked distaste.

''Please?'' Bruwer interjected.

''Mark Twain,'' Coldewe said firmly.

She shook her head.

''Samuel Langhorne Clemens? *Tom Sawyer*? *Huckleberry Finn*? 'The Man that Corrupted Hadleysburg' and *The Gilded Age*?''

She shook her head.

''Is anyone in here aware of Mark Twain?!'' he shouted aloud.

From long experience, No. 10 platoon ignored him. Sanmartin examined the walls, and Kasha purposefully turned her back.

''Am I in Lehi or the temple?'' Coldewe demanded of his audience.

''Please?'' Bruwer questioned.

''Judges 15 or Judges 16. If I'm in the temple, you're Delilah, I need a haircut, and I go for the middle columns, one in each hand. If this is Lehi, the ropes about my arms have become as flax, and Raul there is about to lose his jawbone in a valiant endeavor.''

''Samson, now. All this furor over a jumping frog,'' Sanmartin observed sagely.

Bruwer finally gave in. She collapsed into little giggles over the table. She paused to look at Hans, and broke down again.

''I am refreshed and my spirit has revived,'' Coldewe observed.

Bruwer wrapped her arms over her head.

''Hans, don't you hear a phone ringing?'' Sanmartin asked, opening the envelope. ''I have this from Albert, by the way. The Johannesburg chamber music society is having a recital, and he sent over two entrance cards. He insisted that you come, Hanna.''

She looked up at him sharply. ''And you?''

Sanmartin's smile vanished entirely. He shook his head impatiently. ''I can't. Pretoria, then a night exercise.''

She stood up and quietly walked away.

''I wonder what I did now,'' he muttered.

Coldewe didn't answer. Instead he asked, "Who did you leave in charge?"

"I let Edmund have a crack. You know, between the two of us, we ought to be able to make him an admiral some day."

"You know, Rudi says the same about you."

"Even Rudi makes mistakes." Sanmartin settled into the chair and looked down at the table. "Hans, why did you leave Earth, anyway? I thought you wanted to be a writer."

"Writers want to make statements about the universe in general and mankind in capital letters. Well, the universe is big and doesn't much care, and mankind in capital letters didn't leave an address. Literature these degenerate days is half smut, half academics chasing each other's tails, and the smut is better written. I didn't want people to come after me and say, 'Poor, little rat, he fell into a crack between the leaves and the good, clean earth.' "

Sanmartin put his elbows up and rested his chin. "Hans, have you ever thought you'd like to wipe the slate clean on a world. Just erase it and let it start fresh?"

"Surely. Why do you think I ended up here with you and the rest of God's forsaken?"

"No, I mean really wipe a world clean and let it grow."

"You, my friend, have been out with the slugs and bugs too long."

"Maybe I have, Hans. Maybe I have. What would all your bright, literary friends say about this?" Sanmartin extended his hand in panoramic sweep.

"I think the interdepartmental knife-fights would titillate them. They don't have much to say about slugs and bugs, but our profession they adore. War is futility, occasionally garnished with abject stupidity, or didn't you know?"

"That's what people always want to remember, especially the ones who never want to fight in one. *The Charge of the Light Brigade*."

"Scarlett's Heavy Brigade had their poem twenty years late and poorly written. Who remembers them?" Coldewe toyed with his breakfast kasha. "They see us as automatons to their Napoleon or Caesar. They can't see themselves working the business end of a spear."

Beregov came up. "Scarlett's men were competent. People don't like to remember that. It frightens them. It's something they can't control," he added unexpectedly, holding out an extra cup to Sanmartin.

"Just so," Sanmartin responded slowly, staring at the tea in it.

"Berry, what do you think a good book should be like?" Coldewe asked him.

Beregov thought for a moment. "Keep it simple," he decided finally. "The good guys win, the bad guys get stepped, and the girl gets the hero."

"Be nice if life were like that, wouldn't it?" Sanmartin responded.

STRIJDOM SPOKE RAPIDLY AND FORCEFULLY AT CELL MEETINGS. "We must be be as ruthless as the Imperials. We must destroy them before their preparations to destroy us are complete. We must destroy the *uitlanders*, these cowboys who collaborate with the Imperials in our subjugation. We must strike them and heavily, with the hand of God. And so, I say to you, we shall strike and must strike if the Volk is to survive!"

He was conscious both of his standing in the Order and support from his listeners. On this occasion, that support seemed lukewarm. Van Eeden rose to his feet and was recognized. "But what if the initial attack fails?"

"The forces of the Volk will be mobilized behind us. So long as traitors are not permitted to strike down the armed might of the Volk from behind we shall not fail!" Strijdom said.

Van Eeden shuffled his feet nervously, clearly unprepared to take such a momentous statement on mere faith, however strong. He was the delegate of the Johannesburg cell. Of all the men present he was the weakest link. Strijdom resolved to watch him closely.

"The Volk must be purified. A farm that supplies food to the Imperials will be burned. A home that houses a traitor to the Volk will be burned, and traitors who collaborate with the invaders will be slain out of hand. The last days are at hand, and the elect must cast aside the weak in order to triumph."

Although every man present expected the pronouncement and most welcomed it, there was still a slight buzzing in the room. The chairman, Koos Gideon Scheepers, motioned for silence and gestured once more to Strijdom.

Van Eeden raised his voice. "But if we scorch the earth beneath them, the people of the cities will be the first to starve."

"Then let those sinful folk who will not join our cause perish! I expected more faith, more resolve of you, Aaron," Strijdom said, and Van Eeden subsided. Still, taking his cue from Scheepers, Strijdom softened his voice and became more beguiling than masterful.

"Nevertheless, it is in our power to emerge victorious after a brief struggle, for our initial attack will be overwhelming. While the enemy is stronger, his might is concentrated away from the heartland of the Volk, and we are stronger still in the eye of the Lord." He placed one finger on Kimura's headquarters at Reading.

"God's wrath will descend upon this nest of vipers." He moved his hand to cover the spaceport. "And here as well, for we shall lure the forces of the ungodly to destruction and cast down the seat of their power. God's mighty hand will sweep the ships of the invader from our skies, and we shall triumphantly free the cities of the Volk from our oppressors."

And although not four even of the Elect of the Order knew the details of the plan that Strijdom had outlined, they applauded. Ten minutes later, Strijdom wrapped himself in his coat to attend another meeting, that of the Executive of the Bond, wrapped in the guise of a loyal member of the Bond with his power and glory subdued.

Friday(12)

RETTAGLIA PACED WHEN HE WAS ANNOYED. APPRAISING THE damage, Sanmartin decided they'd have to replace the floor if negotiations continued for another week.

"It's been four days now, Raul. We talk. They jabber. We divide up into committees to work on the text. I polish commas. Ask me how you divide three delegates armed with an ultimatum into committees?" Rettaglia asked rhetorically as he reached the far end of the room and prepared to reverse himself for another pass.

"How do you divide three delegates armed with an ultimatum into committees?" Sanmartin asked.

"The thing that bothers me is that they don't seem to be trying. I expected to have three drafts of puerile nonsense for the admiral to slap down by now. For puerile nonsense I have to rely on Irie and Gamliel. The Boers are negotiating as if it doesn't matter what goes down on parchment."

"Is this really negotiation? Rudi asked me that. Negotiation is dialog between equals, and if they're equal, this is the first he's heard of it."

Rettaglia stared him down. "Even the Boers know that this is the admiral telling the Bond what he expects in return for not transporting the lot of them. Still, I wish the admiral would take this seriously. This is a smoke screen for something, but for the life of me I can't decide what."

The Boers were innocent of the complicated charade of protocol that normally necessitated a week's haggling over the size of the room and the number of chairs. In every other respect, there was stench in Rettaglia's nostrils.

In breaking the delegations up into negotiating teams, Rettaglia had been cleverly maneuvered away from the center of things and kept there. He and de Roux had been shunted aside with a fanatic named Olivier for a keeper. That much had obviously been arranged with Lying Louis. It was difficult to maintain the illusion he and de Roux were strangers, so well did they know each other through Shimazu and so complete was their mutual bafflement.

Rear-Admiral Irie had disappeared halfway through, driving off with his aides and bodyguards in a vehicle with springs sagging. Irie was already back up in *Graf Spee* with unmanifested cargo, a box three-tenths of a meter in size massing 580 kilograms according to the astonished sergeant who had weighed it for the pilot.

Irie had obviously been tendered a bribe, likely in gold. Yet Irie counted for little and was likely to make the slow trip back to Earth in ballast on a freighter when Admiral Lee tired of his presence. It had to be obvious to the Boers that Irie's ability to persuade Admiral Lee to undertake a course of action was sadly limited.

It might be Admiral Lee was meant to have an accident, but if the Bond had even discussed the possibility, de Roux would have mentioned it with hypocritical horror. Even if Admiral Lee fell down a hole, Irie would be in a position to disavow any promises made, however deep his degradation.

"You don't like the idea of Lying Louis being given his head," Sanmartin said.

"That, too," Rettaglia admitted. "Gamliel is cocksure that his friends in the Bond are going to give him something to shove down my throat."

"But they know you can tap into the cells. Either the Bond begins emasculating themselves or the admiral will lose his fine Korean temper and begin rolling heads."

"I know, and the only thing that seems to make sense is that this whole charade is a ploy for the fanatics to discredit the peacemakers.''

The feel of the negotiations was wrong. The thought was puzzling, annoying, even chilling. However the Boers played the game, with four battalions and the warships in the sky they stood to be ground under. The Boers had had ample demonstration of how devastating lightning from the sky could be. There was, however, a maxim that every fish has one good jerk before he's pulled in, and Olivier for one had the look of a man holding the rod instead of the hook.

''At which point Lying Louis dries up and blows away, and the fanatics either take to the hills or end up on *Shokaku* in irons. Surely they can't be that shortsighted? Or can they?'' Sanmartin asked.

''I wish I knew. Did I mention my other mystery?''

''The five hundred eighty kilograms? I still have trouble imagining why anyone would bribe Irie.''

''I want to think the fanatics have miscalculated in triggering this bit of nonsense, and that somehow by the middle of next week the peacemakers will be helping us to hunt them down, with or without a piece of parchment.''

''Do you really believe that?''

''No.''

''So what are you going to do?'' Sanmartin asked quietly.

''Oh, I obey my orders. If the admiral wants to let Gamliel talk, I let Gamliel talk. But the Brothers are getting more and more afraid of their own extremists, and my information is getting better every day. Pretty soon the trap is going to snap and we're going to go hunting. I hope.''

''And if this is just a ploy to knock you out?''

''Can you see them turning in enough weapons to make it credible?''

''No,'' Sanmartin admitted. ''A screen for an uprising, perhaps?''

''Possible, but not likely. I know for a fact the Bond as a whole hasn't taken any steps in that direction. In the Executive, I doubt that a vote for an uprising would muster more than two votes. They aren't stupid. Don't forget, as the admiral continually reminds me, that whatever they do, we still have warships in the sky and four battalions.''

''At night, I have a mental picture of the Bond as a mound of melting gelatin stiffened with steel shot, and I'm wondering what's going to happen when the gelatin runs off. '*Caelum non animum mutant qui trans mare currunt,'* said Horace. 'They who cross the sea change their skies but not their natures.' ''

''There is one quote I remember from Horace, *'Amoto quaeramus seria ludo,'* '' rejoined Rettaglia, who spoke six languages fluently and could get by in seven more.

Sanmartin looked at him blankly.

'' 'Let us put jesting aside and treat of serious matters,' '' he said, and Sanmartin laughed.

''With fortune, you'll have most of Kimura's battalion up here to help you clean out the warrens by next Friday,'' Rettaglia continued.

''That would give us a choice of targets, wouldn't it?'' Sanmartin rejoined, only partly in jest.

Rettaglia sighed. ''All right, Raul. I've kept you long enough. When I get to hell, I'll save you a warm spot. Ciao?''

''Ciao.''

Normally, it would have been Rettaglia's pleasure to pull Strijdom in—if Strijdom were really the master and not a front for someone else—but Gamliel had stirred the waters with a stick. Strijdom had taken out insurance by acting as a subagent for Gamliel. Rettaglia knew without a particle of doubt that if he were to pull Strijdom in and some fact of overwhelming importance didn't occupy Strijdom's mind, in three hours he himself would be occupying a berth on *Shokaku*, and a pistol would probably be waiting. Gamliel never failed to mark the little touches.

Still, there was an adage that the one constant in the crazy, federalized patchwork of Imperial societies is that the rich get richer, the poor get whatever is left over, and noisy colonials get their just rewards.

Rettaglia intended to maximize the odds of that happening.

Saturday(12)

PINNED IN THE COMMO ROOM LISTENING TO SOLCHAVA, FOR THE fourth time in fifteen minutes Matti Harjalo couldn't decide whether all surgeons were crazy or just the ones seconded to the infantry.

Claude Devoucoux had never bothered to conceal his belief that if physicians like himself were running the universe, there would be no place in it for infantry battalions like Vereshchagin's. Harjalo had been inclined to agree. If anyone could do a better job of mucking up the universe than the Diet, it would be a bunch of physicians like Dapper Claude. Before him, Ohta had managed four years and two campaigns without ever losing the touching belief that every line officer carried a field depot in his side pockets. Ohta's predecessor had been spin-dizzy as well, and Natasha Solchava was apparently the craziest of the lot.

Someone having finally told her that her medics were off learning how to be infantrymen, she'd come very near to scraping Esko Poikolainen off on a wall airing her grievance.

He listened to her continue as she appeared bent upon doing, her face almost unrecognizable with fury. The anger in it was real. Vereshchagin, who could charm paint off a wall, had brushed her off.

Exigencies of combat blithely ignored the limits philosophers set on the conduct of war. The laws of war in truth rested upon no firmer foundation than the ancient moral law, an eye for an eye. What one side did, the other imitated, and colonial wars were irregular wars, fought without chivalry, pomp, and circumstance. Against irregulars, it was a hard law that most of the barriers came down, and it was Vereshchagin's opinion that fielding medics who lacked competence to survive in a field environment was murder, which societies define as unlawful killing.

"They are out on your island." Solchava was out of breath and struggling for words. "These are medics, not soldiers. They should be learning to be medics. And he . . . he . . ."

The length of her body through the abdomen and thighs gave her such a flat chest in battle dress that it was easy to think of her as mannish, particularly as she came from Eva Moore's battalion. As he listened to her decry the Variag's arbitrary and tyrannical nature, Harjalo realized that she was not and wondered whether he ought to hang a sign advertising guidance to the lovelorn, which was a hell of a way to end a day.

Outside, Company Sergeant Poikolainen was listening to the Hangman exclaim incredulously, "Solchava? The devil you say! She has a face like a horse and half the personality."

"Colonel Moore is a shrewd old vulture," Poikolainen observed sagely. "And I think Matti's going to shoot her at the first opportunity."

Sunday(13)

IN THE DANK LITTLE MEETING ROOM, THE ABSENCE OF OLIVIER was breathing new life into de Roux's bearing. As he listened to de Roux cast witty aspirations on his fellow negotiators, Rettaglia's unease grew. He could not recall whose idea it was for a Sunday session. The timing still appeared singularly ill.

One anomaly that had piqued Ssu's interest was inexactitude in the obituaries reported in the Boer papers and in the deaths reported to the landrosts. Some sixth sense impelled him to nudge de Roux about the number of Brothers his watchdog committees had eliminated. To his surprise, de Roux denied the charge angrily. Intent, Rettaglia reeled off half a dozen names, studying de Roux's face.

De Roux's anger turned to amazement and distress.

Rettaglia's mouth tightened. The Brothers—some of them—had successfully compartmentalized. The fact they'd successfully sealed off their Executive Council from decisions that were being made meant there was a gap in the information upon which his calculations were based. Equally, it meant de Roux and his compatriots among the Twelve were likely dead men. Rettaglia left him gasping like a gaffed fish and glided to the door to test the lever.

It was fastened. Apparently, some of the Brothers with guilty consciences were distressed by the thought of having Rettaglia free to spin his webs of Satan.

Rettaglia pulled out the little pistol he carried in his sleeve and began to wait, patiently, for the door to open.

IN VENTERSTAD FOUR MEN HIDING IN THE FIELDS SHOT DOWN Arkadi Peresypkin, where he had gone for a tryst.

For a young man, Peresypkin had served under the Iceman for a long time. He had put money in the pocket of Daniela Kotze's dress, almost as if he knew. She remained rooted when she heard the sound of rifle fire, the many against the one.

And as men have done before, they called her whore and traitor and other names. They forced her down roughly to cut away her hair with a knife.

The next morning, before going off on kommando they would whip her through the streets of Venterstad. The people would come from their homes then to jeer, armed with that especial bitterness to the collaborator that only people who have themselves acquiesced and collaborated with an invader can feel.

Her dress would lay where it had been torn from her, the pocket ripped. Unnoticed, feather-light bills would drift away on the wind.

"RAUL, THE BODY?" VERESHCHAGIN ASKED KINDLY.

Sanmartin tried to swallow his bitterness. "The body. Solchava examined the body for me, I'm not sure who else in the battalion she's talking to. The Boers were not very pleased. There was, of course, nothing for her to find. Three witnesses stated that de Roux fired three shots into Rettaglia before he took his own life for reasons unknown, which is preposterous."

The Variag lay the tip of his finger across the bridge of his nose, which was as close as he came to outwardly betraying displeasure. "Please explain for the benefit of us all, Raul."

Unconsciously, Sanmartin squared his shoulders. "Rhett wouldn't go to the toilet without a palm gun and a crystal memory recorder, both of which have disappeared. Tomiyama and Aksu confirm." The corner of his mouth turned down. "They're working for me until the admiral gets around to finding another IO."

"That will suffice. Matti?"

"Three other indicators. Piotr has one man off seeing his girlfriend. He missed a radio check. Venterstad. I talked Piotr out of burning the place down for the time being. Paul ran the spot check you wanted an hour ago. A lot of people aren't where they're supposed to be, two or three hundred. They're probably hiding in the vlei with the lungfish. Couple that with the activity around the perimeters. We had what? A half-dozen Boers out trying to weed our gardens last night? One of them blew his hand off. I thought for a while we were going to have to go get him. What the Boers intend, I don't know. I can guess."

"What do the admiral and Colonel Lynch think?" Henke asked. "Or do they?"

"Colonel Lynch seems to think that we are seeing foxes in so many words. I do not believe that he has passed my evaluation on to the admiral," Vereshchagin replied.

"Can we count on help from other battalions?" Henke asked.

Harjalo spoke up before Vereshchagin could respond. "Not one thing. Ebyl has been dribbled out to repacify the Lakes with a company of Higuchi's. Higuchi is worried sick, not that that will do any appreciable amount of good, but he's got less than nothing to spare. Kimura's are in garrison, split between Reading and Upper Marlboro. The volunteers are worthless."

"It is a serious matter to fritter away a strategic reserve in this manner," said Henke, whose aspect suggested a smoldering fire.

"Agreed, Paul, but Colonel Lynch does not. His rationale appears to be based upon the supposition that Boksburg District is beset with cultists, and that this is the only difficulty facing us. He has instead reiterated his directive that we supply a battlegroup to respond to the complaints of cultist depredations around Boksburg."

Yoshida, usually quiet, exploded for once. "That is insane! There aren't any jungle bunnies there!"

Vereshchagin chided him gently. "Colonel Lynch can be extremely stubborn when he has an idea in his head. Please be constructive, Chiharu."

"So when do they hit us?" Henke asked. "Things seem to have come to a point. Tonight, tomorrow, or the day after?"

"Raul?" Vereshchagin asked.

"Irie initialed the draft of that half-witted agreement in principle a few hours ago. If they don't move quickly, the news will be out all over and discourage recruitment. They've been expecting us to send people up to Boksburg for about twenty hours now, and it's the Day of the Covenant so they won't have to do much to whip people up. Tonight, late, or tomorrow."

"What does the colonel expect us to do when this blows up in our face?" Henke asked.

"The best we can, I suppose," Vereshchagin answered softly. "Paul, what do you want for Boksburg?"

Yoshida could no longer restrain himself. "Boksburg?"

"Colonel Lynch feels that we are deliberately flouting his authority by continuing to procrastinate. Obviously, we must set his mind to rest," Vereshchagin said with a gleam in his eye. "Paul, what will you need?"

"I can leave number sixteen with Piotr, but if I'm going to play a shell game with armored cars, I'll want the rest of mine, the engineers, ground sections from recon, and two sections from Raul."

The Hangman never did anything by halves. Stripping C for Chiba was an obvious choice. The Iceman would be too far away for Henke's battlegroup to succor, and Yoshida would need all of his platoons and then some for his extended perimeter, the hangers, and key points within Pretoria.

"I'll give you Karaev and two sections from number nine," Sanmartin said, calculating swiftly.

"Expect us back for breakfast," the Hangman replied.

"Comments before we break?" Vereshchagin asked.

"Raul?" Harjalo queried mischievously.

"Oh," Sanmartin said. He shut his eyes. *"Ira furor brevis est."*

" 'Wrath is a transient madness,' I think," Vereshchagin reflected.

"Haven't we heard that one before?" Henke asked.

"We've heard them all before," Harjalo said. The Hangman chuckled.

The room emptied silently. One of Malinov's idiosyncrasies was his hatred for the rustling and scraping of chairs, and a battalion sergeant was entitled to idiosyncrasies. Vereshchagin rose to his feet and strode through the door.

At the com, Timo Haerkoennen was scratching the back of his neck with a stylus. He gave Vereshchagin a casual wave which Vereshchagin returned.

Passing by, Vereshchagin stopped to admire the battalion crest where it hung, inconspicuously positioned. There was only one; one reproduction would have been cheapening, a hundred would have been demeaning. A rifle battalion carried no colors. It was a simple enameled emblem on a plaque of wood, worn slightly by the fingers of two generations of recruits. It had occasionally caused problems with the navy; the wood was slightly radioactive.

The salamander on the crest seemed to stare back at him in return: a salamander argent passant regardant, taches sable, oeilles vert, on a field sable. Black on white on black, more yang than yin. Never mind the technical convention that argent was silver and a metal rather than the color white, the heraldry was fitting: a creature born in fire, the color of death, wryly regarding the fields of hell.

"The voice of the Buddha is heard; yet day in, day out, winds roar, and waves surge," he quoted, and passed on.

WHEN HENDRIK PIENAAR SPOKE, HIS NEIGHBORS LISTENED. IT was not the gray hairs on his head or even the light in his watery eyes, but rather the quiet intensity of a man who accepted the mysterious workings of God and listened to His Word.

They knew that Pienaar's father had died on the approaches to Potgietersrust, that his mother and two brothers had died in the camps, that he himself had left on the last ship with a rifle in his good hand that bloody year when God's Elect were driven from the Highveld forever. As for the men who had served in the Styndorp kommando, they trusted Pienaar implicitly.

Many men had spoken already that night. They spoke of the strength of the Imperials, of the hardships, of the dangers. When Hendrik Pienaar spoke, he mentioned none of these.

Instead, he spoke of the *Afwyking*, the Deviation, and the *Ondergang*, the Fall. He told them of the traitors who had lost their faith in their just and stern Lord, who had crawled into their cities to embrace diamonds and gold and forgot God's Word and God's Law. They had huddled in their warrens in their hundreds of thousands when the time of trials came, to lick the spittle of Kaffirs as the hands-uppers had licked English spittle. So it had always been, those who lost their ties to their land were dead in the eyes of the Lord.

He reminded them of the loyal Bantu who had been murdered in their hundreds of thousands. He reminded them of the English who had called themselves South Africans, how in hundreds of thousands they had taken to the ships or went crawling before their Kaffir conquerors when only a pitiful handful of God's Elect had stood forth proudly to fight God's Battle and die; and they were all reminded once more, of how the English invented the murder camps to break and enslave the spirit of a proud, beleaguered people.

Finally, he reminded them of the many years the Volk had spent wandering in the wilderness because of their lack of faith. He spoke of the Greater Trek, in which God had revealed to His people His true design which had made of the Highveld a forge, to temper the Volk for the greater journey across the sea of stars to carve a new Suid-Afrika out of the wilderness. He brought them to the present and told them how one final time the legions of Satan were arming to despoil the people of God of all they had wrought. His neighbors listened.

Singing in the quiet darkness, they walked with him down to the shores of the river called Blood, to reaffirm that first covenant with their God. And as they sang, Hendrik Pienaar, late *luitenant* in the *Regiment Danie Theron* of the Second Republic, despised himself for what he had done.

That evening, the first of the kommandos assembled to strike, as they had struck the ranchers and the mercenaries, and before them the Zulu and the Matabele.

Did the men of Slachter's Nek quail at the might of the mur-

dering British? Did Jopie Fourie? Did the men who swore a Covenant to dedicate their victory to the glory of the Lord turn away from their God? God chose the Afrikaner Nation for a special destiny. This and each Geloftedag is a day upon which the heartstrings of the Afrikaner are tuned in harmony with the great Divine Plan of the Lord; and is there one, single underminer among you who is so dyed in sin as to deny God's Divine Plan for His Chosen People?

Yet on this Day of Remembrance, I look; I see doubt and fear, fear and irresolution in Afrikaner faces. I see faithless, irresolute Afrikaner hearts quailing at the might of a heathen oppressor! Do you have trust in the Lord? Do your irresolute hearts not know that the Lord is sovereign and intensely busy at every turning point in the affairs of His Chosen? That the suffering of the Volk is a testing of us and a sign of His Divine Favor? Remember! For after suffering comes deliverance!

Did the Voortrekkers quail? Were their hearts faithless and irresolute? No, never for a minute! Inspired, selfless, ennobled by their cause, they struck forth into the wilderness like the people of Israel fleeing Pharaoh. They set forth to do the work of God protected by Divine Providence. God called them, God guided them, God raised them up and showed them the path even as He calls to us and guides us this day.

But I speak to you this Day of Remembrance not of these things, but of shame! And sin! And sloth! For the People of the Lord have turned their eyes away from Him, they have bowed their necks before brazen idols, they have sold their children and their children's children into the bondage of Egypt! They have lost their faith in The Lord and His righteousness, they have submitted meekly, cravenly. Must the Lord endure this from His People? I say to you, never! For we are a Volk which has been called to a high estate, which can only be maintained so long as our Volk understands and proves itself to be the bearer of its rightful culture-mission; I say to each of you, lift yourselves, come forth and raise up the hand of the Lord!

> *Excerpted from a sermon delivered by the Reverend Louis Pretorius Snyman, Paulskerk, Johannesburg, in commemoration of the Day of the Covenant.*

ZENITH _____

The pig cleaned up his webbing, and he shined his bayonet
  Some people started shooting, so he shot them with regret
He couldn't work an office, and he couldn't be a clerk
  For pigs who like to whistle like to whistle while they work

Monday(13)

Proclamation From The Provisional Government
Of The Republic Of Suid-Afrika Reborn
To The Afrikaner Volk

In the Name of God and of the dead generations from which we receive our tradition of nationhood, through us, the spirit of our great nation summons us all to our flag to strike for our freedom.

Having organized and trained our manhood through our Christian-national organizations, having patiently perfected our discipline, having resolutely waited for the right moment to reveal that spirit, we now seize this moment, and relying from the first on the strength of our nation assembled, we strike in full confidence of victory.

We declare the right of the Afrikaner Volk to the ownership of Suid-Afrika and the unfettered control of the Afrikaner destiny, to be sovereign and indefeasible. The usurpation of that right by a foreign people and government has not extinguished that right, nor can it ever be extinguished except by the destruction of the Afrikaner name and the Afrikaner Volk. In every generation, the Afrikaner Volk have asserted their right to national freedom and sovereignty. Standing on that fundamental right and again asserting it in arms in the face of the worlds, we hereby proclaim the Suid-Afrikan Republic as a Sovereign Independent State, and we pledge our lives and the lives of all our comrades-in-arms to the cause of its freedom, of its welfare, and of its exaltation among the nations.

The Republic of Suid-Afrika is entitled to and hereby claims the allegiance of every Afrikaner. Until our arms have brought the opportune moment for the establishment of a permanent National Government, representative of the entire Afrikaner

Volk and elected by the suffrages of all true Afrikaners, the Provisional Government, hereby constituted, will administer the civil and military affairs of the Republic in trust for all the Volk.

We place the cause of the Suid-Afrikan Republic under the protection of the Most High God, Whose blessing we invoke upon our arms. In this supreme hour, the Afrikaner Volk must, by its valor and discipline and its readiness to sacrifice for the common good, prove itself worthy of the august destiny to which it is called.

Signed on Behalf of the Provisional Government

Three meters in, the first Afrikaner through the warning wire hit a locust in the blue darkness on what he supposed was a cleared path. As his foot left the mine, an explosive charge blew the body of the mine into the air where it exploded belt-high. Two more Johannesburgers behind him also died. A fourth was on his knees spitting up metal pellets when a shower of projectiles from the s-mortars arrived to pin the storming party for the attention of Mekhlis's 105mms.

Sanmartin was awakened by the rumbling from the mortar pits as the mortars returned fire. Pedestal mountings afforded the mortars a full traverse. Steel plates crafted on NovySibir with trapdoor openings cut into the surface gave them protection. Steel rang off the plates.

Rudi Scheel added his personal signature by flinging something hard and heavy at the door. Scheel whistled heavily through his teeth when excited.

"Outposts five and six are in. The sensors are ringing like chimes. I flipped the safeties on the mine field."

The primary mine field, command activated, was laid underneath the pebble mines the Boer sappers had spent blood to clear. Dead ground around the knoll that hadn't been graded out of existence was mined and sensored beyond belief.

Strapping on his webbing, Sanmartin spared a glance at Coldewe's empty mat. Coldewe was picketed in the Johannesburg staatsamp with Gavrilov and two sections out of No. 10. If the rest of C caught a cold, they would sneeze.

He came into the passageway as the second of No. 10 emerged, Wanjau's team leading. Wanjau was methodically stuffing cotton waste into his trousers with one hand. Isaac hated mortars. One had dropped a dugout on his head once. He smiled. "Colonel Lynch should protest."

Sanmartin made a smile. Even a bad joke was better than screaming out loud, which tended to unsettle people.

The last of No. 11 was already gone, through trenches scooped beneath the steel and concrete of the sidewalks, to cover the perimeter solidly, the s-mortars returning fire undetectably in the darkness and drizzle. No. 11 boasted a dozen s-mortars, nine more than they were authorized. C Company had invested too much in concealing their scattered firing positions to betray them lightly. The civilian telephone was ringing.

Mischa was sitting next to it, a portrait of innocence. Sanmartin picked up the receiver.

"Is this the Van der Schlacht Funeral Emporium?"

"What's up, Hans?" Outside, rocket and recoilless rounds were slamming into the top and sides of the bunker. The sound of scraping metal was likely the phony radar dish going down.

"We have problems."

"I'll keep the matter under advisement." Sanmartin handed the receiver to Mischa. "How many?"

"Two wounded so far, not serious," Mischa answered.

Sanmartin nodded. He leaned back to listen to the chatter on the nets, section by section.

THERE WAS A MINOR EXPLOSION ON ONE OF THE SIDE STREETS out of Coldewe's field of vision. In the predawn, they'd spent an hour affixing directional mines in inconspicuous locations, and overhead, two Hummingbirds were reaping the fruits of their labors.

The Boers who hadn't seen fit to call it a day were aggressive enough. Coldewe and No. 10 had already been forced out of the Burgerstraat. Their position was somewhat delicate. The rocket launchers the militiamen kept trying to set up in what was left of Majubalaan were becoming annoying. The problem for the Boers was still the staatsamp with its thick brick walls of Flemish Bond over a concrete base.

A fortified position is a tactical expedient that allows a small force to pull on someone's nose while his legs are being broken. The Boers would find this out very quick when Der Henker showed up selling crutches. The eager, young Afrikaners still hadn't quite grasped that the first of No. 10 had spent a few hours with a few power saws turning the dark, decorative bricks into loopholes. Reinikka's engineers had done the measurements and left a choice collection of graffiti. Although brick walls were hardly protection against the singleshot rockets the

Boers were tossing away, behind the deceptive facade, Coldewe's riflemen were cocooned in composite matting, snug and at least partially amused by the passages he was quoting from *Beau Geste*.

As Coldewe watched through his slit, a young man in a brown coat jumped to his feet and spilled into the courtyard firing full auto from the hip. He actually got about four paces before the laws of statistics and probability caught up with him in the form of a light machine gun.

HANNES VAN DER MERWE GRIPPED THE HEAVY MACHINE GUN under his fists, wilting in the rain. He waited, praying his nervousness would not be noticed as the Imperials' knoll shuddered under the impact of rockets and shells. He himself had fired off three belts although he'd seen nothing to shoot.

The maps were all wrong. A rumor had gone around that the Johannesburg kommando had been wiped out to a man, and that the other kommando leaders had politely told the Provisional Government's supreme commander to sit on a nail.

Kurt Voerward suddenly pitched backward and flopped, a sniper's bullet in him. Hannes crouched lower, mumbling prayers, waiting for the tank.

At least they had the tank. General Pienaar was somewhere else, but he'd given them that.

FEELING USELESS, MUSLAR LAY FACEUP IN THE RAIN, NUMBED by the sound of battle. He had Beregov and the second of No. 9. Half of them were out on local security. The rest were asleep or playing tarok with waterproof cards, flashing finger signs. The stay-behind party was holed up twelve hundred meters southwest of the caserne and half a kilometer in the rear of the nearest Boers. Although their life expectancy was distressingly short if discovered prematurely, Platoon Sergeant Beregov, whose tarok was unscientific, was obviously far more concerned about being down four hundred yen.

Berry's job was to take his sixteen men and pitch into the back of the Boer horde at an opportune moment. Muslar's was essentially to keep out of his way.

The radio whined. "Sanmartin. Edmund, Berry, we're having some problems. Execute G for Gifu. Acknowledge."

Looking disgusted, Beregov scooped up his cards and issued a few terse orders over the section radio net.

They broke into four-man sections and began heading for the

back side of the ridge eight-tenths of a kilometer away. Otherwise of negligible value, the north-northeastern extension of the sprawling, ill-defined ridge had military consequence. A pack of missile teams there would make the Hangman's desired axis of advance untenable, at least until kind souls put flanking fire where it would do some good.

Sanmartin needed them. He tuned out the No. 9 net, cursing the copters and the Hangman who were somewhere else and cursing the Boer who'd thought of armoring a road train. "Mischa, what's the Hangman say?"

"Forty minutes."

"Are the big boys upstairs ready yet?"

"They're still waiting for the weather to tail off a little more. They say conditions are not optimum."

"Chiba point three. Break. Sanmartin. Rudi, how about the road train?"

"We'll have to take the damn thing out. Now."

"Can we use the mortars?" Sanmartin asked. With dark eyes and matching rings under them, Kyriakos was manning the counterbattery radar topside, shoving the folding grid around with his hands, heedless of the fire. Sanmartin could see Mekhlis wheezing, "Ulcers to your soul and trousers, Kyriakos, give me a fix!" The dummy mortar pits had been blasted out of existence.

"No," Scheel told him, "they got steel plate all over the thing, especially around the road wheels."

Without the Hangman to break things over, Sanmartin's sections were outnumbered ten or twenty to one. The hastily armored road train creeping up the gentle grade cloaked by a curtain of fire was enough to break their backs.

"All right, Rudi, let the 88s take it." The 88s had a distinctive dust signature thrown up by the venturi. They would be pitifully exposed. "Use the mortars and the grenadiers on everything. Yes, I know, don't belabor the obvious. Give me about three minutes on this end to try something. Out."

He turned to his com specialist. "Mischa, we can't wait. Ask the navy if they'll try anyway. Firmly. Especially since it probably won't work anyway. Put me through if they say no."

The Boers were using commercial 81mm mortar rounds with the old-style electronic fuses. Rytov had dissected a few shells they'd turned up searching here and there, and Rettaglia had correlated the batch number with fuse settings. If the ships could blanket the area where the Boer mortars were positioned with charged particles punched through the clouds, it would be very interesting if the Boers had more shells from the batch.

"*Exeter* and *Achilles* say they'll try. There's somebody who calls himself Veldt-General Malherbe on the landline for you."

Sanmartin wrinkled his eyebrows. "What does he want?"

"Something about the manifold destiny of the Afrikaner nation and the effusion of useless blood."

"Put him on hold."

"I've got him on hold."

"Canned music?"

"Got it."

"I'm going up."

As his face emerged in the tainted air, single explosions were followed by two double explosions that caused the building to tremble as Boer mortar shells on the far ridge blew themselves up and took others in sympathetic explosions. A storm of fire burst from the knoll to give the 88 gunners shelter, and a fourth explosion came, larger than the rest, as an 88mm round placed a fireball in the vitals of the Boer road train and lit its fuel. Almost at the same moment, he heard Beregov's voice say, "Beregov. G for Gifu executed. No casualties. Beregov out."

Around them, the Boer fire slackened. C Company had paid for that mad minute, Sanmartin did not want to know how dearly. But the Hangman was coming, and the choppers. If the Boers didn't run now, Cadillacs would eat their flak launchers and helicopters would whistle in. If C Company stayed on Suid-Afrika a hundred years, Sanmartin didn't think they could duplicate the preparation and imagination that had gone into stacking this deck as ice-cold as they could make it.

From her window, Bruwer looked out through a hole in the armored matting Kasha had put up. At the foot of the hill she could see the ruin of the road train. Framed against the sky on the ridge, the drab plastic skin on a burning truck was curling toward the sky in long strips.

VERESHCHAGIN HAD HIS PERSONAL RADIO TUNED TO YOSHIDA, trying to make sense out of the situation and Yoshida. It was somewhat difficult to determine where hysteria began and left off. The Boer assault on the Pretoria facilities had fortunately developed as little more than a holding attack.

With Sanmartin preoccupied, Shimazu was acting as IO, processing a trickle of useful information. The Boers had kept their secret admirably until the phone system lit up like the brothel district when the kommandos discovered they were not being called out for semilicit drill and began franticly phoning their wives.

A price had been paid for that secrecy. Despite a veritable miracle of organization, of five assault groups only the one attacking the spaceport had formed up as intended. The turnout of the kommandos who were supposed to storm the Complex had been so poor that they had been diverted to reinforce the attack on Johannesburg, which Sanmartin had finally reported secure. Bloemfontein had been an even greater fiasco. Instead of collecting in villages outside the city, the Boers had apparently been persuaded by Piotr's incessant patrolling to form up further out and ride in over the farm paths. Ambushes and staccato gunfire from Wojcek's helicopters darting in and out of the rain clouds dissuaded most of them. The shock of finding their assembly areas under mortar fire was enough for the few who ran the gauntlet. One kommando hadn't even made it as far as where the helicopters were operating; a team from the second of No. 2 had set off three directional mines in succession over the stretch of ground the Bothadorp lads were crossing.

Haerkoennen tapped Vereshchagin on the wrist. "Sir, Acting Major Dong, calling in to the battalion net. He's ordering you to come to the line. He sounds very excited."

"Please tell the little catamite that I am busy, Timo. No, wait a moment. What does the little catamite want?" Vereshchagin replied.

"Hold on, I'll ask. . . . Sir, he says that headquarters is under attack. He demands two companies immediately."

"I presume that he means the spaceport is under assault. Matti?"

"Is he crazy? Even if we had two companies to spare, we haven't any transport for them," Harjalo replied. "I would also like to know where the Dutch boys scraped up enough men to hit the port hard considering what they've thrown at us."

"Dong is still on the line, sir. He insists that the order comes directly from Colonel Lynch," Haerkoennen added.

"That's what I thought. When the little sodomite gets excited, he tends to forget details, including the fact that there's a certain separation between him and Colonel Lynch, at least during duty hours," Harjalo commented.

"That was not very funny, Matti. Who over there has some sense?"

"Fuwa seems cool enough."

"Timo, ask the little catamite to put Lieutenant Fuwa on. Then get me Raul."

"Sir, Dong is too busy screaming at me."

"Well, cut him off and get Raul. Matti, should you be leading a counterattack or something?"

"Give it another ten minutes. Yoshida is dithering. Anton, I just can't see how they could get more than a few hundred men there."

"Captain Sanmartin is on," Haerkoennen interjected.

"Good. After I take it, get me Wojcek. Also see if Fuwa is on the line yet. Hello, Raul? What is your situation? . . . You are mopping up there? Good. Listen, Raul, I have a little job for you. Do you have a clear landing zone? . . . Well, get one. The spaceport is under heavy attack, along with everything else. Stuff a platoon and some mortars into Wojcek's aircraft and take care of it for me. . . . Please try not to get yourself excited, Raul. It is a half-hour ride, and you will have plenty of time to think of something. Coordinate with Lieutenant Fuwa. . . . Fine, Raul, any time. Bye."

"There, that was easy," Harjalo said.

Vereshchagin smiled. "Raul is cleaning up the town. A hundred Afrikaners or so elected to hole up in the houses rather than run past Paul. Most are trying to blend in with the civilian population. Raul is searching the houses and scoping occupants for nitrates and gun oil."

"What about Paul. Is he still upset you wouldn't let him pursue?"

"Let us merely say that he is disappointed Chiharu is not handling his end in a more professional manner. I think that we can say that Chiharu has had his opportunity. After you clean up the perimeter, I will want a reserve from B Company."

"May I shoot Chiharu?"

Haerkoennen interrupted. "Sir, Lieutenant Wojcek is on the line. Lieutenant Fuwa is standing by."

"Wait a moment, Matti. Timo, tell Fuwa that I am sending a relief force with Captain Sanmartin. Have him coordinate with Sanmartin and give me Wojcek. Stash? . . . You mentioned to me that you were beginning to run low on ammunition. How would you like to go back? . . . There is just one little errand I have for you. The spaceport is under attack, and I am sending Raul to take care of it. He is busy clearing a landing zone for you now. Please get the transports off and float up to Jo'burg to give him a lift. You will be under his orders. . . . Yes, Stash, the usual thing. A platoon and a pair of mortars. . . . Why thank you, Stash, I will consider that a compliment. Good-bye, Stash.''

He turned back to Harjalo. "Patience, Matti. I know Chiharu is a fool, but if we start shooting all our fools, they might stop letting us have any. Just relieve him, so that we might get on with fighting the war.''

"Which one?" Harjalo asked, running out the door. "The one against the Dutch boys or the one against brigade?''

"Matti, counterattack?''

"*Hai*, O-Anton-san, I'm on my way." Harjalo slithered on his belly out of the tunnel into the rain. The first officer he saw was Mizoguchi. "Mizoguchi, what's happening?''

"We are waiting for Captain Yoshida to seize the kraal and are taking sniper fire. The company has taken nine casualties. At least we have learned them not to hide in ferntrees.''

"The word you want is 'taught,' Hiroshi. Are there any targets worth wasting the mortars on?''

"Negative. I strongly believe that they have had enough for the day and are pulling back.''

"Running" was probably more descriptive of what the Boers were about. To the north, Paul was amusing himself in a small way. Until Yoshida managed to clear the Vlakkraal farm, every Boer that the Hangman's hounds flushed would scamper off into the forest little worse for the ordeal. With No. 10 and the engineers still cleaning up Jo'burg, Paul was short on infantry, and probably on patience as well. Relieving Yoshida might be a kindness. Harjalo reached for his radio receiver.

"Beppu point command. Break. Yoshida, this is Harjalo. Are you in position yet?''

Yoshida was still yammering about snipers.

"Fine! Sversky, are you monitoring? Captain Yoshida has just been relieved. You are in command. If you haven't moved out in ten minutes, I'll relieve you. Yoshida, report to Lieutenant-Colonel Vereshchagin. Harjalo out." He redialed for Henke.

"Date point one. Break. Paul what do you think?''

"Any time you feel you are ready," was the Hangman's cool reply. Der Henker probably wanted to nail Yoshida's thumbs to a cross.

"I've just relieved Yoshida, and I'm up with Mizoguchi. We'll start pushing them. We should be able to cut a few off.''

"I doubt it, but we'll enjoy ourselves anyway," was the reply on the other end.

"Ja, you have that right, anyway. Harjalo out.''

The Hangman's executive officer was a phlegmatic captain named Willem Schwinge, from Maarianhamina. In D for Date, they called him Swinging Dick. He and his crew had died when their side armor was pierced by a missile from a well-concealed launcher. Schwinge and his driver, Jouni Mainninen, were the only two married men in the Hangman's company.

Above them all, Wojcek's helicopters were cutting by on their return from Johannesburg. In the jump seat of the second machine, Tulya Pollezheyev commented, "Say, Coconut, you fly this thing pretty good."

The bearded pilot, an aviation sergeant named Kokovtsov, banked the chopper sharply just over the treetops. He didn't bother to reply. The gunner who doubled as co-pilot was even less talkative. Pollezheyev looked out through the glass at the treetops, close enough to touch.

"When that big gun of yours talks, people have to listen," Pollezheyev opined.

The gunner nodded and continued scanning the terrain below for some sign of movement. The rest of Pollezheyev's team was sprawled out in the catwalk seats sleeping. The shock of combat hadn't hit Pollezheyev yet.

"Captain Sanmartin said we had a half-hour flight."

For all the response he got, Pollezheyev might as well have been talking to the wind. Kokovtsov again altered his course slightly, following Lieutenant Wojcek in the lead helicopter in his efforts to throw off any unseen antiaircraft, and Pollezheyev felt the safety belt tighten around his gut.

Behind them were three light transports, carrying two sections and a pair of mortars. The other two choppers brought up the rear.

"I'll bet that most of the niobium they put into this chopper came from here," Pollezheyev commented.

There were no takers.

"You know, Coconut, this is the third time I rode in this chopper, and I never once heard you say something. You don't talk much, do you?"

Kokovtsov replied out of the side of his mouth. "Parrots talk a lot, but they don't fly much. Me, I fly." He kept his eyes glued to Wojcek, periodically zigzagging to throw off ground fire.

Ahead of Kokovtsov, Wojcek banked his helicopter sharply and almost dumped Sanmartin out of the command seat and through the cockpit over the side. Sanmartin clutched his safety straps without relinquishing his grip on the helicopter's microphone. Wojcek and his were more considerate to their aircraft than to passengers.

"Whistle before you do that, Stash, I'm trying to complete a call. Lieutenant Fuwa? Do you hear me? Sanmartin here. What is the situation there?" Sanmartin said loudly over the hum of the rotors.

"Captain Sanmartin, sir, I hear you very well. At present, we have two companies of the volunteer battalion in position. The third company appears to have abandoned its positions. The fourth company and Hokkaido Company of Lieutenant-Colonel Higuchi's battalion have been thrown in to retake the ground. Elements of Lieutenant-Colonel Higuchi's Ehime Company are arriving by air from Complex. The construction engineer battalion is supposed to be on its way for air insertion, but communications with Admiral Lee and Lieutenant-Colonel Kimura's headquarters have been lost and have not yet been regained. *Exeter*, *Ajax*, *Achilles*, and *Graf Spee* are standing by, but the cloud cover is too thick for effective naval support. They are prepared to launch guided projectile munitions if targets are acquired."

"Has anyone been monitoring the naval channel?"

"No, sir. Colonel Lynch ordered the naval channel to be shut down after an interchange with commander *Graf Spee*."

Kim, the commander *Graf Spee*, was known for his slashing wit. One naval rating had let slip that Rear-Admiral Irie refused to leave his cabin when Kim had the bridge.

Sanmartin tried to hold his head steady to let the blood clear. "Fuwa, request permission to open communications immediately. Something feels rank about this whole mess."

"I shall comply with your directive, sir." There was a brief silence. A moment later, Fuwa came back. "Sir, Colonel Lynch is not available, and Major Dong has denied my request to open communications with the navy in absence of the Colonel."

"Listen Fuwa, this is very important, I think. On my non-existent authority, ask the navy what's going on at Reading."

"I will do so, sir. One moment," Fuwa replied.

Sanmartin said half to himself, "Lord in heaven, I hope I'm not right." He looked over at the pilot of the helicopter. "Stash, hold up. Don't go any closer to the port."

"What?" Wojcek turned around in his seat.

"I said hold up, Stash. Don't go any closer to the port. How long can we hover here before we have fuel problems?"

"About ten minutes."

"Do it."

Wojcek acknowledged, issuing the order. For some reason, Sanmartin began working the other riddle over in his mind, the one that had mystified Rettaglia. What could be packaged in a box three-tenths of a meter on a side that weighed five hundred eighty kilograms? Why would the Boers bribe Irie a week before a war?

A moment later, Fuwa came back on. "Sir, the navy reports that both Reading and Upper Marlboro appear to have been destroyed by small nuclear devices. They have been trying to relay this information to us for the last seven minutes, sir. Major Dong has threatened to shoot me," he added.

"Fuwa, are any of the companies in the perimeter under pressure?"

"One of the volunteer companies has stated that they are pinned down by intense fire, but all elements of Lieutenant-Colonel Higuchi's companies report nothing but noise and fireworks. They have requested permission to pursue. Permission to pursue has been denied."

Sanmartin felt his throat go dry. "Listen, Fuwa, the spaceport is about to be nuked. It's the only thing that makes sense. Get Higuchi and get Lynch. Tell them to clear whatever they can out of there immediately."

"I will do my best, sir."

Wojcek turned, pale as milk. "Everything that isn't in orbit is stored either in Reading or at the port."

Sanmartin said nothing. Instead, he found his mind dwelling on Irie's prize, wondering how well Irie had scoped the thing, what could be that dense. It was too heavy for gold, far too heavy for lead. Solid platinum? Or something that was intended to look like a solid cube of platinum.

"Fuwa, this is urgent! Call Rear-Admiral Irie. Tell him to jettison his platinum cube immediately and clear the area. Tell him every second counts. Tell him there's a nuke inside."

Fuwa betrayed no hesitation. "I shall endeavor to comply, sir."

A few minutes later, Wojcek spoke up. "If we don't land at the port, we can either go back to Pretoria or divert to Complex."

"Is there any fuel left in Pretoria?"

"Some. Not much."

"Head back. Tell the Variag we're coming. What time is it?"

Fuwa interrupted before Wojcek could speak. "Captain Sanmartin, this is Fuwa. Lieutenant-Colonel Higuchi has super-seded Colonel Lynch and begun evacuating personnel. I shall stay to man the communications center. You have been given permission to divert or return. I have relayed your message to the navy with the urgency you requested. They have acknowledged." There was a pause. "I have shot Acting Major Dong. I have nothing further for you at this time. Good luck to you, sir. Fuwa, out."

"Good luck to you, too, you little Jap," Sanmartin murmured. He looked down at his hands and noticed he was clenching his fists. His fingernails had broken skin.

"It's four hours fifty-six," Wojcek stated.

They waited as they flew. "They could have synchronized their watches a little better," Sanmartin murmured, possibly to Wojcek. Four minutes passed. Then there was a brilliant white flash, around them, behind them, that seemed to fill the sky. It was followed by a shock wave that jerked the helicopters about like little toys.

"Any casualties back there?" Sanmartin yelled as Wojcek pulled the chopper on course with difficulty, buffeted by winds.

"Grigori hit his head. He's out, but the rest of us are fine," someone shouted back.

Sanmartin wiped the blood from his chin. "Stash, see if we still have communications. Call Vereshchagin. Tell him what's happened," he said quietly. For the companies that had been swallowed up, and maybe just a little for the companies that hadn't, he started mumbling the words of a paternoster he had learned as a child.

BELOW THEM IN PRETORIA, VERESHCHAGIN WAS SPEAKING TO Haerkoennen. His voice was unnaturally quiet.

"Timo, please contact Rear-Admiral Irie. Find out what the situation is and what his orders are." Vereshchagin had only met Irie once, during an operations briefing on *Shokaku* a hundred years in the past. The import of the tremor that passed through the building had shocked him almost beyond words.

"Sir, commander *Ajax* is responding. He is requesting orders from us." Haerkoennen replied.

"Is the navy aware that Admiral Lee is missing, presumed dead?" Vereshchagin asked.

"Yes, sir. Wait. He says that a nuclear device, estimated to be two kilotons, has destroyed *Graf Spee*. The blast, coupled with the resulting fusion reaction, also eliminated units *Achilles* and *Exeter*. Rear-Admiral Irie was aboard the flagship when the device went off. He, along with Admiral Lee, is missing, presumed dead. Lieutenant-Colonels Moore and Ebyl are the only senior officers to have reported in. Commander *Ajax* states his vessel has sustained moderate damage but is still functional. He requests orders."

Vereshchagin felt himself laugh, until tears streamed down his face. "I am sorry, Timo. Tell *Ajax* to interdict any traffic coming west from Pretoria and Johannesburg along the road net, and to stand by for further orders."

HOURS LATER, IT WAS TIME TO ASSESS. "SO WHAT HAVE WE, Eva?" he asked Moore, acting commander of Complex and of odds and ends thrown off from the inferno that had engulfed the spaceport.

Moore hesitated over her reply. "Forget Reading. Forget Upper Marlboro. Glassy slicks, no survivors. At the spaceport, over and above the ones who got out, you have fifty-seven who are dead and don't know it yet. Most of them are from Higuchi's H Company, they were in advance of the others and fairly quick with a shovel. For the moment, they're functional. They've formed themselves into a platoon. I have sixty-seven more under treatment with varying chances of pulling through."

Raul Sanmartin's warning had enabled Higuchi to send off most of the aircraft with a mixed bag of passengers. Characteristically, Higuchi had refused to board himself. None of the survivors knew why Colonel Lynch had failed to embark.

"Thank you, Eva. Please tell them that I will be by to address them in an hour." It was a promise Vereshchagin meant to keep. It was a matter of pride that just as his battalion kept faith with the living, it kept faith with the dead.

"One personal note, Anton, Claude Devoucoux was in Reading when it blew. I put him there. I sent him off to try and do something about the venereal disease."

Moore had divined that the loss of witty, urbane Claude Devoucoux meant more than all the rest of Reading's dead. It would be better, Vereshchagin quickly reasoned, not to mention the circumstances surrounding Devoucoux's death. It was the sort of brutal irony that made a mockery of war.

Sensing his mood, she told him quickly, "Give my love to Solchava!" and broke the connection.

Solchava had hung the cross and crescent out at the Pretoria hospital. She had her hands full, and a little girl, a spindly thing with a thin, ferret face, had attached herself to her remaining limbs. Her immediate problem was to arrange transportation for casualties military and civilian to Lieutenant-Colonel Moore's facilities at Complex, themselves overflowing.

She had pulled perhaps a third of the staff and was doing as well as might be expected. The Afrikaner medicos—good Brothers all—were mostly out getting themselves shot. The first one to show came as a patient with mortar fragments in his spine from leading an Oxwagonguard squad with more zeal than discretion.

Overall, the situation reported was grim. Ebyl's battalion had ridden out the storm unscathed, positioned in the backwaters of the cowboy country. So had Higuchi's G Company. The survivors of Higuchi's light attack company were reforming themselves into a reinforced platoon, heavy on Cadillacs and light on slicks. Two platoons from his Ehime Company had been left behind at Complex, his reconnaissance platoon had made it out on a heavy transport. Still another platoon had put down an uprising at the ocean tap, albeit at the cost of heavy casualties. Of the other men Higuchi had preserved, Vereshchagin could put together five or six platoons of artillerymen and engineers as garrison forces.

His own battalion had sustained thirty-four casualties serious enough to have been reported, concentrated in B and C Companies. The wastage was remarkably light. Still, Vereshchagin had only the training detachment and strays to fill the holes.

More serious was the loss of the naval units, the runway, and the supply stockpiles. A considerable number of aircraft had been saved, but munitions were short. From this day forward the war would largely be fought on prayers and meditation. On the civil side of the ledger, the cowboys had been decimated, with their leaders wasted. USS had lost more than a hundred personnel in the fireball that enveloped the spaceport.

Vereshchagin felt it important to take a moment to reflect upon Kosei Higuchi, without whom the losses of the day would have been higher. It was perhaps fortunate, in a grotesque way, that Raul's serendipitous flash of intuition had proven out; several survivors remarked that as the last aircraft departed, Higuchi had been removing the ribbons from his tunic to award to the remaining members of the half section he had retained to ensure orderly evacuation.

People reacted in unexpected ways. Certainly there had been

small trace of the fearful little man with an ulcer that Colonel Lynch's staff had derided.

Vereshchagin smiled sadly. There was something poignant and compelling about Kosei Higuchi and seven brown men bearing the last name of Gurung—as did almost everyone in that clan and that company—lined up in a row, keeping their faith to the last with the rituals of their calling.

Haerkoennen interrupted his thoughts. "Captain Yoshida, he's very upset. If you can break for a moment, you can get him off me. Sanmartin is here, too."

"It needn't wait, Timo. Send Yoshida," he commanded.

Yoshida jarred him from his reverie. Haerkoennen had understated. Yoshida was seething over having been relieved.

"Lieutenant-Colonel Vereshchagin, Major Harjalo had no right to relieve me in the manner in which he did, in front of my men, he had no right to relieve me at all, he . . ."

"I believe Major Harjalo ordered you to report to me, Captain Yoshida. Do you know how to report to a superior officer, Captain Yoshida?"

Vereshchagin's voice cut Yoshida finely and deeply. Yoshida drew himself fully erect and saluted.

"Sir, Captain Yoshida. I have been relieved of command, I am reporting as directed by my superior officer for reassignment, sir!"

"Very good. I instructed Major Harjalo to relieve you. I was dissatisfied with your company's progress. I am satisfied with his actions, which were undertaken at my direction. Major Henke will take over B Company in addition to his own for the present. When we find the time, you may sign over your accounts and property formally. At this moment, we are in something of a war. We will find something else for you in a day or so."

"Sir, my company advanced as well as it could under the circumstances prevailing on the battlefield. I protest this action removing me from my command!"

"Your protest has been duly noted. The action stands. Chiharu, you have many talents, but you are not suited to field command," Vereshchagin replied dreamily, as if acting out some scene in a drama.

"Sir, I believe I have been unfairly singled out for opprobrium and respectfully request that I be reinstated. Otherwise, I shall be forced to carry my protests to the brigade commander."

"Captain C, go ahead," Sanmartin commented from outside

the door. "You've got the battalion commander, the brigade commander, and the task group commander all sitting in the same chair. The Boers made a clean sweep."

"Chiharu," Vereshchagin said gently, "we have been hit very hard, and we are going to have to forget about the usual nonsense for a time in order to concentrate our efforts. You are not suited to a field command. I will find you a different manner in which to contribute."

For all his faults, Yoshida was not stupid. For a moment, he stood there. He started to say something, but the words tripped over themselves as he tried to eject them from his mouth. It is a fearful thing, Vereshchagin thought, to see a man so naked.

"I am sorry, sir. I do not know what came over me. I really could not have been myself," Yoshida finally said.

The banality appealed to Vereshchagin. It seemed to represent stability in a disorderly cosmos. It was, however, more than Sanmartin could stand. It had been a long day for Raul Sanmartin. Rudi Scheel had been shot thrice in the chest by a young boy during the mopping up.

"Who were you, Chiharu?" he called through the door.

"Chiharu," Vereshchagin said gently to give him some face, "I am looking for Raul Sanmartin. If you happen to notice him, please send him in."

Yoshida excused himself to permit Sanmartin to enter. As Sanmartin dropped into the seat that fate had provided for the occasion, Vereshchagin used the opportunity to examine the steel he was forging. The tone of Sanmartin's flippancy alarmed Vereshchagin. It betrayed mental exhaustion.

He selected an approach ruthlessly.

"My regrets over Rudi. You have made Beregov your acting company sergeant. I agree. I regret that I can afford you little rest." Lightly, he dismissed the day's events.

"You will retain your position as intelligence officer. Matti and Saki's people will assume other staff functions to the extent we require them. Integrate Rettaglia's personnel and begin training Muslar to assist you." Mizoguchi, who would have been a better choice than Muslar, had been shot through the head and had lost the sight in both eyes. A small, ivory netsuke that had been in his family for generations was in the care of Timo Haerkoennen.

Sanmartin began to say something. Vereshchagin cut him short. "Raul, we are at a linkpoint. We dare not allow a political movement to coalesce."

Sanmartin blinked his eyes, and Vereshchagin moved to deflect his unvoiced questions deftly.

"The Afrikaner masses are poised at the brink of an unknown future. Before they rally around the revolt, we must impress our will upon them.

"It seems strange to speak in abstraction when reality has intruded so chilly, but Piotr has a theory," Vereshchagin commented, the gentle rain following the lightning, "that every once in a great while, an opportunity arises for a few soldiers to tip the scales while thrones and powers dangle naked."

"Napoleon had a dictum that God is on the side of the big battalions," Sanmartin said slowly, to give himself time to think.

"He also said that the moral is to the material in a ratio of four to one. Sometimes," Vereshchagin said carefully, "war is not a test of brute strength, a crisis of attrition, but rather a subtle matching of superiorities against inferiorities at a decisive moment. We are poised, delicately. After today, we cannot negotiate, nor do we have the strength to impose a solution by orthodox military means." He opened his hands compellingly.

"I need a touch of insanity, Raul. We can gobble up Boer civilians turned soldier by hundreds and never touch the heart of the darkness. Where is it? Find me the lever which will break it," Vereshchagin asked him, and waited cruelly while the resolve he had calculated to impart manifested itself.

"By the way," he added, "I must speak with Juffrou Bruwer. Please arrange this."

The sentence galvanized Sanmartin as the glassy sea that was the spaceport had not. Vereshchagin could almost see the interplay of his thoughts in the rippling of his facial muscles. War stripped a man of pretense.

As Sanmartin got up to leave, even before he reached the door, he began to ponder what he had been asking as well as what he had been asked.

When Matti Harjalo saw him emerge, he stepped up to the door and knocked discreetly. Hearing the tapping of a pipe on the other side of the thin panel, he turned the lever down and entered. Vereshchagin was curled in his familiar spider seat, softly striking his new pipe against his knee. He coughed.

"Oh, hello, Matti." He looked at Harjalo closely. "What is that on your forehead?"

"Blood, I think. My own, possibly. Sversky and Kiritinitis were cleaning out the power plant, and I went along. They tried to be careful. The place will be fine after they clean it up a bit. I ought to clean up a bit, myself."

"You should."

"You ought to sleep. Both Paul and Piotr have broken off pursuit, and Yuri and I can handle things. Tomorrow, we're going to need you rested."

"I am sure that I will get around to it, eventually," Vereshchagin said distantly. "How is Solchava managing?"

"Very well, considering. It was a mistake of sorts to let Raul position Coldewe in Johannesburg proper. Between ourselves and the Boers, we pretty well shot the bells out of the place. She and your friend Eva are going to be up to their eyebrows in wounded civs. Hans just sent off another two truckloads." In Johannesburg, the area around Majubalaan had been leveled. Along the Burgerstraat, all the pretty, pastel houses were decorated with pretty, white stars from small-arms fire.

Harjalo wiped his forehead, leaving a white streak. "What's the latest with Piotr?"

"His company was not overly happy about what happened to Arkadi Peresypkin. It is not especially obvious, but they have not been overly concerned with taking prisoners. I have spoken to Piotr." The Iceman's wrath was a quiet affair, which nevertheless translated itself in concrete terms.

"How did it go with Beyers? Yuri said that you spoke with him."

"Not well, particularly. He wanted to resign. I convinced him otherwise, but his attitude was not reassuring."

"In what way?" Harjalo asked.

"Despair and fright, intermingled. He expects to become a corpse. I want to use him, and I cannot." The pipe resumed its monotonous cadence. "I need to use him, Matti. Militarily, we have the initiative for the moment, but in political terms, we are on the defensive." He resumed brooding and found himself staring at the pipe in his hand.

Harjalo looked at him thoughtfully. "Anton, why not let Piotr do intell. He is very good at it, you will recall."

"Piotr, our flashing sword. Sometimes we have a tendency to try to use the sword in every instance, do we not? I sometimes think to myself that if Piotr had a scrap of imagination, he would be dead ten times over. The thought is neither fair nor accurate. Nonetheless, I know exactly what I might expect from Piotr."

"Are you going to give Chiharu political?"

"Tomorrow. As much as we affect to despise it, it is a difficult job to do well, and Chiharu has the instincts for it."

"So what will he advise?"

"Radical relocation. Ship the population to the islands ánd camp them there to isolate the canker before it spreads."

"Moderation in warfare is imbecility. What will you say?"

"What can I? It is a penetrating analysis of our position, and we may have no better choice."

"That may be. Have you heard from Tuge yet?"

Vereshchagin's lip moved slightly in a small and uncharacteristic show of distaste. "Indeed. He appears to have an unrealistic appreciation of his importance at our present junction. I regret to say that he was sufficiently insensitive to hint that he would be happy to mediate with the Bond on our behalf. I believe he has been drinking. His facilities will remain shut down, his civil authority will remain a nullity, and his Complex will remain under my control until such time as I direct otherwise."

Harjalo laughed.

Vereshchagin let his hands rest and closed his eyes. "So tell me, Matti, what choices do we have?"

"Gods." Harjalo flopped heavily into the other chair. "We could pull in our horns, gut the refineries, and bastion Complex. Then they either come over to us or revert to savagery."

"The Boer leaders who are attempting to grasp the reins of power have too much blood on their hands to allow it."

"There's Yoshida's solution. We put the Boers behind wire, scorch everything green and Earthlike, and let the kommandos starve."

"Many will flee, many will fight. It would lead to generations of bitterness and oceans of blood, enough of it ours."

"Or we could just bull through," Harjalo continued stubbornly. "We shake out Rettaglia's contacts for a few leads, trace the Boer kommandos, beat them into the mire, and beat out the embers with a stick. If we move fast enough and strike hard enough . . ." He didn't finish the sentence.

If they could, well and good. If they could not, they would have to grind the Boers down, which would amount to the kind of bloodletting that Vereshchagin's battalion had hitherto avoided. It was true of men and it was true of battalions: too much combat over too extended a period, and they would break. What separated the brave from the cowardly was a matter of a few months, a few hours, a few minutes more.

"What do we have, Matti? Ten companies, to crush a hundred thousand Boers? Still, there is the fourth choice."

"Which is?"

Vereshchagin told him, "When we have one, I will tell you."

"Gods."

"We do what we must. Have you ever thought of getting married, Matti?"

"No, not seriously. I never thought I had anything I would want a child to inherit "

"We have been away too long, Matti. We are losing touch, I think. All of us. And that frightens me. Is that a bottle of wine you have been holding behind your back? If it is, we might as well drink a libation to someone or another."

"It is and we will. To cheer you, I have one bit of low comedy. A few zealots decided to strike a blow at Imperialism by torching the smelter at Mariental. The workers there, Afrikaners all, threw them out bodily."

Vereshchagin smiled, despite himself. Harjalo stood and stretched.

"Is there a message you'd like me to pass along to Natasha?" he asked innocently.

Vereshchagin opened his eyes. "Are you a matchmaker, too? Every second person seems to be trying to thrust me into the woman's arms."

Harjalo smiled a lopsided smile. "No, Anton. You're as surely marked with the sign of Cain as I." He traced the design on Vereshchagin's forehead with the ball of his thumb.

MEAGHER STEPPED UP BESIDE PIENAAR IN THE LONG RETREAT, in the pouring rain. There had been deathly silence in the ragged column as they moved away from the place where the spaceport had been.

"Your English is too good for a farmer," Meagher told him, stepping casually over someone's rifle, cast away.

Pienaar nodded.

"I hope you know where you're going."

Pienaar amiably nodded as he felt the muscles in his lower back begin to tighten. The years were long, and they had a way of weighting down the feet.

"We'll be lucky to arrive with a tenth of the ones we started with."

Pienaar broke his silence. "They are hungry, they stop at the houses. Some will come follow." A handful of his trusted

Steyndorpers were at the back, rooting them out with sjamboks. Even ten years past, Pienaar would have done it himself.

"Fat, bloody chance," Meagher observed dourly. "That was a nuke back there that took out those poor, bloody fools. You didn't know about it, did you?"

This time, Pienaar quietly shook his head. He continued to trudge through the muddy forest steadily.

"Then your orders were to pull back at a certain time, am I not right?"

Pienaar nodded.

"But you were not supposed to say anything to me, is that not also right?" Meagher asked.

Again, Pienaar nodded.

"Someone meant to leave me there, pinning Imps in place when that thing left off, do you think?"

Pienaar nodded a fifth time, moving forward. He tried to ignore the pain in his legs and side.

"You did a good job there. I half expected your little squirts to break and run away like those poor, bloody fools of cowboys. Tell me, Hendrik, are you married?"

"No."

"Were you?"

"Yes."

"Thought so. It shows. Any children?"

"A daughter, many years ago," Pienaar replied, thinking about the child that daughter had been and the wife full of life who had sickened in the plagues and left him nothing but a daughter to remember her by.

"Where is she, now?"

"In a hole in the ground back on Earth. I have a granddaughter."

"Is she as pigheaded as you are?"

Pienaar thought for a moment. "Worse."

"I'll stop prying, then. You're a good man, Hendrik. Too good a man to be a miserable farmer."

Pienaar smiled with the rain trickling down his face and the back of his neck. "For a miserable hireling, you are a good man, too." A moment later, he added, "I am a lousy farmer."

When they halted in the darkness beside the rude path, they had perhaps fifty men. About half of those were Meagher's cowboys, who had literally nowhere else to go.

Meagher unfastened a boot and began pouring the water from

it. "Lord of hosts, we must have squirts strung out over half the continent," he averred.

"They will turn up. Then we can begin to make something of them. Perhaps we will have another chance, half as good," Pienaar reflected placidly.

"Do they know where to go? I don't!" Meagher retorted.

"We have Friends in all the villages, who were too busy to come out today. They will be sure to tell them," Pienaar replied. His voice did little to conceal his opinion of these Friends. He and Meagher had spoken to one another, off and on, throughout the night.

"Did I tell you, Daniel, that we owned a vineyard?" Pienaar began. "Near Kaapstad. My mother's family owned it in 1770. After my brothers were murdered, it should have gone to me and then to my granddaughter, I suppose. I had a lump of earth from it I would have given her, but they would not let me bring it. I flung it from my hand and none of it clung, but I remember."

"We Irish are worse, Hendrik. We can't tell you about last week, but we can name the women Cromwell's dragoons raped."

"When I listen to my granddaughter tell me how we are destroying this world, our future, I tell myself someone has to do something." Pienaar interlocked his fingers powerfully.

Meagher looked at Pienaar quizzically. "So tell me, Hendrik, why are you mixed in all this? It's obvious you despise these people."

"Daniel, we Afrikaners stick together. It is our strength and our weakness. For good or ill, we stick together."

"Ah, Hendrik, my man. You can lie to yourself, I suppose, but not to me. Come now, you've swallowed a dream as much as any of them. 'For I will own the Lord my master, and none other.' Is that not true?" He paused. "You're a hell-raiser, Hendrik, my man. Like me, now, admit it."

"No, you are wrong. I will tell you why I came, Daniel." He took an embroidered handkerchief and wiped some of the dirt from his face. "I am an old man, Daniel. I remember what it is we are fighting for. I know the price we are willing to pay for success or in failure. These are my people, after all. These others? As long as they use me, I will not let them forget."

"Ah, Hendrik, my man," Meagher said thoughtfully, "it should be a crime to grow as old as you or I in a trade such as ours."

* * *

IN THE DARKNESS IN JOHANNESBURG, HANNA BRUWER SAT IN A little chair in a little room, rocking herself back and forth. She had been out walking, helping, until the grief-stricken people had driven her away.

Sanmartin passed himself slowly into the room, easing himself into the other chair. He let his chin rest on his chest. His mouth was dry. Outside, through the window where the splinter matting Kasha had put up had been torn away, the night was black, the outposts manned. Illuminated by the moonlight was the rugged hill D Company had crossed with fire.

He had spent the last four hours seeing to the tasks that remained after the singing of the rifles ceased. On the ragged edge of exhaustion, it was sometimes better to push on into tomorrow than try to sleep when sleep wouldn't come. A bitter fight took three quiet days to settle out, if three quiet days could be had for money or love. Beregov had watched him, finally prying an extra magazine from his left hand to send him off.

Sitting, he noticed the kylix resting in pieces on the floor where vibration from the impacting mortar rounds had shaken it. Bruwer looked at him, mouthing thoughts as they came into her head. "My grandfather, the one who fought in the Wars, told me that once when he was a boy, there was respect that people had for each other. Somewhere, it disappeared, and he spent the rest of his life wondering where it went. We were wrong, weren't we? We lost the land that was ours for more than three centuries, and that means we were wrong, doesn't it?"

He said nothing, and she added, "Now, we will lose this one."

He had no words of comfort. Automatically, he pulled the bolt assembly from his weapon to inspect its freshly cleaned surface for specks of grime he might have missed. The gesture was not lost upon her, and the knowledge was bitter.

The Variag's mold was tight and sometimes it pinched.

Solchava finally pulled the plug on Rudi Scheel close to midnight. His brain waves had flattened, and other people needed her more. He died ten minutes short of the hour.

A list was compiled of the Imperials units lost from service. At the bottom of the list neatly appended was "The Baker Street Irregulars."

Tuesday(13)

*"DE GOD ONZER VOORVADEN HEEFT ONS HEDEN EEN SCHIT-
terende overwinning gegeven!"* The God of our forefathers has
given us a glittering victory, Scheepers said with unintended
irony.

Others around the *krijgsraad* were less exultant.

The banker, Claassen, was outspoken. "Yesterday, we had
four field guns, thirty-six mortars, twenty-nine missile launchers, two hundred twelve machine guns, sixty-two rocket launchers, fourteen antiaircraft launchers. How many do we have this
morning? How many more such victories can we suffer?"

The worst thing, Pienaar reflected, was that Koos Gideon
Scheepers had been in such a fury to give his bright, shiny, new
weapons out that most of the men he had given them to hadn't
been trained to use them. As Claassen knew, most of the heavy
weapons committed had never fired a shot before they were
discarded or silenced. Then too, Claassen was from Johannesburg. Fifty-seven men and boys had died in the armored tank
committed there, and he had known each of them.

Still, the losses in men and weapons were not as bad as they
could have been. Many of the kommandos raised had never
come anywhere near an Imperial soldier, and most of the young
Afrikaners and their weapons would come trickling in over the
next few days. The ones who had seen fire would be the better
for it.

More serious was the loss of ammunition. Claassen had shown
Pienaar the figures. Not one person purchasing weaponry for
the Volk had had the slightest idea how much ammunition an
army of young Afrikaners shooting at shadows could dispose of
in the course of a long day's fighting. A few more such victories
would ruin them.

Claassen followed up his sally with a direct attack on Scheepers. "Indeed," he said acidly, "did anyone think where we
might get more weapons and more ammunition now that we no
longer have a spaceport on this planet?"

Scheepers still had his majority, a much quieter majority. His
éminence grise Strijdom silenced Claassen adeptly.

"If the Volk require a spaceport, we shall build it out of rock
with our hands," he said, as if pointing out the obvious was a
betrayal of the ones who had fallen.

Brave words for a man with no soil under his nails, Pienaar
thought. If there was any more ammunition to be had, it would

come from USS, and the Volk would crawl for it. Pienaar did not have to read minds to know that Claassen's name was being taken down. When Claassen stopped speaking, more from frustration than from lack of something to say, no one came forward to take up the banner that had slipped from his hand.

Even after the eclipse of de Roux's followers, the debate over the formation of a new executive for the Bond and a single government had been acrimonious. Only Strijdom's renunciation of his own candidacy and the acceptance of Koos Gideon Scheepers as a compromise had prevented a complete rift between the various factions that comprised the army that the Bond in some mysterious manner had called into being.

Still, it hadn't taken very long for the politically astute to notice that power in the new government was concentrated in the hands of Strijdom's backers and the young men who clustered around Scheepers. In company with the intense secrecy and confusion surrounding the mobilization, it made one wonder, particularly after the spaceport.

Scheepers began speaking, though Pienaar was too preoccupied to pay it more than the barest of respect. At the end of his address, although they dutifully proclaimed a great victory, to many it seemed barren of rejoicing. The ones who begrudged the cost begrudged the method even more.

Upon Pienaar's return, Meagher met him. "Ah, Hendrik, you're back. What do you have to say for yourself?" Meagher commented contentedly.

"More politics. Someone told Koos Gideon of the help you gave to drafting the proclamation. He requested of me that I extend to you his grudging thanks."

The mercenary returned an impish grin. "Consider it a present, an Easter present belated. Although I still think it might have been wiser to agree on a provisional government before agreeing on a proclamation. How much longer do we sit while they bicker?"

"A few days. Forever. I don't know. Koos Gideon and his generals want to recruit by the thousands, and they are afraid if they let the fledglings out from under their eyes, they'll fly away."

Christos Claassen had said, "What have we? Scheepers, Strijdom, Olivier, and Snyman. Olivier ought to put an ess in his name, and then we'd have four little snakes, as if three weren't enough." Pienaar had been named second-in-command of what they called the Oom Paul Krueger Division, which Snyman would command.

"With all the stragglers telling tales, they'll have a devilish time convincing people yesterday went all that well," Meagher replied acidly. "And is he quite sure a mob of country lads is what he's wanting? There's a story about a Gideon in the Bible he ought to read."

"The Bible is the only thing he does read. It is insane, Daniel. A few of them think we have won and concern themselves with doctrinal purity. The rest seem to think the Imperials should wait until we are ready to stir a finger. I was at least able to tell how to get the recruits here without leading the Imperials to our doorstep."

"You think different?" Meagher asked with a smile.

"If they know we are concentrated, they will find some way to locate us. Then?" He slapped his hands together. "But between ideologues and amateur field marshals, what I say is as welcome as pigs in the choir. The Imperials have two battalions at least. They say they have no spacecraft, but they have aircraft, and it is only a matter of days before they have a good landing strip for them."

"Too true," Meagher replied. "They've just announced that unregistered vehicular traffic is forbidden beginning Thursday at dusk, the inference being that they'll be in a position to interdict it. Between now and tomorrow, Messrs. Scheepers and company are going to be moving everybody and his grandfather. But I'll confess something else I've heard is worrying me more. There's a rumor that Scheepers has been speaking to USS."

"To the USS director. Little rat eyes himself," Pienaar told the mercenary with relish. "I was there when he made the call."

Meagher slammed home a magazine into his rifle before trusting himself to speak. "Do you know, Hendrik, my man? I am beginning to think that perhaps I did the Imps an injustice. All they wanted to do was shoot me."

"Little rat eyes in his sharkskin suit. He welcomed Scheepers with outstretched arms and told us that USS would do nothing to discourage our legitimate aspirations. That was when I reached into my pocket and felt for my purse to be sure it was with me still. But if the devil had ammunition this morning, I am sure he would have gotten a respectful hearing," Pienaar explained dryly.

"Indeed. I'll say no more, Hendrik, but there's a few debts I never got around to settling. Nor have I forgotten about the accident at the spaceport that nearly was," Meagher said, his face drawn tight. He was silent for a moment, before asking, "Do Scheepers and company know who's commanding the Imperials now?"

"They don't, but it is a man named Vereshchagin. A dangerous and subtle man. We have met."

Meagher caressed the trigger housing on his weapon gently as he studied Pienaar's face. "Hendrik, I've had a peek at what passes for an intelligence summary here, and I'm surely wondering how you came by that bit of information."

"I DID NOT EXPECT TO SEE YOU LIEUTENANT-COLONEL VERESH-chagin. It was not mentioned to me that you were coming," Solchava said, unconsciously pushing back a curl of her short, dark hair.

Her voice was ragged with exhaustion. Vereshchagin considered her carefully, for it was at moments such as this that he learned the most about a particular person. "Sit. Relax. Rest. You have the time. Your anesthesiologist and I have conspired," he replied kindly.

She looked at him uncertainly for a moment, then looked behind herself for a chair. The little Afrikaner girl who had been holding her hand climbed into her lap when she sat down.

Briefly, Vereshchagin wondered where the little girl had come from and to whom she should be returned. For the time being she was a mystery, but Albert Beyers had promised an answer by the end of the day and Beyers kept his promises.

"Are you aware of the situation?" he asked her.

"Yes, I am aware of as much as I need to know," Solchava replied. She made as if to rise, but Vereshchagin laid his hand over hers.

"You are too tired to fall asleep, I imagine, but an hour of quiet will do you a great deal of good. Is this what you came to the colonies for?"

She made an effort to smile, and began to speak. "Yes, that is true. That is so. It is not right to give the rich everything they need and the poor no medicine at all. But one can do nothing without money. That is what they say. When I do, I will return," she said, made light-headed by the tension and the exhaustion as she stroked the child's hair. For some reason the words flowed apart from her like water from a spillway.

In her own way, Solchava was ruthless. She simply did not realize it, and perhaps never would.

Vereshchagin smiled secretly, sadly. Even under Vereshchagin's predecessor, who had been forcibly retired to a vegetable patch on Esdraelon, the battalion had always been a lodestone for failed and frustrated idealists like Raul Sanmartin, who was still fighting a battle the Ecologists had lost a generation ago, or dead Willem Schwinge.

Eva Moore, for all her cynicism, was more perceptive than most. As Vereshchagin had suspected, her dispatch of Solchava was not quite the cruel jest it appeared at first glance. Solchava would never return. Her store of learning would be rendered obsolete by the very passage of time she counted upon to accumulate what she sought, and Vereshchagin was convinced she realized this as well.

On Esdraelon or even on this planet, man had not come so far that his course could not be wrenched aside and diverted. There was still a small place for dreams. On Earth, human societies had grown too large to be encompassed by them.

As Solchava continued to speak, with the child holding her tightly, Vereshchagin recognized that it was as if she were talking to a part of herself. While she chattered on about her hopes, her dreams, her great plans, Vereshchagin shut his eyes.

JOHANNESBURG WAS ALSO IN DOWN TIME. AS MISCHA CLEANED a message out of the mailbox, Coldewe drifted over and took him by the elbow. "I'll take it. Is Achilles still in his tent?"

Mischa nodded. "Shimazu's hand-carrying something up, and he's waiting for him."

Coldewe elbowed his way through the door to Sanmartin's quarters in the rear of the C Company bunker and handed him the message. Sanmartin looked at it blankly, making no effort to unfold the printout.

"Hans, that reminds me. Ask Hanna to call Albert. Tell him Andrassy is meat whenever Albert wants him butchered."

Coldewe gave him a peculiar look, but nodded. "What's in the bulletin?"

Sanmartin looked down at the thin plastic in his hands, then began to scan. "Something here from aviation," he said bleakly. "Kokovtsov hit a mounted kommando last night, approximately seventy men, fourteen kay east-southeast of Muldersdrif, at EC 13-4617. . . ."

"What do you call cavalry that's been gotten at by a chopper?" Coldewe asked.

"Infantry. Stop it, Hans," Sanmartin said. "Kokovtsov reported small arms but also light ground-to-air launchers. . . ."

"Hanna's stepmother lives at Muldersdrif, doesn't she?"

"Hans, shut up!" The message slipped out of Sanmartin's hands to the floor.

Coldewe retrieved it silently. "Raul, you're getting tough to live with. What's between you and Hanna?"

"Maybe she figured out what I do for a living. Let it lie." After a moment, he added, "I need to get a handle on Rhett's business, somehow. I need an answer. I don't know what to tell the Variag." His face hardened.

"But do you know what's funny, Hans? I could wipe the slate on the damn Boers. Wipe it clean for something to grow. Rhett and Rudi were all the family I had. Pulling the plug is what I'd like to do, and it's about the only thing the Variag can do that has a chance of working. And all I have to do is not come up with a miracle."

Coldewe let go. Instead he asked, "Who's running things over there?"

"I don't know. I'm not sure they do. But I'll wager a man named Strijdom is the one saying 'Come hither.' "

"Why so?"

"He's smart. He's nasty. He knows what he wants, and he wants it bad."

Coldewe asked, "So what will they do?"

Sanmartin looked away irritably. "I don't know. Lick their wounds. Think of something else. They probably don't know either. Ask Hanna, she knows as much as anyone," he said. He added, "I'm fresh out of miracles, Hans."

Coldewe didn't say anything, and Sanmartin looked through him. "Hans, take over the company for now. You and Berry put some more people out. Keep trying to put a tail on some Boer volunteers. Tomorrow, we're going to pull the plug on the power." Coldewe nodded and left him.

The hours passed slowly. He heard a knock and it was Shimazu. "What do you have, senior intelligence sergeant?" he asked glumly.

"Sir. Acting Major Rettaglia directed me to deliver this disk to you personally in the event of his death. The condition has been fulfilled. I regret the delay."

With that, Shimazu saluted and left.

Sanmartin momentarily studied the little voice from the grave. Then he leaned over and slid it into a mount.

"Version 3.3. Raul, if you are listening to this, hell is broken loose and stalking. Don't try and stop the disk just yet. In five seconds, you will hear a series of rings three seconds apart. On the third, record your full name."

Despite his grief, Sanmartin found himself smiling. At the academy, a habit Rettaglia had broken him of was using his full name.

There was a ringing noise. On the third, Sanmartin exhaled and recorded, "Raul Tancredo Morgan Llewellyn Sanmartin de Sanmartin y ap Rhys." The disk mount clicked.

"Little brother, this is my last will and testament. I don't want to go and I don't like the idea of being gone, but I want you to know I love you. And your smart, little Afrikaner. I haven't got a family or children that I know of, so have the Variag devote anything I have coming to Esdraelon. Mawkish sentiments coming from me, but you understand."

Sanmartin nodded his head as if Rettaglia were present and asking approval for the deed.

"Now, for your legacy. The agent's name will be followed by his net and his controller. . . ."

Rettaglia's final entry was the names of forty-two people he believed were eminently suitable for a good, selective plague. For a moment, Sanmartin felt his eyes misting over, but he checked himself. It was too soon to mourn. Then with the disk of names in his hand, the hazy outline of an idea began to crystalize and form facets.

BEREGOV WAS SUPERVISING THE RELAYING OF MINE FIELDS WHEN Sanmartin gathered him up. Beregov's own mood was not precisely sweetness and sunshine. "Divine wind. You heard?" he asked as they walked down the scarred sidewalk.

Sanmartin nodded. "Before you did, I hope. I'm supposed to be IO. Two aircraft, one *Ajax* knocked down and one our flak launchers took. Miscalculation, do you think?"

Beregov shook his head. "They learned better. We taught them. Recruiting problems. They wanted martyrs," he explained.

"Morning runs are going to look like sniper drills," Sanmartin commented.

"We pulled in how many?"

"Four hundred thirty-seven. Piotr rounded up twenty or so this morning. He's still screening them," Sanmartin calculated quickly.

"Trace them through?" Beregov asked.

"I just spoke to Hans and Yevtushenko. No chance. After they fell apart, they improvised well. They go to one village and get instructions to go to another. Go to Stellenbosch and receive further instructions from a man wearing a white shirt, that sort of thing. We've broken down the phone system pretty thoroughly, but they can still communicate. When we scoop up a batch of volunteers, we can get the first line contact, but they fold the second before we get that far. They have some bewildered cannon fodder wandering about, but by and large they're reassembling without real interference."

Wojcek's helicopters were the only aircraft available for the time being, the Imperials were spread too thin. Intelligence sources had dried up completely. The laager was forming, and any Boer foolish enough to ask questions would find himself outside, or herself.

"Frost it all. . . . You all right?"

"Yeah, Berry. I'm all right."

Beregov thought for a minute. "What are we going to do with the ones we picked up?" he asked, thinking of something else.

"Prisoners? Most of them we'll ship out to the island for the recruits and the stray artillerymen to keep track of."

"The rest?"

"If the Variag approves, we'll have Dr. Solchava give them a physical and let them go," Sanmartin said blandly.

Beregov sucked in his breath. He gave Sanmartin a hard, sidelong look.

"I think we need to fly down to Complex," Sanmartin said.

THE HOSPITAL WAS LOCATED IN A TAN OUTBUILDING. THE TINY biochem section was buried in its bowels off in a basement corridor. The chief of section took his siesta between ten and two, not that Sanmartin intended to solicit his permissions. The fat chemist who'd whipped up the skunk oil was a sharp man. However, on the bio side there was only the senior technician and his self-effacing assistant.

Unfortunately, the little senior technician was so happy to have an audience for his answers that he didn't seem to want to stop for the questions. Sanmartin looked at Beregov and then broke into a burgeoning monologue.

"Senior technician. I want to know what kind of biologicals you have. Characteristics, doses, inoculations."

The man waved his hand airily and set his smoldering cigaretto down in the ashtray. "We got all kinds, captain. Anything anybody wants." He chuckled. "Hey, for most of the stuff we have, one dose is plenty, but listen to me, captain, stop fooling yourself, nobody wants biologicals. If they sent you down to take an inventory, don't even waste your time. Nobody wants biologicals. They put their hands to their mouths and gasp if you even mention germs. Besides, on a mudball like this, how could you control a plague? Take my word for it, captain . . ."

The subbasement to which Lieutenant-Colonel Moore had banished the Wizard Warriors was poorly ventilated. The smoke irritated Sanmartin's sinuses. The senior technician didn't whine well.

Originally, Sanmartin had intended to work it through Moore's adjutant. Beregov had chopped that notion down. Miss Molly's nickname was "Miss Metal" because she had a heart of gold and a head of lead. Sanmartin was beginning to understand why no one else wanted her job. It struck him forceably that Eva Moore's contempt for the biochem section nominally under her control had nothing to do with their mission and much to do with the caliber of personnel.

He counted past ten before he spoke again. "You'll coordinate with the hospital company on the inoculations. We'll need at least a thousand within the first seventy-two hours."

"Coordinate? Coordinate! To us, the Nellies won't even talk much less coordinate. Hey, you wouldn't need a thousand, you'd need a hundred thousand, one for every civ out there if you want to inoculate them. Me, I'd rather see them rot. But let's be realistic, captain, whoever sent you down here didn't know what he was talking about. In seventy-two hours, we'd be crawling along exactly one step ahead of wildfire. If you ask me, it's a silly question, and you can tell that to whoever sent you, too!"

Sanmartin hadn't asked. He found himself weighing judiciously the man's presumed competence as a biotech against his demonstrated incompetence as a human being. The hollow drumming of the man's fingers on the polished metal began to echo the pounding in Sanmartin's head.

"Now, I don't want to poke sticks at this Colonel Vereshchagin," the stubby little man continued, "but if I were in his place, I'd teach these filthy Boers a lesson. Make them pay for what they did! If you ask me, half our problems come from being too kind to civs instead of slapping them hard."

Sanmartin looked at Beregov, who was standing in the place of dead Rudi Scheel. Rudi had had even less regard for semicivs than he did for real civilians. Beregov quietly wrapped one large hand around the dancing fingers and squeezed gently once. The little man held them to his breast then examined them to see if they were all still there. Then eyes opened wider than his mouth, he looked up at Sanmartin. Sanmartin coughed expectantly.

"What was it that you said you wanted, captain?"

Sanmartin wrinkled his nose again. He picked up the ashtray sitting on top of the stacks of papers and pitched it into the wastebasket together with its malodorous contents. Then he leaned on the desk.

"I have a few technical questions about your stock in trade. Please give me answers. Immediately, if not a trifle sooner."

Sanmartin needed facts rather than opinion. If an opinion from the senior technician became necessary, it would be Beregov's pleasure to beat it out of him.

HANNES VAN DER MERWE TAPPED ON THE WALLS OF HIS CELL. A thin coil of fear was wrapped around his stomach. He was more frightened than he had been since he had lost his hat and his machine gun, since the thin spike of the machine cannon on the armored car had gazed in his face and at his upraised arms.

Dirkie Roussoux had been taken. Van der Merwe had heard a single rifle shot, and nothing. The second one was Magnus from the cell adjoining. He had gone a little after Dirkie, and there had been a second shot.

Van der Merwe heard a ringing of keys. A short, stocky Imperial with a heavy black mustache pushed open the door and entered the cell. Behind him was another, standing with an assault rifle where he would have a clean shot. The stocky Imp asked fiercely in Afrikaans, "Are you going to make trouble?"

Van der Merwe shook his head violently. The man relaxed. "That's good. I don't like this either. What's your name?"

"Hannes Mannetjies Van der Merwe. Boksburg," Van der Merwe answered quickly, still tensed, not wanting to anger him.

"Resit Aksu. From Antakya on Earth. That is the city of Antiochii. Antioch. You know, Saint Paul?" Van der Merwe knew Saint Paul. Aksu handed him a cigarette and lit it. He sighed. "I am sorry for you, friend."

"Why?" Van der Merwe asked, coughing slightly. He didn't smoke.

"That bastard Shimazu thinks you're all saboteurs and assassins."

"That is crazy!" Van der Merwe said.

"So is Shimazu, so watch yourself," Aksu advised. "This is what we do with saboteurs and assassins. Bang!" He made a pistol out of his fingers and pantomimed firing it.

"But we're not!"

"Don't tell me. You got a uniform?"

"None of us have!"

"No unit, no uniform. Bang!" Aksu shook his head sadly. The other Imperial cleared his throat. Aksu looked at his wrist. "We got to go."

They crossed in front of the bunkers. Van der Merwe blinked his eyes at the unexpected sunlight. As they stopped in front of one door, Aksu said, "This is where I leave you," and acknowledged Van der Merwe's thanks.

Shimazu was a mild-looking man who greeted Van der Merwe politely. A long ivory-colored rod was stretched across his desk. He put gentle questions, murmuring politely as he listened, pausing only to adjust a machine whose snout was pointed at Van der Merwe's midsection.

Suddenly his face altered. He bent to take a reading from the machine. In a single motion he took Van der Merwe up by the shirt and slammed him bodily against the wall.

"Liar! Atom-bomb murderer!" Shimazu snatched up the rod and pinned Van der Merwe, who had only shaded the truth slightly. "So, you come to plant bombs and tell lies?" He used the rod to cut Van der Merwe's legs from under him and followed up.

For tortured minutes, the whistling stick sought out the recesses of Van der Merwe's body as he cringed and tried to protect his eyes and lips. Occasionally, the rod struck, leaving weals. The words that tumbled from his mouth at the mistake that was being made stayed neither Shimazu's guttural abuse nor the slashing blows.

Suddenly, Shimazu stopped, panting. After a few cautious seconds, Van der Merwe lifted his head a fraction and flung his face aside from a final blow. Shimazu shouted for Aksu.

Aksu entered and saluted. Shimazu tightened his grip on the stick until his knuckles turned white, and spittle flecked his lips. "Take this one. I will shoot him personally," he said roughly.

Aksu saluted. He escorted Van der Merwe around the side of the building until they stopped by a row of freshly covered graves topped by small white crosses. The last one had a name freshly painted on it. There was something like drops of fresh blood by the edge.

"Start digging," Aksu said gently. "I would help, but it is forbidden." He followed Van der Merwe's dazed eyes to the name on the cross. "Was he a friend of yours?"

Van der Merwe began to cry.

"Keep digging, you don't have much time. You want it nice and deep," Aksu said gently.

"He didn't listen!"

"I know. He really is a crazy bastard."

"But we're not saboteurs or assassins!" Van der Merwe said desperately.

"I wish I could help," Aksu said. "Keep digging," he added gently.

"We are not, none of us are! He wouldn't listen!"

Sanmartin walked by, accompanied by Beregov, Tomiyama, and a rifleman.

"Perhaps Captain Sanmartin would help," Aksu said brightly. "If you could convince him, you would save your other friends."

He switched to English. "Sir! Sir, come here, please."

Sanmartin returned the salute slowly. "What is it, Aksu?"

Desperately, young Van der Merwe tried to explain his predicament in mixed Afrikaans and halting snatches of English. Sanmartin listened skeptically.

"Is this true, Aksu?" he asked.

"I believe him, sir. He seems forthright," Aksu replied.

"Company Sergeant Beregov?"

Beregov rubbed his chin. "I suppose it wouldn't hurt to check into it," he answered with doubt in his voice.

"Tomiyama! Look into the boy's story. See what he has to say. If he's telling the truth, I'll deal with Shimazu. If not . . ." Sanmartin let the sentence trail away ominously. Aksu translated faithfully.

"Sir!" Tomiyama said, saluting briskly. Sanmartin returned the salute. "You, come with me!" Tomiyama demanded peremptorily.

After they disappeared from view, Sanmartin asked Aksu, "Judas Iscariot was a Turk, wasn't he?"

"No, honored sir," Aksu laughed. "If it pleases the honored captain, it was a Greek who betrayed the prophet Jesus!" There was a Turkish proverb to the effect that a man who shakes hands with a Greek should count his fingers.

The rifleman dutifully gardened, pausing to erect a little white cross with "Hannes Van der Merwe" freshly painted across the top. He stopped and looked at Aksu and then at a bale of straw inconspicuously placed to the side.

"Rifleman, if you would punctually delay firing for two minutes, our schedule will not be inconvenienced," Aksu decided.

"Honored captain, if you will excuse me, it is necessary for me to look in upon our first clients before attending to the next."

Sanmartin nodded curtly. "How much longer will the first ones take?" he asked. The six were representative of fifty more kept in studied ignorance.

"It will be another hour, possibly slightly more than this, honored captain. If I might suggest, we might switch to the drugs. If the captain pleases, I must go and attend to these matters." Aksu saluted. Sanmartin returned the salute, and he departed.

"This intelligence business is hard on the arms," Sanmartin commented.

Beregov began rubbing his chin for real. "The doc?"

Sanmartin made a face. "I'll talk to her."

"The truth?"

"Enough of it."

"Not too much."

"If I have to," Sanmartin promised, "I'll do the job myself with a rusty spoon." Beregov nodded and walked away, deep in thought. "I want to see that boy's soul," Sanmartin commented to no one in particular. The rifleman sculpting the mound paid him no mind.

In addition to the would-be warriors they had rounded up in clumps, they had another fifty-some acquired in ones and twos without weapons who could claim more-or-less convincingly that they'd been out for a walk in the country. Releasing Boers who had been captured in arms would have aroused too much suspicion.

Sanmartin knew enough about the men who'd called out the Hannes Van der Merwes of this world to guess at how they'd react. It was a virtual certainty they'd try to lure released prisoners back into the bush. Not only would this prevent them from spreading tales of defeat and overwhelming Imperial might among the civil population, but the Boer leaders were an untrusting lot. They would want to do their own interrogations. What Sanmartin needed to know was what the Van der Merwes thought. And ironically, whether they could be depended upon to lie.

"I want to hold his soul in my hand and squeeze it," he added quietly. He looked over at the rifleman. "That patrol into the Empty Land with number nine, you were there."

The rifleman nodded as he continued to shape the little mound with an artist's eye, remembering the dry, empty days.

"Do you remember? Vijer got shot through the scrotum while he was passing water? Oh, how we laughed! We called him 'Deadeye Dick.' "

The rifleman laughed, remembering. That had been on the nineteenth day. Two of the cakes they'd been trailing had committed suicide the day before.

Sanmartin looked in the direction of Reading. "It gives you a different perspective," he said.

The rifleman nodded solemnly. He finished his ministrations and fired a round into the straw.

Wednesday(13)

KEKKONEN SAT WITH HIS BACK TO THE PARAPET, AMUSING HIMself playing ripple solitaire with cards that could be read from either side. Resting his fingers lightly on the triggers of his gp, Sery yawned. Kalle K. was good for two more hands.

As a medium-sized truck approached from Bloemfontein, Sery locked the first round from the roll into the breech with a speed born of long practice and watched languidly. His eyes narrowed as the vehicle picked up speed. He rocked and jerked the safety.

The vehicle didn't brake at the barrier. It crashed through, ignoring fire from the sentinel. As it slowed for the first of the dragon's teeth, Sery saw the fixed expression on the driver's face and ripped the cab with a long, sustained burst from his seven seven.

The truck exploded with a dull roar. Kekkonen clung to the parapet, clutching a second, unneeded pouch in his hand. He whispered softly, *"Jumalan kiitos!"*

Sery absently cleared the weapon and let it rest on its tripod, the barrel pointed skyward. Kekkonen's discarded cards came fluttering down one by one onto their heads. The blackened chassis of the truck lay between the first and second of the dragon's teeth.

That morning, the power from the ocean tap was turned off except for three hours each day for cooking.

* * *

BRUWER SHUT THE DOOR BEHIND HER, HER SLIGHT HESITATION affording Vereshchagin an opportunity for reflection. Her delicate features showed shock and abrasion in equal measure.

A passed pawn, Matti Harjalo had called her, a tiny, inconsequential pivot among thrones and powers. Pawns were seldom predictable. Nevertheless, one made use of the tools at hand.

Vereshchagin ran through his mind every scrap of information Raul Sanmartin had let slip over the months, slapping his borrowed pipe against the palm of his hand gently. She liked gaily colored flowers, he recalled inconsequentially, on a planet that as yet had none. As she let her hand drop from the lever that worked the door, he stood and courteously motioned her into the twin of his worn spider chair.

"Good day, Juffrou Bruwer," he said, standing to take her hand politely.

Bruwer stammered out some form of greeting in return. She seated herself, and he examined her through soft, brown eyes. Her skin was very fair; the bone structure of her body was unusually fine for an Afrikaner. Vereshchagin observed a fresh bruise, very small, on the skin of her left arm a few centimeters below the elbow.

He said carefully, "I express my regret over the death of your stepbrother. He was scarcely old enough."

She stared. After another slight hesitation, she made small words of thanks.

"Please do not thank me. I am insufficiently aware of your feelings to extend either sympathy or pity, and I see no reason to demean your intelligence by pretending that I do. Still, in cutting a tree, I spare a small prayer for the spirit I extinguish. I do no less for a man."

He paused to see if she had any inclination to share her thoughts, then said, "Tell me about yourself," settling himself patiently.

"What do you wish to know?" she countered.

"Your hopes, your fears, your dreams. Whatever it is about you that you would like me to know. I find that I need to see you as a person."

She sat very still, very stiff, with her hands folded in her lap like an errant schoolgirl. "What hopes should I have?" she asked pointedly. "My fears, they are profound. For dreams, I have ashes."

"And of Johannesburg?" he inquired gently.

"I looked out my window as the shells came in. Katrina

wished me to hide, but I stayed where I could see. I felt very helpless, very angry. Afterward, I went out into the streets. Is this what you wish me to say? *Cicatrix manet*.''

"I wish you to say what you wish to say, and I believe you are aware of this. And scars heal, or at least we pretend that they do,'' he added, acknowledging her adage. "It appears you have been much in the company of Raul.''

"I have been learning Latin. Because he is so fond of the language.'' She burst into sudden, nervous laughter, piqued by the thought, by Vereshchagin's odd manner, by the appearance of normalcy. "I'm so very sorry.''

Vereshchagin gave her a curious look with his head tilted, then interrupted gracefully as his ears detected footsteps outside. "It is difficult to picture Raul as devious, is it not? Indulge me one moment. Please come in, Timo.''

She turned, startled. Haerkoennen pushed open the door and set a tray down on folding legs as silently as he had entered. A mound of thin vegetable crisps rested on a small, round plate next to a canister of tea.

Bruwer declined tea. Vereshchagin poured himself a cup and replaced the canister. It was a custom, away from the field, to use round table plates in place of square ones after a combat death.

"Do you know Timo? Juffrou Bruwer, permit me to present to you Senior Communications Sergeant Haerkoennen. Timo, to your knowledge, does Raul speak Latin?''

"No, he does not speak the language,'' Haerkoennen replied disinterestedly.

"But he always . . .'' Bruwer began.

"I am aware that he is familiar with three to four hundred Latin tags, which is not the same.''

Bruwer looked about twice as surprised as Chiharu Yoshida when the first shell had dropped in.

"I have been told that the Eleventh Shock Battalion laid particular stress on 'Roman discipline and Samurai virtue' and expected junior officers to open staff meetings with suitable quotations. Raul fell into the habit of displaying his erudition on other occasions,'' Vereshchagin explained apologetically.

"On Ashcroft, no one much paid attention. Talking to rocks in tongues there is not especially noteworthy,'' Haerkoennen said.

Bruwer put her hand to her head for a moment. "I think then I should learn Latin after all.''

Haerkoennen looked at her gravely. He then nodded to Vereshchagin before he walked out the door with a slight bow.

Vereshchagin followed her eyes out the door. "Timo tends to make his mind up about people quickly, although with great care. We two, however, must question each other."

"I will try to answer, if I can."

"That will suffice. Does Raul care for you?" he asked.

She faltered. "I believe so. I am not certain," she admitted.

"No one ever is. The belief is sufficient. I agree, however."

"He expresses it strangely," she said bitterly.

"I have not informed him of the fact as yet, so he may not be aware. He does have other matters on his mind. We are, as you have undoubtedly observed, on the brink of a war."

"Is what is out there not war enough?" she asked.

"No, Juffrou Bruwer, it is not. There is most of heaven and all of hell between the unstable situation that exists and war. Until the Afrikaner nation has taken up arms or until I say *fiat justitia*, *ruat caelum*, let justice be done though the skies fall, there is no war."

Immediately, he softened his voice. "I realize that the heavens appear to be falling around you. You, Burgemeester Beyers, a few others, are straddling a widening abyss. Still, however likely it may be that war will manifest itself within this next week, it is not yet, and I greatly dislike inaccuracy."

"I do not understand you. Are you saying there is no war?" she asked, the unexpected way in which he expressed his thoughts dulling her intellect.

Vereshchagin ran his thumb across the surface of the pipe he was holding in his hands. "May I clarify? The situation is volatile and unstable. Within a very few days, if no cause intervenes, the fanatics who initiated this sterile conflict will begin to suppress moderation. Yet as a nation, at this moment in history, the Afrikaners have not yet chosen a course of action. Your work with Shimazu, I take it, has given you an understanding of the narrowness of the support the fanatics presently enjoy."

She made no answer for several minutes. "Are you saying that there does not have to be war?" she asked solemnly.

"The spring at its source can be turned by a twig; grown to a river, not even an elephant can cross it," Vereshchagin said. He waited to see if he had gauged her correctly.

"What could intervene? Who could intervene?" she asked.

"I do not know. I do not have a good appreciation for your people's politics," Vereshchagin said, not entirely truthfully.

"The only Afrikaner I am acquainted with of any political stature is Burgemeester Beyers, and unfortunately, events have intruded to separate us. I will not endeavor to guide his actions."

"Are you so callous"—

"Please. Understand. I am the symbol of Imperial authority. The mechanism for resolution must originate within the Volk. Were I to be seen stretching out my hand even so much as a few centimeters, I would ensure that men of blood become your rulers until such time as I harry the Afrikaner Volk into an exhausted submission. You understand, I trust, why it is that I cannot treat with these same men of blood?"

She looked at him blankly.

"Think! They have placed themselves in a position from which they may not agree, they may only dictate; they can now never believe that any man would trust them to fulfill an agreement. They must either rule or be ruled. It is the Afrikaners, equipoised, who must find themselves a voice to which I may listen, and I must show strength before I may show mercy. This I regret. Circumstances compel me to exert unselectively what Raul likes to call environmental pressure."

"If we have no word for peace?" she asked, sitting very still.

"Then I must become a grim teacher. Enough, however. You must excuse me, I have allowed myself to digress. We must discuss your future, rather than any other."

She sat quietly and allowed him to continue, her rebelliousness quiescent.

"You understand," Vereshchagin continued, "that when war comes, you will be forced to choose. In many respects our hands will be no cleaner than those of your compatriots."

She failed to respond.

"Some, many of your people will take up arms. You may join them. Alternately, you may cast your lot with us at the risk of severing yourself from the Volk, perhaps forever. What you may not do is equivocate; for you as for us all there is no third choice."

"I believe you."

"Thank you. I rarely find it necessary to lie."

"If I were to choose the other? What then of Raul?"

"Leave Raul to me."

"Don't you ever stop playing the puppeteer, pulling his strings?"

"Young woman, for years I have had to say, 'This one lives, this one dies.' To make no decision is itself a decision."

"What choice do you leave me? I betray my people or I betray myself."

"I find the word 'betray' inappropriate. I must ask you to enunciate what future it is your people seek before I will permit you to speak of betrayal."

"What future does His Imperial Majesty offer us?" she countered.

Vereshchagin began examining his pipe in his hands minutely. "There is a state secret I shall confide to you. Whatever instructions His Majesty's government gave Vice-Admiral Lee seem to have taken a bath in nuclear fire. I suspect that by the time I discover what those instructions were, we may both be old and gray. For planetary policy, it appears I shall be compelled to rely upon my best judgment."

He gave her a moment to reflect upon that. Her eyes widened.

"You still have a decision abeyant, do you not? Would you care for some advice? Of course you would not, but you are unnaturally polite. In choosing sides, I permit my conscience to guide me. Because it is such a poor beacon, I end up selecting persons I would prefer to associate with."

She laughed despite herself, charmed by such a marvelous answer.

"I will give you one assurance. If you cast your lot with Raul, I will ensure, by means fair or foul, that if Raul ever leaves this planet, you will be aboard the same ship."

"It seems a strange arrangement," she said halfheartedly.

"You cannot imagine how irregular it is."

"I must think. Perhaps I must speak to Raul. For the rest of it, it doesn't matter. Whatever is best."

"Acceptable. Please give my regards to your grandfather."

She stared at him a moment and then left without a word.

A moment later, Harjalo materialized in his accustomed place. "You look terrible, Anton."

"Matti, I do not believe that I have ever done anything quite this foolish. Since the day that Sir Harry Smith conquered the Voortrekker republics at Boomplatz and the British government made him give them back, her nation has been on a collision course with destiny. Stop smiling like that, you will hurt your face."

"Anton, this penchant of yours for testing people to destruction is going to destroy someone you care about sooner or later," Harjalo said, momentarily serious.

"She may pass very well, thank you. You predicted she would. We shall see."

"It isn't her that I worry about," Harjalo said, now quite serious. "Why don't we let them tear each other's throats for the next ten generations. Is it really worth all the lying and conniving to settle a five-yen war on a five-yen planet for a five-sen dividend on USS preferred stock? Wouldn't you like to climb aboard *Shokaku* and steer for Esdraelon?"

"Do you remember what Arto said about Ashcroft?"

Harjalo laughed. "I do! He said, 'Of course this war's important! I'm in it.' "

"I understand the skin graft took well, and all his fingers work." Vereshchagin's face showed sadness. "There was a certain nobility to Arto."

"Well, now you've had your conversation with the little Bruwer."

"Matti, tell me, am I really going as soft as I think I am?"

"Yes and yes."

"But a battalion is composed of human beings, is it not?"

"And if you ever forgot that, I'd have to shoot you and take command myself." He brightened. "Of course, then I could shoot Tingrin, which would almost make it worthwhile."

IRONICALLY, RAUL SANMARTIN WAS ENGAGED IN A SIMILAR MIS-sion.

Seated across the desk from him, in response to his request Solchava protested mildly, "But there is no medical need."

Dislodged by events, the unshakeable air had visibly dropped away from her. Sanmartin picked it up and dusted it off.

"I don't recall saying there was. I said there was a military need, which isn't precisely the same." He held up one of the thickened glassene needles that fitted to the sensors to puzzle out the pattern of the circuitry before looking up. "You understand, we're not exactly doing this for fun and frolic."

"No, I do not understand," she said sharply. "There must be a medical purpose. I do not cut on persons for 'fun' as you say."

He laid the transponder down on the desk between them and reached into his pocket to pull out a document. "Read this through."

She took it from his hand uncertainly and read it through. Solchava was disturbed by the seemingly senseless violence of the past several days, an advantage, but a slight one. He momentarily wondered whether he would have been better off hunting up one of Eva Moore's drones, but rumors ultimately emanating from the little clown in biochem were floating all about the hospital company; the risk that someone there would add four and four and come up with forty-four was too great.

So too, he knew Solchava. The infantry always inherited the dirtiest jobs, and for the moment he despised Eva Moore, who had cared too much and left a job that needed doing to the Variag instead.

Solchava glanced up and exposed the surface of the paper with an unconscious gesture. "This appears to be a consent, like a medical consent in form. He accepts Imperial authority and agrees to any measures necessary to ensure this acceptance. I do not understand."

Sanmartin reached into his pocket and pulled out a wad of documents. "I have thirty-nine more," he said agreeably, "and it looks like a medical consent because I wanted it to look that way." The neat pieces of paper were multipurpose tools. He threw it on the desk.

"There's a signed consent from each of them. Are you going to dispute our right to shove transponders in their rumps?"

She thought this through carefully. "To what purpose will this be done?" she asked, conceding the point.

Sanmartin exhaled deeply. If Solchava had disputed legalities, it would have been difficult to obtain a legal ruling from the brigade advocate, who'd been slagged with the spaceport.

He plucked the scalpel from her pocket and turned it on, adjusting the ruby-red cutting edge to a thickness of one centimeter and a length of two.

"They've been told to stay home, and we mean it. If I give them a parole and we catch them a week from now, gun in hand, we'll shoot every mother's son." He held up one of the transponders he wanted her to insert in his forty Boers.

"These things are inert until I send a signal, at which point we know exactly where these men are." That wasn't all there was to them, but that was as much as Sanmartin intended to tell her. "If they're carrying hardware around in their tails and they're not where they're supposed to be, we'll have an opportunity to persuade them we're serious before we line them up on walls. If they're lucky."

Solchava looked at him bleakly, perhaps thinking of the dying that had already been done. "If they won't be persuaded, as you say?"

"Doctor, whatever pity I have left I ration among the deserving. In this battalion, from this battalion, people get one warning and might consider themselves lucky to have received that." He turned the tiny laser off.

"What would they have done instead? Not sign, I suppose," she retorted.

Sanmartin grinned mirthlessly. "Two men didn't. I expect they'll be on Henke's island for the rest of their unnatural lives." He didn't add that they were probably better off. Instead he laid the scalpel down and looked at her.

"Doctor, when I tell my company what the rules of the game are, we play by those rules. We may bend every last one, but we play by the rules. And some of those are very hard rules, indeed. But I'll make you a deal. Any of these boys we catch with a rifle in the next week we won't bother shooting. They're yours. We'll give them to you."

It was undoubtedly cold-blooded to treat what was intended to be both a strategic and a tactical advantage as a humanitarian gesture, but as Sanmartin had indicated, while he didn't break rules, he bent them.

He picked up the scalpel again and held it out. "You're a surgeon. Cut."

Solchava nodded slowly.

Of course, Sanmartin did have one unfair advantage he was aware of. A small part of Solchava wanted to please the Variag more than anything else, and that was a positional weakness you could drive light armor through.

THE ICEMAN'S COMPANY WAS ROCKETED THAT NIGHT. FOUR ROCKets exploded within the perimeter, but a fifth never came as his mortars fixed the launcher's position and pinned it. Riflemen infiltrating from his outposts were too slow to catch the screen of Boer riflemen, but they did bring back the mangled launcher and two bodies, the eldest of three brothers in a Bloemfontein family.

The last rocket landed in a farmer's field, fifty meters from the room where his children were sleeping. The lord mayor of Bloemfontein was assassinated that night in his bed, having declined Kolomeitsev's offer of a cot inside the perimeter.

Thursday(13)

THREE DAYS HARD WORK BY WHAT WAS LEFT OF THE ENGINEER construction battalion had served to lay out a shuttle strip on Henke's island in addition to facilities for fixed-wing aircraft, but it would require some weeks to make that shuttle strip operable. Vereshchagin did not have weeks at his disposal. Instead he boarded one of the Shidens and rode the plane to its maximum altitude.

He ejected at twelve kilometers. The shuttle from *Shokaku* flying low and slow caught up the wire array streaming from his harness to bring him aboard for the remainder of the journey.

They docked. Thanking the crew, he entered the bay. There he returned without comment the salute of the senior surviving naval officer.

The young commander was eager to make a favorable impression, perhaps overly so. He showed Vereshchagin the arrangements made for the transportation of the more recalcitrant Afrikaners, and after enduring this and other wearisome formalities, Vereshchagin was able to assess the man to his satisfaction. Nodding his head at the prompting of an unseen Muse, he excused himself when they reached Admiral Lee's cabin. Unsealing it, he passed within, a weighted dispatch case under his arm. He left the slightly startled young officer standing in the corridor.

He emerged three hours later without comment and wasted another twenty minutes being civil, declining lunch before entering the shuttle for his return.

Aloft, when the shuttle began to hit atmosphere, the pilot depressurized the passenger compartment and spoke. "Sir, we must release you about three kilometers northwest of the island to account for drift."

Vereshchagin acknowledged. He had expected that.

When the jump light came on, with brief words of thanks, Vereshchagin stepped past the crewman in the gleaming ceramet suit into the thin air. Drifting down, he waited the many minutes for his chute to open and watched the shuttle disappear from his view. Unhurriedly, he began unfastening the weighted dispatch case from his harness.

When he opened his chute and began to check his descent, he let the dispatch case slip from his hand. Guiding his risers toward the slender gouge of the unfinished runway, Vereshchagin watched the case and its contents plummet into the water beneath his feet. The die was cast.

Anticipating his return to Pretoria, Timo Haerkoennen sped out into the hall on his way from Bukanov's workstation.

Bukanov was deep in contingency planning for removing Boers. The text solution was wholesale concentration of the rural populations, leaving the rest as a tightly controlled shield against nuclear attack. An operation to evacuate by force sixty or seventy thousand people from their homes was a shambles by definition, but if the Variag decided to see it through, there was no reason why it couldn't be a well-planned shambles. Bottlenecks would be construction, transportation, and the savage resistance the operation would spawn.

If the Variag did implement it, Chiharu Yoshida would play a major role. Haerkoennen glanced through the open doorway of Yoshida's temporary quarters.

Yoshida was nestled behind the low table, holding the stroke brush, the *tsuketate-fude* at arm's length, waiting patiently for his heart to quiet, glistening *sumi* poised in the ink stone. Familiar both with Japanese culture and art forms, Haerkoennen watched entranced.

Yoshida practiced brush strokes daily. Today, it was simple *hiragana*, to ease the mind.

Tingrin was off to Henke's island in a matter of hours. The Variag wanted someone to whip his prisoners and their warders into line. It would not do either for the more militant Boers to push the rest into cabals or for the former artillerymen to brutalize their charges. His talents would not be wasted.

Haerkoennen watched as, first with the hard, then with the soft of the brush, Yoshida attacked the stark white of the paper, impressing it with his boldness and infusing it with his temper. The inscription that he was copying out was banal—to Haerkoennen illegible—which had nothing to do whatever with the intrinsic merit of the exercise.

Haerkoennen understood Japanese very well. He did not speak it. In Haerkoennen's view, foreigners who spoke Japanese ended up mouthing polite, homogenized phrases of deference and solicitude bearing no relationship to the feelings underlying the words. It was strange the Japanese didn't get along better with the Boers; both were products of closed societies, sheltered and contained. He stepped aside from the open door before Yoshida noticed his presence.

Tingrin's outburst in front of Vereshchagin had been uncharacteristic, not Japanese. In Haerkoennen's opinion, his cathartic reaction to Matti Harjalo's studied brutality might eventually right his shattered imbalance.

And if it didn't, well, there was a war on.

Yoshida completed his flowing lunge with grace and force. He exhaled heavily. He then looked to the result.

The left-hand *ro* was vague, uncertain. Flawed. Yoshida picked up the sheet, divided it into two equal parts with a single motion and consigned the halves to a growing pile of wasted efforts. Another sheet was gone from his dwindling stock. By that much was he diminished.

The *sensei* cleaned and replaced his brushes; from his eyes the glow faded, and once more Chiharu Yoshida paused to consider the cares of the world that had thrust themselves upon him.

COLDEWE LOOKED AROUND, HALF EXPECTING TO SEE THE LITtle Bruwer. "Kasha, you see Raul and Berry anywhere?"

Bruwer had reverted, taking her meals at irregular intervals and hiding like a mouse in Shimazu's office.

"No," Kasha said glumly. "You know what's with those two?"

Coldewe shook his head. Security was bleeding tight any time Kasha didn't know what was going on.

"What's the word on the sneak?" he asked.

Kasha shook her hair free. "He was at the port when the port got it."

Coldewe grunted. It wouldn't be easy to find somebody as loyally dishonest as Grigorenko. "We're pulling in the surveillance teams in an hour, and they're going to be hungry."

"No problem."

"You see Bruwer?"

Kasha shook her head in an emphatic, semispastic manner.

As far as Coldewe knew, Bruwer hadn't spoken to Sanmartin for several days, not since seeing the townspeople of Johannesburg sweeping up their sons and lovers—occasionally their wives and daughters—from the streets. A few of them had spit at her, one had thrown a stone and hit her on the arm.

Two strong and silent types, Coldewe thought to himself venomously. Sanmartin had forgotten what little he'd learned about being a human being, and Bruwer hadn't learned enough to forget. He allowed Kasha to shove a cup of tea in his hands. The warmth from the tea seeped into his body, but it didn't erase the chill. When he stomped into quarters, the weariness of the night and the long morning still clung to his body like a shroud. He leaned against the doorframe.

"Hello, Hans. Luck?" Sanmartin asked. He moved to one side of the room and rested the palm of one hand on the wall as high as he could reach.

"I have twelve teams covering twenty-four farms and villages. Maybe tomorrow we'll pick the right twenty-four."

"No. Bring them in. We'll need them rested," was Sanmartin's clipped contribution as he walked back to the other wall.

Coldewe didn't ask and didn't argue. Sanmartin spared him a look. "You get some rest, too. You look like you were walking all night."

"I was. I will. What about you?"

Sanmartin didn't answer. A chess game was set up on a low table. White was partway through a variation on the Max Lange Attack: old, perilous, still one of the most complicated openings in chess. Coldewe palmed a fallen knight, then set it aside and lay down on his hammock.

"This is where you are," a feminine voice said.

Coldewe made an effort to open his eyes. Bruwer was another one aligned on an edge. "I'm sorry about your stepbrother."

She ignored him. "I asked Kasha to show me in," she said, to which of them was not clear. She sat down gingerly in the room's only chair, saying nothing. Sanmartin continued his minute inspection of the cracks in the wall.

Coldewe sat up and folded his arms. "All right, both of you, I don't care anymore whether you drive each other crazy, but you're starting to make me nervous. I'll referee if you like."

Sanmartin turned his head.

"So what happens, now? Have you a Latin saying for it?" Bruwer asked him sharply.

"*Homi homini lupus.*" It was from Plutarch. Man is a wolf toward man. "You don't understand, do you? We kill a few more, and a few more after that. It's gangrene. If we don't cauterize it, it'll spread. I wish we'd gotten a thousand more, that might have set a few people thinking. Lord of heaven, some of the silly toads out there probably think they won a victory."

"But you cannot win either!"

"We'll call it a victory. Bet?" he said evenly.

"No, you are serious. You are hiding something," she said, studying his face.

"Yes. And I'm not the only one. What do you think this is? Some kind of silly game out of Hans's romances?"

She was close enough in the narrow room to hit him. She rolled her fist and struck him hard across the side of the face.

His head snapped. Then looking at her, he deliberately took the emotion from his voice. "You'll hurt your hand like that. If you want to do it, do it right. Use a piece of pipe." He walked away. As she angrily turned to follow, Coldewe materialized beside her and grasped her wrist firmly. She attempted to wrench it free and was surprised by the strength in his frail shoulders.

"You don't understand. He's right about that, anyway. Try gulping air, you look like you're going to pop."

She sighed. The anger drained out of her. "He is so changed. Is it because of Rudi and Major Rettaglia?"

"What do you mean changed?" Coldewe asked, taken aback.

She struggled for words and looked to the floor in embarrassment.

Coldewe tilted her chin up so he could look at her. "I actually think I understand. Circumstances have changed. He's no different. Not since he arrived, not in what counts. Not yet." He looked into her blue, blue eyes. "You don't think the Variag gave him a company because he won a spelling prize? His mother taught him what little he knows; she was a professor before she got listed. She gave him a transit ticket on his birthday and went out to the Plaza Federale to talk herself into a twenty year sentence. If she hadn't made him join up, they'd probably be in the same cell. His father you know about."

She nodded her head mutely.

"He doesn't start off thinking the universe is friendly, and he doesn't start off thinking the universe is fair. Since then, the Variag's had him." Coldewe thought for a minute.

"You've met the Variag. He's kind and gentle, but ask Kasha how this battalion cleaned NovySibor. Reds and Whites, kinsmen and countrymen once removed, they couldn't stand each other, and this battalion got the job after Ishizu lost more men in the cross fire than he was prepared to tolerate.

"He had them identify each other's fanatics and sent the Iceman on a ratissage. The Iceman culled fifty agitators aside and lined them up on the walls, two by two. They got buried with military honors, their families got transported, and the survivors got an appreciation for what constitutes acceptable behavior." He released her arm to leave behind finger-width marks of red.

"They were averaging two or three a day on their own. The Variag was a little more selective about it. Raul and I haven't been around as long, but we both did things on Ashcroft that weren't exactly friendly. That's what they send us out for. We finish wars other people start. Your boyfriend knows that. He doesn't need you to tell him. I don't think he likes it much.''

She hung her head. ''In the villages, wives are pushing their husbands out the doors to fight.''

''Yesterday, he got a call from Albert Beyers's wife, who is probably the only woman on the planet with a half gram of sense. Her son wanted to join up, and she told Raul to come pack him up and salt him away until the idiots stop playing with people's lives.''

He gestured toward the departed Raul. ''Consider it a compliment that you're the only one he likes enough to lash out at. I'll talk manners into him. Maybe some sense, too. But if you're still collecting Latin quotes, he's got a favorite that he used to use on Ashcroft all the time, *mutatis mutandis*.''

''Necessary changes having been made,'' she translated.

It was said that there was once a particularly gentle Viking who was known as ''the children's man'' because he would not impale captive children on the point of his spear, as was the custom among his companions.

Friday(13)

''MATTI, IF WE NEED TO LAY OUR HANDS ON SOME QUALITY electronics, where would we go?'' Vereshchagin asked as he waited for the remainder of his senior officers to appear.

''Anything that Koryagin doesn't have squirreled away is down at Complex if it exists at all. Lord of heaven knows, we stole enough, Yuri and I. Why?''

''You might call it curiosity.''

''Curiosity, say you. Are you going to tell me what you and Raul are about? You've been quiet for three entire days. Raul has been bustling about like a busy little bee, and it didn't take him and Beregov flitting off to Complex to tell me that there's some strange scent in the breeze.''

''Patience is occasionally a virtue, Matti.'

''I know. I play my lines better when I haven't read the script. I assume you know that the cowboys are in trouble down south. Some sort of fungal infestation is ripping through their wheat. It looks like it could be native, but—''

''The timing is suspiciously apt.'' The Boers could grow no wheat, only glutenized sorghum and millet.

"Correct." Harjalo's frown deepened. "I hear Yuri's foot-steps, is it that time already?"

The echo of the slight hobble in the battalion sergeant's tread was distinct. Lassotovich's hard-luck team had missed return, and Malinov looked older than his years.

"Yes, Matti. I think that it is time," Vereshchagin replied.

After he had them assembled, Vereshchagin examined the G Company commander and Ebyl's representative before turning his attention. "Have you something, Raul?" he asked formally.

"We have three camps located. We can hit them tonight. Not before."

The look on Harjalo's face at the appearance of this rabbit was priceless. Ebyl's man, a sleepy-faced lieutenant named Ohlrogge, glanced up from the table with sharp interest.

Sanmartin looked at the other faces around the table and se-lected Matti for a foil. "Matti, do you remember all those in-nocent little Afrikaners I let go?"

"At the time, I thought your circuits were warped. Out of forty of the little toads, forty are out there shooting at us by now. Myself, I'm a little tired of hearing 'We're just poor little Dutch boys.' "

Sanmartin smiled, a thin, cold wraith of a smile. "Twenty-seven of them anyway, we picked up the rest with apologies. The twenty-seven may be out shooting at us, but we sent them out in the big, wide world with transponders in their funda-ments. I triggered them three hours ago. We won't be able to pull the same trick twice, but we may not have to. For myself, I've logged in an excursion to Krugersdorp."

Harjalo studied his face. "Rettaglia was right," he said fi-nally. "There is an underhanded side to you. Have we had a better offer today, Anton?"

"Not that I recall," Vereshchagin said guilelessly. He looked around the room. "Elandslaagte Farm for you, Paul. You may have number twenty-six Gurkha platoon and you may have the aircraft first. Nelspruit for Piotr. Ebyl has two companies within striking distance; they are yours and the Gurkha provisional platoon as well. Raul may have number twenty-seven platoon. The recon and the engineers will be divided among you. The rest of the Gurkhas will go to local security. Mask and quaran-tine. Matti, please remain behind," he declared firmly, and no one asked him why. After a moment, he asked, "Well, gentle-men, what are we waiting upon?" with a hint of his old vivacity.

Sanmartin stood up from his chair. This one was going to be different, Hans had said. This time, the good guys would win.

"Did I play up too much?" Harjalo asked after the room had cleared.

"No, you did just right, Matti," Vereshchagin said wistfully. The games we play to make soldiers of them, he thought. The ones that live, he amended. "Matti, the commander of G Company is eager, but sadly lacking in experience. I shall need you to quietly take a hand to keep him healthy and occupied."

"Raul?"

"Is growing up. He will have Lev along. I think that we shall let him manage on his own."

By the time Sanmartin returned to Jo'burg, *Ajax* had done three timed passes over Krugersdorp and the surrounding forest and broken the pictures down into half-meter stills. Yevtushenko and Beregov had them out of the cannister and neatly on the floor for examination with a magnifier, examining them on their knees. Yevtushenko brought four teams from the recon platoon.

"You didn't waste time," he commented, elbowing his way in to peer at pictures of the church.

Krugersdorp was the smallest of the three targets. Although difficult to access, the town consisted of a bare four dozen buildings. The Boers inside the town would be concentrated without the breathing room necessary for a successful defense.

"They're inside, all right. In the village," Beregov said flatly. He pointed to one of the offending stills. "If this isn't a bunker, I'll buy it and deed it to my grandchildren."

"Lev?"

"Too many people floating through. Look at the foot traffic up to the warehouses along the northeast rim. Barracks. Maybe a few people in the forest where we're getting a dappling effect," Yevtushenko replied judiciously.

"What about bunkers?"

"I see one at either end. Three more covering the road. There's dead foliage covering them, with traces of plastic netting showing on the infrared shots."

Sanmartin stood and stretched. "Berry, I think we have the makings of a plan."

THE SUN WAS FALLING, WHICH MADE IT AN UNUSUAL HOUR FOR an exchange of views. Vereshchagin's two guests were clearly somewhat ill at ease.

Nadine Joh had survived her sister. James McClausland,

"Little Jim," had stepped into his father's place. Between them, they could speak for as many of the ranchers as mattered.

Vereshchagin invited them to sit. "I am prepared to tell you that efforts are in progress to end the conflict with the Afrikaners. In order to ensure a genuine peace, I require your assistance in restraining your colleagues and their followers."

This statement was clearly not one Little Jim had expected. "What are you, some creeping Boer-lover? There isn't a family that doesn't have its dead. They killed my father! They killed a couple thousand Imps! They're out there laughing with guns in their fists, and you talk about making peace?"

Nadine Joh smiled a worldly, cynical smile that her mouth hid. Vereshchagin blinked his eyes.

"It is rather trite to so state, but killing a few thousand more Boers will not return your father. We have bled the Boers rather badly, and we will do so again. However, your cooperation, although helpful, is not essential.

"You might be interested to learn that the USS director moved about a great deal without an adequate explanation for his movements. This was coupled with a slight shortfall in his company's ammunition stocks which he apparently did not expect us to monitor. I had him shot fifteen minutes ago."

Young McClausland, scion of a great house, had no idea what that meant. Nadine Joh did. Yugo Tuge had continued to believe almost up to the moment he was strapped in his chair that it was merely a matter of working out the proper arrangement. He had died very badly.

"I dislike having people maneuver behind my back," Vereshchagin continued. "I am not disposed to wage a genocidal struggle against the Afrikaner nation. I am concerned with channeling energies into positive paths. Do we understand one another?"

Vereshchagin left young McClausland to the Joh's tender ministrations and turned his back on the cowboy country to concern himself with more immediate problems.

WHEN DARKNESS FELL, THEY MOVED OUT SILENTLY IN SINGLE file. It was an easy three-kilometer walk to where the tilt-props would be waiting to carry them further.

Sanmartin had his three rifle platoons plus a recon section. Coldewe and Okladnikov, the other arm on the pincers, would rendezvous with the armor, an engineer team, three mortars, the fourth recon team, and the Gurkhas.

Beregov had been left behind with the fourth mortar, still more of Higuchi's orphans, and a fair percentage of the heavy weapons that had stuck to Matti Harjalo's fingers. His task was to maintain the illusion that C for Chiba was where it was supposed to be for the benefit of any toads in the bushes.

Wheels had been set into motion, to grind swiftly and exceedingly fine. Nocturnal activities were occurring on a massive scale. After the big birds lifted Sanmartin off, they would go back to pick up the Iceman. The Gurkha provisional platoon would spearhead the Iceman's assault. Radiation sickness was beginning to consolidate its grip on them. They didn't walk well, but they were very, very angry. Ebyl's companies moving north along the Red River Road from Chalkton were the hammer that would smash the largest of the three laagers against Kolomeitsev's anvil. The third objective was the Hangman's. Ground-attack aircraft and copters would fly off just before contact was made.

It was about 25°C, but it felt cold to Sanmartin. It was better to think about the approach march.

The tilt would ground eleven kay out. From the stereoscopic photos *Ajax* had transmitted, parallel to the Paarl River the ferntrees at ridge-level were thirty meters high; that was almost as good as a road on a planet that did not have Earth's woody vines and shrubs.

Once off the ridge, Sanmartin and No. 11 would let themselves in through the back door quietly, liberally equipped with unauthorized silencers. Karaev's platoon would provide flank support until they were actually inside. They would then seize an isolated group of four houses and seal off the northeast end of town. Gavrilov and No. 10 would be the stopper, spread to fire up anyone breaking out toward the mines.

When the back door was taken care of, Hans and Sergei Okladnikov would beat down the front.

Based on the tracking from *Ajax*, the Boers were wandering from the village up into the forest the villagers had planted almost casually. Sanmartin hoped that they were equally casual about answering the doorbell. If they weren't, Yevtushenko might have occasion for a little knife work.

It was the sort of harebrained scheme that might actually work. He had said as much to Hanna.

That had been the hardest task, sitting down and telling Hanna what he had done, what he was about to do. He remembered leaving her, sitting on her bolstered bed, looking into the wall with her hands squeezed together.

Abruptly the tilt-prop set down.

Moving silently, left around the first tree and right around the second, Sanmartin's column crept through, trusting to night goggles. Entombed as they were in utter blackness, even starlight magnification was useless, and only the black wands they carried gave illumination, painting the night in vivid burgundy red.

In front, Yevtushenko paused ritually every ten meters to check his compass bearings with a quick flip of his wrist. Although he had a feel for the slope of the terrain, he didn't depend upon that alone to navigate. Padding softly through the night with a step that never altered, he counted his steps in his mind so that he knew exactly how far he had come.

The virgin ridges were crested by true, double-canopied rain forest, a silent, magnificent cathedral of somber black and green. The thick pillars of the trees flowed up into the sky like green spikes. Running streams of water ran down scaled trunks spread to cut off the starlight twenty and twenty-five meters over their heads. A second roof formed at ten meters where a different species of ferntree topped out.

Jan Snyman walked with Muslar's No. 11 platoon, as a medic's aide to Mario Vincente. "Who picked this route?" he asked the man who came up next to him in a whisper. "He has a taste for shit."

"I don't know," Sanmartin answered, more or less inaudibly, "but we ought to shoot him." Scandalized, Vincente hissed "*Sjuut!* No noise." Sanmartin clapped a startled Jan Snyman softly on the back and moved up in the column.

HAERKOENNEN LOOKED UP FROM THE COM. "MAJOR KOLOMEIT-sev thinks he may have lost the benefit of surprise. He requests instructions."

"Tell him to use his best judgement, Timo," Vereshchagin directed inexorably.

Haerkoennen held his hand over the mike. "Sir, I am certain he will continue his mission as planned if I say this. Why risk the casualties?"

"Timo, it will cost us less in the long run if they remember that they were beaten this night rather than tricked into surrender or defeated by a germ."

For nine hours, twenty-seven men with transponders had been silently spreading the disease that would fragment the Boer armies, but it would be best if their sons remembered the plague as a mercy that spared the Volk further evidence of the Imperials' wrath.

"A few thousand men," he added, including Ebyl's battalion and the others, "cannot control a world, even this one. The leaders on the other side recognize this. In adversity, it is their strength. What they do not realize is that we can reshape the situation to make it possible for us to control it."

Haerkoennen nodded, satisfied, and began to deliver crisp instructions to the Iceman.

On the outskirts of Nelspruit, the hour struck. A swarm of little men, angry and sick, scrambled out of the forest screaming "Ayo Gurkhali." Five of them went down, a man named Ale, a Pun, and three Thapas. Then the rest were among the startled Boers of the Bethlehem kommando, who had dug themselves into a shallow position like pigs in a sty for companionship.

The Bethlehem men who bolted were the lucky ones. The others learned about the downward-curving Gurkha kukris. Jankowskie's No. 1 platoon left Higuchi's orphans to finish the men of Bethlehem and passed through.

At that hour in Johannesburg, Hanna Bruwer rose up and changed her clothing, putting a gray pullover and dark trousers on her body, sturdy shoes on her feet. Passing through the silent structure, she left by the door and made her way to the southeast outpost, waving to the two little Gurkhas manning it. As they had strict orders not to fire on her under any circumstances, they waved back. Threading her way down a hidden path through the wheat, she guided her feet toward the silent, deserted streets.

She paused at No. 27 Viljoenstraat, thinking about what Raul Sanmartin had said. Perhaps it was foolish to allow him to be so close that he could hurt her, but there it was. He had said that just as there was a balance in nature, there was a political balance in men that could not be tipped too far, too fast, without incalculable consequences. This was true.

He had told her what he had planned. He had also told her personal things with the thought that he would not come back.

He had left, she remembered, weighted by implements of his trade, having pushed into her unwilling hands as much trust as he could fairly give her and perhaps a little more.

She rapped on the door very softly. Inside, there was the faint glow of a light, but nothing more.

"It is only I, there is no one else," she said in Afrikaans in a muted voice. "It is safe for you to open."

The glow of the light disappeared. Albert Beyers opened the door with a hard look on his face. "Come in quickly," he replied in the same language. When the door had closed behind her, he bolted it and chanced making a light. Behind him was his wife, holding a heavy stone rolling pin in her hands.

"Have you no sense?" Beyers demanded in a harsh whisper. "What possessed you? Do you not remember there is a curfew?"

"Hush, Albert," his wife replied more calmly. She craned her neck forward a few centimeters. "You are the Bruwer girl, I recognize you now. You must pardon my eyesight. I must have lenses inserted and have not troubled to do so. What is it?"

"Heer burgemeester, I have a task for you," Bruwer said as she seated herself heavily and began massaging her calves, the tensions of the last week weighting her voice oppressively.

Beyers's wife made as if to leave. "No, you stay!" Bruwer said. "This concerns you as well."

She began to explain.

SHUFFLING THEIR FEET THROUGH A RUDE PARODY OF A SENTRY round, bored sentries stood outside a rude parody of a bunker close by the forest edge of Krugersdorp. Above them rose the spine of the southernmost ridge, sheltering the vale where Krugersdorp lay. Although a sentry round was more appropriate to guarding a post office than to manning an outpost, it passed the time and made the young miners feel military.

As the two of them came together, there was a series of small sounds in the brush ten meters away, and they spun away from one another to flop on the ground like drunken marionettes.

One man sitting outside the bunker to escape the heat climbed the top step without his weapon, his face wreathed in anxiety. As his body straightened, a thin, whirling splinter of plastic caught him squarely in the chest. He toppled back.

Two shadowy forms emerged from the forest cover at a dead run. As the first reached the step, his feet came out from under him on a wet spot, and he desperately maintained his balance long enough to empty his magazine through the open doorway before crashing to the bottom.

The clicking of the bolt was echoed by duller thuds as the rounds sprayed around and off the inside walls. Yevtushenko regained his feet with infinite care; two of the escaping rounds had passed back out the door close by his head. Shining his light within, he saw three huddled figures. He removed his knife from where it stuck out of the corpse between his legs, and he passed within momentarily.

Coming out, he saw Thomas standing at the top of the steps with the silliest grin on his pinched face. Without any trace of an expression, Yevtushenko loaded another magazine. He wiped the blood off his knife on a dead Afrikaner's trouser leg.

Sanmartin moved out from cover to join them. "Well, we're here," he said softly. Yevtushenko nodded.

Sanmartin looked up toward the thin spire of the church tower looming over them, shrouded in the darkness, before looking back to Yevtushenko.

"Lev, as the hedgehog said to his wife, let's go easy."

OKLADNIKOV CURSED FREELY. THE DRONE OF THE TRANSPORT'S engines muted his comments.

When the light attack went in by air, most of the time the big transports could find themselves a nice, clear patch to settle on so that he could drive his vehicles off like a gentleman with his cuffs buttoned, but "most of the time" was like egg roll. Egg roll yesterday, egg roll tomorrow, but never egg roll today. Everything in the vicinity of the designated landing zone that wasn't swamp was either hot and bothered or forested over. Coldewe's Gurkhas and even the mortars and slicks could move between the trees, but the only good place for the Cadillacs to insert was right in the middle of the river.

Okladnikov felt his stomach part company with the rest of his insides as the transport abruptly lost altitude. Squandering his store of maledictions freely, he worked his way through the generation of Boers immediately preceding the one that had settled Suid-Afrika in a flat monotone as the tail opened out and the ring chute deployed.

He was still cursing when the ring chute opened and dragged his Cadillac out the rear of the aircraft, to plop it into the pond from an altitude of two meters.

The armored car bobbed up and down, more or less gently. Okladnikov concluded his litany in a harsh whisper as he released the catch that held the chute to the vehicle. A small wave washed over the vehicle's hull as the next Cadillac came down, the second transport roaring overhead with a scant four-meter clearance. Okladnikov grinned as he began to loosen the straps that held him in place. If he pulled a Prigal and the engine didn't catch, he'd drift halfway out to sea.

He shoved his head out the hatch. Coldewe was waiting on the embankment.

"Hey, Sergei. The road looks all right. Zerebtsov's boys took out the picket."

The logging road was crooked as grandmother's snake and

probably mined. As for the picket, the Boers had the theory down but their execution left a lot to be desired. The computer on *Ajax* had tracked vehicles all over the planet, and even after the ban on traffic had gone into effect, they'd continued driving reliefs out to spare the little lads' feet. The last time through, a Hummingbird had been along to watch where everyone got out.

"Anybody hurt dropping?"

Coldewe grinned white against the darkness. "One and a half casualties."

Okladnikov gave him a hurt look. "How do you get half a casualty?"

"Salchow dropped in the top canopy and lost his rope. Zerebtsov's boys are too busy giggling to get him down."

Okladnikov guffawed as he shepherded his wet vehicles ashore. The Gurkhas climbed aboard, and they started down the trail in close formation. In front, the little utility vehicle heading the column dipped and yawed. Occasionally, the engineer in the passenger seat would look up from his equipment and heave a handful of flour over the side to mark anomalies for the trailing vehicles. Where the roadbed wasn't firm, the blower in front kicked up a small cloud of dust.

"Think they'll know we're coming?" Okladnikov asked of Coldewe.

While Coldewe was considering a reply, the driver of the utility vehicle veered right and then suddenly widened his swerve. The stream of particles from the blower touched off the mine; the counter in the mine held up under the ion bombardment just long enough to trigger the explosion almost under the front wheels. The vehicle flipped neatly on its side and skidded away as about three meters of the roadbed disappeared, the explosion shredding the silence. The engineer rolled over and sat up clutching his shoulder from where he had been flung; the blood belonged to the deceased driver. The shattered wheel spun badly, trailing strings of melted plastic.

Coldewe replied, "They just might."

Six kilometers away, Hendrik Pienaar awoke and found that he was unable to return to sleep. He scratched his gray beard moodily and put his boots on, pausing to ruminate.

Sometimes a feeling was worth more than a thousand textbooks of military tactics. He had such a feeling, but it refused to place itself in words. It was a feeling he could not remember experiencing since the missile boat had pulled him off the beach at Hoedjes Bay in the final days.

* * *

THOMAS MOVED UP TO THE FIRST OF THE CONCRETE STRUCTURES and glanced up at the walls. A handful of small windows broke up the creamy surface at ground level. They were closed.

"Praise be for air conditioning," he whispered under his breath. He shined his black light in the window and saw long rows of bunk beds.

"Three and three," Thomas whispered inaudibly. Looking around the side, he saw Yevtushenko test the door. Satisfied, Yevtushenko took a small tube of glue from his pouch and squirted it in the lock mechanism. He nodded to Thomas, his profile rendered grotesque by the mottled outline of his mask.

Holstering his submachine gun and flipping the black light into his pouch, Thomas removed instead a suction cup that he attached to the window and tested for a secure fit. Then he unsheathed his cutting bar and slashed a rude diamond in the glass around the suction cup. Sheathing the cutting bar, he held the suction cup and rapped the diamond with the back of his gloved hand. It came away, and he set it aside.

Then he reached up to his harness and felt among his stock-in-trade for the smooth shape of a plastic-cased chem grenade. Removing the safety pin, he counted to three, stuck his arm in the hole, and lobbed the grenade in the center of the room, where it bounced under a bunk and exploded with a soft pop.

Yevtushenko calmly handed him four strips of tape slashed from the roll he carried in his pouch. Inattentive to the men dying inside, Thomas carefully taped over the hole in the window. He then cut a small piece of his own tape to cover a small cut in his sleeve made by the knife-edged glass.

He rejoined Yevtushenko at the next of the barnlike concrete structures where two other team members were already at work. Another team was hard at work on the other row.

Inside, Hendrik Pienaar wondered what it was that his senses were telling him as he flexed and unflexed his stiffened muscles. It might be that they were saying that he was an old man, he thought sourly.

Suddenly, in the big room next to his own, Pienaar heard a pop and a slight hissing sound. Without a thought in his head, his body took him through the window at his bedside, rifle in hand. Rolling, he straightened up to hear a clicking sound and fired by instinct a short burst at a crouching blur of a figure.

The dull roar of the rifle shots that killed Yevtushenko were the first intimation Krugersdorp had that it was under attack.

* * *

ON THE OUTSKIRTS OF KRUGERSDORP, ANOTHER OF YEVTU-shenko's men, Zerebtsov, was mildly surprised that the Boers camped in the forest had no prepared positions and only a few sentinels. Better still, the ones they had were making themselves obtrusive.

There were perhaps a hundred fifty or a hundred seventy-five of them, possibly two small kommandos. Someone in the circle of tents had spent a few opportune minutes trying to start up a balky truck, allowing Okladnikov's slicks to position themselves.

Setting aside his night glasses, he wriggled back to sketch out a quick map for the slicks. Salchow made one intelligent, if inappropriate, observation. "Why shoot them up? Why not just drop the artillery?"

His corporal looked at him as if half a night in a tree had addled his wits. "Those are mortars, not prayer wheels. These dumb Boers are scattered over half the forest and every last one is lying down. You want ants, you stir them with a stick first. His quick ears detected something that sounded like faint rifle fire. "I think we better get moving," he said, even before his radio began spitting out its message.

SACKED OUT ON A CHURCH PEW, DANNY MEAGHER SAT UPRIGHT, recognizing the same sound. He kicked over the bunk nearest him, dumping its startled occupants on the floor.

"Get up! Move, move, move, if you want Christmas to come!" He grabbed one man by the shoulder. "Don't bother with your clothes. Get up in the bell tower and ring it loud." He draped his webbing over his body in a well-practiced motion and snatched up a weapon to fling it at its owner, who was contemplating Meagher's madness from the safety of his coverlet.

He bent to lace his boots and looked up to find Pat staring back at him remorselessly, readied for battle with an ease that was born and not taught.

"Cover my back," he told the younger merc as he opened the door to the street. Outside in the darkness, he tried to pinpoint the sound of a developing firefight over the noise and bustle at his back.

The whole town might have been dead for ought else he heard. Overtop his head in the tower, that poor fool of a naked cowboy was ringing the church bell for all he was worth.

* * *

WHERE COLDEWE HAD LEFT THE FIRST OF THE MORTAR CREWS, Mekhlis listened to the ringing as well, then opened a channel.

"C point one. Break. Mekhlis. The church bell?"

"Sure. Take it out. Sanmartin out."

Mekhlis's crew had already lowered the hydraulic spade-feet of the utility vehicle and elevated their firing tube. Mekhlis whistled to the second utility vehicle positioned wheel-to-wheel to act as a limber. Number five was already shifting a case of ammunition into the hands of number four.

Mekhlis checked again to make sure the computer had adjusted the extension of the feet to compensate for irregularity in the ground. He ran the firing calculations quickly. His crew dropped nine HE rounds a distance of 4,327 meters, give or take a hair.

THE RINGING FROM THE BELL OF THE PIETERSKERK ACROSS THE street also awakened Elise Louw. Huddled in her bed, she wondered what it might portend. Abruptly, she ran to her window and threw it open in time to see part of the church explode outward in front of her eyes. Chunks of masonry crashed through the wall. Clouds of billowing dust and smoke emerged from everywhere.

As Louw fled, three more rounds ripped the top off the bell tower. She ran to the next room. Hearing the sounds of weapons firing through the shattered window, she crept back against the wall.

Outside her window, Danny Meagher shook his head. Twisting it, he observed Pat, similarly prone, bleeding about the face from a succession of small cuts. To his back, the mortar fire that had torn the guts out of the church halted punctually.

He rose to his knees and crawled over to see what was behind the ruined door. With its blast confined by the walls, the mortar had turned the inside into a charnel house. For a second time on Suid-Afrika, Meagher commanded a unit that no longer existed. Pat jerked his head toward the darkness.

"A church, yet. Colonel Vereshchagin's lads are not a trusting lot. Well, let's blow, Pat," Meagher said at last.

As an afterthought, he said, "Friend Hendrik, we purchased him a few minutes. I suppose we ought to look in and see if he's all right." Pat climbed to his feet and shrugged, setting off at a dogtrot through the streets, Meagher at his heels.

* * *

AS THE BOERS IN THE TWO LITTLE KOMMANDOS BEGAN RAISING their heads, the slicks went in, gun slicks leading, to give a few minutes personalized attention to the uneven rows of little green tents.

Zerebtsov watched seven-sevens wrapped in the bulky shrouds of their coolant jackets move in tandem with the gunners' helmets to play over the startled Boers. They held down opposition for the s-mortars on the trail slicks to do the real work. Unhurriedly, he and Salchow took out four unusually active individuals in the confusion.

The slicks abruptly wheeled and sped off in an unexpected direction, firing Parthian arrows. The astonished but relatively undamaged Boer contingent reacted with enthusiasm. Expected and understandable, this was also silly. As light and flimsy as the slicks appeared, the extreme slant to their armor left them largely invulnerable to small arms fire and everything else being thrown at them. Not so the Afrikaners.

Half of them were standing up, blazing away, when Zerebtsov called in fire from all three mortars and let them use the Hummingbird to see the fall of shot. A sixty-second barrage and a follow-up five minutes later blew the bells out.

Zerebtsov observed the damage critically and spoke again to his radio. "Twelve point one. Break. You got mines, right? Scatter a dozen shells worth, same coordinates, and we call it a day." The slicks had already shoved off to give Okladnikov's Cadillacs a hand, and Zerebtsov made to follow. What was left of these Boers wasn't going to be of much use to anybody until long after the fight for Krugersdorp had been settled.

The guns fired the mission before they prepared to shift back and pound assigned targets inside the town. Out of habit, Mekhlis and his crew lifted the spade-feet and began to displace to a new firing position. Before his vehicles had traveled a hundred meters, three rounds of accurate counterbattery fire from the center of town landed squarely on the position they had just vacated.

The town was awake. Number four in back whistled loud and long.

DAWN ARRIVED ABRUPTLY IN THE FOREST. FOR ABOUT AN HOUR, it penetrated the canopy as a strange, luminous gray part-light without reds or shadows. Then suddenly, each leaf emerged in iridescent light as sun's rays infused the water droplets.

The forest was green.

Chekhov had said somewhere that the best description of snow he ever heard was one given by a schoolgirl. She said, "The snow was white."

Waiting in the gray half-light to the side of the stunted excuse for a road, Coldewe tried to recall other tidbits from his vantage point on the back of Okladnikov's Cadillac. Okladnikov flipped open the hatch and stuck his head out.

"Hello Sergei. Of interest?"

Okladnikov shook his head. "I just came up to feel the breeze."

Coldewe nodded. He let his eyes drift downward until they fixed on the tires. "Did you know that they once made those things out of rubber?"

"Like chewing gum," Okladnikov replied noncommittally, his interest in matters historical nonexistent.

"No alveoli, just a long tube full of air."

Okladnikov made appropriate noises.

"What we need are the ravens, to set the mood," Coldewe said, feeling the night breeze brush against his face, listening to the gunfire.

"Sure, sure," Okladnikov whispered as the firing intensified. Seven spaced clicks from Sanmartin's radio spared him further.

He watched Coldewe mask himself and returned a casual salute. The Hangman's company had a few rituals all its own. As the engine purred into life, Okladnikov shut the hatch and opened a channel to his vehicles.

"Hear me, my brothers. The winds of Paradise are blowing. Where are you who long for Paradise?"

They moved out to crash the barriers.

SANMARTIN WAS FIFTH THROUGH THE HOLE. PASSING DOWNward to the second level, he felt his knees shake as one of Muslar's riflemen put a stick grenade down to clean out the cellar.

They knew house drill. On either side of the street, starting from the top, a section would clean out dividing walls with shaped charges and clean up the rooms with grenades. Machine guns at street level and on the rooftops kept the party private.

It was a little rough on the nonfighting Boers, but a lot of fighting Boers were billeted in the cellars. It was a lot rough on them.

Every movement sent a cloud of blue wafting through the interior of the house. Sanmartin had them dusting the upper floors with incapacitant grenades for the time being; the blue powder was everywhere. He could see the particles adhering to the walls, the floor, the surface of Muslar's mask. Incapacitants were about the most humane weapon known to man. They worked fairly well in confined spaces. Sanmartin intended to use them until the first Boer turned up in a protective mask, and then things would be a lot rough on the nonfighting Boers as well.

Muslar had his assault rifle resting in the crook of his right arm. With his left he held up the engineer's axe he had taken from Tyulenev after the big dummy had stepped in a hole and wrenched his knee.

From the corner of his eye, Sanmartin saw a side door flung open and slammed his body onto the plaster chips, squeezing a burst. Incongruously, a naked man with a rifle stumbled over the towel blocking the door's lower edge and fell into the space where Sanmartin's fire intersected with rounds from the steps above. Behind the man a woman sank to her knees untouched, dropping the sheet she held in front of her body. Gingerly, she reached down to shake the man's arm, and her hand came away red. Sanmartin raised to one elbow. He turned to Muslar.

Muslar was flaccid on the steps. The rifleman stooped over his body shook his head and pointed to his cheek and chest, indicating where return fire Sanmartin had never seen had gone in. The first hit had ruptured Muslar's aorta. As Sanmartin watched, Muslar's face settled out, exsanguinated. He died without lifting his head. Gently prying fingers apart, the rifleman bent to take up the big axe from where it stood stiffly wedged against the rail.

Sanmartin sprang down to the landing and absently scooped up the Boer's rifle by the barrel to smash it against the wall. Billowing blue dust had taken the girl; she slumped. Unconscious, naked, she looked elfin, childlike. Innocent. He felt a sudden urge to kick her. The team leader recovered Muslar's weapon.

"Atque in perpetuum, frater," Sanmartin chanted softly.

From the steps below, he heard someone ask, "You coming, captain? The armored cars are here."

He hurried to a window and looked far down the main street.

The barriers on the side streets had been designed to stop straying cattle, not armored cars. As AP rounds from the mortars crumpled the bunkers on either side of the main road, Okladnikov cut in his sirens and swung his Cadillacs in from the fields. His gunner hosed down the buildings on either side with high-velocity flares for lurking missile teams and impact-fused projectiles for everyone else. The barrier came apart like wet paper.

They hit the main street, and Okladnikov formed his vehicles into a tight diamond, guiding left. Shifting fire, they cleared the streets on either side and ripped the facades. Twenty meters from their entry point, the red light of an errant rocket flared briefly. Stabbing white fire smashed the Boer with a launcher against a wall and the wall behind the Boer before the light armor darted down another side street and away into the night. Behind them, Coldewe's Gurkha infantry consolidated a position, rounding up dazed Boers, military and civilian.

Sanmartin pulled his head inside.

VINCENTE ALMOST SEEMED TO BE ASLEEP, WEDGED AGAINST the concrete steps. Snyman listened to the light chatter over the radio, waiting for his own name or Vincente's.

Dead bodies looked nothing like what Snyman had expected. Some of them were very young. Any lingering faith in martial glory that Orlov hadn't kicked out of Snyman's soul had been erased by the sight of Cornelius du Toit kicking up his fat legs with a bellyful of caseless 5mm killing him a centimeter at a time. The old burgemeester had guested in Snyman's house several times.

Du Toit had always esteemed himself to be one of the heros of the First Republic reborn. Still, it was no way to die. Vincente had eased him with a shot of opiate.

A few prisoners passed, frightened. Each of them had his arms taped and a loop run around his throat. A Boer light machine gun was firing down the length of the street, trying to buy time. Captain Sanmartin had wedged a section of No. 9 platoon in next to No. 11.

Across from him, Snyman saw an 88mm team from No. 9 move around the side of the building out of his field of vision. Curious, he stuck his head around to see and immediately felt Vincente's long fingers hook his harness and jerk him back. Machine gun fire splintered plaster where his head had been. He looked back at Vincente.

Vincente tapped his radio as he lay back down. "Hey! No hurry. You made two trips already, why rush? They're good boys. They'll tell us when they want us." He closed one eye. "Orlov tell you you could stick your head around up high like that?"

Synman nodded and wetted his lips.

"Say, 'Mario, I owe you a beer.'" Vincente closed both his eyes and folded his hands over his chest. "Dignity, kiddo. Dignity. Don't let them take that away. Hey, you listen to the radio and give me a kick in the ribs they call our number."

He fell asleep and began snoring.

De Kantzow's team was supporting Miinalainen's 88mm. "Nine point two slash three. Break. Fripp, you and Mother Elena get frosting lost?" he sang out into his wrist mount as the machine gun fire stripped the paint off the walls over his head.

Without lifting himself, de Kantzow expertly directed a grenade from the launcher slung under his rifle through the shattered window and reloaded. The small projectile had no discernible effect on the volume of fire. In the open field, the Boers were a mob. Wedged into the houses, they had to be smoked out one by one, gutter fighting.

De Kantzow knew the center of the town was holding. Someone had welded the Boers together well enough to regroup and try to cut their way out. Although crippled, they'd stopped Colewe's Gurkhas stone-cold. Spotted, the Boers weren't especially hard to deal with. To spot them, there was one sweep sensor per section. There was also the old-fashioned way, which was to stick your head up and see if it got shot off.

Thursby crawled over from where he was lying, dragging his light machine gun. "Hey, Filthy DeKe!" he whispered.

De Kantzow ignored him. "Do you frosting hear me, Frippie?" he yelled, and listened for a reply. What he heard was a familiar voice singing slightly off-key.

> By that stone, there runs a flood,
>   the bells of Paradise, I heard them ring,
> The one half runs water, the other runs blood,
>   and I love my Lord Jesus, above anything . . .

"Frippie, you frosted turtlehead, is that you frosting singing frosting Christmas carols?"

The singing broke off. "Prayer and patience, Deacon. Jerusalem was never built in a day."

De Kantzow clicked off mouthing obscenities. He rolled over to look at Thursby shrugging off plaster from the ceiling. "Now what's your frosting problem, Thursday?" he whispered.

"DeKe, there's gold back here. Little bars. Lots of it."

"So?"

"So? Is that all you can say? So?"

"So. You can't screw it. You can't drink it. You can't even frosting crawl with it. Has it skipped your frosty, feeble mind that maybe I don't want to spend the rest of your unnatural life mucking out frosting latrines for Berry because you got itchy fingers?''

"But DeKe . . .''

The unseen machine gun ripped through the building, knocking away what was left of the glass in the windows. De Kantzow turned his back on the speechless Thursby and keyed his radio. "Nine point two slash three. Break. Hey Fripp! You and Mother Elena stuffing sheep out there?''

The triple blast of Yelenov's s-mortar, finally positioned, resolved the question to de Kantzow's satisfaction.

Snyman watched a half-dozen Boers tumble out the door of the ground floor with their hands held high, coughing from the smoke and dust. Fripp leaped up and darted forward. Like thistledown, the surrendering Afrikaners scattered as rifle fire broke out from the floor above indiscriminately. Fripp's head snapped back as four bullets smashed into his body.

Thursby and de Kantzow raked the upper level. Snyman watched Yelenov jump out in the street and carefully pump three s-mortar rounds through each of the wide big windows, stepping calmly back to reload. As he nerved himself to come across, Vincente waved him back.

"Mine, kiddo!'' And he was gone.

Yelenov braced beside the smoking doorway. "Help him check out inside,'' Vincente shouted, kneeling beside Fripp, who was obviously dying.

Snyman found himself on his feet. When he reached the far side, Yelenov grabbed him by the shoulder and pulled him against the wall. "Get out of the light,'' Mother Elena told him petulantly, his own submachine gun poised in the crook of his arm and the s-mortar dangling from its strap. Then he vanished inside.

Stumbling, Snyman followed and flung himself beside Yelenov. Over his head, dawn streamed through the cracks in the floor above.

"Headquarters,'' Yelenov whispered. He leveled his submachine gun and fired a dozen rounds through one unopened door. "Cover me,'' he said, moving across the room to kick the door in.

Sheepishly, Snyman thumbed his weapon off safety. The little room was empty. Responding to Yelenov's hand signals, he moved to where he could cover the stairwell. Cautiously, Yelenov explored what was left of the upstairs. He reappeared almost immediately.

"Want another trip? The guy at the top of the steps is still breathing, looks bad. Forget the rest. I'll tell Vincente." Yelenov tapped his radio. "Chiba point one. Break. Yelenov. Building fourteen is a headquarters, secured, lots of documents. Yelenov out." He darted past Snyman back out into the street without awaiting a reply.

Snyman recognized his father in the man in the black uniform at the head of the steps. The elder Snyman was unconscious, breathing shallowly with blood oozing from a small hole in his temple. Jan Snyman climbed the steps and ran his hand across his eyes. He began unfolding his A-frame, using his fingers to brush away little bits of hardened foam.

Yelenov reappeared. "Vincente's busy. Can you manage?" he said, flipping through his pockets absently for another sheaf of grenades. He looked down at the Boer and looked at Snyman quizzically. "He looks like you. You know him?"

Snyman nodded. "My father. Help me slide him on."

He spoke as they worked. "He would have loved me very much if he had known how to go about it. Perhaps he would not be here if I had not joined. Then again, perhaps he would, he was very much a patriot. Still, I am old enough to be responsible for my actions. I suppose he is old enough to be responsible for his."

Once they had him on the A-frame, Snyman immobilized him with the foam. Then he got underneath, lifted the apex, and settled the weight over his hips while Yelenov folded the legs.

"Guide me down," Snyman directed.

Yelenov did so. They reached the street, passing Fripp and three dead Afrikaners. De Kantzow met them.

"What's the word?" Yelenov asked in his soft voice.

"We're going to frosting leapfrog. Three minutes." De Kantzow looked at Snyman. "We've got two more frosting bleeders and a couple who can move. Think you can get them back?"

"Vincente left his A-frame for one, and I see half a door for the other," Yelenov said.

Snyman nodded.

"Frosty straight. Tell the walkers they're on a frosting errand of mercy. But don't get too close, they all got frosting runny noses." He tossed Snyman Fripp's assault rifle. Snyman cleared it and went through a quick functions check. De Kantzow looked over at Thursby, kneeling beside a ragged hole in the wall providing covering fire for another team. "Thursby's frosting busy," he said, and bent to use Vincente's foam dispenser to weld a wounded Boer to the broken door himself.

Snyman stepped over to look at de Kantzow's impressed stretcher bearers. "We are going to take these wounded men back for treatment. If you give me difficulties, I will shoot you," he said in Afrikaans.

Yelenov made a comment. "It would be easier if one of these turtles took the one on your back."

"No, I think that I will have less problem if I show that I myself am helping. Also, I want to." Snyman looked up at him, his eyes showing white against the green skin of his mask. "I owe Mario a beer. Maybe two."

Yelenov said softly, "When this is over, you look us up."

"I will," he promised.

AS BRUWER'S INTENSITY WANED, BEYERS THREW UP HIS HANDS. "This is madness. Four months ago, no one knew my name."

His wife examined Bruwer closely. Bruwer sat gripping the arm of the chair with her left hand. The sleeves of her pullover were carefully rolled. Veins crossing her wrist stood out, blue and pulsing.

"Hush, Albert. The child is right," his wife said.

Beyers stopped wringing his hands to consider this possibility.

"I understand that Vroew Reinach threw a stone at you the other day. I would ask you to forgive her. She is a bit of a goose, really, but she did lose her husband." Beyers's wife looked at her own husband. "You must excuse him. At his age, men need a full night's rest."

Beyers had ceased to wring his hands. Instead he rubbed the fingertips of one hand across the palm of the other softly. "What do you think, Mother?" he asked his wife quietly.

"Some men seek out greatness. You waited to have it come along and shake you by the neck."

With her hatchet face, it was clear that she had never been a beauty. Beyers had had other reasons for marrying.

"The war will be over," she continued. "Either you beat this into the farmers' thick heads, or someone else will. But no prancing about, lining up supporters and all the things you politicians do."

"You are right, Mother. Who would have thought it?" Beyers said quietly.

"I did, or I wouldn't have married you." She glanced at her timepiece. "I should think that there are a number of men who owe you favors, but the phones are turned off and there is the curfew. How should we begin, Hanna?"

Bruwer held up a small radio. "With this. But if you could excuse me for a moment, first," she said haltingly. "I feel I shall be sick and your carpet is too pretty for me to ruin. Not the infection," she added hastily.

"In there," Beyers said, pointing. Bruwer rose and left.

As they heard the sound of running water, Beyers turned to his wife. "How do we thank her, Mother?"

"Don't thank her, use her. Make her the landrost or even the burgemeester, God willing. Who else can you trust?"

Beyers laughed. "And what about you, Mother? What office would you hold?"

"None, thank you. I'm too busy keeping my children and their father from acting the fools they were born," she said primly.

"Mother, would you come to the fort with me today?" he asked formally.

It was a local conceit, of recent and unknown etymology, to refer to the Johannesburg Staatsamp as Fort Zinderneuf.

THE CHURCH WAS BUILT OF STONE, LIKE A MEDIEVAL CASTLE. Snaking past the ruins of the bell tower as resistance crumbled away, Coldewe darted inside, following his own grenade with two of the Gurkhas close on his heels.

The little Gurkhas were pathetically eager, but it was mostly "Follow me. Do what I do." Still, for peasant boys off to earn a little money and see the wide worlds, they caught on to the essentials.

The north wall was pockmarked, 88 hits. Overhead were the stars, disappearing in the gray light of morning. A stray round had desecrated the dominee's living quarters, but there was a cellar or crypt that appeared intact. On impulse, Coldewe started down the steps, pushing open the door.

Inside were two dozen Boers. A few were civilians. One tall girl with a very pallid face was standing up clothed in little more than a shift. A young man was seated in one corner with one arm bandaged, holding a light machine gun across his knees. Several of the men were holding grenades. Two of them removed the pins as Coldewe entered and let them fall to the floor.

The two Gurkhas looked to Coldewe uncertainly. Coldewe shrugged.

"Good day, I am Hans Coldewe, from Tuebingen," he said in his less than fluent Afrikaans.

The young boy nodded politely.

"Who's in charge?"

No one spoke up. Coldewe pointed to the tall girl in the shift. "What's your name?"

"Elise Louw, Heer Coldewe."

"You are in charge of these people. Have them stack their weapons along the wall there. Take them to the Van Rensburg house. Do you know where that is?"

She nodded.

"I'll send Bahadur to help you. If the armored cars stop you, tell them that I sent you." Bahadur was the taller of the two Gurkhas, the only one whose name Coldewe knew. He looked around at the faces.

"Find the pins to those grenades." he directed. He pointed to the two Gurkhas who hadn't understood a word. "You two, help them."

The young boy nodded again without ever changing his slack expression. He lay his light against the wall neatly at a tilt with the muzzle up. Several men began scrabbling in the dust for the pins. Louw had the others follow the boy's example.

Coldewe turned to his Gurkhas. "Bahadur, show these people to the Van Rensburg house." He pointed to the other. "You, guard these weapons!" Both of them straightened and snapped off crisp rifle salutes. The shorter man took station stiffly by the wall.

As he stepped outside into the warm air, Coldewe realized that they were clearing the last buildings, and that he'd almost become the last casualty.

He made a mental note to check up on Louw.

On the outskirts of town, No. 10 was strung out in a broad wedge. To the right of Tulya Pollezheyev's team, there was nothing but trees to the sea.

On either side of Pollezheyev, cleared ground rose gradually to slight crests half a kilometer apart. Down the middle ran a soggy depression that would have been a stream on a respectable world. Except within the depression's confines, the rest of No. 10 had a clear and murderous field of fire. The depression would draw Boers like a magnet pulls iron. Sitting in water up to his assets, Pollezheyev was sited to fire down its length.

The first Boers streaming out of the stricken town passed in no particular order. Marksmen from the other arm of the wedge took most of them. They let the survivors by. Pollezheyev wanted something better.

He spotted one group of three men, clustered together and moving purposefully.

Reaching down to squeeze off, he was momentarily distracted

by a little girl with golden hair. She skipped along in her ruffled dress across the meadow. Pollezheyev hesitated.

The girl said something to the men that he couldn't make out, pointing emphatically toward Pollezheyev's positions. The command group melted away into the mire leaving the little girl alone to admire the scenery.

"The devil!" Pollezheyev observed with feeling.

Shocked by the narrowness of his escape, Danny Meagher watched the girl skip away and then began crawling a body-length at a time toward the inviting forest a few hundred meters off. Halfway across, he heard overhead an engine's sound and froze.

A solitary Shiden flew obliquely by at a low altitude, spewing a stream of little pellets from the ruptured pods on its hardpoints. Meagher felt a few of the motes cascade over his body, then heard the tiny sounds as the pebble-sized mines armed themselves. He turned his head backward to see Pat's unsmiling face. Pienaar was behind him.

"Ah, Pat, Hendrik," he said, "my mother told me once there'd be days like this."

Saturday(13)

"HOW ARE WE DOING, TIMO?" VERESHCHAGIN ASKED, WAITing.

Haerkoennen pulled his headset off and tried to make sense out of the conflicting signals he'd been monitoring. "Major Henke has cordoned the farms and is quartering. They are gassing the tunnels. Captain Sanmartin is still cleaning up in and around Krugersdorp. Major Kolomeitsev has broken off pursuit to complete refueling."

And to have his shoulder dressed. The Iceman was a difficult man to kill; if he acquired the same reputation here as he had on other worlds, it would not be long before the Boers still full of fight were scratching crosses on their bullets.

Haerkoennen glanced at the time. Fourteen minutes more. To Haerkoennen's experienced eye, it appeared the Variag was out of courtesy.

"I wish I were with them," Vereshchagin said very softly. "Casualties?"

"Eighty-seven at last count. One aircraft, three vehicles. Less than we expected."

"But more than we can afford. What would you say, Timo?"

"If they don't know they're beaten now, they never will."

At Elandslaagte, panicked Boers had tried to break away east along the road. *Ajax* had found them, spewing chickenseed until the very aluminum in the vehicles began to burn. Survivors from Elandsslaagte, Nelspruit, and Krugersdorp who didn't give themselves up would spread disease all over creation. Albert Beyers knew as much about the tactical situation as anyone on the planet. If Beyers hadn't convinced himself by now, he never would.

Haerkoennen had been around the Variag too long to imagine that Beyers's sudden shift was entirely fortuitous, but one way or another, they'd have worked the trick. Shimazu, Tomiyama, and Aksu had broadcast teams out, letting some of their prisoners speak to their former colleagues. Haerkoennen had no doubt that they could put on a fairly convincing prancing pony show even if Beyers had a change of heart.

The key to live biological operations is controlled dispersal. Uncontrolled dispersal creates infection foci that the slightest mutation can turn into a pandemic. Harjalo had done some reading in the last few hours.

Psittacosis strains are uniformly marked by extreme contagion; apart from the odium attaching to live biological operations from the Wizard Wars, the difficulty of controlling dispersal normally rendered use of PS strains unacceptable, but war is rarely normal.

The Psittacosis[37] strain Raul had let loose when he triggered the transponders was distinguished from other PS strains by its low lethality and delayed onset of symptoms. Infection settled in the respiratory system and was spread by coughing or spittle. The illness was characterized by high fever, disorientation, and muscle ache, with complete convalescence requiring several months. Strain-specific immunization was ninety-eight percent successful.

The thirteen Boers who had abided by their paroles had been snatched up and quarantined before they became infectious, with apologies and compensation. Eva Moore had quietly arranged to have Solchava brought down for a plague presentation. There were some jobs even too dirty to pass off to the infantry.

Moore had said that Solchava's face had gone dead, pale white in the course of it. Moore had also said without a trace of self-pity that when her own time came, there would be no hell too deep for her.

Haerkoennan glanced down again. As for Beyers, thirteen minutes more and they'd be sure one way or the other.

Vereshchagin tried to smile.

Haerkoennen missed what he had to say, pricking his ears up at a signal. "Muravyov, sir. For you." He listened for a moment. "His number three Cadillac, the one that took the rocket."

Vereshchagin nodded. "Inform him that Prigal has been reinstated as a superior private by my order. What did Prigal have to say for himself?"

"I'll ask." Haerkoennen did so and awaited a reply. "Prigal figured Johan had gone to sleep at the switch, so he took it upon himself. Johan will be all right. Muravyov also mentions a pay discrepancy. Prigal got around to admitting he's been getting paid as a superior private. He was afraid to mention it before."

Vereshchagin made a face. "Please ask Muravyov to inform Superior Private Prigal that the battalion sergeant is not accustomed to making mistakes. Nor am I."

"Acknowledged. Surgeon Solchava has returned from Complex. She has requested permission to see you as soon as is possible."

Vereshchagin nodded distantly as he watched Beyers appear before the camera and begin to speak.

Beyers was leaning on the table in front of him. He spoke softly at first. "My friends, my enemies. My name is Beyers. Some of you I know. Some of you know me. Others among you know my wife. She is my conscience."

Beyers had made the journey to Pretoria as if it were to Calvary instead, as in one sense it was. He kept his speech slow and formal. Behind him, he felt rather than saw the presence of his wife and the young Bruwer. They were well matched, both of them, far too somber. Beyers felt it was the curse of his race that they took things so seriously that men died for them.

"My colleague of Bloemfontein is dead, murdered by Afrikaners. His deputy resigned two days ago in fear for his life. My colleague of Pretoria resigned last night, his deputy as well. I am the last."

Both resignations had come under duress, but Beyers saw no obligation to muddle his tale.

"Both Pretoria and his deputy have promised to pay several million yen, to ease the sufferings of our people. For this I thank them with all of my heart."

That, too, had come under duress.

"But as I have said, I am the last representative. For this reason, a duty is mine. I have a story which I must tell you. It is a story of shame, a shame affecting each of us."

The population was huddled in their homes. The papers stopped printing. Power came on for them to cook, and they were hearing only the news that Ssu's surviving censors released to supplement the wild rumors and wilder speculations that passed from hand to hand. No artifacts flowed from Complex. Men tried to purchase from dwindling stocks of goods with money in which men placed no confidence, the ablest among them realizing what had been lost when the warehouses filled with goods from Earth were destroyed with the port.

When vehicular traffic ceased, isolation was added to other fears. The rumors had been ugly.

When the power came on, out of habit they turned on their televisions. They saw and heard Albert Beyers.

Beyers spoke in that style of brutal frankness that the worst of the Boer politicians affect and the best discover naturally. He spoke. From time to time he paused, to read from a list of names, of the dead, of the wounded and captured, fifty names at a time, Afrikaners and Imperials.

There were three things he told his people.

He told them of the Order; the Order had made itself an unholy parasite on the Bond, itself a cancerous growth on the body of the Afrikaner Volk. He told them how the Order had made its unholy alliance with USS in order to wage its war on the Imperials, how the Order had murdered Reading and the spaceport in the name of a past that was dead.

He told them of the cost. The cost was measured in the battles that had been fought, for if the deaths of a few men were acts that cried out for vengeance, the death of a few thousand was something that called for searching one's heart; he told them as well of the infection, the psittacosis fever, that had been spread among the shattered, deluded fighting Boers in retribution.

Finally, he explained to them the proposal he had made to Lieutenant-Colonel Vereshchagin. Vereshchagin's counterproposal had been replete with sticks rather than carrots, and Beyers made no effort to disguise this. What he spoke of instead was amnesty, of autonomy in local affairs, of rebuilding. What he emphasized instead was that he intended to have a peace for which no more would die.

And he paused to read names from time to time. Even Afrikaners who reviled his name listened, if only to hear the names of the dead, the wounded, the captured.

He intended to speak until night fell or he collapsed at his post. He offered hope.

* * *

"IN THERE, YOU SAY?" SANMARTIN SAID TO HIS PRISONER. LIKE most of the ones they had taken in the course of the night, this one was disposed to be agreeable. Sanmartin pointed to the nearest soldier who didn't contrive to look busy. "You, look after him!"

The young rifleman rammed the barrel of his weapon up the back of the Boer's coat, twisting it to tangle the foresight in folds of cloth.

"Please do not move. Otherwise, I must explain the expenditure of ammunition."

Sanmartin cupped his hands and shouted toward the mine entrance. "Raul Sanmartin, captain, First Battalion, Thirty-fifth Imperial Rifles. Please surrender yourselves."

"I regret to say that we shall not," was the reply.

"If you don't, we're going to blow you out of there. Suicide is silly. Also useless."

"Not entirely useless. My last task is to be sure that the ammunition stockpiled here does not fall into your hands. It is my ammunition, you see," the man said in a cultured and somewhat pedantic voice. "My name is Claassen. You may perhaps recognize it from the *Geloftedag* Proclamation."

Sanmartin registered the name. "Don't be silly, Christos. You're not one of Scheepers's merry chuckleheads. We're cleaning up tonight. It's over, and we're going to want a few people to pick up the pieces," he shouted back.

"Still, I believed. I still believe. I have committed my honor, Heer Sanmartin. There is a proverb that I learned once that you might perhaps understand. 'The wine is bitter, but it is our wine,' " was Claassen's reply. He punctuated it with small arms fire. He turned to Olivier having made his point. Olivier was shaking with fear.

"Do you want to go? It only takes one of us, and I'm sure they won't harm you," Claassen said quietly.

Olivier shook his head, not trusting himself to speak.

Claassen nodded his head wearily. "Down the shaft then with you. We all die sometime. In order to be brave, I suppose that you must first learn how to be afraid. I still think that you were an idiot to get yourself mixed up with this Order nonsense, but I suppose God won't mind."

Olivier held his left hand clutched in his right, his fingers curled rigidly, as he tried to control the twitching. Many of the ones who had been the loudest had been the first to fall away when the Imperials struck back, but not all.

"There are special weapons in the vault. Almost the last ones we have," he said, his teeth rattling uncomfortably.

Claassen pondered this. "We can call them atom bombs now, there's no one to hear. Do you know the combination?"

"No."

"A pity. Ask Strijdom if you see him before I do." His eyes softened. "I would not have used them in any case."

Olivier nodded, acknowledging the sentiment. "If it comes to it, you pull the switch. I don't think that I can," he said, attempting to command his fear. He looked out the entrance between the supports suddenly. "Who is that?" he exclaimed.

Sanmartin approached, waving an embroidered handkerchief. "Don't shoot. This is a flag of truce, and I'm not armed."

"Come in," Claassen said with a gesture. "Are you here to surrender?"

"Not hardly likely."

"Are you not afraid we will take you prisoner?" Olivier said in labored English.

"Again, not hardly likely. Abuse of an emissary is a class three war crime. You're better off taking a shot at the emperor. It means your family gets transported without civil rights. Transportation with civil rights is bad enough. You're Olivier? You have two small daughters." Sanmartin shook his head. "When they get dumped off somewhere, they can support themselves by begging, stealing, or prostitution. Kinder to cut their throats."

"I assume you are here for some reason," Claassen said dryly.

"It's over, Claassen, and I can use you to help put things back together. Your people are going to need a few honest men." He pulled a small radio out of one pocket. "Here, Albert Beyers can tell you better than I can."

He looked at Olivier. "You can stay for all I care. But your family gets transported with civil rights either way, and they might like you along."

"What about the ammunition? We cannot leave it for you!" Olivier protested.

"Oh, that. Just so." He reached into another pocket and pulled out a detonation charge. "Go ahead and make it a professional job, but if you're not out in an hour, we'll blow the place for you."

He turned and walked out into the sunshine.

Forty minutes later, he asked, "Any sign?" The engineer lieutenant, Reinikka, shook his head.

"All right," Sanmartin said resignedly, "clear the pithead."

"Hold it, they're coming!" Reinikka said suddenly. "All that work wasted."

"Now that we've gone to the trouble, it does seem a shame. What did we set that charge for, an hour?" He watched Claassen and Olivier walk toward them with their hands raised. He cupped his hands and shouted, "Hurry up!"

They used the mining equipment to pump in a slug of electrolized water. With four minutes to spare on the charge, Reinikka fired an incendiary round from an 88 to flash the liberated hydrogen. They heard a muffled tremor and a huge dust cloud shot out.

Sanmartin detailed Moushegian and another engineer. "Stay behind and check for radiation. Send the bill to USS."

"THIS MAN, BEYERS, OF YOURS IS SHARP, HENDRIK. HE CERtainly makes what you've done sound dirty. Do you think I should switch over, now? I've done poorly on picking sides of late," Meagher observed, listening.

"I didn't know you knew Afrikaans, Daniel," Pienaar replied absently.

"You would have if I'd meant you to know." He thought he recognized a name. "Le Grange, isn't he the footballer?"

Pienaar didn't know and said so with no great enthusiasm.

"Some hearts will break if he is," Meagher said darkly. Beyers finished with a series of names and a different voice began speaking.

"You were right, Hendrik, it's your friend, Vereshchagin. A subtle man, as you say. When you come right to it, the deal he's offering is better than the one I'd give if I were wearing his shoes after the kicking he gave us."

Pienaar made a show of interest. "Will the Imperial government ratify, I ask?"

"As your Dr. Beyers so aptly expressed it, by the time the Imperial government drafts a response, the porridge will be very cold indeed."

Pienaar growled. "What is Beyers saying now?" he asked.

"It isn't him at the moment. That man Ssu has one of Scheepers's pups on to bear witness to the truth. A simpleton they captured who obviously knows too much for his own good and is eager to share it."

Beyers had called men by name, telling one to repent, another he was infected, a third to come home. Some listened. As for the committees of safety he had called upon to disperse, many of these who were not on them, and some who were, were more than ready to see them disappear. Members on more than a few had already begun to even old scores. Pienaar said morosely, "Scheepers just announced that it was a court-martial offense to listen."

"Indeed. I'd still like to know why you elected him your little tin god. Half the world must be listening out there." Meagher jerked his thumb toward the encampments. "Does the man really think they care whether he forbids them to listen or not?"

"I don't know what the man thinks anymore. When the whole crew of them get together and start puffing away at each other, good sense flies out the window," Pienaar said.

He had spoken to Scheepers, bone-weary, in the bright, hard sun of morning before the rains came. Scheepers had been surrounded by his minions, insulated from the disaster, isolated from the events he sought to influence.

"You were the last man out of Krugersdorp!" Scheepers had said aloud, as if the act had been something heroic and Krugersdorp had been something other than a tangled, bloody fiasco. Pienaar had looked from one heroic face clustered around the generalissimo to another, then to his own arthritic knees and torn feet. If Pienaar's escape from Krugersdorp had been something not quite miraculous, Scheepers's own departure from Elandslaagte had been dearly purchased.

"My horse got away," he had answered truthfully. "I can't run as fast as I could as a young man." Poor Koos Gideon had puffed up just like a frog. That silly, dangerous man Strijdom had hissed like a snake. Pienaar decided that when the devil came to take his own on the day of judgment, Scheepers would be there to make an uplifting speech.

The memory brought half of a smile to Pienaar's blistered face. "Good sense just flies out the window," he repeated to Meagher, who was patient with an old man's maunderings.

"You'd better catch it and send it back to them," Meagher said in reply. "Your man, Beyers, will break in to read some more names shortly. The Imperials run smooth graves' registration, and it's sobering. At a rough count, the names from last night are running about twenty to one against. Demoralizing, that. And then there's the plague we're all infected with. Psittacosis, the man says. Nasty stuff. Has your little tin god figured out what we're going to do about that?'' He smiled sweetly. "Do you know, Hendrik, I've never seen a war stopped over the tele before.''

Pienaar continued to stare off into space. "Don't be foolish,'' he growled petulantly.

Meagher laughed a little. His voice was playful, but his words were deadly serious. "It's over, Hendrik. Now the silly men get desperate, and the rest of us start thinking for ourselves. This may be a personal idiosyncrasy of mine, Hendrik, but I greatly dislike being used. And it strikes me that some of us have been used pretty shamelessly.''

Pienaar didn't answer, and for a moment Meagher was afraid that he hadn't heard. Changing the subject, he said, "Do you know, you were so slow getting here this morning that I was starting to think that you'd met with a misfortune.''

Nearly enough, Pienaar thought. Imperial aircraft had caught up with the first truck he'd ridden and turned it into a torch. The burns were on his arms and face. "I stopped at a farmhouse to telephone my granddaughter,'' he said aloud.

"That sounds like a breach of security to me. Wouldn't Koos Gideon be annoyed?''

"You do not know the half of it, Daniel,'' Pienaar answered soberly.

"Well, what did she have to say?''

"She has a mind of her own, that one. She wanted to know if I had gone crazy.''

"So what did you tell her?'' Meagher asked, curious.

"When I found out what she had done, I asked her the same.'' Pienaar wagged his finger. "Be quiet, Daniel. I need to think.'' He wrapped himself tighter against the driving rain and began thinking as a soldier, as a man.

It was a clever trick the Imperials had fastened upon them, to open the fourth seal. Pienaar knew of the rider on the horse of pale green; his name was Death. With his handmaids typhus, cholera, typhoid, and dysentery, he had swayed the course of a thousand campaigns and capriciously toppled dynasties. Power was given him over the four parts of the earth.

The thoughts tripped over themselves, one after another. Pienaar did not consider himself a reflective man, but he knew that he was as ruthless with himself as he was with others.

In haggard faces around this woeful encampment, already he could see traces of fever. Some of these belonged to men from different camps. It might be another day before its victims realized, but then the panic would set in.

On the planet of Suid-Afrika, space quarantine and the absence of native diseases had left them unprepared. Massing in the camps had left them concentrated. Pienaar did not know how the Imperials had spread the disease among them, but this was unimportant. The fact remained that it had been done swiftly and effectively, and that they would not escape the blow. He had lived to see the Afrikaner nation broken on the Highveld. He knew a defeated army.

Koos Gideon and his puppet masters had failed to consolidate a hold on these men. The shattering to which they had been subjected and the numberless dead had eroded their faith.

That faith would not be afforded an opportunity to return. The guerrilla bands that Strijdom planned would not now come into being. Once these kommandos scattered, the dispirited survivors would carry away no memories of proud victories against the Imperial fist, only fear that cold, hard professionals had fostered, and the seeds of infection.

Frightened men by the score would turn themselves over to the Imperials for treatment; farms and villages would close their gates to the others who would be harried by Imperial wolfpacks across the face of the land, their trail marked by the refuse of the sick and the dying.

Under field conditions, the mortality rate might be twenty, thirty, seventy percent? Only the Imperials knew. They had not said, and camp rumor would make it far higher.

Pienaar knew that the ones who had not declared would rally to Albert de Roux Beyers. His voice was clear, and his hands were free of the stain of defeat and savage losses, the shame of atomic murder. And the moment that the war became one of Koos Gideon Scheepers and his ragged "Order" against Beyers and his voice of hope, that war was lost.

Even so, maddened until original causes were forgotten, brother would strike brother. Hands-uppers would swell Imperial ranks to compel bitter-enders to make an end to the suffering; bitter-enders would murder hands-uppers in hatred and bitterness. Fever and famine would stalk the land as men were sundered from their fields and their homes. The Volk would be divided, and exhaustion would sap them as a nation.

In the end, there would only be a bloody shadow of a land, and Afrikaners who would bleed. Only the most ruthless of men could contemplate this; yet wars were not started by ruthless men so much as by small, frightened men who sheltered their eyes from what the Lord plainly intended for them to see.

The Volk could flee, someone had said. They could strike out into the wilderness, trusting in the hand of God to feed them as had the original Voortrekkers.

And they could starve, a nation of jungle bunnies.

Pienaar looked at his hands and thought of his own infertile fields. Any man who dreamed of turning his back on the Imperials and trekking out into the wilderness had done his farming in coffeehouses.

There was nothing to debate, to chop logics. Pienaar had the ruthlessness to see this clearly. He did not have the ruthlessness to force this upon his people.

He knew as well that there were men who would not recognize this. He also knew that there were men, a few, who did not lack that final ruthlessness, for reasons of their own.

Having considered, Pienaar turned toward Meagher with cold dispassion.

"My granddaughter has done her part and what she did was right," he said enigmatically. "Now I must do mine." He took off his hat, vainly trying to shake some of the water from it. Then he said, "My Irish hireling friend, Koos Gideon will call a meeting soon. I think that it is time that we talked."

WHEN THE TIME CAME FOR SCHEEPERS TO CALL HIS GENERALS together, Pienaar was searched at the door, roughly, for weapons. It pleased him, ever so slightly, that Scheepers, or perhaps Strijdom, was so afraid for his tattered skin.

Both of his feet were swollen, the right one so much so that his right leg was almost unusable. It occurred to Pienaar for the first time that perhaps he really was an old man. He set his lips together. There were a few things that the old men couldn't very well leave to the young ones.

Strijdom was speaking, but for some reason Pienaar heard not a word. Instead, he looked around the room and smelled the stink of fear. Many were coughing. It struck him how few of the ones who had started were left. As the Lord willed, perhaps it was better that way.

With Claassen gone, there was not one of them that Pienaar considered a friend, and perhaps this too was better.

Strijdom was speaking about guerrilla warfare, unconscious of any irony. One of the weaknesses endemic to Afrikaner military units, even the beloved *Regiment Danie*, had been the tendency to gloss over awkward facts with vague exhortations and appeals to the Lord, not that this motley collection of frightened schemers could be considered military any longer. Pienaar looked at his watch and waited another thirty-eight seconds before he rose to his feet and began hobbling steadily to the platform where Strijdom was speaking.

"Veld-General Pienaar, you are out of order!" Strijdom erupted uncertainly.

Pienaar bore down upon him stiffly. Strijdom took one step back. It was enough.

"You, be quiet!" Pienaar said with the same voice he had used to frighten recruits. "We have heard enough. Now, it is time that we all started to be truthful to one another."

Turning his back to Strijdom, Pienaar spoke to them all, for them all.

"Let us stop this pretending that we are playing with toys instead of men's lives. We have been beaten. Perhaps we were not beaten as fairly and chivalrously as we might like, but it is not a game and we can hardly complain after what we have done. Yes, what we have done, for we are all stained with that sin."

"You traitorous underminer!" Strijdom blazed, motioning frantically to his security men.

"Yes, you be quiet! I'm tired of hearing you slander better men than yourself. Go on Hendrik," one man said, unexpectedly.

Refreshed from this cup, Pienaar took a deep breath and one last time, he assumed the mantle of faith and the words as he set out to win over his audience.

"Glibly, your kind speak of traitors. You shall not silence the truth that is within me! Yes, I remember well all of your kind, they made their brave noises about what a true Afrikaner must be, and when the Bantu rose up in their wrath and desperation, they fled across the seas and left us to fight their battles. I knew you then and I know you now. I will not be silenced, for I know you, Satan!"

He threw off one restraining arm imperiously, as if he were once again a youth of seventeen, the old medals rippling softly on his tunic.

"Oh, come now, Hendrik," Scheepers began timidly, "we are all in this together. We must all stick together and be loyal to one another. Do you not think that there is a man here that the Imperials would hesitate to hang?"

"And what of it!" Pienaar demanded. He looked from one man to another. "For weeks I have kept my silence, and my faith bids me to keep it no longer. I recall those self-styled true Afrikaners crawling like maggots behind us, whispering, slandering those of us who fought and were sickened by it. Now, when I look around me, I see fear! Fear in the faces of brave men who are afraid lest some viper say that they are not true Afrikaners! Is there doubt in my heart? Yes, there is doubt because the road we have led our people down is the wrong one, and we do not have the courage to turn aside. We have been beaten, we have been outtricked, and I for one will not condemn our people to pay the price for our mistakes. I say to you, if we do not lead our nation back from the brink of the pit, then God will turn his face against our nation for our hatred and our crimes, our sins and our pride.

"Who are you, Koos Gideon, to condemn our people to death and suffering? All the blood on your hands, all your brave dogmas, will that bring back so much as one? Bow your head! Bow them all of you and pray that the Lord will forgive us for what we have done!"

He had them now. He could feel it. Out of the corner of his eye he saw Scheepers cowering, Strijdom flushed with rage so that he could not speak. In that instant, Pienaar knew that God had answered his prayers truly, by cleaving Strijdom's lying tongue to the roof of his mouth so that truth might this once be spoken. It was then that Pienaar's old, grim humor began to reassert itself.

Psittacosis.

Parrot fever. The very thing for a roost of jackdaws.

Pienaar flashed his broken, yellowed teeth. "God is my witness, and I am His servant. I have buried my father and my brothers. I will fight no more in this unhallowed cause. Look out there, all of you! Can you not see the fever come to take our young men? Can any of you doubt that we would not have suffered such terrible defeats if the Lord had hallowed our cause? For our sinful pride and ambition, will we cast aside everything our people have built? You prattle of guerrilla war. I know it. We are beaten before we have even begun. Let be. If it is our lot to be ruled by Imperials and by men like Beyers who have the bravery to speak out with words which none of us wish to hear, then let His will be done. For this delusion, let us spend no more Afrikaner blood. For now, we ourselves must make a harsh peace and reknit the sundered fabric of the Volk in this fair land."

Malan, who was master-at-arms, recovered his courage. Hearkening to Strijdom's ample gestures, he fired one shot into Pienaar and let the pistol drop from his hands with a shiver.

Pienaar fell to his knees. He tried to say something, but no words came out. Malan made a sudden chopping motion with his left hand. One of his gunmen stepped behind Pienaar. He shot him once in the back of the head.

"So will perish all traitors!" Strijdom stuttered exultantly, abruptly recovering his speech.

Meagher was outside watching. The mud in his mouth tasted rancid. It tasted of blood.

Why would the sons of the Irish go off to die in other people's war? Pienaar had wanted to know. There was a fairy tale, of course.

The Children of Erin were the Children of Lir, transformed by jealousy and poverty not into mincing swans, but into wild geese, swift and proud, to fly for a thousand years from one field of strife to another. And when the Children of Lir came home from their wanderings, the Christian voice of the bell they heard. Their feathery plumage fell away and they regained human shape as men bony and wrinkled, feeble with hair of gray. Men ready to be peacefully buried by the saintly Kemoc, side by side, with an earthen mound over their heads.

Danny Meagher picked up his rifle and spat the earth from his mouth. He was not ready. At the sound of the first shot, Meagher said, "That's what we were waiting for, boyo." He tapped Pat Shaunessy and vaulted from concealment, gunning down the two guards at the door expertly with a burst of automatic fire. Shaunessy reached the door and kicked it from its hinges. Stepping inside, he cut down the two gunmen standing stupidly over Pienaar's body and two of the delegates standing behind.

A third gunman beside the wall opened up wildly, and Shaunessey slid to the floor, emptying the rest of his magazine high into the ceiling. Hard on Shaunessy's heels, Meagher put five rounds in the gunman's chest with a caress across the trigger. Turning to Scheepers, who was still wringing his hands, Meagher said simply, "I won't be lecturing you, boyo. If you see my friend Hendrik, give my regards, though I don't expect the two of you will be going the same direction." Meagher shot him gently, and before Strijdom could finish drawing the pistol from his sleeve, Meagher shot him dead as well.

Calmly reloading, he gunned down Malan and then picked out seven of the stunned delegates and shot each one of them through the head. Bleeding slightly from a graze, he bent to check for signs of life from Pat Shaunessy. After a second, he straightened.

"And a fine day to the rest of you," he said as he gaily vaulted out the window.

Sunday(14)

"I UNDERSTAND PIOTR RAZED VENTERSTAD THIS MORNING," Vereshchagin said.

Malinov nodded.

"Piotr always did have a fine hand for detail."

Malinov let his face relax into a troubled frown. "Redzup is making calls."

"Yes, he is preparing audits. Albert Beyers made us at least one convert, the assistant treasurer for the Order."

"Conviction?"

"In a manner of speaking. De Roux was his brother-in-law."

Malinov nodded again.

Vereshchagin could hear Redzup's monotone through the paneling. "Your concern has been confiscated. You will not report to your office. You will report tomorrow to the Pretoria caserne to turn over your computer codes, and thereafter on a daily basis. You will continue to receive your pay so long as you undertake no activities inconsistent with your status as an Imperial employee."

Redzup and Liu were having almost as much fun as they had running the banking system on NovySibir.

Malinov rose to leave unhurriedly. In between Redzup's staccato phrases, Vereshchagin heard a timid knock at the door.

"Sanmartin. Beregov wants me to tell you he has a new nickname now," Malinov said with his hands curled in the spider chair, the other spider chair.

"Which is?" Vereshchagin asked politely.

"Little Vee."

"He will grow into it."

"Might. Do you want me to stay?"

Vereshchagin shook his head. "If I am going to be high admiral, I ought to have a desk, do you think?" he said smiling.

Malinov nodded a final time and levered the handle with a calm dignity. Harjalo almost fell over as he opened it.

"My timing appears to be precise, today," Vereshchagin said as Harjalo entered the room with his head down like a bull. He pointed an accusing finger. Vereshchagin nodded gently, and Malinov closed the door on his way out.

"You told Solchava it was your idea . . ." Harjalo began with quiet venom as the door latched itself.

"The responsibility is mine," Vereshchagin responded, the tiredness showing in his eyes for once. "She will return to the hospital company tomorrow as soon as Eva decides who might be sent in her place.''

Harjalo stood there with his finger extended and his mouth open, but no words came out.

Vereshchagin picked up the kukri the senior surviving officer of the Gurkhas had presented and spun it in his fingers. ''Come now, Matti. I know that your advantage over Raul is that you have been reading my mind for years, but wherever did you get the idea that I could not read yours? As I told Raul, very few of us have real choice of paths in this life. I have none left to me, and I am not sure that you do either. If you will kindly lock the door, I still have that half bottle of whatever it is sitting here somewhere. You look as if you could use a glass.''

Harjalo closed his mouth and looked down at his hand as if it had misfired. Vereshchagin reached into his ruck and pulled out the flask in question and a pair of glasses. He filled one and handed it to Harjalo. ''The Bond is beginning to disintegrate as an organization. I do not expect that its offshoots will be greatly longer lived,'' he observed.

''It's over, then,'' Harjalo exclaimed.

Vereshchagin looked at him. ''Come now, Matti, you know better than that.'' He held up his own glass with one hand and stared through the clear fluid.

''Despite our pious hopes and intentions, in two days' time, we will have half a dozen infected villages. In four, we will have at least a dozen. Albert Beyers has already let emergency contracts to put fences around Pretoria, Johannesburg, and Bloemfontein. It will not help, but the possibility cannot be overlooked. He will need a military force of his own. We have a few people we might lend him, an Afrikaner lad named Snyman in particular. After the disease has run its course, we may expect a resurgence of violence. More blood, perhaps a lot more blood, will be spilled out. Ultimately, we will discover whether we have correctly gauged the tide of history.'' He smiled unexpectedly, striking ice into Harjalo's soul with his sad, haggard eyes.

''In four days, you will become battalion commander. We will absorb what we can of the Gurkhas. We will give Coldewe his company, and Sversky as well.''

Harjalo pondered this, closing his eyes and then reopening them. ''So tell my why, Anton. For once, I can't read your mind,'' he said slowly.

''The battalion? Consider, Matti. I will have four years, perhaps five, to alter the face of this planet. Do you think that I will be retained in His Imperial Majesty's service after what I will have done? I assure you, I will not.

"As for Natasha, she looked out at the worlds through colored lenses. I broke them on her face, Raul and I, and I watched her eyes bleed. She will forgive, she might perhaps forget, but something will have died and I am not Christ to raise the dead. We do what we must, Matti."

"And shoot the ones we can't reform," Harjalo finished for him.

"She is resilient. She thinks quite highly of you, as I am sure you are aware." He broke off. "Eighty-seven casualties," he said to fill the awkward silence.

"Plus a few more on the other side." Harjalo closed his mouth, then opened it to say, "Anton, what are we doing here? Now, I mean."

Vereshchagin unfolded his hands and let his pipe swing freely, to give what was intended as a serious question appropriate consideration. "We are laying a new foundation for a society, Matti," he said, "using what is salvageable from the old."

"Doesn't happen often, does it? Tuesday is Christmas. Isn't that strange?" Harjalo said, making a mental note that there had to be another pipe somewhere on the godforsaken globe.

"Which reminds me," said Vereshchagin, a polite lie. "Are you aware that among the battalion assets that Lieutenant-Colonel Higuchi salvaged from the spaceport were his pipers?"

"Bagpipers? Gurkha bagpipers?"

"In kilts. They are actually quite good. I have heard them play *Alamein Dead* and *Lord Lovat*." And *Flowers of the Forest*.

"Bagpipers?" Harjalo repeated incredulously.

"We have never had a band before," Vereshchagin proffered with a childlike innocence. "We have the rest of today and tomorrow to teach them *The Little Tin Soldier* and *The Whistling Pig*."

SANMARTIN STEPPED OVER TO THE WOULD-BE REFUGEES THAT the Border Police and a few of Beyers's men were screening for plague. He singled out one man wearing ill-fitted clothing, a hawklike man with two day's stubble of beard on his face and a touch of gray in his hair.

"Aren't you a bit old for this sort of thing, old man?"

"Too right you are, lad. Shocking thing, disgrace is what it is. They had no right to call me up at my age," Meagher said jauntily.

"You look remarkably like the photo we have of Danny Meagher."

"Ah, you flatter me, lad. By all accounts, he's a much handsomer man."

Sanmartin smiled, thinking of the story of Yoshitsune and Benkei.

"My name is Sanmartin, Raul Sanmartin."

Meagher's eyes lit up. "Captain Sanmartin, I'm pleased to have met you. A name for yourself you've made. From C Company, Johannesburg, I recall. Call me Dan, I ask you."

"I'll do that." He looked at Meagher. "What do you think?"

Meagher considered this carefully. "Well, Raul, I've seen cowboys, Boers, and Imperials now. You're a right set of bastards. I'm not sure there's a penny's worth of difference between you, but I'm hardly one to speak," Meagher said. He reached into his pocket and pulled out a plastic envelope. "A friend of mine asked me to deliver this, it's addressed to his granddaughter, a woman named Bruwer. It occurs to me that you could give it to her as well as any and better than most."

Sanmartin glanced at the name. He nodded. It would make a good reason to see her now that the Variag had told Mischa to stop monitoring her line. Beregov had sent a simple message. "Talk to her. We need to rechristen the still."

He remembered the rest of the story of Yoshitsune. Yoshitsune's military skill had made his brother shogun, but a shogun fears nothing more than an overmighty vassal. A hunted fugitive, Yoshitsune disguised himself as a servant to his retainer, Benkei. He was recognized by a captain of his brother's guardsmen.

"You look like Yoshitsune," the captain exclaimed.

Benkei immediately began beating his revered master about the head and shoulders, crying out, "How dare you look like Yoshitsune!"

The captain let them go, for whatever reason. "Good luck to you, old man," he said, turning away. "Get yourself checked and injected."

SEVERAL HOURS LATER AS THE BULLDOZERS PLOWED UNDER THE bundles gently laid in holes gouged from the earth, Coldewe delivered an epitaph, chanting crisply the opening lines from Heine's poem,

> *Verloren Posten in dem Freiheitskriege,*
> *Hielt ich seit dreissig Jahren treulich aus.*

Ich kaempfte ohne Hoffnung, dass ich siege,
Ich wusste, nie komm ich gesund nach Haus.

He translated, ''Forlorn post in freedom's war/ Held true by me
for thirty years/ I fight without hope, that I conquer/ I knew I
would not come home sound.''

Behind him, Koryagin was singing,

''We're having a war and we want you to come!''
  So the pig began to whistle and to pound on a drum.
''We'll give you a gun, we'll give you a hat!''
  And the pig began to whistle when they told him that!

The wailing of a dozen dead cats was brought to life. Gurkha
handlers were torturing them. Koryagin's grasp on the melody
was none too sure, and the attempt that the pipers made to
follow was both valiant and vain.

Coldewe watched the soil scatter itself over the ragged corpses.
''Now and then indeed it might come to pass/ that such a wicked
rascal likewise knew so well/ to shoot—I cannot deny—/ the
wounds gape, and stream forth my blood,'' he said, translating
Heine's last stanza to himself.

A little humor, a little horror, a lot of sweeping up, that was
war, Rudi Scheel had once said.

Wars are sometimes over and they debited his pay,
  They took away his hat and they took his gun away,
They told him they were thankful and they split him north to
      south
    As they fried him with a whistle and an apple in his
      mouth!

Coldewe listened. ''It's not Heine, but it'll do,'' he said, watching the bulldozers scar the thin soil. He joined in the last verse.

The pig bought a planet and he earned it with his sweat,
  He filled it full of corpses just to liquidate the debt.
He taught the people manners and it didn't take him long
    To teach them how to whistle and to sing The Whistle
      Song!

About the Author

Robert Frezza was born in 1956 at Bolling Air Force Base and grew up around Baltimore, Maryland. He graduated from Loyola College in Baltimore with a B.A. in history and was commissioned as a second lieutenant through the ROTC program. He then went on to the University of Maryland Law School to learn a trade and avoid ending up as a second lieutenant in infantry in Alabama.

After serving on active duty for three years in Germany as a captain in the Judge Advocate General's Corps, he went to work for the Army as a civilian attorney. He currently holds a position as the Deputy Chief of the Personnel Claims and Recovery Division of the U. S. Army Claims Service and is a graduate of the Army Management Staff College.

A third-generation Baltimore Orioles fan, he enjoys reading, theater, and arguing military history. He lives reasonably quietly in Glen Burnie, Maryland.